ID0955643

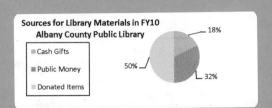

FAR CRY

FAR CRY

JOHN HARVEY

An Otto Penzler Book
HOUGHTON MIFFLIN HARCOURT
BOSTON NEW YORK
2010

For information about permission to reproduce selections from this book,
write to Permissions, Houghton Mifflin Harcourt Publishing Company,
215 Park Avenue South, New York, New York 10003.

www.hmhbooks.com

First published in Great Britain in 2009 by Random House

Library of Congress Cataloging-in-Publication Data
Harvey, John, date.
Far cry / John Harvey.
p. cm.
Originally published: London : William Heinemann, 2009.
"An Otto Penzler book."
ISBN 978-0-547-31594-2
1. Police — Great Britain — Fiction. 2. Missing children
— Fiction. I. Title.
PR6058.A6989F37 2010
823'.914 — dc22   2009029048

Printed in the United States of America

DOC 10 9 8 7 6 5 4 3 2

All my pretty ones?
Did you say all? – O hell-kite! – All?

— WILLIAM SHAKESPEARE, *Macbeth*

FOR

PETER COLES

a small thank you
for many years of
unstinting help and advice

FAR CRY

I

1

Ruth sets down her cup, crosses the room and opens the drawer. The kitchen floor strikes cold, even through her slippered feet. February. At seven this morning, when she first stepped outside, it had still been dark.

The envelope is where she left it, buried beneath receipts for old electricity bills, scribbled notes from the woman who comes Tuesdays and Thursdays to clean and which she has never yet discarded, recipes torn from this or that magazine: an off-white envelope, self-sealing, buckling a little at the corners. Inside is an ordinary postcard showing a map of south-west Cornwall coloured largely green; on the reverse side her name, hers and her ex-husband's, Simon's, are written above the address in a careful, painstaking hand. *Mr and Mrs Pierce.* The old address in London, NW5. The message alongside slanting slightly, left to right.

> *Dear Mum & Dad,*
> *Went to the beach again today. Big waves!*
> *Kelly and I are going to surf school tomorrow.*

Hope you're both okay. See you soon.
Lots of Love, Heather
XXXXXXXXX

Even though she knows it by heart, Ruth reads every word slowly, carefully, taking her time. *See you soon.* For a moment she closes her eyes. Here and there the map is decorated with illustrations: Truro cathedral, a cow standing over a pail of milk destined to be Cornish cream, St Michael's Mount, the rocks at Land's End.

Midway between Cape Cornwall and Sennen Cove, close to a zigzag of coast, a small dot has been made with a ball-point pen, and when Ruth holds it up, as she does now, towards the kitchen window, the afternoon already beginning to fade, she can see a faint pinprick of light through the hole the pen has deliberately made. *This is where I am*, written in small letters that curve out across the ocean. *This is where I am*: an arrow pointing to the spot.

It's not certain how long she stands there, staring out, staring down, the card in her hand. Then, with a small catch of her breath, she slips the card back into the envelope, the envelope back into the drawer, and, glancing at the clock, turns quickly away. Time to change into her shoes, pull on her coat, collect her daughter from school; her other daughter, Beatrice, the one who is still alive.

2

———

Will Grayson hated mornings like this: this time of the year. Not so dark that when the alarm went he could guiltlessly ignore its call and steal, as long as the kids remained asleep next door, ten, fifteen minutes more, but just light enough, the sky beginning to break at the far horizon, to prise him from his bed.

Alongside him, Lorraine stirred and for a moment he turned back towards her warmth, her hand reaching sleepily for his as he kissed the smooth skin of her shoulder then rolled away.

Downstairs, he pulled on his running gear and laced up his shoes, Susie's first cry reaching him as he slipped the bolt on the door and stepped outside. A few stretching exercises and he set off along the narrow road towards the end of the village, the path that would take him between the fields towards the fen.

Though there were times when he would deny it, disclaim responsibility, it was Will whose decision had finally brought them here, this small, strung-out village in the sparsely populated north of the county, where everything beneath the widening sky seemed to be water, sometimes even the land.

Lorraine, it was true, had been prodding them, even before Jake, their first child, had been born: wanting them to move out of the city, away from the small terraced house with its pinch-sized garden and damp walls. Somewhere in the country where they could find more space and room, fresh air, somewhere healthy for the kids – she had always talked of two, at least – to grow. And Will had half-agreed but had hung back, uncertain, valuing the push and flurry of Cambridge proper, the proximity of friends, and dreading the long commute into work, the backed-up lines of barely moving traffic. Maybe they should stick fast, stay where they were, extend upwards if she liked, a loft conversion, plenty enough of those. But then, driving east from Ely, having looked at something in the town – no bigger than where they already were and close to twice the price – they had been attracted by a *For Sale* sign pointing away from the main road, not an estate agent's board, but one the owner had put up himself; a builder with an eye for design who had bought the land two years before and built this place – simple, clean lines, pale wood and glass – as a dream house for his wife. His dream, as it had turned out, not hers.

Will liked the wooden porch that ran the length of the building at the rear, the comfortable feel of the rooms, the high, broad windows with views out towards Ely cathedral and the slow-setting sun.

'So what do you think?' he'd asked Lorraine, and read the answer happily in her eyes.

Once the novelty had worn off they were certain they had made a mistake. The drive to the police station where Will was based, close to Cambridge city centre on Parkside, took even longer some days – most days – than he had reckoned and in the long hours that he was away, Lorraine, marooned with only a barely crawling child for company, felt as if she were going slowly out of her mind. Sometimes not so slowly at all.

'Okay,' Will said. 'Sell up. Cut our losses. Find somewhere else.'

They stayed. Gradually, almost grudgingly, Lorraine found other women in the village, other mothers, with whom she had common cause; Will's move, as detective inspector, into the Major Investigation Team was confirmed, taking DS Helen Walker with him as his number two, a working relationship that had sparked and flourished now for close on five years. How much longer Will could hang on to her before she was heading a squad of her own, he wasn't sure.

Something had been itching at Helen lately, he'd noticed, making both tongue and temper sharper than ever, and maybe that's what it was. A lack of recognition: too long spent trailing in his wake.

Forty minutes after setting out on his run, Will was back at the house, muscles aching, head clear, vest sweated to his skin; a quick shower and a brisk towelling and then into the kitchen for breakfast, Jake spooning Rice Krispies into his mouth as if there were no tomorrow, Susie managing to get more of the glop from her bowl into her hair than anywhere else.

Will poured himself a second cup of coffee and spread marmalade on his last piece of toast; Lorraine was upstairs putting the finishing touches to her face. Three days a week she worked in the admissions office at King's College and on those days she dropped Susie off with the registered child-minder, before taking Jake to the local primary from where the minder would collect him at the end of the day.

Will swallowed down the remainder of his coffee, rinsed the mug at the sink, then stooped to give Jake a quick hug and kissed the top of his head. 'Have a good day at school, okay? Work hard.'

'Okay.'

Susie put her arms out towards him and he managed to kiss her cheek without getting cereal from her sticky fingers all over his shirt.

'Dad?' Jake's voice stopped Will at the door. 'This evening, when you get home, can we play football?'

'Sure.'

Leaving the kitchen and living room curtains open would give them all the floodlighting they would need. Jake would be Manchester United, varying between Rooney and Ronaldo, while Will was doomed to be Cambridge United. A lopsided contest at best.

When Will stepped out into the lobby, Lorraine was almost at the bottom of the stairs.

'You off?' she said.

'Better be.'

'Home late?'

'No more than usual.'

She slid inside his arms and when he bent his head towards her she kissed him lightly on the lips and stepped away. 'Later, okay?'

Will laughed. 'On a promise then, am I?'

'You wish!'

Still laughing, he pulled his topcoat from the rack and headed out the door.

As often, Helen was there before him, leaning against the roof of her blue VW in the police station car park, enjoying her last cigarette before entering the building.

In the past few years she had tried patches, hypnosis, Nicorettes, even acupuncture, but the longest she had been able to abstain had been three months: one more particularly grisly case, one more set of early mornings and late, late nights and she had tumbled off the wagon and back on the nicotine.

She straightened as Will approached, squinting slightly against the light, surprisingly bright for so early in the day, so early in the year – Helen, wearing black trousers over red ankle boots, a grey sweater under a blue wool coat, her newly lightened hair pulled back – and Will thought, not for the first time, what a good-looking woman she was and wondered why men – if that was her preference, which it seemed to be – were not forever beating a path to her door.

Perhaps they were.

One sour and oddly possessive relationship aside, she had rarely, if ever, confided in Will about the vicissitudes of her private life – and only then because she had been hospitalised and feeling especially low.

'Hi,' Helen said cheerily now.

'Hi yourself.'

'Kids okay?'

'Fine.'

'Lorraine?'

'Likewise.'

Helen grinned. 'Got it made, haven't you?'

'Have I?'

'Beautiful wife, lovely kids, clear-up rate second to none.'

Will frowned. 'Is there a point to this? Or is it just your normal common-or-garden goading for a Monday morning?'

Helen tilted her head sideways. 'There's a point.'

'Because if it's about your promotion, I've told you I'll support—'

'It's not my promotion, long overdue as that might be.'

'Then what?'

'Mitchell Roberts.'

'What about him?'

'He's being released.'

'When?'

'End of the week.'

'Jesus!'

'Supervision order, but . . .' Helen shrugged.

'Jesus!' Will said again. 'Jesus fuck!'

Helen ground her cigarette butt beneath her heel and followed him between the cars towards the entrance to the building.

3

It had been the height of summer, three years and some months before. A Norwegian lorry driver, ferrying a load of wood chips south along a flat stretch of the A10, had pulled out to avoid a small figure stumbling haphazardly along the side of the road. The driver had slowed to a standstill and waited, uncertain, watching in his mirror – a stranger in a foreign country, delayed already on his journey from the port at Immingham and not wanting to get involved.

As he hesitated, the figure – a girl, he was almost certain – pitched sideways towards the verge and was still. He swore to himself softly, shut off the engine and climbed down from the cab.

She lay with one leg stretched towards the road surface, the other buckled beneath her; the soles of her feet were bloodied and torn, cuts encrusted with gravel and gobbets of earth. She was wearing an oversized waxed jacket, unfastened, dark green and stained with oil, and nothing else. Her hips, barely pubescent, angled sharply against the thinness of her skin, and a few wisps of hair lay dark between her legs. Her breasts, little more than a boy's, lightly rose and fell above the contour of her ribs. Her eyes were closed.

Without moving her, the driver covered her body as best as he could, then hurried back to the lorry and his mobile phone.

The first police car, north from Ely, was there in seven minutes, the ambulance in ten; Will, who had been attending a meeting at the Constabulary Headquarters in Huntingdon, arrived as the paramedics were lifting the girl on to a stretcher. She was too terrified to speak to anyone, even to say her own name. When Will leaned cautiously towards her, smiling encouragingly, she flinched.

It was several hours before they discovered her full name: Martina Ellis Jones. She lived with her mother and three siblings on an unofficial travellers' site a mile or so from Littleport, a patch of unpromising land between the Old Croft River and Mow Fen.

When Will drove up the narrow road, little more than a lane, later that day, the sun sagged low in the sky, a deepening red splintered sharply with cloud.

Four caravans had been arranged in a rough circle, as if to keep out hostile elements and a searching wind. A bonfire, all but extinguished, smouldered on a patch of ground near the centre, an assortment of bicycles and children's toys nearby. There were two cars just outside the circle; a third car, propped up on bricks and lacking its wheels, was further back down the lane.

When Will knocked on the door of the first caravan, a dog growled low in its throat and then, when he knocked again, began to bark; a voice from within shouted at it to stop, quickly followed by the sound of something being thrown and then a yelp before the silence resumed. Nobody came to the door.

Hostile elements – Will realised that was him.

By the time he'd reached the third caravan, his impatience was beginning to show: kicking low against the door, he called a warning about impeding the police in their inquiries. That and the girl's name. Another dog started barking, different from the first; a different voice ordered it to be quiet, threatening the Lord knows what punishment, and it did.

Slowly, the door swung open.

The man standing there, his height causing him to crouch a little inside the frame, had a mane of silver-grey hair that spread across his shoulders and a nose that had been broken not once but several times. He was wearing a ragged pullover over a collarless shirt and black trousers with a piece of fraying rope for a belt; there was a polished walking stick in his right hand and he leaned his weight against it as he stood. For a moment, Will saw the dog between his legs, then it was gone.

'Martina Jones,' Will said.

'What about her?' The voice was cracked and harsh. Will would have put him at sixty or more if it hadn't been for the brightness of his eyes.

'She lives here?'

'What's it to you?'

'Does she live here?'

'Aye,' the man said, 'when she's a mind.'

'Maybe I could come inside?' Will said.

The man didn't move.

There were signs of life stirring around them, adult voices and children's too; people beginning to show themselves, show an interest in what was going on.

'Martina,' the man said. 'What's she done now?'

'Now?'

The man looked back at him, no flicker in those eyes.

'What did you mean, now?' Will asked.

'It's no matter.'

'You suggested . . .'

'I know what I suggested.' He tapped his stick against the floor. 'The girl, where is she?'

'In the hospital. Huntingdon.'

'Serious then?'

'Serious enough.'

The man cursed and smacked the stick hard against the caravan side, setting off a young child crying inside. 'What happened?' he asked.

'She was found walking along the main road, the A10.'

'In Christ's name,' the man said, slamming his stick against the caravan again, 'haven't I warned her enough?'

'Warned?'

'Against wandering off.'

'Martina's mother,' Will said, 'is she here?'

'Never mind her.'

'If she's here . . .'

'You're talking to me, that's good enough.'

'You're Martina's father?'

He laughed. 'Do I look like her father?'

Will raised both shoulders in a shrug. 'Is he here then? The father?'

'If he were, I'd take his head off with this stick and feed it to the blasted crows.'

A youngish woman appeared behind him in the doorway, a baby, sticky-mouthed, at her open breast.

'What is it?' she said. 'Is it Martina? Did he say Martina?'

'Get back inside, woman, and for God's sake cover your-self up.'

'Someone should come to the hospital,' Will said. 'You and Martina's mother. There'll be questions to answer. How she came to be where she was. A few other things.'

He said nothing about what had appeared to be bite marks on the tops of the girl's shoulders, the weal across her buttocks, the thin line of drying blood down the inside of her thigh. That would wait for later.

*

The silver-haired man's name was Samuel Llewelyn Mason Jones, Martina's grandfather and the patriarch of a loose conglomeration of sisters, brothers, cousins and common-law spouses that moved up and down the eastern side of the country more or less at will. Cleethorpes, Hunstanton, Wisbech, Market Rasen; Lowestoft, Colchester; all the way down to Canvey Island.

Martina's mother, Gloria, had had Martina when she was just sixteen; there had been three other children since, two boys and a girl.

'Running wild,' Jones said, 'the lot of 'em. It's me as has to keep 'em under control.'

Will thought about the rough weal on the girl's behind, the rope around the grandfather's waist; about other things that might or might not have happened, things the older man might or might not have done.

Martina, it seemed, was forever running off, a habit, a compulsion: sometimes she would go no further than the edge of a nearby field and hide; at others she would lie down in an old farm building, the back of a tractor, an empty oil drum that had rolled on to its side. Most times, not always, she would come back of her own accord. Usually the same day. On this occasion she had been gone since late the previous afternoon.

'You didn't report her missing?' Will asked.

Jones looked back at him as if he were some kind of fool.

'You went looking for her?'

'Of course we did. All on us. Not a bloody sign.'

'She stayed out overnight.'

Jones looked at him evenly. 'Somewhere.'

'You know where that might be?'

'Ask her, why don't you?'

But Martina was not talking, not to her mother or her grandfather, not to the doctor or the nurses, certainly not to Will. Nor, when she arrived, to Helen, either. She lay there, uncomplaining, eyes squinched up tight, as they examined her internally and took swabs from various parts of her body.

She was no longer a virgin. She had had intercourse recently and, apart from some small abrasions, probably the result of her size, there was no evidence to suggest it had been other than consensual. There were faint traces of semen, along with saliva, on the backs of her legs and her chest.

When the grandfather was told, he showed little surprise, but grunted and looked across at the mother. 'The fruit,' he said, 'don't fall far from the tree.'

Will questioned him further, while Helen talked to Gloria, and then, fruitlessly again, Martina. Other members of the family were spoken to while officers made a thorough search of the caravan. Social workers were all over the other children like flies at midsummer.

It was only on the third afternoon, when Helen had all but despaired of Martina saying anything at all, that the girl mentioned Mitchell Roberts' name. Just Mitchell at first.

'Tell Mitchell,' she said. 'Tell him I'm okay. He'll be worried about me, else.'

4

————

Mitchell Roberts kept a small place up towards Rack Fen: a garage and workshop fashioned largely from breeze-block and corrugated iron, with a single-storey dwelling out back. It was less than a mile from the Joneses' encampment; a similar distance from where Martina had been found.

In one corner of the workshop Roberts kept a small stock of supplies for farmers who stopped by to refuel with diesel or replace a blown tyre: animal feed and fertiliser and galvanised feed scoops. From behind the till he sold cartons of long-life milk and cigarettes, boxes of cereal and chocolate bars well past their sell-by date; cans of Pepsi and 7-Up that were lukewarm because the refrigerator was always on the blink.

Will had asked about Roberts before he and Helen set off, had him checked out on the computer. At first pass, nothing known officially, no record. Seemed he'd taken over the establishment three years earlier, after it had lain in disuse for almost as long. Word was that he knew his way round a John Deere as well as most and could be relied upon in an emergency. In a part of the country where talk for talk's sake wasn't rated highly, he was considered sociable enough; ready if needed to down tools and pass an opinion on the weather – deteriorating – water levels – rising – and the way the price of fuel was shooting through the roof. Hadn't going into Iraq been meant to settle all of that?

What kind of a life he had once the lights were off and the pumps were locked, nobody knew nor cared. Till now.

Will's jacket lay along the rear seat and his shirt was sticking to his back; beside him, Helen had her window wound down and her fingers trailing in the air. The temperature in the car showed twenty-six degrees.

The waxed coat Martina Jones had been wearing was double-wrapped in plastic inside the boot.

Will brought the car to a halt well to the side of the road, nearside wheels in the dirt, and a lone crow hopped a short distance away and continued pecking at something on the ground.

'God!' Helen said, pushing the car door closed and looking round. 'Can you imagine what it must be like? Living out somewhere like this?'

Will followed her gaze round the flat, almost bare landscape, the small rise to the west that some optimistic cartographer had labelled the Croft Hills.

'I don't have to imagine,' he said.

Helen shook her head. 'Where you live, it's a metropolis compared to this.'

The man who came towards them from the building was medium-height, with pale sandy hair, wearing a plaid shirt beneath dungarees that had missed more than one turn in the wash. Forties, Will might have thought, mid to late forties, if he hadn't already known Roberts to be fifty-two.

Roberts looked from Will to Helen and carefully back again. 'You must be lost,' he said.

'You think?'

'I know just about everyone lives round here and I in't seen you afore, so 'less you're visitin' someone out by Home Farm or got some burnin' desire to see the Hundred Foot Washes, I'd say, yes, you're lost.'

'Think again,' Will said.

Roberts glanced over his shoulder at nothing. 'You're police then,' he said.

Will held his warrant card out for him to see. 'Mitchell Roberts?' he said.

Roberts nodded. 'Accordin' to the Inland Revenue and a few other interested parties, yes. Most folk call me Mitch.'

'She called you Mitchell,' Helen said.

Roberts blinked. 'She?'

'Tell Mitchell not to worry, that's what she said.'

Roberts took half a pace back, hand reaching down towards his hip.

'Hurt your leg?' Will said.

'Tractor chassis fell on it a while back. Some days it hurts more than most.'

'When you're nervous maybe?' Will suggested.

'Am I nervous?'

'You tell me.'

'I don't . . .' He smiled. 'I don't know what this is about. Some woman tellin' me not to worry.'

'Not a woman,' Helen said. 'Not exactly.'

'You said . . .'

'More a girl.'

'I don't know any . . .'

'Martina.'

'Who?'

'Martina Jones.'

'No, I'm sorry, I . . .' Raising a hand towards them, Roberts shook his head.

Will snapped the lock on the boot and, taking out the coat, still in its plastic wrapping, carried it towards him, folded over one arm. When he was almost level, he lifted the coat up for him to see.

'Well,' Roberts said, a look of relief spreading across his face. 'Thank heaven for that. Thought I was never going to see that coat again.'

'It's yours?'

'Yes, it's mine. Know that thing anywhere, trussed up or not.'

'You're sure?'

'Sure as I'm standing here.' He smiled. 'Recognise just about every damn mark.'

'Would you care to tell us how it came to be out of your possession?' Will asked.

'Out of my possession? Why, that little girl stole it, that's how.'

A nerve began to beat alongside Will's temple. 'Which little girl is that?'

Roberts looked at him. 'The one you was tellin' me about, I suppose. What'd you say her name was?'

'You don't remember?'

'No, I don't remember.'

'Martina,' Will said quietly. 'Martina Ellis Jones.'

Roberts scuffed the earth with his toe. 'I never knew her name.'

'But you gave her your coat.'

'I never give her no coat, she stole the coat, I told you that.'

'When was this?'

Roberts gave it some thought. 'Must be three, no, four days ago now.'

Will and Helen exchanged a quick glance.

'Suppose you tell us,' Helen said, 'exactly how Martina ended up with your coat.'

'You want to come inside?' Roberts said, shuffling a little to one side. 'Get out of this heat. Got some pop in there or I can make a brew.'

Neither Will nor Helen had moved.

Roberts cleared his throat. 'She'd come by here,' he said, 'her and her brothers. Sometimes another girl, too. They'd walk across the fields.' He pointed towards a narrow gap in the low hedge, what might have been the beginnings of a track. 'Gyppos, diddicoys, whatever you like to call 'em.' He spat. 'Sometimes they'd have money, stole from their mother's purse likely as not, buy 'emselves a Pepsi or such. Caught one of the boys stealin' a brace of Mars Bars once and took my boot to his backside. Chased 'em all off. Told 'em if they tried that, any one of 'em again, they could stay clear of my place an' not come back.'

'And did they?' Will asked.

'What?'

'Come back?'

'After a spell.'

'Martina,' Helen said, 'did she ever come here on her own?'

Roberts swallowed and wiped a hand across his mouth. 'Once in a while.' Given the temperature, the way the perspiration was running freely down his face was no surprise.

'Like the day she went away with your coat?'

'Yes. Like that.'

'Tell us what happened that day,' Will said.

Roberts blinked the sweat away from his eyes. 'Nothin' to tell. I'd been working on this trailer best part of the afternoon, went back to the house to wash up and there she was.'

'At the house?'

'No. Sitting up in there on the counter, bold as you like, eatin' a Twix. I remember sayin' to her, I hope you're goin' to pay for that.'

'And did she?'

'Oh, yes.'

'She had money?'

'How else was she goin' to pay?'

Will looked at him. 'You took her back into the house?'

'Why would I do that?'

'Maybe to get the coat?'

Roberts shook his head. 'That coat always hung from a peg right in there.' He pointed through the open workshop door. 'I can show you if you'd like.'

'Later,' Will said.

'Why did you give her the coat?' Helen asked.

'I didn't give her the damned thing. I told you. She took it while my back was turned an' run off with it, that's what happened.'

'Now why would she do that?'

'How should I know? Her kind, see something they can lay their hands on an' it's gone.'

'Her kind?'

'You know what I mean.'

'Hot, wasn't it, four days ago?' Will said, more conversational than anything else.

'I dare say.'

'Hot like this?'

'Just about.'

'Yet she took your coat, this heavy adult coat, where was the point in that?'

'Like I said, if it ain't nailed down . . .'

'Come on,' Helen said, fixing him with her eyes. 'You can do better than that.'

'I don't see what you mean.'

'You don't see what I mean? When that girl was found, running, running scared, half out of her wits, your coat aside, she was naked as the day she was born. Not a stitch on, not a stitch.'

'I don't know 'bout that.'

'You don't think that's why she took your coat? To cover herself. After what had happened.'

Roberts pressed his hand harder against his leg.

'What did you do with her clothes?' Will asked. 'Burn them? Make a bonfire somewhere? Or are they still back in the house?'

'Look,' Roberts said, 'I don't know why . . .'

'Souvenirs,' Helen said, 'isn't that what you call them? Isn't that what you like? Your kind?'

Something sprang to life in Roberts' eyes. 'Fuck you!' he said. 'You bitch! Fuck you, fuck you, fuck you!'

'Mitchell Roberts,' Will said, 'I am arresting you . . .'

Helen had been right. They found Martina's cotton underpants, torn at one corner and badly stained, pushed down towards the rear of the box chest that served to hold Roberts' own clothes. Martina herself, unsurprisingly, was all over the place in what she said. One minute Mitchell hadn't touched her, hadn't laid a hand on her; another, he had forced her to do things, threatened to report her to the police for stealing if she didn't agree. Mitchell loved her; she loved him, she really did. She hated him for hurting her. It wasn't Mitchell who'd done those things to her at all, it was someone in a red car who'd stopped to give her a lift home. It was her grandfather. Really, it was.

They'd been looking at him, of course, the grandfather. Questions, evidence, intimate samples, DNA. The broken skin and the bruising to his granddaughter's buttocks, Samuel Jones readily pleaded guilty to. Discipline, that's what she'd needed. Too little too late, and that's the truth. Jones staring back at Will with all-too-clear eyes, as if daring him to disagree. Daring him to ask why she'd spent nights sleeping in the back of a straw-strewn trailer instead of the comfort of her own bed; why she'd trekked across open fields and skirted drainage ditches to Mitchell Roberts' home, not once but several times.

In the end there was nothing to suggest that Jones had abused his granddaughter sexually; he had simply, to Will's mind, driven her into the arms of someone who would do that for him.

'You can't blame him,' Helen said. 'Jones. Not for what someone else did.'

'Can't I?' Will said.

An analysis of both the bite marks and traces of semen on Martina's body left Mitchell Roberts' defence with nowhere profitable to go. Concerned, however, as to how Martina might stand up if she were called to give evidence in court, the prosecution accepted two guilty pleas of indecent assault and one of unlawful sexual intercourse with a girl under thirteen, and Roberts was sentenced to five years' imprisonment.

Since which time, by Will's estimation, he had served a little over half. Less than enough. Will would have been happy if once they'd locked him up they'd thrown away the key.

5

She hadn't thought she would ever marry again, not after the divorce. A divorce Simon had tried to talk her out of at first, keen to prove he understood what she was going through, what she was thinking. Surely this was the time when they needed to stick together most, for mutual help, support? Lacking close family – his parents having both died when they were comparatively young and his only brother long settled in South Africa – and enjoying no more than cursory relation-ships with his colleagues, without Ruth, Simon had been in danger of floundering. His forthright exterior in danger of falling apart.

But Ruth had surprised herself – and Simon, she was sure – by sticking to her guns, and once he saw there would be no altering her mind, no going back, he had, to give him credit, been more thoughtful than she might have expected, conciliatory even, and, in the event, being awarded her decree nisi had been like having a tooth removed under anaesthetic, no more troubling than that. You walked in and only minutes later, or so it seemed, you walked out, admittedly with your tongue unable, for now, to stop touching the place where, for years, that particular tooth had been. Searching for a twinge of pain that was not really there.

She'd told her parents about Andrew first, driving up to spend a weekend with them in Cumbria; her father barely looking up from whatever he was repotting in the conservatory, merely nodding acceptance as if it were what he'd been expecting all along; her mother leaning forward in her chair and taking both of Ruth's hands in hers: 'If you're sure, you're really sure . . .'

Friends from work, the ones she considered close enough to tell, had shown not much more surprise than her father; had thought it what she needed, someone to help her refocus her life, someone new. Even those few friends she and Simon had shared, when they heard, for the most part agreed she was making the right decision.

Even when she had finally plucked up the courage to tell Simon himself that she'd met somebody else, he'd been more reasonable than she'd had any right to expect. Oh, not straight away, of course, not immediately – but once he'd got over the initial surprise.

They had met in a café near the Angel, not so far from the local government offices where Simon worked. Ruth had phoned him just two days before: she was coming down to London to do a bit of shopping, maybe they could meet for a coffee or something? Making it all seem as casual as she could.

'Of course,' he'd said. 'How about the afternoon? Shall we say three? Three-fifteen? I'm supposed to have a meeting but I can always shunt it around.'

And when she'd asked was he sure, not wanting to make a mess of his day, having cold feet if the truth were told, he'd laughed her down.

'Come on, Ruthie, always time for you, you know that.

Besides, it's been a long time. If I don't see you soon I shall forget what you look like.'

Ruthie: how she hated it when he called her that.

At first glance, Simon had scarcely changed at all. Still neat inside his soft grey suit. But he was thin, she noticed, thinner than before, his cheekbones more prominent, and there were worry lines around his eyes.

What was he now? Forty-two? Forty-three? When she had looked at herself in the mirror that morning she'd seen a woman who, in a kind light, might just pass for forty-five. She was thirty-eight.

'Sorry to keep you waiting,' Simon said.

Ruth gave a quick smile to show that it was perfectly all right.

She had felt only a little awkward sitting there, in that busy interior, surrounded by people who were mostly younger and more casually, more fashionably dressed than herself. Men and women pecking away at their laptops or having brightly animated conversations in several languages, voices raised above the intermittent shrill of the coffee machine and the rhythmic jousting of world music through the speakers.

'Another coffee?'

'No, thanks. I'm fine.'

He smiled and turned in the direction of the counter, returning minutes later with a small flat white.

'Decaf now in the afternoons, I'm afraid. Get too hyper otherwise. Start throwing things around the office.'

'I doubt that.'

He smiled. 'You'd be surprised.'

'I would,' Ruth said.

When they'd learned what had happened to their daughter he had lost his temper certainly with those he blamed, but almost never with her. And later, while they were still trying to come to terms with what had happened, he had taken himself off and cried quietly in corners, as if his grief were something not for sharing. Real and immediate and his own.

'So,' he said, taking a sip of his coffee, 'what is it exactly?'

'Nothing special, I told you. I was just coming down and . . .'

'Ruth, you live just outside Ely, not at the ends of the earth. You must have been in London half a dozen times in the past eighteen months if not more. If you'd wanted to see me, just to chat, find out how I was getting on, you could have done so easily.'

'Simon . . .'

'No, that's all right. It's fine. Remaining friends, it's not what you wanted. And I respected that. I understood. A clean break. Easier, much easier. For you, at least.' He made a small sound through his nose. 'We deal with these things in our different ways.'

Oh, God, Ruth thought. She pushed the spoon around the inside of her empty cup. 'I've met someone,' she said, her voice so low that Simon had to lean forward, his expression suggesting he hadn't heard or didn't understand.

'I've met someone,' she said again, too loud this time, and the young woman sitting next to them – Spanish? South American? – glanced up from the book she was reading and smiled.

It took Simon a few moments to respond.

'You mean, as in . . . Yes. Yes, of course you do. And it's serious?'

'Yes.'

'Well . . . well, I don't know what to say. I'm surprised, that's all. I thought maybe, whatever you had to tell me, it was about your family – your dad, I know he's not been too well – I thought perhaps you were moving up to Cumbria to be closer to them.' He shook his head. 'I didn't expect this.'

'No.' She laughed, self-consciously. 'Not exactly love's young dream.'

'That's not what I mean.'

'Simon . . .'

'I thought you wanted to be on your own. I thought that was the point.' His fingernails, she noticed, were bitten almost down to the quick.

'It was,' she said. 'Believe me. This was the last thing in the world I expected to happen.'

'Almost.'

'Sorry?'

'Almost the last. Not as unexpected as . . .' A shadow passed behind his eyes.

'Simon, I'm sorry, I . . .'

'No, no, congratulations. Really. I mean it.'

'Thank you.'

'So, where did he come from, this Prince Charming? This Lochinvar?'

'Don't mock.'

'I'm not.'

'Perhaps I should never have told you. I'm not sure why I did, it just seemed important, that's all.'

'Yes, of course. I understand. Least, I think I do. And I'm pleased, pleased that's what you felt. Pleased for you, too. I really am.' Squeezing out a smile, he leaned across the table and aimed an awkward kiss at her cheek.

'I should be going,' Ruth said. She felt flustered, un-comfortable, conscious of the young woman next to her looking on with unfeigned interest, and wished she had never come.

Outside, they stood for a moment on the pavement, side by side. There was an odd pallor to his skin, she thought, as if lately he had not been much exposed to the light.

'Simon,' she said, 'you are all right?'

'Me? Yes, of course. Of course I am, what did you think?'

And he was on his way, threading through the traffic that

spread in both directions along Upper Street in a slow-moving, never-ending trail.

She had met Andrew through a friend, Catriona, a jolly fifty-five-year-old with whom she volunteered at the Oxfam bookshop, Saturdays and Thursday afternoons. Between studying part-time for her Postgraduate Diploma in Information and Library Management and working three days a week at a little arts and crafts shop near the cathedral, it helped fill in the time.

Catriona and her husband, Lyle, had retired to Ely two years before; Lyle, laid off after two decades in the engineering department of Rolls-Royce Aerospace, had chosen to spend part of his redundancy money on a vintage 27-foot motor launch, which he kept moored on the marina.

Catriona was good at talking Ruth into accompanying her to the latest foreign film at the Maltings or the new exhibition at the Babylon Gallery – Ruth had once let slip that she used to paint herself, so Catriona was forever bowing to her greater knowledge and asking Ruth to explain the inexplicable. She had even cajoled Ruth into going along with herself and Lyle to the occasional Ely Folk Club evening at the Lamb, where Lyle joined in the choruses far too loudly after too much beer. And then, of course, there were trips along the Great Ouse, Lyle as proud of the pulling power of his craft's 80-hp diesel engine as he was of its oak frames and teak planking and traditional coir-rope fender.

They had listened, both of them, to Ruth's story and decided, good-hearted people that they were, that she should not be allowed to wither on the vine. Get out and meet people, make new friends, a new life. Ruth had already arranged to shadow one of the staff at Ely library for five hours a week, but Catriona had something less bookish in mind.

At dinner parties she and Lyle would introduce her to what

they clearly saw as eligible men, for one reason or another unattached: a widower who had recently lost his wife to cancer; a Cambridge academic, never married, with an interest in liturgical history; a folk musician whose speciality was the penny whistle.

And then there was Andrew. Andrew Lawson.

Four-square, seemingly dependable, the head of a local primary school, on that first evening he was close to self-effacing. The only time he became particularly animated was when describing a new mentoring scheme in which year five and six pupils read to the younger ones from years one and two.

'Ruth used to be a teacher,' Catriona had said, oiling the wheels.

'That was a good while ago,' Ruth said.

But Andrew's interest was caught. 'Here in Ely?' he asked.

'No. In London.'

'Secondary?'

'Primary.'

'Still, pretty tough all the same. Most of the kids round here, the villages especially, have them eating out of your hand.'

'That's because,' Lyle boomed, 'they've never learned to use a bloody knife and fork.'

Everyone laughed and the conversation moved on.

Ruth was surprised when, four days later, Andrew called her at home. 'Catriona gave me your number, I hope you don't mind.'

Even more to her surprise, she found she didn't mind at all.

Of course, he'd been married before. It had lasted ten years, almost as long as her own. Andrew's wife had fallen in love with a young New Zealand woman who had briefly been teaching at his school and whom he'd invited home several times out of kindness, not wanting her to feel isolated and alone.

When it became clear where her affections were leaning, his wife moved out of the family home into a flat of her own. Andrew kept his head down: there was a new round of SATs tests to prepare for, an Ofsted inspection looming, the budget to be readied for the next governors' meeting, a new special needs coordinator to be appointed.

Eighteen months later his wife was on her way out to New Zealand with her lover and as far as Andrew knew the pair of them were still living on the South Island, in Dunedin, a place which Andrew, in a rare coarse and less than cautious moment, had once described as being just a fingertip away from the arsehole of the world.

At least they had never had children: that was a blessing.

When, later, Ruth asked him why, he told her that for the first few years they had both said it was too soon, too early, they should wait, and then, after a few more years, neither of them had mentioned it at all.

Ruth had become pregnant with Heather not long after she and Simon had married, almost without thinking about it, something that just happened. She had been twenty-six.

It was not the easiest of births and afterwards Ruth had suffered quite badly from post-natal depression. For a time, she'd come close to rejecting Heather altogether – something for which she felt forever guilty – and if it hadn't been for Simon the whole situation might have imploded.

It wasn't until Heather was practically a toddler that she and Ruth had really bonded, though Simon had remained very much a part of her life, closer perhaps than many fathers.

They talked of having another child, but Ruth was frightened and Simon wary. 'We're happy now, aren't we,' he said. 'As we are? Why change things? Eh, Ruthie? Why take a risk?'

'I envy you,' Andrew said. This was some little while after their first meeting, after they had begun talking about the possibility of getting married themselves. 'I shouldn't say it, probably shouldn't think it, no right, but I do. You and Simon. What you had with Heather.'

'Even after what happened?' Ruth asked.

Andrew looked at her, seeing the residue of pain he could never hope to clear from her eyes. 'Yes. Even after that.'

It wasn't so very long after the wedding – Catriona jubilant in a suit of shocking pink with orchids in her hair; Lyle, florid-faced, taking none-too-secret nips from a silver flask – that Andrew suggested they had a child themselves.

'Andrew, no! No, that's ridiculous. It's not . . . Besides, I'm too old.'

'Not necessarily.'

'I am. You know I am.'

'Let's see.'

Beatrice was born almost exactly a year after they were married, and for all that Ruth was by then thirty-nine, there were no complications and it was a relatively easy birth.

Simon, when he heard – she had to tell him, had thought it through, talked it over with Andrew, and decided it was the only thing to do – was magnanimous: he sent a card with congratulations, a bottle of Moët, and a selection of knitted bootees and such from the Baby Gap near where he worked.

Ruth, feeling awkward and oddly beholden, sent him an effusive thank-you note and pictures of the baby, but to these Simon made no reply.

Five months later she received a letter. Brief and to the point:

Have taken your advice – the advice you gave me long ago – sold up here and gone into private practice. Wish me luck. And if ever you need someone to look at your accounts . . .

There was no phone number, no address.

Ruth had not heard from him since.

*

33

With Beatrice there were none of the difficulties she had experienced with Heather. From the moment her mouth found the breast, gumming the nipple with surprising force, feeding was no problem, any more than weaning her off on to the bottle was later. She put on weight, she grew, her eyes followed Ruth happily around the room.

She was a lovely baby, a loving child, and remembering how she had been with her first-born, Ruth felt even more guilty than before.

She hid this from Beatrice, of course, overcompensating with love and affection, and hid it too, as best she could, from Andrew, though not always with success.

'What's this?' he asked one evening, when Beatrice was five years old, holding the envelope out in front of him gingerly, as if it might burn.

'You know.'

'Hmm?'

'You know what it is. You know very well.'

Like a sour magician, he turned the envelope round between finger and thumb and shook its contents out, the card with its green map of Cornwall floating towards the table where Ruth was sitting and landing face down.

Soon. See you soon.

'I thought . . .' he said.

'You thought what?'

'I just thought after all this time . . .'

Ruth laughed, a scoffing humourless laugh. 'How long is it, then, Andrew? Do you know? Do you even know?'

'Ruth, come on, that's not the point. The time, it's—'

'Of course it's the point. You want to know how many years? How many months? How many days?'

'Ruth, look—'

'No, you look. Look at this.' She was shouting now, beside herself. 'This stupid bloody card with its cows and its cathedrals and fishing boats and her writing . . . look, her writing, here, read it, look, read it for yourself.' Brandishing it in his face, pushing it at him, close, until he had to duck away. 'See you soon, that's what it says. See you soon. And you thought I'd forget. Forget. Because of Beatrice, because of you, because of my perfect bloody life, you thought it would be like – what? – a bad dream? Something that happened to someone else? And you think that if I stopped looking at this, this card, if I never took it out of the envelope, out of the drawer, it would all change, I'd forget all the sooner?'

Andrew stood there, shaking in the force of her anger, eyes angled to the floor. Ruth never lost her temper in that way, almost never swore.

'Here.' She thrust the card at him again. 'Take it. Go on, take it. Tear it up. If you think that's what makes the difference. If you think looking at that is what makes me think of her. Go on. Tear it into little pieces. What are you waiting for?'

She pushed the card towards him again, hard against his face, so that he had little choice than to take it from her hand.

'Go on,' she said. 'Tear it up.'

Without looking at her, he let the card fall through his fingers to the floor, then turned and walked away. The post-card was returned to its place in the drawer, from where Ruth would take it, from time to time, and neither she nor Andrew ever mentioned it again.

Though there were times, after an especially tiring day and one more than usual glass of wine, when she would rest her head against his chest and want to talk to him about Heather, to tell him what she was feeling, and Andrew, to his credit, would put an arm around her and listen and kiss the top of her head as if he understood.

Only when he'd had a particularly difficult day at school – an especially long meeting with the local authority, an argument over extra funding — would she feel him tense up against her and they would stay there on the settee, silent and uncomfortable, muscles cramping up, until one or other of them would stumble out something about the time and needing to get an early start in the morning and they would get up then and go about their various tasks, the lights, the locks, the bathroom jobs, the bed.

But Beatrice was a sweetheart, Beatrice was a darling, good at her lessons, popular at school. Ruth loved her, admired her, felt proud, and, yes, she loved Andrew too. Of course she did.

How lucky she was, despite everything, she reasoned, to have had two beautiful daughters, be thus twice blessed. And to have known two kind and loving men, quite different, but loving and supportive all the same, when there were people out there who lacked either, or both, and for whom happiness was always, for whatever reason, out of reach.

Surely, knowing that, she should, beneath it all, be happier than she was?

6

———

Liam Noble had been the division's Sex and Dangerous Offender Intelligence Officer for nine months; operating within MAPPA, Multi-Agency Public Protection Arrangements, his focus was on the management of high-risk offenders in need of varying levels of supervision after their release from prison.

Noble had previously worked in Probation and before that in Social Services, a career path which made him, as his superiors had pointed out when he was appointed, ideally suited to the task in hand.

'At least,' as one had said, 'you know how the buggers think.'

To which Noble had almost retorted, the buggers think just like you and me. Except that he knew there were occasions when that wasn't strictly true. And, as he had discovered, being able to get some way inside the minds of those probation officers and social workers who sat across from him at MAPPA meetings was as apt to confuse as clarify. Affiliative, his manner of dealing with colleagues had been described in his last appraisal; affiliative rather than author-itative. The unspoken suggestion being there were times when a little more direction, a touch more directness would be appreciated.

Noble was trying for a little directness when Will Grayson knocked on his door; an irritatingly circular conversation with a senior social worker about the advisability of applying for care proceedings in order to protect the stepchildren of a recently released offender.

'Will,' he said, relieved at the interruption. 'Come on in. Take a seat. I'm just about finished here.'

'No,' he said into the telephone, 'I think you should go ahead and make the application. Definitely. Do it today. There's no sense in leaving those children at risk.' He listened for a moment, and then: 'Yes. Yes, right. You'll let me know.'

Setting down the phone, Noble let out a slow breath of satisfaction before turning towards Will. 'No need to ask why you're here.'

'Pass the time of day?'

Noble laughed. 'Mitchell Roberts, right?'

'When were you going to tell me?'

'I thought you'd find out soon enough.'

'And you've known for what? Months?'

Noble shook his head. 'Six weeks.'

'I thought the prison service had to give three months' notification?'

'Level Three offenders they do.'

'And Roberts isn't Level Three? He's not high risk?'

'Not high risk enough.'

'Tell that to Martina Jones,' Will said. 'Tell that to the next twelve-year-old he gets his hands on.'

Noble sighed and sat forward in his chair. 'There's no indication Roberts is a serial offender, no history of anything similar in his background. What happened was an isolated incident.'

'Bullshit.'

'I'm sorry?'

'People like Roberts, there's a pattern. You know that as well as I do.'

'There's a first time, too.'

'And you think that's what this was? You've read the transcripts of the trial? Seen the pictures? That doesn't happen out of the blue. The only reason we don't know about it, either he was clever or he was fucking lucky or he was both.'

'Will, Will, getting angry doesn't help.'

'It helps me.'

Noble looked at him carefully. 'Just suppose for a minute you're right, there is another alternative, of course.'

'Which is?'

'CID wasn't as smart as it might have been.'

'What's this, Liam? Passing the buck? Spreading the blame?'

'Not at all. But if there is something there, something in Mitchell's past, which I doubt, how come it's never come to light?'

Will held his tongue. When they had first taken Roberts into custody, he had been questioned about a number of other unsolved cases involving young girls without anything germane coming to light; and then, once the CPS had agreed the charges relating to Martina Jones, other matters had been allowed to fade away, more pressing things taking their place.

'The thing is this,' Noble said, 'if you include when he was on remand, Roberts has served more than half his time. He's successfully completed the sex offenders' treatment programme. The parole board found him truly contrite. He realises what he did was wrong.'

'Wrong?'

'Yes.'

'And you believe that?'

'Yes. Until he gives me reason to think otherwise.'

39

Will was quick out of his chair. 'He gives you reason, it's going to be too late.'

Noble thought this was another conversation that had just about run its course. 'He'll be on the sex offenders' register. For the first six months he'll be living in approved premises and reporting to his probation officer regularly. We'll be keeping a close eye on him, don't worry.'

Will looked back at him from the open door. 'Not as close as I will.'

'For God's sake, Will . . .' Noble began.

But he was gone.

It was Wednesday morning, two days after Helen had passed on the news of Roberts' impending release. She was sitting on the only clear corner of Will's desk, taking advantage of his absence to make a personal call, mobile to her ear. 'Yes,' she said, encouragingly. And, 'Yes, really? You would? Here?' She laughed. 'I don't think Will would like that.' And she laughed again, low in her throat and loud.

'That's a dirty laugh if ever I heard one,' Will said, entering.

Helen murmured a quick, 'Gotta go,' snapped her phone shut and swivelled round, showing rather more leg than she'd perhaps intended.

'Sorry. Just needed to make a call.'

'That's okay.'

'You know what it's like out there, all that racket, everyone's ears flapping.'

'Private then?'

'Sort of.'

'Who's the lucky guy?'

Grinning, Helen raised a mocking eyebrow. 'Wouldn't you like to know.'

'Probably not.'

Helen slid down from his desk and smoothed her skirt along

her thighs; she was wearing a sombre business suit in solemn black, black shoes with a slight heel, her hair, as was usual these days, pinned back.

'You in court later?' Will said.

'For my sins.'

'Curtis Chambers?'

'The very one.'

Chambers had got into an argument with a nightclub bouncer, driven off to his friend's house and borrowed a gun, a converted starting pistol that as often as not misfired, gone back to the club and, after more heated words and a deal of pushing and shoving, had taken the pistol from his pocket and shot the bouncer in the head. Miraculously, the man had survived. Chambers had been arrested three days later and charged with attempted murder, unlawful wounding and being in possession of a firearm in a public place. Now he was pleading self-defence.

'Open and shut, isn't it?' Will said.

'You'd think.'

Will eased himself down into his seat. 'I went to see Noble,' he said.

'About Roberts?'

'Yes.'

'Maybe not so wise.'

'You think so?'

Helen shook her head. 'Come on, Will. You know what I mean. You've got to let it go. Besides, they'll be all over him.'

'They?'

'MAPPA. He's not going to be able to turn the wrong way down a one-way street without someone knowing.'

'Nice idea,' Will said. 'Unfortunately they've got him pegged as Level Two. Not sufficiently high risk. Few months in a hostel, nice little chats with his probation officer. Keeps his nose clean, tells them what they want to hear and then when they wash their hands he can slip back beneath the radar.'

'I wonder,' Helen said.

'What?'

'Why it's got to you this much? There've been other cases since this, similar. Too many, God knows. Why let this one get under your skin?'

'I don't know. The fear in that girl's eyes when I first saw her? Roberts when we questioned him? Standing there with the sweat running off him, lying to his back teeth. That leering little smile. Like he was remembering.'

'It's out of our hands, Will. There's nothing we can do.'

Will looked up at her and didn't answer.

He took his time. Didn't go barging in. Even found a way to chat to Roberts' probation officer, nothing official, no big deal, simply passing the time of day. Apparently, Roberts had turned up neat and on time for his first appointment, no problems about his accommodation, everything fine, eager to find work, get a job, start earning for when he could rent a place for himself. There was a garage owner who had been prevailed upon to take on ex-offenders before and might be again. Owned one of those fast-fit tyre and exhaust places. More than one, in fact. And by all accounts Roberts knew his way round most vehicles blindfold. Good with his hands.

Will watched him from where he was parked a short way along the street: Mitchell Roberts in shapeless cargo pants and a dark sweater, a pair of work boots on his feet. His sandy hair, always fair, had been cut so short that in the keenness of the morning light he appeared to be almost bald.

A free man out for a stroll, rolled newspaper in one hand, reacclimatising himself at his own speed, in his own time, pleased to be back in the world.

Will kept him in sight and, when he judged the distance between them was sufficient, he slid out from behind the wheel, locked the car, and followed.

Not hurrying, Roberts' route took him across two main roads and a busy intersection, and then past the new Museum of Technology, by which time Will thought he knew where he was heading: Stourbridge Common, a broad patch of open ground alongside the River Cam.

He watched as Roberts chose a seat with his back to the water, unfolded his newspaper and began to read.

Without causing him to look up, several cyclists went past at intervals, using the approved path, then a small group of workmen on their way back from lunch, returning to one of the small factory units clustered around Mercers Row; some teenage boys, playing the wag from school, started kicking a football around towards the far side of the common; a silver-haired couple in tracksuit tops and white shorts passed close by him on their way to the tennis courts beyond the bowling green.

Roberts lit a cigarette.

Time passed.

A young woman went by pushing a pram, baby asleep inside, a toddler making reluctant progress behind.

From one of the pockets of his cargo pants, Roberts took a paperback book, found his place and proceeded to read.

It was the best part of forty minutes before the first of the children from the nearest primary school appeared, taking the bridge across the river and then the path that led out towards the Newmarket Road. Four or five boys, aged nine or ten, pushing, pulling, arguing, yelling at the tops of their voices, oblivious of anyone save themselves. Two girls followed, book bags in their hands, each listening to a single headphone from the MP3 player clutched in the taller one's hand. A few parents with children then, the women gossiping, kids lagging behind, laughing, calling names.

Roberts was alert now, the book still open on his lap, but his eyes everywhere.

As Will watched, a fair-haired girl, purple anorak over a white blouse and a green pleated skirt, screamed as one of the boys snatched the hat from her head and sent it skimming close to where Roberts was sitting.

Before she could retrieve it, Roberts, moving with surprising speed, had scooped it up and stood, arm extended, holding it towards her.

'Here. Here you are.'

Will read the words on his lips.

The girl hesitated, then darted forward and, not quite looking at Roberts' face, took the hat from him and backed away.

'Say thank you,' her mother called.

'Thank you,' Will imagined the girl saying, though he couldn't hear the words.

As she ran back to where her mother was waiting, Will's eyes were fixed on Mitchell Roberts' face, the smile that lingered, the cat that had just had sight of the cream.

'What the hell were you thinking of?' Liam Noble asked.

They were on the stairs between the first and second floors at Parkside, Noble on his way up towards CID as Will was leaving.

'Now?' Will said, scarcely breaking his stride. 'Going home. I promised Lorraine I'd be back before she put Susie to bed.'

'Will, wait . . .'

He stopped and turned.

'You know what I mean,' Noble said.

'This afternoon?'

'Yes, this afternoon.'

'Keeping an eye on a potential reoffender. Someone has to.'

'Not you.'

'No? Well, until somebody else steps up I might just have to do it myself.'

'It's none of your business, Will. Not any more.'

'Yeah, well . . .' He swung away and continued down the stairs.

Noble caught up with him close to the ground floor and stopped, blocking his way. Voices drifted up from the lobby, one of the duty officers making the same point again and again.

'Look,' Will said, 'I don't see why you're getting in such a state. I didn't speak to him, I didn't interfere. I doubt very much if he even knew I was there. And as soon as I got back here I sent you an email outlining what I think are very real concerns.'

'Our concerns, Will, not yours.'

'Only just out and one of the first afternoons he's free, he's out there, hanging round some school, I'd say that was cause for concern, wouldn't you?'

Noble shook his head. 'I've read your email, Will, looked at the map. Roberts was a good half a mile away from that school, if not more.'

'Half a mile away on a route some of those children take . . .'

'Will, Will, there are children everywhere. You know that as well as I do. We can't fit him with blinkers, keep him on a leash.'

'More's the pity.'

'If he'd been loitering close to the school, any school, a playground somewhere, anything that would be breaking the terms under which he was released, we'd apply for an emergency recall to prison. No hesitation.'

'Fine. Just show me how you're going to know.'

'I've told you. We're monitoring him at a level commensurate with the risk involved . . .'

'You're what?'

'. . . and any rise in those risk levels will be properly assessed and responded to.'

'By which time he'll have done it again.'

'I doubt that very much.'

'You do? Then you should have seen the look on his face this afternoon.'

'Stay away, Will. Steer clear. Please don't force me to go over your head.'

Will fixed him with a stare. 'I'll do my job, Liam, as best I see fit. I suggest you do the same.'

Skirting round Noble, he pushed his way out of the building and into the car park. If Helen had been there, waiting by her VW instead of still being on her way back from court, he might have bummed a cigarette, his first in years. Instead, he got into his car and turned the key in the ignition, letting the engine idle while he switched on the radio: another teenage suicide in South Wales, the number now not so far short of twenty. The Welsh Assembly, the report continued, had voted to increase its spending on youth welfare with the aim of decreasing the suicide rate by ten per cent in the next three years. Too bad for the other ninety per cent, Will thought, presumably they could just go hang.

Replacing the radio news with a CD by the Arctic Monkeys, he turned the volume up loud and, with a swift look over his shoulder, pulled out into the evening traffic.

7

By the time Will arrived home, Jake was sitting up to the table, labouring over baked beans on toast; Susie was strapped into her high chair while Lorraine, despairing of her daughter's wayward attempts to feed herself, patiently spooned a mashed-up mixture of chicken, rice and vegetables into her mouth. Music dribbled from the radio.

Will bent and kissed Lorraine on top of the head, then leaned forward to kiss Susie's cheek; when he ruffled his son's hair and went to kiss him, too, the boy turned his face sharply away.

'What's wrong?' Will asked.

Jake hunched his shoulders and made no reply.

'What's got into him?' Will asked his wife.

'I was about to cook him stuffed pasta and he said, no, he wanted beans on toast, and then, when I asked him to switch off some television programme he was watching and come and get it, he threw a tantrum and I had to practically drag him here and sit him down and now you'd think I was trying to poison him.'

Will sighed. 'Come on, Jake, there's a good boy. Eat your tea.'

Jake pushed a soggy piece of toast from one side of the plate to the other with his fork.

'Jake . . .'

'It's okay,' Lorraine said. 'Leave him. If he wants to go to bed hungry that's his lookout.'

Will took a carton of orange juice from the fridge, poured some into a glass and drank it down, then went upstairs to change.

When he returned, wearing a faded sports top and an old pair of jeans, Jake was still sitting sullenly over his plate, arms folded in defiance, and Lorraine was in the process of unfastening Susie from her chair.

'Take her for a minute, will you?' Lorraine said, holding the child out towards him. 'She's falling asleep.'

Smartly, Lorraine lifted Jake's plate away from under his nose, swept its contents into the bin with his knife, and deposited it in the sink.

'Right, young man. Upstairs and into your pyjamas, wash your face and hands and clean your teeth.'

'But . . .'

'No buts. If you're good and quick your dad'll read you a story before turning out your light.'

'But you promised . . .'

'You heard what I said, now go.'

Wrenching his chair round noisily, head down, the weight of the world on his shoulders, Jake trudged from the room.

Will and Lorraine exchanged weary smiles.

'Busy day?' Will asked.

'No more than usual. You?'

'Don't ask.'

'Fancy a cup of tea?'

'Love one.'

Lorraine went to fill the kettle at the sink and Will shifted Susie's position against his chest, surprised as ever at how little she weighed, how fine her bones.

Will, there are children everywhere.

He buried his face against the top of Susie's head, eyes closed, breathing in her smell.

An hour or so later, supper finished, they were in the living room, curtains drawn, idly watching the TV.

'How's Helen?' Lorraine asked.

'Fine as far as I know. Why d'you ask?'

'I thought I saw her in town today.'

'Ely?'

'No, Cambridge. She was with some man. Near the market square.'

'With?' Will eased himself up a little in the chair. 'How d'you mean, with?'

'With, as in . . . you know. You know what I mean.'

'How could you tell?'

Lorraine smiled. 'One minute they seemed to be arguing. The next she was all over him.'

'All over . . . ?'

'Kissing him.' She grinned. 'Tongues.'

'And this was the middle of the day?'

'What if it was?' Lorraine said, amused.

'She's not some teenager.'

'And you're not her father.' Lorraine laughed. 'If I didn't know you better, I'd think you were jealous.'

'Now you're talking daft.'

'Will, for God's sake,' Lorraine said, laughing. 'Calm down. Chill.'

'I'm fine. Okay? Fine.'

For some minutes they sat in silence, staring at the screen.

'What did he look like, anyway?' Will asked.

'I don't know. Your sort of age. Maybe a bit older. Leather jacket. Dark hair.'

'One of us? Another officer?'

'I don't know. Why don't you ask her?'

'Maybe I will.'

Lorraine knew better than to say any more.

'Are you watching this?' Will asked a while later, nodding towards the television.

'No, are you?'

'No.'

He used the remote to switch off the set. 'I'll go on up,' he said.

Some minutes later, when she hadn't followed, he came back down. Lorraine was standing outside on the back step, coat round her shoulders, smoking a spliff, the smell sweet on the night air.

'How's it going to look,' Will asked, 'when you're arrested for possession?'

'For you? Pretty bad. You'll have to resign, I imagine. The children'll be taken into care.'

'Over my dead body.'

'They may not go that far.'

She took a last drag and turned towards him, her hip pushing against his groin, his hand moving down her spine through the thin material of her dress. When she kissed him her mouth was full of smoke.

Next morning, Will had a meeting at police headquarters in Huntingdon: *Towards a Policy for the Handling and Management of Confidential and Covert Human Intelligence Sources.* Human Intelligence Sources. What used to be called informants. What used to be called snouts.

By the time he got back to Cambridge his ears were clogged with high-minded promises, evasions and officialese: the difficulties of balancing compelling issues of public interest with the need not to compromise ongoing investigations or subsequent court proceedings; the importance of protecting the identity of sources, if necessary by applying for an exemption to prevent the release of information requested under the Freedom of Information Act, 2000.

One precept stuck in his mind: in order to tackle crime effectively and make the community safer, there are times when it may be necessary to infringe upon the human rights of the individual.

He thought he might quote that at Liam Noble next time they crossed paths.

At lunch-time, Will found Helen was sitting on one of the benches near the edge of Parker's Piece, the swathe of open ground that faced away from the police station on Parkside. Collar turned up against a chilling wind, she sat with the inevitable cigarette in one hand, a take-away cup of coffee in the other.

A weak sun was visible between the clouds.

'Not taking solids these days?' Will said, sliding on to the bench alongside her.

'I had something earlier.'

'You can have one of these if you want.' He was unwrapping the foil package he'd brought from the car: ham and cheese sandwiches with mustard and tomato.

'Lorraine make those for you?'

Will shrugged. 'She was getting Jake's lunch anyway.'

He held one out towards her and she shook her head. 'What happened to Pret A Manger?' she asked. 'Fancy chicken and avocado and a cinnamon what-you-call-it?'

'Too expensive.'

'On your salary?'

'Lorraine wants to take the kids to Center Parcs at Whitsun. It's not cheap.'

Helen took a last drag at her cigarette, wafted the smoke away from Will into the air, and ground out the butt beneath her shoe.

'She saw you the other day,' Will said.

'Lorraine did?'

'Snogging some guy in the market. Tongue right down his throat, apparently. Wonder the poor bloke could breathe.'

'Bollocks!'

'They probably came into it. Sooner or later.'

'Fuck off, Will!'

Will laughed.

'No, I mean it. Mind your own damned business.'

'Okay, okay. But if you don't want people to pass comment, perhaps you should stop getting carried away in public.'

'Yeah, well. Easy for you to say.' Helen reached into her bag and tapped another cigarette out of the pack.

'You don't need that,' Will said, hand on her arm.

'Don't tell me what I need, Will,' she said, shaking him off. 'You're not my doctor. Not my bloody father, either.'

'That's what Lorraine said.'

'Well, she's right.'

'I'm your friend, least I thought I was.'

'You're my boss.'

'Can't I be both?'

She looked at him. 'Maybe.' Lighting her cigarette, she inhaled deeply. 'Whichever you are, doesn't give you any right to comment on my love life.'

'Okay. Fair enough.'

He went back to his sandwich; Helen drank some of her coffee. An ambulance went fast past the sports centre away to their left, sirens blasting, heading for the Newmarket Road.

'Is it serious?' Will asked. 'This bloke?'

'Maybe.'

'How serious?'

She cast him a sideways glance. 'Enough for him to want to leave his wife.'

'Oh, Christ, Helen!'

'It's all that's out there, all you'd want to shag anyway – gay blokes and married men.'

'He's not on the force?'

Slowly, she nodded, avoiding his eye.

'Who?'

'It doesn't matter.'

'Who?'

'Declan.'

'Declan Morrison?'

Helen nodded.

'God, Helen, what did you do? Line up the ten most unsuitable men and then pick the winner?'

Helen grinned. 'Something like that.'

'He's been married what? Twice. Two kids this time around. Story is, even before the second was born he was going over the side.'

'Stories, Will, rumours. That's all they are.'

'And now?'

'Now what?'

'This a rumour?'

Helen shook her head in annoyance. 'Don't.'

'Don't what?'

'Don't preach.'

'Okay.'

Will rewrapped the uneaten half of his sandwich and slipped it back down into his coat pocket. Declan Morrison had transferred into the Cambridgeshire force from Sunderland three years before; a transplanted Irishman by way of Liverpool and then the north-east, he had arrived at Parkside with a couple of warnings for insubordination hanging over him, one accusation of using excessive force that had subsequently been withdrawn. Will had met his wife on a couple of occasions, small and shy, pretty in a Claire's Accessories kind of way.

Morrison himself was broad-shouldered, an inch or two under six foot, a few pounds overweight. He gave the air of not suffering fools gladly, doubting authority, forthright enough to relish calling a spade a fucking spade.

Will tried to picture him and Helen together, then rapidly shunted it from his mind.

'How on earth did you ever get tied in with him anyway?' he asked.

She smiled ruefully. 'He must have caught me in a weak moment.'

'You mean, like when you were breathing.'

'Very funny.'

'Well, why couldn't you just – I don't know – do it and get over it? Move on?'

'Ah, Will . . .' She leaned against his arm, hand over his, '. . . you know I'm a great romantic.'

'And this is what? Beauty and the beast?'

'He's nice. Really. When you get through all the front, all the bluster. I like him.'

Will looked unconvinced.

'And he's great in the sack.'

'I don't want to know.'

'Not jealous, Will?'

'No, you can have him.'

Helen laughed, spilling coffee down the back of her hand and on to her skirt. Will got to his feet and she fell into step beside him, the concrete and glass of Parkside inviting them back.

'You really think he'll leave his wife?' he said.

'That's what he says.'

'Don't they all? When they want to go over the side?'

Helen's face tightened. 'Do they, Will? You tell me.'

54

They walked the rest of the way back to the building without speaking.

Mitchell Roberts took a bus out to Histon, walked around the thirteenth-century church and moat and then the site of the old Chivers jam factory at Impington, before catching a bus back. In the city, he sat for a while on a low wall close to the bus station, smoking a cigarette, before heading off along Sidney Street towards Magdalen Bridge. Fifteen minutes later he'd changed direction and was strolling between the stalls in the market, pausing to look at a piece of old silverware here, a set of knives there, a collection of old sepia postcards. When a young schoolgirl in uniform, white ribbon in her hair, walked close behind him, holding her mother's hand, he scarcely seemed to notice.

Following him into the twist of narrow streets and passages between Market Street and the Guildhall, Will thought he'd lost him, until Roberts stepped out of a shop doorway and stopped right in front of him.

'Inspector Grayson.'

'Yes.'

He was leaner than before, the lines in his face deeper; there were liver spots on the backs of his hands.

'Bit of shoppin'?'

Will shook his head.

'Not a coincidence then?'

'No.'

Roberts nodded slowly. 'Saw you the other day. In the park. Takin' an interest, that's nice. Sense of responsibility, I dare say. Only right. Since it was you got me put away.'

Several of his teeth, Will noticed, were stained yellow; one, near the front, was badly chipped at the edge.

'You did that yourself,' Will said.

'Ah, yes.' A smile curled round Roberts' mouth. 'That poor girl.'

Will held himself under control. Just.

'You got children?' Roberts asked. And when Will didn't answer: 'I'd like to see 'em some time.'

The only thing Will could do to stop himself from punching Roberts in the face was to turn hard and walk swiftly away.

8

———

She sees her. Heather. She has never told her husband. She has never told either of her husbands. She doesn't know for certain what they would say. Except that neither would believe her.

Andrew, she thought, would listen a trifle wearily and then, making an effort not to be patronising, try to explain it away: a projection of loss, the result of too much dwelling in the past. If only she could bring herself to get rid of some of those things of Heather's she'd clung on to, or, if not that, at least lock them away. Out of sight, out of mind. And she should talk to the doctor, why didn't she do that? Probably there were some pills. Or therapy, that was always an option. Even yoga.

Simon, on the surface anyway, would be more understanding. He was the one, after all, and not her, who had joined those support groups, gone to meetings, spent hours exchanging experiences on the Web. He would advise her, Ruth thought, to do the same. Share. Don't keep it all inside: that's the worst thing she could do. Talk to other sufferers, other victims – for that's what they were. They were victims, too.

Except that sharing, sharing Heather, now, was the last thing Ruth wanted to do. And telling anyone — Simon, Andrew, anyone — would be a betrayal. A severing of trust. And once she lost that trust, Ruth feared — her greatest fear — Heather would not come to her again.

A face seen at the window, the wave of a hand from a passing train; a group of schoolgirls standing waiting impatiently at the crossing, Heather's the only face partly turned away; at the pool, a shout and a splash and then that familiar crawl, feet kicking up so much spray.

But those are only the glimpses, the moments she's vouchsafed, the little proofs that jolt Ruth's heart. Proofs she dare not allow herself to question, lest they disappear.

What she longs for are those rarer times Heather comes to her when they're alone. Bright and chattery sometimes, full of who said what or who did this in class, who was Star of the Week or who had to stand in the corridor outside, who pushed whom in the playground, who was horrible and called her names, who's her new best friend. Then at other times she's quiet and will barely talk at all — like the other week when Ruth was standing in the kitchen, early evening, no one else at home, Andrew having relented and taken Beatrice into Cambridge to see a rerun of *The Bridge to Terabithia* at the Arts Cinema, and suddenly there was Heather, reflected in the dark of the window, walking slowly towards her, smiling. Only stopping when she was right beside Ruth and then reaching for her hand, her fingers small inside Ruth's palm, nails bitten down.

They had not talked then, scarcely a word.

Ruth had asked her if she wanted a drink, nothing more, some juice or hot chocolate, maybe a biscuit, but Heather had shaken her head. She was happy. She was fine.

Sometimes when she sees her — like that evening in the kitchen — it's Heather as she was then, ten years old, just ten, her birthday barely past; dark hair, darker than Ruth's own, and long, long enough to reach almost halfway down her back. Like Rapunzel, she said. Like Rapunzel in the tower. Washing it was a nightmare, getting it properly dry something worse. Knots and tangles that would never untie.

And sometimes when Ruth sees her she is older – not as old as she would have been had she lived – but in her early teens, around thirteen.

As if she had stopped growing when Beatrice was born.

II

1995

9

Ruth closed her eyes. Another day with year four: thirteen girls and seventeen boys, eight different nationalities, five religions, nine children learning English as an additional language, six who are eligible for free school meals. Another day conjuring up some enthusiasm for this term's project on the Egyptians: mummies, masks, a giant wire and papier-mâché model of a pyramid and a forthcoming trip to the British Museum.

Heather, who went to one of the other local primaries, had been on to her from the moment she'd stepped through the front door. 'Mum, why can't I? Why? Why? Just tell me why?'

And when Ruth, after fielding the same arguments as the day before and the day before that, had retreated behind a simple, declarative 'Because', Heather had flounced off to her room with much muttering and slamming of doors.

Ruth made herself a cup of Milo with warm milk and sat watching the blue tits and the occasional robin peck at the fat balls dangling from the cotoneaster bush at the bottom of the garden.

She was still there when Simon returned early from work, having decided, after a meeting on the possible extension of parking provision for the north of the borough, not to go back to the office.

'Where's Heather?'

'Upstairs sulking.'

'What about now?'

'The same as before.'

Simon loosened his tie, pulled off his jacket and draped it over the back of a chair, gave his arms a stretch, and took an already opened bottle of Sauvignon blanc from inside the fridge.

'Join me?'

Ruth shook her head. 'Not just now.'

'It's what I need.'

'Hectic day?'

'Boring. Felt myself nodding off this afternoon on at least two occasions.'

'You could always leave. If you're really bored, I mean. Pack it in.'

'And do what?'

'I don't know. Set up in private practice. Accountancy. You're qualified.'

Simon tasted the wine. 'Too risky. Mortgage like ours, I like to know what we're earning, month on month.'

'If you're really unhappy, we could sell up, find somewhere smaller.'

'No, it's okay.' Aiming a kiss at her head as he leaned past her, he just missed and kissed air. 'Just a bad day. Bad week. It'll be fine. Besides, you don't really want to move again, do you?'

'Not if we can help it.'

'Well, then.'

Something over two years ago they had sold their high-ceilinged, three-bedroom flat in Muswell Hill and, with the help of one of Simon's old friends who was a mortgage adviser, bought a three-storey house on the fringes of Kentish Town – compared to Muswell Hill, a grittier part of London that still didn't seem to know if it was on the way up or down, a book-shop, admittedly, and a new organic grocer's, but Iceland and Greggs and a busy Poundstretcher, and more charity shops than you could shake a stick at. Still, as Simon pointed out, they were closer to Ruth's school, close to the tube and – importantly, and rare for London – there was a choice of halfway decent secondary schools, which meant that even if they couldn't finally finagle a place for Heather at Camden School for Girls or LSU, there were a couple of comprehen-sives that would do the job.

'You sure you don't want some?' Simon asked, topping up his glass.

'Sure.'

One of the first things they'd done after moving in was to open up the side return to accommodate a new kitchen-diner. That and a new coat of paint on the walls. Of course, the bathroom could do with having everything pulled out and being replaced – and Simon was very keen on having an en-suite in the main bedroom – but all that could come in time. For now they were settled.

'Maybe we're being a little harsh,' Simon said. 'Unfair on Heather. This holiday.'

'We?'

'Yes, you know. Laying down the law. It's only a week, after all.'

'Ten days.'

'Exactly. What's ten days? She's spent as long as that before now with your mum and dad, in the Lakes. Longer.'

Ruth could barely contain her incredulity. 'I thought we'd agreed this wasn't the same.'

When Heather had come home, fairly exploding with the

news that her new best friend, Kelly, had asked her parents if she – Heather – could go with them on a camping holiday in Cornwall and they had said, yes, of course, the more the merrier, Ruth's reaction had been, well, ambivalent. Simon's had been this side of apoplectic.

'You know perfectly well I don't like the idea of her palling up with that girl anyway, but the thought of her going away with the whole damned family . . .'

'Come on, Simon,' Ruth had said. 'They're not that bad.'

'No? Mrs is a great lumpen bloody breeding machine, always wandering around with a fag stuck in her mouth and looking as if she's about to pop . . .'

'She's perfectly nice . . .'

'And he's either living off disability benefit or one way or another bumping up the black economy . . .'

Almost despite herself, Ruth had laughed. 'As far as I know, he's got a perfectly good job as a builder. And he doesn't look in the least bit disabled.'

The truth of it was there were a number of nice, polite middle-class girls in Heather's year, all of whom came from homes where there were plenty of books on the shelves and where they had piano lessons or played the flute and went to Guides or Woodcraft Folk, and for whom stir-fried fresh noodles with organic chicken and vegetables were more of an everyday affair than a Big Mac with fries. And those were the girls both Simon and Ruth wanted Heather to spend time with. Instead of which, in the last few months at least, she had chosen Kelly.

So without quite coming out and saying they disapproved, they'd both done their best to discourage the friendship from developing further. Tea after school and the occasional play day were just about acceptable, but, though Heather had pleaded and cried, sleepovers were not.

And now there was the issue of the holiday.

'You're really changing your mind?'

Simon smiled. More of a smirk than a smile. 'It occurred to me, I've got a few days owing. You'll be off anyway. If Heather's down in Cornwall, we could nip over to Paris for a few days. Further, maybe. Avignon. Montpellier. Just the two of us. What do you think?'

Ruth was smiling now, too. 'And for this you're prepared to sacrifice your only daughter to ten days in the bosom of Kelly and her family, warts and all?'

'Oh, I think so,' Simon said, leaning back. 'Don't you?'

10

Heather was upstairs in her room, the walls a barometer of burgeoning change: ponies, kittens, the sky at night; a poster for the Royal Ballet's production of *The Nutcracker* alongside one showing the members of Boyzone looking moody and cool. Certificates for swimming, punctuality and the recorder. Party invitations. A blown-up photograph of Heather and her granddad on a ledge halfway up Helvellyn, laughing into the wind. That had been before her granddad's trouble with his knees.

Among a collage of other photos Heather had made on the outside of her wardrobe door, for Ruth two stood out: Heather in a flowery dress top and blue polka-dot pedal pushers, alice band in her hair, happily astride one of those gloriously old-fashioned fairground horses – every bit a little girl – and then Heather only six months later, got up for the school disco, mauve vest gathered at the top and close fitting enough to show the beginnings of breasts, skin-tight cropped jeans, a suggestion of make-up around her eyes.

Never mind that most of that evening, Heather had scarcely danced at all, but raced around, shrill-voiced, with her friends; and when she had danced it had been as one of a circle of girls, lip-syncing the words, following the others in the swirling movements of their arms, the swing and dip of hip and shuffle of their feet – the only contact with boys to push them aside with scorn – the beginnings were there, unmistakable, the first glimmerings of the rest of her life.

Ruth, standing amongst the other mums and few reluctant dads, all there to chaperone, had felt an ache and looked away.

Now Heather was sitting at the centre of her bed, legs crossed, head down, arms folded across her chest. The bed itself, for a change, was made: duvet straightened, pillows puffed. An old doll leaned against one corner of the bedhead, discarded or placed there purposefully, Ruth couldn't be sure. Most of her daughter's clothes seemed to be in the drawers appointed for them; shoes and trainers were lined up along one wall. Books stood, somewhat haphazardly, on the shelves; comics with girly picture stories were piled on the floor. Homework lay unfinished on her desk.

'What are you doing?' Ruth asked.

'What's it look like?' Heather snapped.

Ruth caught her breath and refused to be drawn. 'I don't know,' she said calmly.

'There's nothing to do,' Heather said, throwing all the emphasis on the 'to'.

Ruth looked around. 'You've got loads of books, games – there's that jewellery kit your Aunt Vicky sent you . . .'

'That's not what I mean.'

'Well, what do you mean?'

'You know.'

Ruth knew well enough. Heather's friend Kelly had her own television in her room; most of her friends, if she were to be believed, had televisions in their rooms. One or two even had computers, too.

'How'm I supposed to do my homework,' the refrain went, 'if I haven't got my own computer?'

'You don't need a computer to do your homework. There's reference books galore in the house and if that fails there's always the library.'

'Oh, yeah, I'm bound to go wandering off down there just to look something up, I don't think.'

'And besides, if it's really important there's your father's computer downstairs.'

'Which he's always using, whenever I want to go on it. Either that or you're looking up something about the Romans or the Egyptians or something boring for school.'

'That's not true.'

'No?'

'No.'

It was a dialogue that had been rehearsed and repeated too many times. But Ruth and Simon had talked it over and were clear: when Heather was older and having access to a computer would be genuinely helpful, they would buy one for family use and set it up in the corner of the living room so that she could get help with her homework in the early evenings and at weekends. What they didn't want was Heather squirrelled away in her room and going online without them knowing what she was doing – that would not only be irresponsible but would cost them a small fortune into the bargain.

'Why don't you come downstairs?' Ruth said.

'What for?'

'We want to talk to you.'

'What've I done now?'

'Nothing. We just want to talk to you, that's all.'

'You're talking to me now.'

'Your dad and I. Come on. Come down, there's a good girl.'

Heather loosed off an elaborate sigh and, levering herself off the bed, followed Ruth downstairs.

Simon looked up from the paper. A department store had collapsed in South Korea, killing over five hundred people and things were starting to look bad in Iraq.

'Hello, sweetheart.'

Heather scowled.

'What it is,' Ruth said. 'What we wanted to say . . . ask, really, just to be sure . . . this holiday in Cornwall, with Kelly, you do still want to go?'

'Er, ye-es.' Heather's eyes spread wide.

'Well, we thought . . . maybe we'd been a bit . . . I don't know . . . a bit mean, overcautious, and . . .'

'And I can go?'

'Yes. That is, probably. Almost certainly. We'll have to check with Kelly's parents, of course . . .'

'Oh, Mum! Mum, that's brilliant! Fantastic!' And she flung her arms around Ruth and hugged her hard.

'It was your dad, you know,' Ruth said, when she stepped away. 'He's the one you should thank. It was his idea.'

'Really?' Heather looked across at her father doubtfully.

Simon sat up and smiled. 'I'm not an ogre all the time, you know.'

He held out his arms and Heather walked towards him, turning her face aside for his kiss.

'We'll have to talk to them, of course. Kelly's parents. Just to sort out the arrangements. Make sure it's still all right with them.'

'Of course it is.'

'I know, I know. But it's still a conversation we need to have.'

'Oh, Dad.'

'What?'

'Nothing, it's just . . .' She swung her head. 'I'll go and phone Kelly, let her know.'

'You don't think I should talk to her mother first?' Ruth said, but she was gone.

Ruth sighed. 'I just hope we're doing the right thing.'

'Four days in Avignon. Food. Wine. Bit of culture thrown in. We might just catch the end of the festival.'

'That's not what I mean.'

'Ruthie, come on.' Holding out both of his hands. 'What's the worst that can happen? She'll stuff herself on too much ice cream and dodgy pasties and fish and chips and come back with a taste for *EastEnders* and saying "i'n it" at the end of every sentence.'

'God, you're such a snob!' Ruth said, laughing.

'And you're not?'

Smiling, she squeezed his hands.

'You'll go round, won't you?' Simon said. 'Talk to them. No point both of us going.'

'They're not contagious, you know.'

'You prepared to bet on that?'

'Bet on what?' Heather said from the doorway.

'Nothing.'

'I spoke to Kelly, she says it's cool. We can have midnight feasts and make fires on the beach for barbecues and that, and Kelly says there's this van that comes round every night to the campsite with these great pizzas, and her brother's got this surfboard he might lend us and I might even be able to borrow Kelly's wetsuit 'cause she's going to get a new one and . . . and you're not listening, are you?'

'Yes, I am.'

'No, you're not. You're just standing there with that dopey expression on your face.'

'I'm happy, that's all.'

'What for?'

'For you.'

'You're weird,' Heather said and pulled a face.

Ruth went round after school two days later, taking Heather with her. Mrs Efford – Pauline, Ruth just called up her name in time – came to the door with her youngest clinging to her like a small bush baby, all hands and feet and staring eyes. It wasn't impossible, from the way her clothes hung around her, that she was pregnant again already.

'Ruth. Great, come on in. I'll get the kettle on for a cup of tea.'

'Oh, no. Not just for me.'

'No probs. I was gonna make one anyway.'

The hallway was booby-trapped with buggies and scooters and bicycles in various sizes and smelt of chip fat and cigarette smoke. 'What did you expect?' Simon asked when she told him later. 'Eau de Givenchy and walnut oil?'

A girl of five or six was sitting with her face up close to the television screen, watching a game show that seemed to involve Noel Edmonds, though Ruth was sure she'd read somewhere that he'd had a stroke and nearly died.

'Tina,' Pauline Efford called. 'Turn that thing down.'

Without taking her eyes from the screen, the girl manipulated the remote so that the voices were little more than excited whispers.

Heather had disappeared up to Kelly's room the moment she had arrived, slamming the door behind them.

Pauline came in with two mugs of tea, her own bearing the legend, *Best Mum in the World*. She settled the baby against one arm of the settee with a dummy into her mouth and reached for her cigarettes.

'Terrible habit, I know,' she said when Ruth declined. 'Keep tellin' meself I should give up, but with Alan smoking I don't stand a chance.'

'Kelly doesn't . . .' Ruth began.

'Smoke? No way. If she did, she'd catch the back of my hand.'

Ruth sipped her tea.

'She's fair made up, Kelly, 'bout your Heather coming with us. Someone her own age. There's other girls on the site she sometimes pals up with, but that's not the same. And Lee, he's near fifteen now and off on his own most of the time. Don't want his little sister hangin' round, gettin' in the way. No, they'll have a great time, the pair of 'em. Won't want to come home.'

'You wouldn't let them . . .' Ruth began, then faltered.

'What's that?'

'Well, wander off on their own. Too far, I mean.'

Pauline waved smoke away from her face. 'Nowhere much they can go, 'cept down the beach. Camp's in a field, two fields, right away from the road. The main road. There's buses, of course, down to Land's End or over to Penzance. Not many. Couple of times a day if you're lucky. Otherwise it means using the van and Alan always says he's driven all that bloody way he don't want to drive no more'n he has to. That tea too strong?'

'No,' Ruth said, forcing herself to take another gulp. 'No, it's fine.'

In under half an hour it was settled. Heather would go round for a sleepover on the Friday school broke up, taking her case and all her things with her, so they could get off to an early start the following morning, Alan keen to beat the rest of the traffic. Ten days later, they would return. Nothing simpler.

Ruth was just negotiating her way back along the hall, having agreed that Heather could stay there for another hour and play, when the front door opened and a youth stepped inside wearing a grey sports top and wide jeans low on his hips. His hair was dark and, Ruth thought, surprisingly long, and his eyes, in the brief moment he looked at her, were a soft almondy brown.

'Hello,' Ruth said. 'You must be Lee. I'm Heather's mum.'

He grunted something that might have been 'Hi', and, head down, pushed his way past.

11

———

When Ruth walked her daughter round to the Effords' house on the final day of term, carrying her suitcase for her, Heather was in such a state of high excitement that she came close to walking into a lamppost and on several occasions tripped on the uneven paving stones.

Drained by her last day of teaching, Ruth herself stumbled on the path leading to the Effords' front door.

'Been at the gin already?' Alan Efford asked with a grin.

Broad-faced and shaven-headed, he stood in the doorway in his work clothes, arms bare, speckled with plaster and paint like a Pollock painting.

'Job like yours,' Efford said, 'looking after these little buggers all day, nobody'd blame you if you had.'

Heather ran past him and into the house.

'Don't know how you do it,' Efford continued. 'Not have the patience, me.'

Ruth realised she was staring at him stupidly, saying nothing.

'Here,' he said, moving towards her, 'let me take that.'

'No, it's all right, I . . .'

Reaching down for the suitcase, his arm brushed against the back of her hand and, involuntarily, she flinched.

'Come on in for a minute. Pauline's somewhere about.'

She could smell the sweat on him, barely dried, and the tobacco on his breath.

'Come on, don't be shy.'

She followed him inside.

Wearing an old-fashioned apron over sweatshirt and jeans, Pauline was pushing clothes into the dryer. Hunched up close to the high chair, Tina was looking at the *Beano* at the same time as feeding Alice from a jar.

'Take the weight off your feet,' Efford said. 'I'll make us some tea.'

'No, it's all right, really.'

'No bother,' Efford said. Reaching past Pauline for the kettle, he gave her behind a generous squeeze.

'Hey!' Pauline shouted, swatting at his hand. 'Leave my bloody arse alone!'

Efford winked at Ruth. 'Not what you usually say.'

Lee, wearing an Arsenal shirt, headphones clamped over his ears, wandered into the kitchen, barefoot.

'Wanna cup?' his father asked.

With a shake of his head and a glance towards Ruth, the boy turned and disappeared.

Ruth prised a piece of jammy crust from one of the chairs and sat down.

'Sugar?' Efford asked.

'No, thanks.'

'Sweet enough, eh?'

For no good reason, Ruth felt herself starting to blush. Taking the mug of tea from his hand, she spilt some before she could set it down.

'Oh, I'm sorry,' she said, blushing all the more.

'No probs,' Pauline said. 'Blend in with the rest.'

'Biscuit?' Efford asked, holding out a packet of custard creams.

Ruth said no and then said yes.

'Tina,' Pauline said, 'will you leave that stupid comic be and concentrate on feeding Alice. Way you're goin', she'll die of bloody malnutrition.'

'So,' Efford said, taking a seat across from Ruth, 'bet you'll be pleased it's the holidays, yeah?'

'Yes. Simon and I, we thought we might go away for a few days while you're all in Cornwall. France, maybe.'

'Second honeymoon, eh?'

'Wouldn't say no to one of those meself,' Pauline said, 'long as it weren't with 'im.' She laughed and the laughter turned into a coughing fit that only gradually eased.

'Drop more tea?' Efford asked.

Ruth shook her head. 'What time are you leaving tomorrow?'

'Five? Somewhere round there.'

'So early?'

'He was born early, weren't you?' Pauline said. ''Fraid he'd miss something else.'

'Any later,' Efford said, 'an' you're stuck in traffic all the way from Bristol to sodding Truro.'

'I was just thinking I might come and wave her off,' Ruth said. 'Heather. Her first time, you know, away on her own.' She smiled, self-deprecatingly. 'Bit silly, really.'

'Up to you,' Efford said, 'but if Kelly's anything to go by we'll be lifting your Heather into the van with her eyes still glued shut.'

There was a scurrying of feet outside and Kelly came bursting into the room, Heather at her shoulder. 'Mum, Mum, can we have some hot chocolate? An' biscuits, yeah? Upstairs.'

'All right, but you can fetch 'em yourselves. I'm not cartin' 'em all the way up there.'

'Thanks, Mum.'

The door closed as quickly as it had opened and they raced away, Heather not seeming to have noticed that Ruth was there at all.

Ruth woke at four-thirty without having set the alarm. Turning on to her side, she struggled with the thought of getting up and getting dressed, but before she could decide Simon had rolled towards her, arm heavily across her shoulder, and she stayed where she was, eyes open, listening to his breathing and telling herself Alan was right, there was little point in going, and even if she did, Heather would certainly not thank her. By then it was gone five and too late anyway and Ruth continued to lie there, certain she would never now get back to sleep.

When she woke again, Simon was on his way back into the room, humming tunelessly, tea and toast on a tray.

'Happy holidays, Ruthie.'

'Whatever time is is?'

'Half-eight, a little after.'

'They've been gone for ages.'

Simon rested the tray near the foot of the bed. 'Be pulled over at motorway services somewhere by now, sampling the Great British Breakfast.'

Pushing herself up, Ruth nudged back the pillows and settled the duvet. 'We're going to miss her terribly, you know that, don't you?'

'Miss who?' Simon said, smiling.

When Heather phoned that evening, as Ruth had made her promise, she was so excited about everything, words tumbled over one another into near incoherence. But the jist of it was the campsite was great and looked out right over the sea, almost anyway, and the tent she was sharing with Kelly and Tina was cool. Dead cool. Kelly's dad was lots of fun, always making them laugh, and the pizza they'd had for supper was brilliant.

'I hope you won't forget to clean your teeth properly,' Ruth said, wanting to bite back the words almost as soon as she'd said them.

The silence at the other end of the phone was her admonition.

'Do you want a word with your dad?' Ruth asked.

'Not now, Mum. We're off down to the beach. Kelly's waiting.'

'But surely it's already dark?' Ruth said.

Too late. Heather had gone.

'She sends her love,' Ruth said, going back into the room where Simon was sitting.

'Hope you gave her mine.'

'Of course.'

Ruth sat down and picked up the paper. Simon was leafing through Alastair Sawday's book of special places to stay in France, looking for interesting bed and breakfasts around Avignon.

'We could hire a car,' he said, 'Aix is only an hour or so away. And there's Arles, just down the road, more or less.' Simon made a mark in the book. 'Didn't Van Gogh do a lot of his stuff there? Him and Gauguin, just up your street.'

'Maybe,' Ruth said, unconvinced.

Neither of them were artists who appealed to her a great deal. Although the actual paintings in the Van Gogh Museum in Amsterdam, as opposed to a million reproductions, had impressed her more than she'd anticipated, Ruth found the work a little too self-dramatising; and as for Gauguin, his high-jinks with Polynesian fourteen-year-olds, she thought, would have placed him on the paedophile register nowadays rather than the fine art syllabus.

She was about to say something to that effect to Simon, but

thought better of it, Simon having moved on from Arles to Aix-en-Provence.

They did go to Arles and also to Aix, Ruth almost relieved to find that, although the Musée de l'Arles had one of the best collections of Roman sarcophagi to be found anywhere in the world, neither it nor any of the other museums and galleries had any of Van Gogh's paintings on display. In Aix-en-Provence, however, she was delighted to discover a number of small exhibitions devoted to Cézanne – an artist she found herself far more in sympathy with – and especially excited to find it was possible to visit the studio where he had done some of his most famous work.

Ruth had once given over the best of her spare time, evenings and weekends, for a month, attempting to reproduce a Cézanne apple, only to have it looking, after all her efforts, like nothing more nor less than an apple. Whereas Cézanne's apples were that and something else. Something she could never come close to achieving.

No matter. They ate wonderful food everywhere they went, hired bikes, walked up into the hills, slept – and occasionally made love – in the heat of the afternoon, then sat out in the evening with glasses of chilled Sancerre, gazing into the haze of purple dusk. Heather, in her campsite on the Cornish coast, seemed all the miles away she was and more.

There were two public telephones at the site and, after that first evening, it had been Ruth or Simon who had phoned at an appointed time, Heather waiting inside the box for the call. Sometimes, if both phones were occupied, there was a short wait but no more. Alan Efford, who had a mobile for his work, had said Heather could use it if there were a problem, but so far there'd been no need.

'I want to send you both a card,' Heather said one evening, 'but I don't know where to send it to.'

'Send it home,' Ruth said. 'Then it will be there when we arrive.'

Simon suggested stopping off in Paris on the return journey, prolonging the holiday for two more nights. They stayed at a comfortable if fading hotel on the Île St Louis and after a long, slow breakfast in the small courtyard, Simon allowed himself to be dragged across Paris to the Musée Marmottan Monet, Ruth having discovered, more or less by chance, that two large paintings by the American artist, Joan Mitchell – one of her especial favourites – were temporarily on display. Huge canvases, ripe with purples, greens and blues: Monet's garden at Giverny, conceived in the most abstract of terms.

Ruth stood in front of them, quite still, until her calves ached, marvelling at the skill of eye and hand that could make something so coherent, so perfect, so much more than itself, while Simon paced, less than patiently, from room to room, coughed discreetly and tapped, from time to time, the face of his watch.

'Thank you,' she said outside, kissing him impulsively on the cheek. 'Thank you, that was wonderful. It really was.'

That evening they ate duck with honey and figs in a small restaurant in the Marais and, walking back to their hotel, close to the Seine, she took Simon's hand. 'We should do this more often.'

'Hold hands?'

'You know what I mean.'

'I know. And now Heather's getting older, maybe we can.' He gave her hand a squeeze.

The bar on the western end of the Île looked inviting, with its wicker chairs and round, marble-topped tables set out on the curve of pavement.

'It's still early,' Simon said. 'We could have a nightcap, what do you think?'

'That would be nice.'

'Warm enough to sit outside?'

'Yes, I think so.'

Simon asked the waiter for cognac and coffee, Ruth a glass of white wine. A boat went slowly by, barely seeming to disturb the near-black water, music playing, couples waving from the side. It was several moments before Ruth realised that her phone was ringing inside her bag.

'Hello?'

She would always remember that moment, the coloured lights reflecting in the water, the marble of the tabletop cool beneath her wrist, the words that, despite the distance and the slight tremble in Alan Efford's voice, were impossible to misunderstand.

'Yes,' she said. 'Yes, of course. Right away. As soon as we can.' And breaking the connection, she put aside the phone.

'What is it?' Simon said. 'What's wrong?'

'It's Heather. She's gone missing.'

12

The minute they'd had their lunch, half a Cornish pasty each, iced buns and salt and vinegar crisps, the two girls were fussing round Pauline for money to go to the shop.

'What for now, for heaven's sake?'

'Ice cream,' said Kelly.

'Chocolate,' said Heather.

'Well, which is it? Make up your minds.'

'Both,' the girls said, almost in the same breath, and laughed as if that were the funniest thing they'd heard.

Heather's parents had given her spending money, but somehow she'd managed to get through most of that within the first few days: endless trips to the camp shop for sweets and fizzy drinks her mum always said would rot her teeth, and sparkly gimcracks from the accessories shop on their one trip into Penzance. A gold chain with her name spelled out in fancy letters was her special favourite, the one she'd have to do her best to hide when she got home for fear of her mother throwing a small fit.

'Mum!' Kelly said. 'Come on.'

'All right,' Pauline sighed, fishing into her purse, 'but this is the last time. And bring something back for your sister.'

'Let me come with you,' Tina said, springing, eager, to her feet.

'Drop dead!' Kelly responded, and snatching the money from her mother's hand, ran off out of the tent, Heather close on her heels.

The shop was a long single-storey building with weathered green walls and mesh shutters across its windows, selling everything from Calor gas cylinders and barbecue briquettes, through cans of Coke and packets of oven chips and fish fingers, to toothpaste and postcards of Land's End and Sennen Cove. Positioned at the head of the entrance road between the camping and caravan fields, it was a focal point for anyone and everyone, not least the gang of eight or nine mid-teen boys who lounged around in a variety of surf tops and shorts or cut-off jeans, none too surreptitiously smoking cigarettes and occasionally summoning up the energy to engage in a bad-tempered game of soccer.

As Kelly and Heather emerged, brandishing virulent purple Slush Puppies, flip-flops on their feet and skimpy near-bikini tops on their tanned, skinny bodies, several of the boys made noises of derisory appreciation.

'Bog off!' Kelly called in their general direction, then, lowering her voice, to Heather, 'There. I told you he fancied you.'

'Who?'

'The grungy one with the spots.'

'Thanks a lot!'

Kelly doubled over with laughter, and then, seeing her brother walking towards them, added, louder again, 'So does Lee. Don't you, Lee?'

'Don't I what?'

'Fancy Heather.'

'Do I, bollocks!' And, pushing two fingers into his open mouth, he mimed throwing up.

'Gross!' Kelly said and, giggling, the two girls hurried off.

Pauline finally contrived to get the baby off to sleep and took the opportunity to have a nap herself, leaving Alan to amuse Tina, which he attempted first by playing catch with a poorly inflated beach ball – pretty much a waste of time, he would say, as Tina seemed incapable of catching anything, not even a cold in the middle of an epidemic – then settling down to play snap with an old pack of cards which kept sticking together at crucial moments, the resulting shouts waking Pauline and the baby in quick succession.

Not so many minutes later, Lee slouched back into the shelter of the main tent, one of those familiar looks on his face that announced he was too bored even to complain about his boredom. Soon after that, Kelly and Heather emerged from their smaller tent in shorts and T-shirts, Heather also wearing a loose cotton top, swimming things and towels stuffed down into a pink and blue rucksack.

'And just where d'you think you're going?' Alan asked.

'Swimming.'

'Not now you're not.'

'Dad . . .'

'No, I'm sorry. No.'

'Besides, it's too late in the day,' Pauline put in. 'It'll soon be time for your tea.'

'We've only just had lunch,' Kelly said.

'Please, Mrs Efford,' Heather said, 'it's not as if we'll be going far. That little cove, you know? The one we saw from the path.'

'You can't go there.'

'Why ever not?' Kelly challenged.

'Because you'll break your bloody necks climbing down,' Alan Efford said. 'That's why.'

'Dad, come on! We're not babies, you know.'

Weakening, Alan Efford looked towards his wife for support.

'Maybe if Lee went with them,' Pauline offered.

'As if,' Lee said, scornfully. He was sitting in the corner, cross-legged, untangling the headphones of his Sony Walkman.

'Go on, Lee,' Pauline said, chivvying him along. 'It won't hurt you.'

'No way.'

'Don't bother,' Kelly said. 'We don't want him with us anyway.'

'Right,' her father said, fed up with the lot of them. 'He goes, or the pair of you stay here. That's all there is to it.'

Kelly looked at Heather, who shrugged and sighed.

'Come on, Lee,' Heather said. 'It might be fun.'

Lee called her a name under his breath.

'You,' Efford said, jabbing a finger in his son's direction. 'Get up off your sorry arse and go. Now.'

'Dad . . .'

'Just do what I bloody say.'

With an elaborate sigh, Lee lurched to his feet. 'Come on then, if we're going.' Slipping his headphones into place, he moved out of the tent.

'Thanks, Mr Efford,' Heather said. 'We'll be careful, honest.'

'Just don't be too long, that's all.'

'We won't.'

And they were gone.

The best part of an hour later, when Alan Efford went with Tina across to the shop – a lolly for her, cigarettes for Pauline and himself – there was Lee, kicking a ball around with half a dozen other boys.

'What the fuck d'you think you're doin' here?'

'What's it look like?' Lee replied.

Efford caught him a clip round the back of the head and several of the other lads laughed.

'You're supposed to be with your sister.'

'Yeah, well . . .'

'Well, what?'

'She kept mouthin' off, didn't she? Her an' that Heather, gigglin' all the time and prattin' around. I told 'em to shut it or else.'

'Or else what?'

'Else I'd come back an' leave 'em to it.'

'So that's what you did?'

'Yeah.'

Efford aimed another blow at his head, but this time the boy ducked and backed away.

'You wait,' Efford said. 'You just bloody wait.'

But by then the fog had started to roll in off the sea. And by the time Efford got back to the tent, waves of mist had spread across the entire campsite, and the coastline, no more than a field away, had all but disappeared.

'I'll ring his bloody neck!' Pauline Efford said, when she heard what Lee had done.

With a curse, Efford pulled on his cagoule and thrust off out into the mass of grey. The beginnings of the coast path were barely legible at his feet. When he called the girls' names the fog seemed to swallow them whole. Less than thirty minutes and he was back.

'Can't see your hand in front of your bloody face. Lucky not to go arse over tip off the edge.'

'Christ, Alan, what're we gonna do?'

'Wait. What else can we do?'

The sea fret showed little sign of fading and out of the west a slow, fine rain had started to fall.

'They'll get soaked through,' Pauline Efford said. 'They've not got proper coats with 'em or nothing.'

'Rain's what you want. Wash this bastard stuff away.'

Instead, the rain seemed to cling and become one with the mist and they continued to sit inside their tent in near-silence, the low, almost animal sound of the foghorn blurting out of the darkness.

'Fuck!' Efford said, picking up one of the enamel pans and hurling it through the flap of the tent. 'Fuck! Fuck! Fuck! Fuck!'

At the anger in her father's voice, Tina began to cry, her sobs setting off the baby, exactly as Pauline had said they would.

Another hour passed. Wet and miserable, Lee slunk back into the tent.

'Where the hell've you been?' his father asked. 'Look as if you've been dragged through a hedge bloody backwards!'

The boy didn't answer, but shucked off his waterproof and dropped it, sodden, to the ground. Most of the colour seemed to have gone from his eyes. 'Kelly's not back?' he said.

'What's it look like?'

Lee turned his head away. 'I'm sorry,' he mumbled. 'I'm sorry, I know I shouldn't've . . .' The words ran to a stuttering halt and he stood there, slump-shouldered, staring at the ground, frightened now and close to tears.

Alan Efford had already contacted the police.

13

They came in two four-by-fours, slow across the field, wheels sending up small plumes of muddied earth. Trevor Cordon, the officer in charge, was angular, long-faced and sombre-eyed, older than Alan Efford by some few years, trousers tucked down into faded green wellingtons. He listened, nodded, made notes in his book: by now the girls had been gone the best part of five hours, rising six, and night would be closing in. With low cloud and enough of the mist still lingering, there was little sense calling in the coastguard helicopter till first light.

Cordon knew the cove the girls had been aiming for, down the coast towards Sennen and not easily accessible: a difficult scramble over rocks before a steep section of cliff, the final descent requiring a length of fraying rope that had long ago been attached to an iron bracket hammered into the face. The council were forever putting up notices warning of potential dangers, all of them promptly defaced before being pulled up and sent tumbling down on to the small triangle of sand, where they were pressed into service as impromptu surfboards or broken into kindling for makeshift barbecues.

'Don't you worry, sir,' Cordon said. 'They'll have taken shelter when the fret came in, I dare say. From what you've told me, I doubt they'll do anything too daft. And they might well get back yet under their own steam. Just in case, though, I'll have my lads go a ways along the coast path while they still can. If they don't turn up, my guess'd be, our best chance of finding them is come morning. Cold and wet and more'n a little sorry for themselves, but hopefully none the worse for that. One blessing of all this cloud, temperature'll not drop much more than this. They'll not freeze.'

Efford glanced across at his wife, who looked away.

If the girls had panicked, Cordon thought, run off blindly instead of finding shelter and staying put, one wrong step could have sent them over the edge, while another might have seen them plunging down into any one of a dozen old open mine shafts, some fenced off, others camouflaged by gorse and bracken.

Some of the shafts, he knew, went out as far as four hundred metres beneath the Atlantic, the deepest of them going down a hundred and fifty metres below sea level. No sense in making matters worse, he kept that knowledge to himself.

When the girl's mother offered him a mug of tea, he accepted and gratefully.

Townies, he thought, the bane of his life: coming down from London or Birmingham or wherever without a bloody clue about where they were or what they were doing; wandering up on to the moors or out along the cliffs without a thought the weather might change in a moment or what the ground was like underfoot. Women in high heels he'd seen before now, turning their ankle out on the coast path and having to be winched home, stupid sods – Cordon would have left them there, let 'em limp back of their own accord.

'Yes, my love, two sugars if you please. That's grand.'

It would be a late night and an early morning and Cordon hoped to Christ it would be good news in the end and not bad. One of the girls, her parents had been informed and they were on their way back from abroad – the Lord alone knew what agonies they must be going through.

Little that the Pierces said in the course of their journey had much coherence, their thoughts filled with dread, conversation between them brittle as old bones. Ruth had managed to speak to Alan Efford once, the signal breaking up constantly: Heather and Kelly had set out together with Lee to go swimming; after some kind of a row, Lee had come back on his own, a thick fog had come in swiftly off the sea and the two girls had got lost. What else was there to know?

The first flight from Charles de Gaulle took off no more than twenty minutes behind schedule, but already Simon was chewing his fingernails. Ruth avoided his eye, not wishing to further jar his nerves and quicken his temper, or engage in yet another painful and fruitless discussion about what had happened, another litany of guilt and blame. In her heart, she hugged Heather to herself, whispered words unheard to keep her safe from harm.

Above Gatwick, the plane circled with agonising slowness as it waited for a slot to land.

Finally down and through customs, all attempts to garner fresh news failed; both telephones at the campsite seemed to be permanently engaged and Alan Efford's mobile was either switched off or lacking a strong enough signal.

Filling in the forms at the car hire counter, Simon twice made mistakes, finally ripping the form in two and having to start again.

'D'you want me to do it?' Ruth asked.

'No!' Simon shouted in her face. 'I don't want you to bloody do it. Why don't you go and get us some coffee? Do something useful for a change.'

They were on the road in half an hour, the M23 to the M25 to the M4. Three hundred miles and the rest. Provided they didn't encounter any major hold-ups, shared the driving, kept stops to a minimum, they should be there in six or seven hours. Early to mid-afternoon.

Ruth tried Alan Efford's mobile again, and again there was no reply.

The weather that morning was a mockery: bright and clear, the sky a perfect Sunday painter's blue, the islands off Cape Cornwall standing out sharp and clean; no vestige of the previous day's mist remained.

The man who walked into the lifeboat station overlooking Sennen Cove was no more than medium height, neither young nor old, his weathered anorak, waterproof trousers and cap not marking him out as any different from scores of others.

He stood for some moments, uncertain, unassuming, the lifeboat man on duty anticipating a question about tides or similar.

The voice was quiet at first, indistinct; a mumble of words like marbles caught in the mouth and little more: something about two missing girls. 'This search,' the man said again, voice louder, 'these missing girls – they're not . . . they'm not . . . anything to do with you?'

'Not really. Not direct.'

'Okay, only . . . only I know . . . know where one of 'em is.'

The lifeboat man looked at him curiously, uncertain whether to believe him or not, but hooked in nonetheless. 'Where's that then?'

'I've got her, haven't I?'

'You've what?'

'Been looking after her.'

'What the hell you talkin' 'bout?'

'Lookin' after her, like I said.'

A crank most likely, the lifeboat man thought; more than a touch of singsong to his voice once he'd got himself started; one of them crackpots, come out the woodwork whenever something happens like this. Even so . . .

'The girl, she's all right?' he asked warily.

'Oh, yes. She's all right.'

Crackpot or not, he knew he should call it in. 'Hang on there,' he said, reaching for the phone. 'Just let me talk to someone about this.'

When the message was relayed to him, Cordon's response was to the point. 'Tell him to wait there till we arrive. Tie him down if you have to. Tie him to the prow of the fucking boat.'

Less drastically, they offered him tea from a flask and found him a stool where he could sit and look out across the sea, pore over the charts for that stretch of coast.

As soon as Cordon saw the man he thought he'd seen him before, not knowing, immediately, when or where. Down by the harbour in Penzance, perhaps, watching the *Scillonian* come in to dock; on the quayside in Newlyn, leaning on the rail as catches of monkfish and mackerel were unloaded. Gibbens, Cordon thought his name was, though he couldn't remember who had told him or how he knew. Francis Gibbens. The name felt right on his tongue.

'Mr Gibbens?'

The man seemed startled to be addressed directly.

'You've got some information about one of the missing girls, I believe?'

'You the police, then?'

Cordon showed him his card.

'I dare say,' Gibbens said, his smile showing a mouthful of yellowing teeth, 'there'll be some kind of reward.'

*

94

Even in a four-by-four they could only go so far. Leaving the vehicle where the track petered out, Cordon and two other officers followed Gibbens along an uneven path between patches of purple heather, bright in the morning sunlight. In front of them the sea today seemed benign, low waves lolloping harmlessly in towards the shore. Some foolish bird twittering above, barely audible through the rattle of the helicopter flying low, further along the coast. The first of the search parties would be making its way from Cape Cornwall, careful, slow.

Cordon felt the peaty soil give beneath his feet.

'How much further?' he asked.

Gibbens moved with the ease of familiarity, the speed of someone half his age.

They crossed the main coast path and down a sloping field to where a mass of granite rock twisted upwards like a man's head. Circumventing this, Gibbens pushed his way through a mass of ferns that rose to near shoulder height.

One of the officers lost his footing and cursed loudly, causing his companion to laugh.

'How much bloody further?' Cordon asked again. If this turned out to be a wild goose chase he'd personally drag Gibbens up to the old lookout point above Sennen Cove and push him off.

They straddled a sagging stretch of rusted barbed wire, turning right along another track that followed the contours of the cliff, and there suddenly below them, on a patch of partly cleared scrub, were four goats, one tethered, the others wandering free. Further along, where the land levelled out, still a long fall down to the sea and hidden from the main coast path above, were the roughly painted walls and roof of a wooden shack, reinforced here and there with sheets of tarpaulin and a few irregular plates of corrugated iron. To one side, a large fishing net, strung out between wooden poles, hung over a makeshift garden.

'You live here?' Cordon asked, incredulous.

Gibbens grinned.

A ginger and white cat lay sunning itself outside the door.

There was no lock, no key, just a wooden latch attached to a piece of string. Cordon followed Gibbens inside and stood quite still for several seconds, allowing his eyes to grow accustomed to the lower levels of light. The interior was cool and steeped in shadow, not easy to pick out the shallow figure wrapped in blankets on the narrow bed.

'There she is,' Gibbens said proudly. 'There's my girl.'

My girl, Cordon thought. Interesting.

The contents of the room were taking shape. Trestle table, a couple of straight-backed chairs, tea chests filled with clothes and the Lord knew what else. Flotsam and jetsam from the shore. Gas canisters. Several small wooden carvings on the walls. A jug of water taken from the barrel alongside the front door.

Cordon bent low over the girl and, with a rare and silent prayer, touched the tips of his middle fingers to her left temple, the pale, almost translucent skin high to one side of her head. His certainty had been, since he had first stepped into the room and seen her lying there tightly wrapped, cocooned, that she was dead.

Real or imagined, then, the faint pulsing against his hand?

Bending lower, he put his face in front of hers and felt the ghost of a breath against his cheek.

'Coastguard chopper,' he snapped, straightening. 'Now. And get the hospital alerted. Do it.'

As the officers backed hurriedly outside, reaching for their mobiles, Cordon's gaze went from Gibbens to the girl and back again.

'There's no signal,' Gibbens said. 'Not down here. They'll have to go back up the cliff to where you left the car.'

'There's another girl,' Cordon said. 'Lost in that damned sea fret. D'you know where she is?'

Nodding, Gibbens pointed towards the door. 'Out there,' he said with a quick nervous laugh. 'Out there.'

Out there was vast and still, in some respects, unknown.

14

Kelly in hospital, safe but sore, dehydrated, medical staff running tests, keeping a watchful eye, the search for Heather continued. The coastguard helicopter had been joined by another from the Royal Naval Air Station at Coldrose. Police, assisted by teams of volunteers, were combing the land either side of the coast path between Cape Cornwall and Sennen Cove. Members of the local caving club had been called in to assist in the search of the old mining shafts in the area close to where Kelly had been found.

A police liaison officer had been appointed, Ann Dyer, a young constable with a diploma in social work, tall, slender, confident, firm yet polite. 'If the Pierces get through to you again,' she told Alan Efford, 'let me speak to them. You've enough to cope with as it is.'

When Ruth phoned from the forecourt of a garage outside Bodmin, he passed his mobile to her without a word.

'There have been some developments,' Dyer said, 'but as of present, I'm afraid your daughter, Heather, is still missing. We're doing everything we can.'

'Developments? What developments? I don't understand.'

'Perhaps it will be easier to explain when you arrive. You'll come straight to the campsite?'

'Of course.'

'Do you need directions or . . . ?'

'No, no, that's fine.' Ruth, wanting to know exactly where her daughter would be staying, had bought an OS map of the area before they left for France.

'Good. I'll meet you there.'

'But listen . . .'

The connection was broken.

The distance was not great, sixty miles, but on those roads – narrow and twisting beyond Penzance – it took a good hour and a half. Behind the wheel, Simon, patience already over-stretched, cornered too fast, swearing beneath his breath.

Alan Efford, meanwhile, had come back to the campsite with Lee and Tina, leaving Pauline and the baby at the hospital. Periodically, Tina would break out crying for no clear reason; Lee continued to look sullen, saying little or nothing. Chain-smoking, Efford paced up and down.

When he saw the car approach, he stopped and pushed a hand up through the stubble of his hair. 'I'm not looking forward to this one fucking bit.'

'Don't worry,' Ann Dyer said. 'Let me handle it.'

Simon braked too hard and the car slewed sideways, danger-ously close to one of the tents.

'Mr Pierce, Mrs Pierce, I'm Police Constable Dyer. Come over and sit down and we can talk. Maybe you'd like some water? A cup of tea?'

'I don't want to sit down,' Simon said, 'I've been sitting down all fucking day. And I don't want tea either. I want to know what you're doing to find our daughter.'

'Mr Pierce, I can assure you . . .'

But he wasn't listening. 'As for you,' he said, pointing at Efford, 'you fucking moron . . .'

'Simon!' Ruth called out. 'Simon, don't.'

'You stupid, ignorant bastard! This is all your fault.'

'Mr Pierce . . .' Dyer set a hand on his arm. 'It's not helpful to talk about fault or blame. What happened is nobody's fault.'

'Nobody's fault? My daughter – our daughter – goes missing while this fucking idiot is supposed to be looking after her and it's nobody's fault?'

'Mr Pierce . . .'

'And that stupid fucking son of yours who let them wander off on their own, where's he?'

'Leave him out of this,' Efford said.

'Oh, yeah, leave him out. Never mind the fact if it wasn't for him . . .'

'Mr Pierce,' Dyer said, 'I can quite understand why you're angry, but it isn't helping the situation at all. Now if you'll please back off and calm down . . .'

Shaking his head, Simon turned grudgingly away, only to swing suddenly round and charge at Efford, arms flailing, fists raised; Efford took half a pace back and, with the shortest of swings, punched him hard in the face.

Simon staggered back, blood streaming from his nose.

'Enough!' Dyer said, placing herself between them. 'That's enough.'

Fishing a tissue from her pocket, Ruth leaned towards her husband, who was down on one knee, a hand to his face.

'That bastard,' he said thickly. 'I think he's broken my fucking nose.'

The nose, when Dyer examined it cursorily, didn't appear to be broken, but come the next morning, she thought, he'd be sporting a fine bruise. Serve him right. She told Ruth to walk him round the field a couple of times until he'd properly calmed down. 'Come back in five or ten minutes,' she said, 'and then we'll talk.'

'We need to know what's happened,' Ruth pleaded.

'Of course. Of course you do. But let's all take a few minutes, okay? Let tempers cool. Then, I promise you, I'll bring you up to speed.'

When they'd gone, Efford apologised to her for what he'd done.

Dyer smiled. 'Wasn't as if he gave you a whole lot of choice.'

'He's got a right to go off on one. His position I'd do the same.'

'But it's not your fault. What happened.'

Efford shook his head. 'I should have known better than to have let them go all that way on their own.'

'You didn't. Your son went with them. He's almost what? Fifteen? Sixteen? You weren't to know he was going to walk off and leave them. Any more than you were to know the fog would come in so fast.'

Efford sighed and lit another cigarette.

'You've got your daughter back, at least,' Dyer said.

'I know. So tell me why I feel like shit.'

'Because you're feeling guilty, that's why. Your kid was found and not theirs. Until we find her, you will be, reason or not.'

'And if you don't?'

'We will.'

Ruth and Simon Pierce were heading back across the field, Simon looking somewhat abashed, his immediate anger abated, both anxious for news. When they were seated, Dyer outlined as succinctly as possible all that she knew.

The fact that Kelly had been found and not Heather struck them like a slap in the face. Ruth looked across at Alan Efford, wanting to say she was pleased his daughter was safe, but not being able to force out the words.

'This man,' Simon said. 'The one who found Kelly. He didn't see Heather at all?'

'Apparently not.'

'And you believe him?'

'No reason not to, not so far.'

'But if the girls were together?'

'It looks as if somehow they got separated in the fog.'

'Is that what Kelly says?' Ruth asked.

'I'm afraid we haven't really been able to talk to her yet. Not in any detail. She's still too weak.'

'And this bloke,' Simon put in, 'the one who found Kelly. There isn't anything . . . ?'

'We're talking to him now. Making sure there's nothing we've missed.'

Gibbens was clinging to his story with the tenacity of the inherently truthful or the simple-minded. He had gone outside way after dark; one of the goats had chewed through the rope by which he kept them tied up at night and was butting its head against the door. Securing the animal again he heard a faint sound, a sort of mewing, from higher up the cliff, and thought one of the several cats he kept around and fed had got itself trapped; climbing up, he discovered it was not a cat but a girl, barely conscious amidst the bracken. She had fallen from a higher path – tripped, possibly, on the barbed wire – and rolled to where he found her. Carefully, he had picked her up – no weight at all – and carried her back down to the shack.

Her clothes had been soaked through, T-shirt ripped and torn; there was blood on her face and on her hands. Blood also from cuts to her leg, low down and high on her hip.

'You undressed her?' Cordon asked.

'Yes, of course.'

'Completely?'

'Like I said, everythin' was wet through. Sodden. She'd have died of cold else.'

'You wrapped her in blankets?'

'After I'd washed her, yes.'

'Washed her?'

'She'd been bleeding, like I said. I washed her with a cloth, just gentle like, before putting her to bed. Tried to get her to drink somethin' too, water or milk, but no, she wouldn't. Just brought it back up.'

'Why didn't you send for help straight away?'

'An' leave her? I couldn't do that. Waited till morning, till I was certain she was all right. Fit enough to leave. That's when I went for help.'

'Why the lifeboat station? Why not use a public call box, 999, emergency? Ask for the police?'

Gibbens shrugged. 'No reason.' For the first time since the interview had begun, he looked away.

'You've been in trouble, that it? In trouble before?'

'Am I in trouble now?'

'I don't know, are you?' Cordon leaned back.

'No.'

A police car delivered Pauline Efford back from the hospital in Penzance and prepared to ferry her husband in the opposite direction. Before leaving, Alan Efford took a step towards Ruth, as if to say something, but changed his mind. But when Pauline neared the tent, baby Alice on her hip, Ruth went impulsively towards her and gave her a hug.

'Kelly, how is she?'

'She'll be fine. Considering. They'll keep her in overnight, just to be sure, you know, observation, but yeah, she'll be fine.'

Ruth squeezed one of her hands. 'I'm so glad.'

'Thank you,' Pauline said through the beginning of tears. 'Your Heather – they'll find her soon. Bound to.'

'Yes. Yes, I expect you're right.'

Ruth gave Pauline's hand another quick squeeze and turned away.

An officer in overalls was approaching purposefully across the field and Ann Dyer moved to intercept him, the conversation close and quick.

When Dyer turned towards Ruth there was a small plastic envelope in her hand.

'Do you recognise this?' she asked.

Inside the envelope was a gold chain with letters spelling out the name HEATHER at its centre. The clasp was broken and, here and there, the links of the chain were dark with mud.

Ruth stared at it, mesmerised.

'Do you recognise it?' Dyer asked again.

Ruth shook her head. 'No. I'm sorry, no. I've never seen it before.'

'You're sure?'

'Yes, of course.'

'It isn't Heather's? Your daughter's?'

'No.'

'Yes,' Pauline Efford said quietly. 'Yes, it is.'

'But how . . . ?'

'She bought it, in Penzance. With her pocket money. She thought – she thought it was lovely.'

No way to stop the tears now, both women crying, and Simon hurrying from where he'd been standing further along the field edge, looking out. 'What? What is it? What's happened?'

Slipping the envelope down into her pocket, Dyer reached for her phone.

15

Alan Efford had drawn Cordon over to one side, the thought gnawing at him since his daughter had been winched up into the helicopter on a stretcher, ready for the journey to hospital; ever since the liaison officer had spelled out the circumstances in which she had been found: Ann Dyer stating the facts as she knew them, her tone neutral, giving each word equal weight, first this and then that.

His face, when he spoke to Cordon, was pale, save for a ragged spread of stubble.

'For fuck's sake, I need to know.'

'Know what?'

'What you're not telling me.'

'And that is?'

Cordon could have read it in his eyes if he had not already known. A father's thoughts and fears. Hadn't he been a father himself? Still was, though there was little enough to show. The occasional postcard, the odd guilt-driven phone call, his son's voice remote and wavering like something caught in the wind, on the tide. Scraps for which he had to be grateful. Would it be better if there were nothing now at all?

'He didn't touch her,' Cordon said.

'He took off all her clothes. Stripped her naked. Of course he fucking touched her.'

'Not in that way.'

'That way? That fucking . . .'

'Her clothes were sodden. She was wet through. Cold. Without him she might have died.'

'He . . .'

'He did what he had to do. Be grateful.'

End of conversation. Cordon turned smartly away. He had asked the doctor who had examined her and been reassured: no signs of sexual activity, recent or otherwise, no traces of saliva or semen.

I washed her with a cloth, just gentle like . . .

It nagged at him all the same: was there more to Gibbens than met the eye? A man who had opted, as far as one can, for the life of a recluse; whose need for companionship, conversation, was almost nil. A few goats, stray cats, the sound of the sea.

To Cordon it didn't seem so bad a life: in some respects, just a more extreme version of his own. The way the job got under your skin, leaving an aversion to humankind.

A preliminary trawl through local records had thrown up nothing and neither could Cordon pinpoint how and why he had known Gibbens' name.

Later that day, the pink and blue rucksack was found, caught up in an overhang of bracken, only a little further along the cliff from Gibbens' shack. Both pairs of swimming costumes were still inside, towels, two pairs of goggles.

Still no sign of the second girl: with each hour, Cordon knew, it was less and less likely she would be found alive.

*

Heather's parents had found accommodation in St Just, the nearest town and a few miles inland, a room in one of several pubs that overlooked the war memorial and the small central square. Striped wallpaper and heavy curtains, tea bags and sachets of instant coffee, biscuits wrapped in cellophane, a plastic kettle which leaked steam and was dangerous to touch, a small television with near zero reception. On the walls were photographs of helmeted miners clustered in groups, waiting to go underground, along with the text of one of John Wesley's speeches, delivered in the local Methodist chapel, promising fire and brimstone, hell and damnation.

Ruth sat, closed in on herself, repeating Heather's name over and over beneath her breath; staring at the phone and waiting for it to ring.

Simon had asked if he could join one of the official search parties, but had been rebuffed: let us get on with our job, sir, it's best. In some kind of placatory gesture, one of the officers had taken them along the coast path in the direction the girls had been walking and they had stared down at the small curve of beach towards which they'd been heading, Ruth's tears impossible to control.

Now Simon paced, made cups of tea he never drank, kicked the bedposts, punched the walls, went out for a bottle of Scotch and brought it back, snapped off the cap and splashed some liberally in a glass, swallowed a mouthful down too fast then spat it back into the sink.

Recriminations were rife.

'How many times did I tell you this would happen? Something like this. Hmm? How many times? Bloody disaster. Disaster waiting to happen. I knew it. Just knew it.'

'Simon, Simon. You're not making any sense.'

'Aren't I?'

'We didn't know, we couldn't know anything.'

'No?'

Ruth shivered. 'Not anything like this. And anyway, you were the one who jumped at the idea. Great, you said. Heather off our hands for a change. Let's go off and enjoy ourselves. You could hardly wait.'

'That's not true.'

'Isn't it?'

'I jumped at the idea, as you put it, because you'd been agonising about it, week after bloody week – maybe we should let her go, what harm can it do? What harm? What fucking harm!'

'Simon . . .'

'They're nice people, that's what you said. Nice! Never mind they haven't got a book in the house and their idea of intellectual stimulation is watching *EastEnders* and reading the bloody *Sun*.'

'God, just listen to yourself. You really think it would have made any difference if they'd been down here working their way through the Booker shortlist or reading the *Telegraph* from cover to cover? You think that would have made them more careful, more aware?'

'It might.'

Ruth laughed and shook her head and when her mobile rang she half-tripped on the rug in her scramble to pick it up.

'Yes,' she said. Then, 'Yes,' again, and 'Well, all right, I suppose,' and 'Oh, good. Good. I'm glad.' After listening a few moments longer, she said, 'Thanks. Thank you,' and 'Wish her well,' and set the phone back down.

'That was Pauline, wondering how we were. Kelly's a lot better, it seems, sitting up and talking . . .'

'Heather. Did she say what happened?'

'She doesn't know. They got separated in the fog, that's all she can tell them. The police have talked to her and they're going to talk to her again.'

Simon turned towards the window and looked out. A couple

were sitting inside their parked car, doors open, eating fish and chips. Three men in shirtsleeves and a young woman in a skimpy top and shorts were standing outside the pub opposite, enjoying the sunshine, laughing, beer glasses in their hands. Kids on skateboards were practising their moves around the memorial.

'I'm going out,' he said.

'Where to?'

Simon shrugged and reached for his coat.

'You want me to come with you?'

'You want to?'

She hesitated. 'One of us better stay here.'

'They'll contact us if there's anything.'

'I'll stay here just the same.'

'Suit yourself.'

When he had gone, Ruth sank back on the bed and closed her eyes. Minutes later, or so it seemed, there is Heather, running towards her, crying, holding out her hand. They are in the garden, the small shared garden in Muswell Hill. Playing. Except that it isn't playing, not for Heather, not really. She's being a gardener, helping Mummy repot the geraniums; both hands held carefully round the handle of the trowel until the trowel slipped and the pot spun and fell against the path and cracked along the edge and there was blood and, of course, tears. Mummy kiss it better. Plaster, of course you can have a plaster, but let's first run it under the tap. Nice cold water. There. Now pat it dry. No, it's all right, it won't hurt. I'll be careful. Mummy won't hurt you. The plaster passing round the stick-like finger twice. No more gardening today. Heather's head leaning against her as they settle back indoors on the settee, her bony elbow pressing against Ruth's thigh. There, that better? Ruth lowers her head until she can feel her daughter's hair soft against her face and inhale her smell, her scent. Something twists deep inside and pulls, like a small fist tugging at her guts.

Alan and Pauline Efford are taking it in turns to be at the hospital, alternating that with looking after Tina and the baby: Tina morose and difficult to amuse, prey, still, to sudden bouts of tears; Alice, as if sensing the general mood, grizzly and complaining, refusing the bottle, refusing her food.

Alan takes them down to the beach, but this is worse: the shrill and shriek of gulls, the laughter of other children as they run in and out of the waves, build sandcastles, play catch.

Your kid was found and not theirs.

The reproach in Ruth's eyes; the hatred in Simon's.

Back up at the campsite, Lee sits, cross-legged, in the tent. He has been to see his sister once, early on, not since. He sits with his hands over his headphones to amplify the sound, the same track on his Walkman, again and again. Portishead. 'Glory Box'. The singer's voice, small and clear, almost childlike, pitched against the distortions of synthesiser and guitar, pleading for a reason.

Heather has been missing now for two nights and two days and already dusk is closing in.

Wandering around St Just, Simon has found himself in some kind of grassed-over amphitheatre where he sits amongst signs of picnicking, struggling to control the images that flicker through his mind. Crossing the square earlier, the area outside the pub more crowded than before, he had caught himself staring at a girl in a short, sheer dress, following her movements as she threw back her head and laughed and performed an odd little three-step dance, the light seeming to reflect from the bare skin of her legs as she moved, the curve and swell of her calves and thighs, the hem of the dress barely covering her behind. As he drew closer and she turned again, sweeping the hair from her eyes, he saw that she was little more than a child, twelve or perhaps thirteen, and he swerved away, ashamed at what he had been feeling, what, remembering, he still felt.

Upstairs in their room, Ruth sank to her knees and, for the first time since she was herself a girl, not knowing if she believed or not, she prayed. If there is a hell, she thought, remembering Wesley's words, it's now and here.

16

They found her almost by accident, early the following morning. A volunteer with one of the official search parties – a student spending his summer vacation working as a lifeguard on the beach at Sennen – lost his footing at the entrance to one of the old engine houses a short distance from the coast path; the stonework gave way beneath his feet and sent him tumbling down, clawing at air, until he landed, badly winded, on a jagged shelf some twenty feet below. When he opened his eyes and they had become adjusted to the low levels of light, there she was, outlined along the crumbling shelf opposite, the girl they were looking for – who else could it be? – her head lolling back against the rusted wheel of some old winding gear that had fallen years before.

Unable to climb back up, no handholds to speak of and his ankle badly swollen from the fall, he shouted himself hoarse until someone heard – not one of the search party but a middle-aged woman striding out purposefully towards Land's End and beyond – compass, map case, binoculars, rucksack on her back.

Help soon arrived; a rope ladder was secured and lowered down and, still shaken, the student climbed slowly out. Within fifteen minutes, a helicopter was hovering over the scene: then Land Rovers, four-by-fours, Cordon pacing.

Only two walls of the engine house were still standing, together with the chimney alongside, all in a state of serious disrepair. Along with the others that dotted the coast it had been searched before, torches shone around, lamps lowered down, without the body being noticed.

How?

Two men in climbing gear, helmeted, photographed the body as it lay, before strapping it securely on to a stretcher and steadying it on its way to the surface.

Cordon held his breath as the stretcher was lowered to the ground. The skin, where it was visible, had already taken on a greenish hue, patches of marbling on the calves and upper arms. A gash across the forehead had scabbed thickly over and there were scratch marks to both sides of the face, where the blood had dried in spidery lines. There were scratches also on the legs and arms, and signs of bruising, too – such as you might expect, Cordon thought, from a fall. The long-sleeved cotton top, once pale blue, she'd worn over her T-shirt, was torn and darkened here and there by what could have been oil, but was, in all probability, more blood.

Her feet were bare.

There was no doubt it was the missing girl.

An end, Cordon thought, and for him a beginning.

Ruth and Simon had had breakfast downstairs in the rear bar that doubled as a dining room, and then gone back upstairs. Since his previous outburst, Simon had been unusu-ally quiet, squirrelling his thoughts away to himself. Ruth had walked to the newsagent's shop on the next corner, bought a *Guardian* for herself and a *Telegraph* for Simon and brought them back to where they now lay on the chest of drawers, largely unread.

The small radio in the corner of the room was tuned to Radio 3 and, through a whisper of interference, mimicking the pianist's own mutterings, Glenn Gould was playing his way through the *Goldberg Variations*.

Ruth had spoken to Ann Dyer, the liaison officer, earlier, phoning her first thing, and been told that, as yet, there were no new developments. So when there was a knock on the door and she opened it, half expecting the landlord, or someone wanting to clean the room, she was taken aback to see Dyer standing there, serious faced.

'Mrs Pierce . . .'

'Has something happened? Heather, you . . .'

'I think I'd better come inside.'

Ruth stepped back unsteadily, hand towards her throat, as Dyer stepped past her, closing the door at her back.

Simon stood, marooned, between window and bed.

'A little over an hour ago,' Dyer began, 'the body of a young girl was found . . .'

Ruth vomited through her fingers and Dyer, moving quickly, caught her before she fell.

With Simon's help, she manoeuvred Ruth towards the bed and sat her down, head towards her knees. Leaving Simon to hold her steady, she ran a flannel under the tap.

'It is Heather,' Simon said. 'There isn't any doubt?'

'I'm sorry,' Dyer said, with a shake of the head.

Without warning, Ruth's body arched sharply forward and she vomited again.

Cordon reached the headland and turned back into the wind. A pair of sparrow-like birds, olive-brown stripes, rose up, one following the other, from the heather, their high-pitched, trilling sound turning in the air. Warblers, is that what they were? Pippets? Plovers? Time was, he would have known. His father, patient, then patience fading – look, just look, will you? – size, shape, plumage, colour; patterns of behaviour, movement, song.

Size, shape, patterns of behaviour – being a policeman was not so different.

The old mine workings had been the first focus of the search, the shaft openings into which the girl might have fallen, the walls behind which she might have sought shelter. Lives enough had been lost there down the years, what was one more?

Her body broken at the wheel.

They had searched, but not well enough. It happened.

He knew of an incident some few years before when a body had been dumped in a small area of woodland close to two adjoining farms. Specialist search teams – not volunteers – had gone over the area twice before the body was discovered at a third attempt. The police psychiatrist had told Cordon it was a known phenomenon: individual officers not wanting to be the ones to discover the body and their fear of so doing so causing them to look without really seeing.

Cordon wasn't sure if he believed that or not.

He walked on and then stopped. From where he stood, the engine house was framed against the sky, blue showing clear through the empty, arched windows on its surviving walls, the mortar and stone of the tall chimney patterned like the neck of a giraffe.

What if, when the initial search had been carried out, the body had not been there? Suppose she had died somewhere else? The body hidden and then moved? A different picture altogether. And one which the autopsy would, to a large extent, prove or disprove. Even then, depending on the circumstances and the pathologist's tenacity and skill, there might still be a sliver of doubt.

Never make up your mind too soon, his father had always drummed into him: identification usually involves a process of exclusion; few birds are identified on positive evidence alone.

Time was, Cordon had known things for sure. Not often, not now.

Simon Pierce had volunteered to identify the body on his own – no need for Ruth to be put through this – but she had refused. Fearing the worst, he had held tight to her hand, but, a small cry, a gasp of air aside, Ruth had managed to keep herself in check.

Her daughter's face as she gazed down – scabs and scars freshly cleaned, blood wiped carefully away – was close to perfect in her eyes.

'She's so young,' she said quietly. 'She looks so young.'

Only when she was outside, in the white-walled, soulless corridor, did the tears come; long, wracking sobs that tore at the inside of her throat.

Simon bent over her awkwardly, embarrassed, concerned. 'Ruth. Ruthie. Come on, it's all right. Let's go outside.'

Cordon stood at the far end of the corridor, close by the door, watching, not wanting to interfere or be drawn in, yet taking on at a distance – is that what he was doing? – some small share of her pain.

'Ruthie, come on . . .' Simon said, leading her as he would a child.

Outside, the air hit her like a fist.

'It'll be all right, you see.'

She lifted her head towards him, as if seeing him for the first time, her face shrunken by tears, head shaking from side to side. It would never be all right again.

'As far as we can determine,' Cordon said, 'Heather must have taken shelter after she and her friend, Kelly, had become separated in the fog. Whether she fell on to the lower ledge immediately, or later, when perhaps she tried to move, we don't yet know. Perhaps we never will. Not exactly.'

They were sitting on a bench outside the hospital on St Clare Street, a few hopeful seagulls loitering on the low stone wall close by. Simon, who rarely smoked, lit a second immediately after the first. Ruth sat with her fingers intertwined, the skin between the knuckles all but white.

'As far as you can determine,' Simon said. 'Does that mean it might be something else? Some other explanation?'

Cordon shook his head. 'I'm probably being overcautious. This side of the inquest . . . well, you learn to bite your tongue.' He allowed himself a quick, self-deprecating smile. 'I shouldn't worry, Mr Pierce. I'm sure everything is as it seems.' Cordon was on his feet. 'Once again, please accept my sympathies for your loss.'

'Her clothes . . .' Ruth said suddenly. 'Heather's clothes.'

'They'll be returned to you in due course.'

'But surely, if you know what happened, there's no need . . . ?'

'It's all right, Mrs Pierce, simply a matter of routine.'

17

Cordon drove out to Cape Cornwall, parked to the side of the narrowing road before it tipped down the hill, and walked on past the car park staffed by National Trust volunteers waiting eagerly to take his money – something sanctimonious, almost evangelical, about some of them that set his teeth on edge. Once, one of them had even come running after him, angered by his all too evident penny-pinching, waving a cluster of brochures outlining the Trust's good works in his wake.

They did a fair lemon and orange marmalade, Cordon knew that, thick cut and at a price.

He took the steeper path, a quick scramble up to the chimney at the summit, a listed relic of the old Cape Cornwall mine. The day he had to follow the easier route that wound cautiously round was the day he would pension himself off, start looking more seriously at those stair lift ads that littered afternoon TV.

A family of four had colonised the single bench at the top, binoculars passed from hand to hand in search of seals, their blue-grey bullet heads sleek above the waves, or sea birds on the Brison Rocks, just offshore to the south, razorbills and guillemots.

Cordon found a smooth ledge with leg room sufficient to his needs and sat, gazing out. Here the Atlantic divided, south past Land's End towards the English Channel, north into the Bristol Channel and the Irish Sea. Over his shoulder, the family were delving into their pack-up, a late lunch, sandwiches and fruit, bottled water and a Thermos of tea. Somehow, Cordon had neglected to eat since the urgent call that morning had scuppered his plans for breakfast: thick rashers of bacon already on the grill, mushrooms waiting, sliced, beside the buttered pan, coffee on the stove. He hadn't felt hungry since and now he did.

The father said something that made the children laugh, girl and boy, both under twelve; the mother laughing, too, all happy in each other's company.

Though his own father had not been much of a one for jokes, Cordon had been happy to be in his company nonetheless; treks along the coast or inland across the moors, each path surveyed, planned out in advance; notebooks in which his father encouraged him to log the details of the trip – geological features, weather patterns, animals, birds. In a fit of late teenage rebellion, he had thrown them out, torn at the spine and tossed on to some skip: he would have done almost anything to have had them still. His father, too, dead these eleven years at seventy-three, no age, these days, at all.

Cordon missed him a little each and every day.

There was movement behind him as the family began packing away their things, readying themselves for the off. His own son was somewhere across that ocean, uncontactable, living a life of his own.

The pathologist's initial examination of Heather Pierce's body revealed only injuries that were consistent with a heavy fall; no evidence of sexual or other assault. There was nothing conclusive to suggest that the body had been moved after death nor that any of the injuries had been caused post-mortem. So much for Cordon's theories.

And now his superior was happily poised to tick the box beside Accidental Death.

Jimmy Lambert had tiptoed past Cordon on his way to promotion with the silent finesse of a Siamese with velvet paws. Now he was DS Lambert, Detective Superintendent, an oak desk with walnut inlay that he'd liberated from an auction house about to go down the tubes, and a view down towards the Penlee House Museum and the Wherry Rocks off the Promenade. Seagull shit on his window ledge a couple of fingers deep.

The end of another day and he'd had a taste of Scotch, maybe two, Cordon could smell it on his breath.

'So, Trev, open and shut, yes?'

'You think?'

'Does that mean you don't?'

Cordon shifted his weight from one buttock to another, the granite out at Cape Cornwall softer than the chairs Lambert kept on the wrong side of his desk. 'Too many questions not answered.'

'Such as?'

'How she got there, more than eighteen foot down, that for openers.'

'She fell.'

'Maybe.'

'You think what? She was pushed?'

Cordon gave a slow shrug of his bony shoulders.

'What else?' Lambert asked without conviction.

'The time. How long she'd lain there.'

'Since the night she disappeared . . .' Lambert began ferreting amongst the papers on his desk. 'Here, the estimated time of death . . .'

Cordon had no special reason for faulting Wilding, the local pathologist, aside from a tendency to view the shortest path between two points as correct. That and the fact that if Lambert swung a bit of weight, bar perjury, he could be talked into almost anything. Cordon heard Wilding liked his whisky with a leavening of water, whereas Lambert, he knew, preferred his straight, the two of them at the bar at the Ship's Apostle often enough after closing, exchanging pleasantries with the owner and his lady wife.

'That engine house had been searched and given the all-clear – you don't think that strange?'

'Careless, that's what I call it. Careless and casual, too casual by half.' Lambert shook his head. 'Use volunteers, sometimes that's what you get. A shame, but there it is. And besides, Wilding seems pretty clear she died where she was found.'

Cordon took a breath. 'I'd like to send the clothes off to Forensics, nevertheless.'

'What in God's name for?'

'They do these tests, I thought you might have heard. Blood, semen, saliva.'

Face reddening, Lambert was halfway out of his chair, pointing. 'Don't play clever buggers with me, you sarky piece of shit.'

Nice, Cordon thought. 'Nothing shows up,' he said, 'all tests negative, so much the better. Nothing lost.'

'Save a chunk of my budget I can ill afford to lose.'

Cordon fixed him with a look. 'That's what it is then, the money? Accidental death cheaper all round.'

'Fuck you, Cordon. There's not one scrap of evidence leads to an offence, nothing suggesting any fucking third-party involvement at all.'

'Not yet.'

'Jesus. Jesus Christ. You don't fucking give up.'

'It's my job.'

Lambert held his head in his hands and looked like a man for whom the next drink was just too far out of reach.

'All right,' he said eventually, 'send them off. Waste of time and bloody money though it is.'

'Yes, sir. Thank you, sir.' Cordon not entirely successful in hiding the smile playing at the corners of his mouth.

'And Cordon . . . Trevor . . .'

'Jimmy?'

'Next time you talk back to me like that you'll be back in fucking uniform.'

18

As ever, Forensic Science Services were backed up. Time seemed to go on hold. The temperature rose: twenty-five Celsius, twenty-seven, twenty-eight. The wind was averaging a mere six miles per hour out of the east. Even at night it was fourteen, fifteen: nigh on impossible to sleep.

Simon Pierce shifted position for the umpteenth time, pillow damp, the sheet sticking to him like a second skin. When, finally, he gave up, it was twenty to five and the light was already filtering through from outside. He drank water from the tap, swilled it round his mouth and spat it out.

Having drifted off at last, Ruth lay on her back, head to one side, a small whistle of breath accompanying each rise and fall of her chest.

The previous night, after an indifferent dinner and too much wine, they had argued fiercely about their daughter's funeral, almost come to blows. Simon held strongly that cremation was the only reasonable course. Reasonable and best. 'We'll take her ashes, Ruthie. Bury them in the garden, maybe, plant a tree. Or scatter them somewhere if you think that's better, somewhere she loved.'

But to Ruth cremation was anathema: Heather's body, already torn and bruised, going into the fire while they stood in some soulless chapel and watched as the coffin slowly disappeared from sight. She wanted their daughter to be buried, not in a churchyard, but in a meadow or woodland, surrounded by flowers and trees. A green burial. Somewhere beautiful, full of life.

'And what?' Simon had said. 'You think somehow that's better? You think that'll make a difference?'

'Yes.'

'She'll rot, Ruthie, that's all that'll happen. Decay and rot. Down into the earth till you don't know where the fuck she is.'

'No,' Ruth had almost screamed. 'No, she won't. She won't.' She believed that with all her heart and soul.

As Simon stood looking at her now, she rolled on to her side, stirred, and blinked open her eyes.

'What are you doing?'

'Nothing. I thought I might go for a walk.'

'What time is it?'

'Getting on for five.'

Ruth eased herself into a sitting position, pillows behind her, the sheet across her breasts. Simon was splashing water into his face at the sink, pulling a comb through his hair, preparing to brush his teeth.

'Why don't you go back to London?' she said. 'There's no reason for us both to stay. Not now.'

'Come with me then.'

'I can't. There's the inquest.'

'That might be ages away. You can't wait here till then. You'll go crazy.'

'Maybe.' For a moment, she smiled. 'I just don't think I can leave, not this soon. Not after . . . I feel I'd be leaving her, leaving her behind. Heather. It doesn't make any sense, I know, but . . .' She shook her head and sighed.

Simon sat on the edge of the bed. 'I don't know,' he said.

'Go on,' Ruth said. 'Go home.'

'If you're sure.'

'I'm sure.' He wanted to leave, she knew he did, she read it in his eyes if not his voice.

'Why not let your mum and dad come down? They've offered, after all. At least then you'll have some company.'

Ruth shook her head. 'I'm better on my own.'

Simon got to his feet. 'Okay, if that's what you want. But come with me now, come for a walk.'

Reaching up, she squeezed his hand. 'You go. I might just try and doze for a while if I can.'

Ten minutes later, less, he was ready and dressed and bent to kiss her on the forehead as he left. Instead of lying back down, Ruth remained where she was, staring at the wall opposite, the space between the windows, seeing nothing, only what wasn't there, the loss kicking deep inside her, deep, deep inside, tying itself into a knot until all she could do to release it was spread her arms wide, her arms and legs, throw back her head and howl like someone possessed.

The girl knocked at Cordon's door a little after ten that morning, spiked-up hair, pale skin, silver ring through her upper lip – new since Cordon had last seen her – and enough studs and rings elsewhere to start a shop of her own. Black T-shirt, black canvas jeans; white lipstick, blood-red finger-nails. Her mother had christened her Rose, but she preferred Letitia – joy and happiness – irony didn't come into it.

Cordon had first seen her when she was just thirteen, cross-legged on the bed in her druggy boyfriend's squalid flat, injecting heroin straight into the vein. Now she was all of sixteen, older than she might otherwise have been, and helped out by walking Cordon's springer spaniel most weekends and on the occasional summer evening. Pocket money, cash in hand. Cordon didn't ask questions as to where it ended up.

'Take the dog for a walk,' she said.

'She's got a name.'

'I know.'

Under the table, the springer had jumped at the sound of her voice, tail beginning to wag.

'I was thinking I might take her myself,' Cordon said.

'Whatever.' She turned back towards the door.

'How did you know I'd be here anyway?' Cordon asked.

'I didn't.'

'Then . . .'

'Took a chance.'

'Trouble at home?'

'What makes you say that?'

'No reason. Just asked.'

The dog was nuzzling into her now, head pressed against her leg.

'You take her,' Cordon said. 'She prefers you to me.'

The girl shrugged and ran her fingers through the hair on the animal's head and down on to her neck.

'How come you're here anyway?' she asked.

'Pulled a sickie.'

She looked at him warily, uncertain whether or not he was taking the piss. What Cordon was doing was biding his time, waiting for FSS to come through, reinterviewing material witnesses, everything by the book – the book as he knew it: Lambert keen to shunt him on to other things and Cordon digging in his heels as hard as he could. Showing his face around the office more than necessary was not a good idea.

'We'll be off then,' the girl said.

'Letitia . . .'

'What?'

'You had any breakfast?'

'What's it to you?'

'I was going to do some toast, that's all. Join me if you want.'

Almost grudgingly she agreed. 'But no questions, right? No, how's your mum, how's college, none of that crap.'

'You still going to college?'

'Okay, Kia, come on, we're out of here.'

'Stop, stop. It was a joke.'

'Some joke.'

'I won't say a thing. Don't want to know, don't care.'

'Yeah, right.'

While Cordon cut bread and placed four slices beneath the grill, then took jam and peanut butter from the cupboard and Flora from the fridge, Letitia wandered around, looking cursorily at this and that.

A former sail loft, basically a long single room with a kitchen at one end and a bed at the other, lavatory and bathroom partitioned off, Cordon had bought it before rumours of a new marina had started to be taken seriously and already stupid prices had become stupider still. Broad windows gave him unimpeded views out across the bay, from Newlyn out beyond Penzance to Marazion and St Michael's Mount.

'What's this?' Letitia asked, holding up a CD that had got separated from its cover. 'Worth listening to or what?'

'Depends,' Cordon said.

'What on?'

'Try it and see.'

It had been one of those relationships that had been going nowhere even before it had started; a woman Cordon had met on an ill-advised visit to the Arts Club in Penzance, psychologically short-sighted enough to believe she could turn him around, bring him out of himself, whatever that might mean.

One of the few things she had left behind, the odd illusion aside, was an album of quiet chamber jazz, clarinet or saxophone, bass and guitar. Jimmy Giuffre, 1956. She had used it to meditate, relax. Later, Cordon, intrigued, had tried to follow it up; a list on the back of an envelope somewhere: Giuffre leads to Brookmeyer, Brookmeyer to Gerry Mulligan, Mulligan to Chet Baker and Chico Hamilton, Hamilton to Eric Dolphy. All those connections neatly linked by arrows. His father would have been proud.

The CD Letitia was handling – *Out to Lunch* – he had played the other night, the night after Heather Pierce's body had been found, the aggravated squawk of Dolphy's saxophone approximate to his mood, but enough to send the dog deep under the bed with paws over her ears.

Letitia set it to play and after half a chorus switched it off.

'What the fuck d'you call that?'

'Music?'

She ate hungrily, piling on the damson jam, shooting a look at Cordon every once in a while, as if daring him to tell her off for not eating all her crusts.

'I'll be going then.'

'Here,' reaching into one of the drawers. 'Best take a key, I'll most likely be out. In fact, hang on to it, it's a spare.'

'Trust me, do you?'

'Shouldn't I?'

She looked around. 'Not much here worth nicking.'

When she and the dog were out of earshot, he got the music going again, volume down. She was a nice enough kid, Letitia, he liked her: a mum who was a registered drug user herself, a father she rarely if ever saw, two brothers in foster care, several members of her extended family on probation or in jail, it was a small miracle she hadn't been in any more trouble than she had. But, up to yet, her head was back above water, she had survived.

Heather Pierce had died.

Good parents, solid middle-class home, good school; broadsheet newspapers, books, not too much TV, piano lessons most likely, art classes, organic food; all the proper values instilled. Every advantage: every hope.

And then this.

An accident.

Unforeseen.

An accident, is that what it was? What it had been?

. . . not one scrap of evidence leads to an offence, nothing suggesting any fucking third-party involvement at all.

Lambert was eager to sign it off as such, the last thing he wanted at this point of his career, an undetected murder on his books, yet somehow Cordon was unable, unwilling to let it go. He had interviewed the principal witnesses, such as they were: Francis Gibbens, first and foremost; Kelly Efford's parents, her brother, Lee; Kelly herself, this carefully, her mother present. When Kelly had been told of Heather's death she had sobbed and sobbed and then closed in on herself, refused to speak, refused food. The doctor attending had thought it best to keep her in hospital longer, for her own safety if nothing else.

Cordon spoke to the student who had discovered Heather's body, the members of the search team who had gone down into the engine house previously and seen nothing – sworn blind that after careful looking there had been no sign. But then, Cordon reasoned, they would, wouldn't they? Anything less – a quick, hurried flashing of torches hastily lowered into the dark – would have amounted to a dereliction of duty they would not have wanted to admit.

Hour upon hour of questioning and nothing germane: just some feeling that wouldn't shake free. And Lambert, not so many steps away from getting Cordon relieved of his duties where this investigation was concerned, shunted permanently aside.

Christ, Cordon thought, a battle of wills between them, is that what it had become? Needing to prove, against all the odds, that he was right all along and Lambert was wrong? How pathetic was that, if so? If that's all it was.

19

At first Ruth had found it hard, almost impossible, to venture on to the coast path close to where Heather and Kelly had got lost, where Heather had been found. But now, especially with Simon gone, she found it difficult to stay away.

Wearing sandals, a loose wrap-around skirt over bare legs and a sleeveless cotton top, sun hat on her head and sun screen jostling against a bottle of water in her bag, she took the Cot Valley path down from St Just towards Porth Nanven and sat with her back against a boulder, high above the shore, looking out.

A container ship, outlined, like a child's drawing, against the horizon, moved slowly left to right towards the Bristol Channel; closer in, a small boat with an ochre sail tacked and tacked again, searching for a wind. She had promised Heather they would go sailing, some friends of Simon's who kept a yacht down on the south coast and kept inviting them – something else they would now never do.

Tears ran soundlessly down her face and, dipping her head, she used the loose flap of her skirt to wipe them away.

Time to move on.

A steep climb – a scramble – up on to the southerly path left her temporarily short of breath, sweat in her eyes and running down her back. Hands on hips, she stood, purple flowers open-mouthed amongst the spiny gorse, the ground hard and baked beneath her feet. The first time Heather had seen the sea – no, stop, stop! – had been in Dorset, a weekend away, Heather – what? – six months old and in a sling; Simon had held her above the waves, the water splashing cold up against her kicking legs and feet and making her shriek with fear and delight.

Ruth's mouth was dry.

She took the bottle of water from her bag and drank before continuing.

A couple of hikers travelling in the opposite direction, serious, the full gear, stepped aside to let her pass.

Blocked by a fall where some of the old mine workings had caved in, the path wound back on itself and climbed again. There were farm buildings, grey roofed, in a small dip where the land levelled out. Fields divided by stone walls. The path between them was dotted with rabbit droppings, lined with cow parsley and nettles, straight as a die: however much she might try to tell herself later she took it by accident as much as design, she would know it was a lie.

Alan Efford lay on a blanket outside the tent, face down, head resting easily on folded arms, legs slightly parted below blue trunks, muscular thighs, the brush of hair growing across the top of his shoulders startlingly blond in the light.

By the time she'd decided to turn away it was too late.

'Ruth?'

'Yes, hello, I . . .'

'Felt someone was there.' He pivoted into a sitting position, legs loosely crossed, peering into the sun.

'I thought Pauline might be here. I thought . . .'

'No. She's gone into town with the little 'un to see Kelly at the hospital. Took the van.'

'And Lee?'

'Off somewhere. Since – you know . . .' Efford shook his head. 'Wasn't what you'd call sociable before, but now, get a word out of him between breakfast and lights out an' you're doin' well.'

'He'll get over it.'

'You think so?'

'He feels responsible. Don't get me wrong, I'm not saying that he is, just that . . .'

'I know. I know.' He looked away.

Ruth made a small pattern in the ground with the toe of her sandal. 'I should go.'

'No. Why?' He moved sideways across the blanket, making space. 'Here. Take the weight off your feet. Sit down.'

'No, it's okay . . .'

'You're sure?'

'Sure.'

A trio of teenage boys, sun-bleached hair, freckles, went past them in wetsuits, laughing, surfboards under their arms.

'Simon,' Ruth said abruptly, 'those things he was saying, blaming you for what happened, all those wild accusations, it was just the heat of the moment, you shouldn't let it . . .'

'No,' Efford said. 'He was right. His place I'd've felt the same. It was my responsibility. My fault.'

'But you weren't to know . . .'

'I'd already told them they couldn't go. It was too late, too close to getting dark.'

'But the fog . . .'

'No. I told them and then I let them change my mind.'

'Children do.'

'I know. But we're s'posed to know better, right?'

For a brief moment, Ruth closed her eyes. 'I never said, not to you – I spoke to Pauline, but I never said, about Kelly, I'm so pleased she's going to be all right. Pleased . . .' She touched a hand to her face, her skin seemed to be burning up. '. . . It's such a inadequate word. It's wonderful, that's what I mean, wonderful that she's okay. If only they'd both . . . if they'd both . . .'

She turned her face away, shaken by tears.

'Ruth . . .'

The tears became sobs and her body shook.

Efford pushed himself to his feet and hesitated, uncertain, before moving closer. When he touched her, a hand consolingly on her shoulder, she jumped and he stepped away, but she turned towards him, body trembling, her face pressed close against his chest.

Without thinking he kissed the top of her head. 'Let's go inside.'

She stumbled against him and he caught hold of her arm.

The interior was shaded, cooler, busy with rolled bundles of clothes, mattresses, sleeping bags, plastic cups and plates, things for the beach.

'I'm sorry,' she said, wiping her eyes. Her nose had run and she rubbed at her cheek.

He reached out both hands towards her.

'No,' she managed. 'That's not . . .'

His mouth brushed past the side of her face, her neck slippery with sweat, his teeth and tongue on her skin; the pair of them losing their balance, falling back, his hand reaching up inside her skirt.

'Oh, God!'

Legs wide, with thumb and finger he opened her like a shell.

'God!'

She wanted him inside her, his weight against her, fucking her hard.

'God!'

When she came it was like the tide, shuddering against him time after time, heels hooked fast behind his legs, fingers locked behind his neck, holding him down.

Released, ragged and wet, they lay side by side, her head angled sideways, resting on his chest, his breathing slowly merging with hers. Against all the odds, she slept.

After a while, he slid carefully out from underneath her, found a towel and rubbed it over his belly and between his legs, went outside and lit a cigarette.

He was still sitting there when Ruth emerged some forty minutes later, face flushed, unable to look him in the eye. The force of the sun had lessened, the sky streaked with cloud.

'You okay?'

She nodded, uncertain.

'Sit yourself down. I'll make a cup of tea.'

'No, it's all right . . .'

'Yeah, come on. Bit of time before the kids get back and all hell breaks loose.'

Ruth sat and waited; if she could have trusted herself to reach the other side of the field without stumbling, she might have walked away.

'You want sugar?'

'No, thanks.'

'Cigarette?'

She shook her head. For a short while neither of them spoke. Kids played around some of the other tents; adults walked down towards the shop holding toddlers by the hand.

'Kelly,' Ruth said quietly, 'she's starting to feel better?'

'Yeah. Yes, she's fine. Cries a lot still, off by herself. Won't talk about it, what happened. Gonna take a while. The hospital reckon she should maybe see someone when she gets back, some kind of psychiatrist, a shrink.'

'I think it's me,' Ruth said, 'needs to see the shrink.'

Efford grinned and shook his head. 'Not you.' He reached across and ran his fingers down the inside of her arm. 'Don't have to worry. Not goin' to tell anyone. Okay?'

She nodded. 'Okay.'

Not so many minutes later, tea finished, she was ready to go. A clumsy hug and quick goodbye, Ruth's legs threatening to buckle beneath her as she walked.

20

The temperature next day had dropped by two or three degrees, the atmosphere more biddable, a breeze drifting in off the sea to the south-west. One glance up at the sky and Cordon reached for his old waterproof in case; that part of the coast, the saying went, more changes to the weather than a whore's underthings.

Quaint word, Cordon thought, underthings, conjuring up something complicated and old-fashioned; frills and furbelows.

The path down off the cliff was no stranger to him now, the goats still there or thereabouts, heads down, cropping at sea beat and bracken, tips of gorse. The same cat, ginger and white, that he had seen before, sprang away when he approached and regarded him reproachfully from a distance.

At first Cordon thought Gibbens wasn't there, but he was only slow in coming to the door.

'Mr Gibbens . . .'

Taking off a pair of wire-rimmed glasses, a crack across one lens, Gibbens blinked towards the light.

'I wonder if I could take up a little more of your time?'

There were another two cats inside, one tabby and a black, feigning sleep on an old rag rug in front of a paraffin stove, unlit. The tabby raised its head enough to squint at Cordon with one yellow eye.

Gibbens lifted away the tattered paperback he'd been reading from the chair opposite his own and set it carefully on the floor. *Crime and Punishment*. Another of those classics of world literature Cordon had been saving against a rainy day.

His eye caught the beginning of the blurb: *A troubled man commits the perfect crime*. Maybe he should read it sooner rather than later: research.

'Bit of a hobby?' Cordon asked, with a nod towards the book.

'Crime or punishment?' Gibbens said with an uneasy smile.

'Reading.'

'Off and on.'

'You remember when we met, I knew your name. Rang bells, somewhere in here.' Cordon tapped one side of his head. 'I've realised why.'

Gibbens looked at him, saying nothing, fingers spidering the edge of his spectacles.

'You had a son. Took his own life. Six, close to seven years back.'

Gibbens blinked and held his breath.

'Hanged himself, wasn't it? One of the struts beneath the fish quay over by Newlyn.'

Gibbens nodded, the smallest of movements, barely perceptible.

'I'm sorry,' Cordon said.

Gibbens breathed on to the lenses of his spectacles and polished them against the soft front of his shirt.

'You got any boys?' he asked Cordon, a few slow moments later.

'One.'

'Still living?'

How the hell did he know? 'Travelling. Central America somewhere, last I heard.' He didn't say that was nine months ago. Gap year, Cordon thought, that was what it meant.

'See the world,' Gibbens said.

'Something like that.'

The black cat stretched and yawned, extending its claws.

'The night you went out and found the girl – Kelly – I'd like to run over what happened.'

'Thought I did that already.'

'Humour me. Tell it again.'

Gibbens told his story, more or less exactly as before.

'And the other girl, Heather . . .'

'What about her?'

'When you stumbled over Kelly, brought her back, you didn't see anything of her?'

Gibbens shook his head.

'Or look for her? You didn't go out later and look for her?'

'How could I? I didn't know she was there.'

'Kelly didn't say?'

'Kelly didn't say a thing.'

'So as far as you knew, she'd been on her own?'

Gibbens nodded.

Cordon sat tall, straightening the muscles of his back. 'According to what I've been told, when you went into the lifeboat station the following morning you spoke of the missing girls.'

'That's wrong?'

'Missing girls. Not girl. How come?'

'Heard it on the radio that morning, local news. Stand on that chair there and keep hold the aerial, you can just about pick up a signal.'

Cordon rose, uncomfortably. 'Let you get back to your book.'

Gibbens watched him to the door. Outside, one of the goats was taking a dump on the stones, each offering perfectly formed.

He was told there was a good chance he'd find Ann Dyer in the Midshipman Ready, saloon bar as was. He looked right past her at first, silver jacket, jeans, dark hair pulled back and piled high, held in place with a silver comb. She was sitting up to the bar, half an ear cocked to the barman's line of chat, what looked like a gin and tonic close by, lime rather than lemon, plenty of ice, condensation on the outside of the glass.

When Cordon went to sit on the stool beside her, she rounded on him sharply, ready to tell him to piss off and leave her alone.

'Oh, it's you.'

'Sorry.'

She had the grace to smile; a senior officer, after all.

'Alan Efford,' he said, small talk not his forte, 'what d'you think of him?'

'How d'you mean?'

'Impressions.'

She thought a little, sipped her G&T. 'Physical, short-tempered maybe; useful to have on your side in a fight.'

'Violent, then?'

'Not necessarily, no. Not without reason.' She told him about the incident with Simon Pierce, which he'd already read in her report.

'Never see him step out of line with the other kids?'

'What way?'

Cordon shrugged. 'Any.'

'Can't say that I did. Sorry.'

'Why sorry?'

'Thought you wanted me to say something else.'

'Wanted? Interesting choice of word.'

'You're looking for homicide, that's the talk.'

'Doing my job.'

'No matter what?'

'No matter what.' Cordon eased himself down from the stool.

'Why don't you stay?' Dyer said. 'Have a drink.'

He gave it due consideration for longer than he should. 'Some other time, perhaps.'

'Yes, sir.'

By the time he had reached the door, she was back in conversation with the young man behind the bar.

21

Ruth had done her best to shut what had happened with Alan Efford out of her mind, an aberration. Concerned at how long it was taking before the inquest into her daughter's death could be reopened, she asked Ann Dyer, who told her she thought it was something to do with forensics; nothing out of the ordinary, unfortunately, just the pressure of work on the service. But why didn't she talk to Detective Inspector Cordon? He could set her straight.

Cordon met her in St Just, the park behind the war memorial, a bench, tastefully engraved by the local youth, in the shade.

'What the liaison officer said is right. Till we get the results back from the FSS – the Forensic Science Service – I'm afraid everything's on hold.'

'And this is what? Heather's clothes?'

'Yes, as I explained to you before.'

'But what happened to Heather, it was an accident.'

'Almost certainly.'

'Almost?'

'Mrs Pierce, I'm sure you can understand. We have to rule out any other possibility. Having the clothing examined is simply part of that process. As I said, a matter of routine.'

'I still don't see what they're expecting to find?'

'It depends. Blood, certainly. There might be hair, saliva . . .' He gestured into the air. 'Everything has to be tested and checked to make sure nothing comes from a third party.'

'A third . . . ?'

'We have to make sure no one else was involved.'

'Involved? Involved how? You think somebody might have pushed her? Is that what you think? Heather might have been pushed? It wasn't an accident at all?'

'No, no, that's not what I'm saying.'

'But you did. You said . . .'

'Mrs Pierce, all I said, we have to be sure. As sure as is possible. At the inquest, the coroner will want to know that all the appropriate inquiries were made. It's his duty, and ours. And until the results are in we have to keep an open mind.' Shifting his position on the bench, he smiled. 'Another day or two, that's all it will be.'

'And if there is anything, anything untoward, you'd let us know?'

'Of course. First thing. You have my word.'

'Thank you,' Ruth said, relieved. Cordon, as ever, amazed at how easy it was to lie.

They had to wait not two days but three. When it came, the report was clear: no significant traces of a third party were found on the clothes of the deceased.

Lambert lorded it as if his lottery ticket had just come home. No other winners. Jackpot. Cordon kept his head down, took his ribbing as best he could.

Lambert then opted to make the police report to the inquest himself, not quite trusting Cordon to toe the party line.

'Did the police, at any stage,' the coroner asked, 'consider the possibility of homicide?'

'We did,' Lambert said.

'And did you come to any conclusions?'

'After a thorough investigation, we found no evidence of third-party involvement whatsoever.'

'And the injuries to the body, Superintendent?'

'As the pathologist's report has made clear, they were entirely consistent with the deceased having fallen into the engine house where the body was found.'

'The scratches to the face and arms . . . ?'

'Sustained, we believe, after the deceased had become disorientated due to a sudden and severe fog coming in off the sea, and had lost her footing amongst the gorse and bracken close to the coast path.'

The coroner looked at the papers before him.

'When the engine house was searched earlier, the body of the deceased was apparently not present, yet when the building was searched again two days later, the body was discovered – do you have any satisfactory explanation for this?'

'Other than the possibility that the earlier search wasn't carried out as thoroughly as it should have been?'

'Other than that.'

'No, I'm afraid not.'

During recess Lambert paced up and down, smoking one cigarette after another – how much more open and shut does it bloody have to be? It didn't take long to find out.

'Having considered the pathologist's report,' the coroner said, 'and after listening carefully to all of the evidence presented – the police evidence in particular – I am led to the conclusion that the most likely cause of death in this unfortunate case was a serious blow – or blows – to the head, sustained when the deceased fell into the disused engine house where her body was found.

'Since, however, after all the evidence put before me, I am unable to determine with any degree of certainty exactly what did occur, I see no alternative than to record an open verdict in this case.'

'Fuck!' Lambert said beneath his breath.

Ruth bent sharply forward, eyes closed, and, close alongside, Simon, who had returned to Cornwall for the inquiry, reached for her hand.

Only when he was outside the court did Cordon allow himself the merest of smiles.

Every exhibit, each item of clothing had been separately bagged and labelled, showing the names of all those who had seen or handled them and in what circumstances; all of the witness statements, together with photographs and any other material evidence, were similarly labelled and secured. Cordon himself took care to supervise the process by which everything was boxed and sealed before being taken to the property store and handed over to the officer in charge.

'I know, don't tell me,' the officer said.

'What's that?'

'Guard it with my life.'

'You'd best do better than that.'

Cordon waited while the officer signed in the box, lifted it from the counter – 'What you got in here, a body?' – and carried it back into the store.

Outside, the weather showed little sign of change; still warm, a scattering of high cloud but little wind, nothing so far presaging rain. People were going about their business with the same haste or ease. In their room above the pub, Ruth and Simon were packing their things, ready to take them down to the car. Ever since the verdict, Ruth had felt she was sleepwalking, unable to focus, unresolved; Simon resorted to small outbursts of anger, attempts to engage in conversation that broke down all too soon.

'Got what you wanted,' Lambert had said scornfully, seeing Cordon outside the court. 'Much fucking good it'll do you.'

Cordon kept his mouth closed. What he wanted were answers: answers he knew might never come.

When he got back to the flat it was empty – no click of the springer's paws on the floor as it bounded towards the door; Letitia had let herself in and taken the dog for a walk. Everything else was in its place. He poured himself a small Scotch and carried it to the window. The sun off the water took on a metallic sheen.

. . . unable to determine with any degree of certainty exactly what did occur . . .

He picked another CD from the shelf, programmed the track he wanted and set it to play. Eric Dolphy soloing, un-accompanied, on bass clarinet.

'God Bless the Child'.

When Letitia turned the key in the lock, Cordon was fast asleep and snoring.

III

III

22

Summer that year was brilliant and short-lived, a heady cluster of days in which the sun shone from first light to last. The temperature hovered close to twenty-four degrees, the relative humidity was high – pushing up towards the nineties – but the wind was a mere five miles per hour out of the east. Hot and still. A careful listener could have heard the thwack of ball against willow wafting in from the parks.

Walking, as he rarely did, along the banks of the Cam as it wound behind the great colleges, and watching the visitors punt lazily along in the imagined manner of languid under-graduates, Will briefly allowed himself to think that perhaps this was, after all, what a true summer was like.

Cambridge – England – at its best.

Was it, fuck!

A fifteen-year-old boy chased through the city centre by a gang of up to a dozen youths, cornered, kicked and finally stabbed to death, all for the wrong word, the wrong look, for not showing enough respect; another stabbing, in a small town to the east of the county, a jealous attack on a fourteen-year-old girl who had wandered off into the alley behind the youth club with the wrong boy; a domestic dispute which spilled over into the street and resulted in a passer-by who tried to intervene being assaulted with a length of metal pipe.

The abject and the everyday.

That was Will's England.

When the heat broke it was with a sudden storm and lashing winds. In some parts of the county there were warnings of flooding if the rivers broke their banks, in others the possibility of drought, the spectre of standpipes in the streets.

And just when he thought it couldn't get any worse, a body was found between Grantchester and Trumpington, near the edge of Seven Acre Wood. A young man of seventeen had been stripped and beaten and then tied in a cruciform position to the branches of a tree, ribs showing through almost translucent skin; his once white shirt had been fastened around his genitals and was heavily stained with blood. His face and chest had been smeared with shit. His eyes were closed. No movement, no sign of breath.

It was only when the paramedics carefully lowered him on to a stretcher that they realised he was, in fact, still alive.

Somewhere, the Church of St Andrew and St Mary at Grantchester, perhaps, bells began to sound, summoning people to evensong. And was there honey still for tea?

Will, together with the other senior officers in the Major Investigation Team, pooled resources, prioritised, pushed overtime up to and occasionally beyond acceptable limits. He worked long hours, longer than usual, pulled double shifts, returning home irritable and short-tempered, too often letting the children feel the rough side of his tongue without reason, too tired to eat, too tired to explain.

And through all of this, the image of Mitchell Roberts flickered fitfully at the far edge of his vision, like a piece of grit caught in the corner of his eye. *CID wasn't as smart as it might have been,* Liam Noble had said, landing the ball squarely back in Will's court. There hadn't been the time or resources to concentrate properly on him then, nor were there now. At night he fretted and twisted and turned and when he finally woke, still exhausted, more often than not it was with a throbbing head.

'We can't go on like this,' Lorraine said one morning, shifting Susie from one hip to the other. 'Something's got to change.'

Nothing did.

She took both Jake and Susie to her parents in Saffron Walden. 'Just for a week, Will, a break for all of us. Give you a little space. Ten days at most.'

There were air fresheners in every room and a knitted cover across the toilet seat; ready-to-heat meals from Waitrose on Hill Street. After three days Lorraine came back alone, leaving the children to be spoiled rotten.

She and Will went for dinner at the Old Fire Engine House in Ely, a taxi there and back, celery and stilton soup, beef and shallots braised in port and Guinness and a bottle of Côtes du Rhône. Will could only just find room for a portion of old-fashioned sherry trifle.

He opened a second bottle of wine when they got home and they sat out on the porch with the windows open, listening to an old Cowboy Junkies CD of Lorraine's; finally making love right there on the varnished boards, Lorraine's skirt pushed up way past her waist, half-naked the pair of them and only a passing fox disinterestedly looking on.

23

Ruth found the heat oppressive. She took to wearing loose linen dresses and floppy broad-brimmed hats that made her look, she realised somewhat sadly, like a character out of Katherine Mansfield or Virginia Woolf: a mildly eccentric maiden aunt who wandered in and out of the edges of the story, haunted by the memory of some beautiful young man who had gone off to war and not returned. Ruth had this vision of herself drinking sour lemonade and being surrounded by a gaggle of nephews and nieces; pitied and then ignored.

She wrote poetry, Ruth thought, this other version of herself: Georgian poetry in the style of Walter de la Mare or Rupert Brooke. Gardened or kept bees. She rather liked the idea of keeping bees.

Unable to find the old Penguin paperback of *The Garden Party* she had once owned, she sought out Katherine Mansfield on the shelves of the library where she worked. But tales of so many lives truncated and unfulfilled made her ill. After a short while, she moved on to Virginia Woolf instead, but in her current state of mind this was scarcely an improvement. Mrs Dalloway driving herself to exhaustion in achieving what was, in truth, mundane – the perfect dinner party, which knives, which glasses, who would sit where; Mrs Ramsay struggling to catch moments of time like fireflies that could be kept in a jar then taken down and examined, as if the meaning of life might then be revealed.

We perished, each alone.

Little wonder that Woolf had filled her pockets with stones and walked out into the waters of the River Ouse.

Each alone . . .

Ruth felt she understood.

There had been times, after Heather had died, when taking her own life had seemed to Ruth the only way to survive. That blackness that would finally absolve you of all pain.

She had always thought of herself, in the most basic of ways, as Christian; believing not just in the tenets of the religion, but the existence, somewhere, of a God. A God to whom, in emergency, one prayed.

Ruth had prayed.

Prayed for a miracle.

Prayed – God help her – for Kelly to be the one who had died and not Heather.

In the end she had stopped. Not in believing in the possibility of another, spiritual world; nor believing there was no life after death. What she ceased to believe was that there was anything she could do to interfere, to influence or intercede.

Wait. Remain open. That was all.

She was good at waiting, Ruth decided. What else was there to do? She had waited and, through the efforts of her friends and none of her own, Andrew had come along and with him the chance of renewed happiness, companionship, a relationship that, while it had neither the highs nor lows of her marriage to Simon, offered stability and a measure of understanding. She still went to the cinema with Catriona and sometimes Lyle or Andrew or both would join them; she caught the train up to London for the occasional exhibition; she ventured downriver on Lyle's boat. Once in a while, at Andrew's suggestion, they would play bridge, the four of them, but Ruth, never good at cards, found working out in whose hand the remaining trumps lay a near impossibility.

'Never mind,' Andrew would sigh, after they had gone three or four off for the umpteenth time. 'It's only a game.'

She had stopped painting after Heather died and when she tried again – a new set of oils to spur her on – all she could achieve were the dullest of still lifes. An attempt to free herself up and paint something more abstract, in the style of the Joan Mitchell canvases she had seen in Paris, ended in disaster. A morass of unconnected squiggly lines that lacked reason or rhyme.

So she shopped, cooked, ran Beatrice here and there, checked her homework, washed and ironed her clothes, tried to keep her temper whenever her daughter flew off the handle for no apparent reason or got into one of her impenetrable moods. She listened dutifully as Andrew complained about some new directive from on high: more tests, fewer tests, sex education for the under-nines.

That was her life now – perfect yet becalmed.

She would persevere with her diploma course in library management and by the summer of the coming year she should be able to stop working at the arts and craft shop and get a job in the library full time. That was something, surely? Something to look forward to. There were hundreds of people – thousands – so much worse off than herself.

She was sitting one evening, alone, just dark enough to switch on the standard lamp, a book open in her lap, the new Rose Tremain, a glass of white wine on the small table by her side. Beatrice was already in bed, Andrew out at a governors' meeting – 'Don't wait up, you know what these things are like. It'll probably go on for hours.'

Suddenly she set down the book and went across to the chest at the far side of the room and retrieved an album from the bottom shelf, where it lay beneath some linen napkins and a set of table mats Andrew's sister had given them and that they'd never used.

Inside the album were photographs that had been taken, mostly by Simon, years before, the years after Heather was born. Each new stage documented closely, as if preserving it in time. Back in those days Simon had rarely had the camera out of his hand.

Ruth sat back in her chair and began to turn the pages. Heather in a buggy at Alexandra Palace, a quadrant of north London spread out behind her. Heather on the swings, one hand pointing at the camera, the other clinging on for dear life.

'I always liked that one,' the voice said from over Ruth's shoulder.

'Yes,' Ruth said, only a little startled. 'Me too.'

'Where is it? Highgate Woods? I can't remember.'

'I think so.'

'Daddy's pushing me. Look, you can just see his hand.'

'Oh, yes.' Ruth had failed to notice.

The breath was warm on her cheek, the back of her neck, just above the collar of her blouse.

She turned another page but Heather was no longer there.

Just the image, postcard size in Kodachrome: a small child with a glass-eyed bear. The air in the room was cold, as if a door somewhere had been left open.

'Oh, Heather,' Ruth said and closed her eyes.

She didn't open them again until she heard the sound of Andrew's key in the front door lock.

24

Summer moved on. On his drive into work that morning, Will had noticed some of the trees already beginning to shed their leaves. It promised to be a quieter day than usual, things ticking down. The number of outstanding cases was coming under control.

That illusion lasted till mid-afternoon, the call to emergency services being logged at 16.17. The caller's voice was high and shrill and difficult to understand; five years old, he was having to stand on tiptoe to reach the telephone where it was fixed to the wall.

When the woman on the switchboard finally pieced together enough of what he was saying and had established his address – the boy reciting it by rote, good boy, well taught – she told him, as calmly as she could, to stay right where he was, not touch anything, not anything at all, and someone would be there right away to help.

The first ambulance was at the scene within seven minutes, the first police cars inside twelve; Will himself arrived just as the area surrounding the house was being cordoned off, officers in protective clothing beginning to go about their tasks.

The house was detached, thirty, perhaps forty years old, part of a small, once more prosperous estate, with a pebble-dash front that was looking tired and starting to fade. A child's tricycle lay on the gravel path leading towards the front door. Two tubs of geraniums, scarlet and white, stood either side of shallow steps, with matching hanging baskets above, fuchsia and lobelia curling haphazardly down. The door to the side garage was closed.

An officer came out of the house as Will approached and from the look on his face, Will knew what he was about to see inside was not good. The first stuttering line of blood splashed out across the parquet floor and up on to the wall beside the now open door. There was more blood in random patches on the stairs and the adjacent wall, and, clear on the banister rail, a bloodied hand mark where it had been gripped tight.

From another room, Will could hear the sound of a child's inconsolable sobbing, a breathless litany that rose and broke but never stopped.

The woman's body was on the first landing, arms and legs splayed wide where she had finally fallen, the pale green of her summer dress darkened here and there with blood. There were a number of smaller wounds along the insides of her arms – defence wounds, Will thought – and her throat had been savagely cut.

The rooms on the upper floors were empty, the beds neatly, carefully made. In the boy's room, the books were shelved, the toys stacked and put away. His dressing gown was folded, with his pyjamas, across one end of his narrow bed.

They found the man in the garage, hanging. A length of plastic-coated wire had been looped over a central beam and secured. The drop just high enough once the stool had been kicked away. There was blood on his hands and blood on his face and in his hair and blood on the rope where he had knotted it and pulled it tight. Also bloodied, a broad-bladed kitchen knife lay on the concrete floor, the kind of knife used for carving Sunday joints, roast leg of beef or lamb, loin of pork, boned and rolled.

What happened here? Will asked himself. A man attacks his wife in a frenzy, kills her and then himself. Jealous rage, is that what this was? His mind was starting to spin. She was leaving him? Having an affair? Leaving him and threatening to take with her their son, their only child, born when she was what? In her mid-thirties? Neither of them in the flush of youth.

A crime of passion, then.

Will thought back to the woman's face, drained of all colour, plain: passion spent.

Paul and Linda Carey, forty-one and thirty-nine years old.

Ordinary people, ordinary lives.

It would be another day before the results of the autopsy revealed Paul Carey's stomach to contain a quantity of partly digested sleeping pills, sedative-hypnotic barbiturates, Seconal and Nembutal evenly mixed.

Will spoke to Paul Carey's father, Michael, when he came down from Northumberland to identify the body.

Michael Carey was a few months shy of seventy, straight-backed, square-shouldered, with a full head of greying hair. Born into farming, he had turned his back on the land at seventeen, joined the army as a junior cadet and worked his way up to the rank of major. On retirement, he had bought a plot of land in southern Spain, where, with only limited assistance, he and his wife had built a villa, which

Paul and his wife had infrequently visited on holiday. Then, when his own wife had died suddenly, following a stroke, at sixty-three, Carey had sold up in Spain, returned home and bought a pair of old farm labourers' cottages a few miles from where he had been born; these he was in the process of renovating and knocking into one. The farm his family had owned for four generations, and on which he had been raised, had been sold to a property developer and now housed upwards of fifty stone-clad three- and four-bedroom dwellings for commuter families from Newcastle upon Tyne.

'She never took to us, you know, Linda,' Carey said. 'Oh, she was polite, like. Very proper. Ps and Qs, you know what I mean? But no warmth. No . . .' He made his hand into a fist and tapped it against his chest, above his heart. 'Nothing there. Not for me, at least.'

They were walking past the bowling green on Christ's Pieces, teams of men and women nattily got up in white, skips standing at the head, cajoling and calling advice, signalling the woods to within inches of their target.

'I asked her once, came right out with it, and, to do her credit, she didn't shirk. "It's you," she said, "you and Paul. The way you are with him. As if he can never do anything right. Never be good enough. Not for you. And he resents it, I know he does, but he hasn't got the guts to say. And that's your fault, too."'

He shook his head and, although they were walking more slowly now, his breathing accelerated.

'I remember once we were on holiday when Paul was just a lad, Scotland it would have been, the west coast. Talisker perhaps, Struan, somewhere round there. Someone had made a rope swing over this piece of water, one side of the rocks to the other, and all these lads were taking it in turns to swing across. Calling and hollering, you can imagine. Great fun they were having. The shout that went up whenever one of them loosed hold and took a tumble down into the water.'

He stopped and looked at Will evenly, weighing up whether to continue or let it be.

'Paul must have been ten,' he said. 'Eleven at best. A year or so younger than most of these lads, but no more. "Go on," I said. "Get up there with the rest. Get in line. Take your place." He would not. He was scared. "You great jessie," I said. And he must've read the disgust on my face.'

They set off walking again, Carey with his hands behind his back, upright, Will keeping step alongside.

'You say things . . . you say things and then you wish later you never had. Do anything you could to cancel them out, but of course you can't. You have to live with it and so do they.'

'Yes,' Will said. 'Yes, I know.' Remembering the times he had lost his temper with Jake, often without reason; words blurted out in haste that he had wanted to swallow back the moment they were out of his mouth.

They sat on a bench and Carey removed his jacket, folding it neatly before setting it down, then turning back the cuffs of his shirt, once then once again.

'Paul and Linda,' Will said, 'did you have any inkling of how things were between them?'

The older man shook his head.

'And the fact that Paul apparently took his own life . . .'

'It beggars belief,' Carey said heavily. 'All of it. It beggars belief.'

They sat for a while longer and then Will walked back with him to where Carey had parked his car.

'There'll be an inquest?' Carey said.

'Oh, yes.'

'Anything you discover . . .'

'You'll be informed.'

Carey nodded briefly and they shook hands, Will waiting while he drove away.

25

It took Helen Walker a good thirty minutes to drive out to Huntingdon, where five-year-old Carl was now living, at the discretion of Social Services, with his maternal grandparents, Bill and Barbara Connors. Had it not been for the plague of roadworks on the A14 it would have taken less.

She had been out to the house – a two-storey semi near the town centre – once before, but with little success; the most basic questions aside, Bill Connors had left everything to his wife, who was clearly too distressed to answer coherently. This time Helen was hoping for more.

Barbara Connors pressed a finger to her lips as she opened the door. She was a small, neat woman with an oval face and gently greying hair.

'Carl's sleeping. He's only just gone off. I try and get him to sleep for a little while in the afternoon if I can. I don't want to wake him.' She pointed towards the rear of the house. 'We won't disturb him if we go through there.'

A small conservatory had been built on to the back of the kitchen and Barbara Connors had been sitting there reading, her glasses resting on a thick paperback beside one of a pair of wicker chairs.

'Bill's out playing golf, he didn't think you'd mind.'

'Of course not, that's fine.'

'Twice a week since he's been retired. Him and the same three pals. Has to miss it for any reason, he just sits around and mopes.'

Helen nodded understandingly.

'You'll have some tea? I've got the kettle on, ready.'

'Yes, thank you, that'd be lovely.'

All this politeness was doing her head in.

Left alone, Helen looked out at the garden, partly paved, a straggle of small roses dangling over the neighbours' fence to one side; a small bird she couldn't identify washing itself energetically in a stone bird bath; late tomatoes sagging on the vine.

'These past few weeks,' Barbara Connors said, returning with a tray, 'it's been so hot. If you don't water everything night and morning it shrivels up and dies.'

She set the tray down carefully on a glass-topped table: teapot, cups and saucers, sugar, milk in a Cornish ware jug. Three different kinds of biscuits, fanned out around a plate.

'You look,' Barbara Connors said, as she passed the tea, 'as if you've been in the wars.'

'Oh, this?' Helen's hand went instinctively to the side of her face, a bruise high over her left cheek that make-up couldn't adequately hide, yellow darkening into mauve. 'It's nothing.'

The older woman smiled. The backs of her hands were slightly swollen, Helen noticed, as if she suffered, perhaps, from arthritis. That apart she looked fit and well. Spry. Sixties, Helen guessed, middle-aged these days, not old. But young enough to bring up a small boy?

'Carl,' she said, 'how's he getting on?'

At first Helen thought she hadn't heard.

164

'He cries a lot,' Barbara Connors said eventually. 'That's only to be expected, of course. Keeps calling for his mummy and daddy.' She shook her head. 'I don't think he really understands. What happened. I don't think he understands.'

Helen nodded and waited for her to go on. The tea was weak and slightly scented, Earl Grey mixed with something more standard.

Barbara Connors set down her cup. 'We brought all of his toys over from the house, his little bed, everything. Put them upstairs in the spare room. We thought that's what he'd like.' Leaning forward, she drew a tissue from her bag. 'He won't go up the stairs. Just won't. No matter what. We tried carrying him, Bill and I, between us, but he wriggled and kicked and tried to bite. We've made up a bed for him down here, for now. We didn't know what else to do. The social worker says he'll get better in time, settle, get used to being here. The worst thing we can do, she says, is push him too hard.' She twisted the tissue between her fingers. 'That's where he found her, his mummy – our daughter – on the stairs.'

Helen smiled sympathetically, sensing there was more to come.

'They'd been trying for a baby more or less ever since they were married, you know. I don't know what the problem was, Linda never said, not in so many words. But they went to doctors and everything, I do know that. Even talked about IVF, read up about it, went along to the clinic and what have you, but in the end they decided against it. I've never really been clear why.'

She picked up her cup but didn't drink.

'They both had busy jobs, I suppose that was part of it. Good jobs with good money. After a while I think it was a case of, instead of fretting let's enjoy what we've got. Holidays, that's what they went in for. Egypt, America, the Bahamas. I thought they might move house, buy somewhere bigger, you know, out in the country. But no, they seemed content with where they were. And Linda always kept it looking nice – she had help, of course, working full time the way she did – but that was Linda, everything neat and in its place.'

She paused to sip some tea.

'They seemed to have stopped thinking about starting a family. Linda never talked about it to me, at least, not the way she had before, and then, suddenly, there she was, pregnant. I don't know who was more surprised. A shock to the pair of them. I mean, Linda had stopped, you know, taking precautions, there didn't seem to be any point, but even so . . .' She smiled. 'It changes everything, doesn't it? Especially when you're used to doing what you want when you like. A baby. Independence, that goes out the window.'

'They weren't totally happy about it, then?'

'Oh, no. They were, they were. Of course they were. Overjoyed. Paul, especially. I mean, Linda loved Carl, of course she did, she was his mother, it's only natural that she should. But Paul – he was besotted, he really was. He'd sit with little Carl and play with him for hours. Always reading to him – those picture books, you know – carrying him round on his shoulders. It was lovely, lovely to see . . .'

She turned her face aside. Helen knew she was crying, without needing to see the tears.

Barbara Connors stood hurriedly, turning away. 'Carl, I'd best go and check that he's all right.'

Moments later, Helen heard the splash of water at the downstairs sink. Several houses away, a lawnmower whirred to life. Reaching across for the pot, she topped up her cup and added milk.

'Poor lamb,' Barbara Connors said from the doorway, 'he's barely stirred. This whole awful business, it's worn him out.'

'I just helped myself,' Helen said. 'I hope you don't mind?'

'No, of course not.'

'How about you?'

Barbara Connors shook her head and sat back down. 'I'd best wake him before too long. Sleeps overmuch now he'll not go off tonight.'

Time to push on, Helen thought. 'Paul and Linda, before this terrible thing happened, there'd not been any tension between them? Something out of the ordinary, I mean.'

'No. No, I don't think so.'

'No major arguments? Disagreements?'

'Not that I know of.'

'And you would have known – if there was anything serious?'

'Yes. Yes, I think so.'

'You and Linda, you were close?'

'Oh, yes.'

'Talked on the phone, that kind of thing?'

'Yes. All the time. And twice a week I'd go over, Mondays and Fridays, look after Carl when there wasn't nursery.'

'How about Paul? You got along?'

'Yes.'

'And there was nothing . . . ?'

Barbara Connors was shaking her head.

Helen sat forward a little in her chair. 'Mrs Connors – I don't like to ask you this – but is there any chance Linda could have been seeing somebody else?'

'Seeing . . . ? You mean, having an affair?'

'Yes.'

'Good God, no!'

Helen was surprised by the strength of her reply.

'You seem quite certain.'

'I am.'

'Shocked, even.'

'I suppose . . . No, not shocked, at least not in the way I think you mean. I know these things happen. They always have. It's just . . .' Embarrassed, she tugged at the pleats of her dress.

'Linda – it's not that she wasn't interested in, you know, sex, it's more that, well, as I understand it, for some time before Carl was born, they – she and Paul, they didn't . . . Oh, dear, I'm not expressing this very well, am I?'

'They didn't enjoy a very active sex life,' Helen offered, helpfully.

'Yes, that's right. That's why Carl – when he came along – it was such a lovely surprise.' Another tug at the recalcitrant folds of her dress. 'They'd been on holiday. Egypt. Around the time, you know, Carl was conceived.'

'Something about the sun, perhaps,' Helen said. 'All that afternoon heat.'

'I'm sorry, I don't . . .'

'It doesn't matter. I was being flippant, I'm sorry.'

Barbara Connors forced a smile.

'How about more recently?' Helen asked. 'After Carl was born. Did things change between them? In that way? They didn't try for another child?'

Barbara Connors was looking at something out in the garden, concentrating quite hard. 'I got the impression – I may be wrong – but I got the impression that Paul – I mean, he was always very affectionate – but I think what he really wanted most of all was a cuddle. A kiss and a cuddle and that was enough.' She cleared her throat. 'And who's to say there's anything wrong with that?'

'No,' Helen said softly. 'No, indeed.'

'That cat from next door,' Barbara Connors said, 'it will keep coming and doing its business in our begonias.'

Helen sat in the car, lowered the window partway and lit a cigarette. She and Declan had been fooling around the previous evening, Declan several pints to the good before he arrived and Helen with a bottle of wine just opened. She'd been flirting with him, knowing they were going to end up in bed, but just holding back, prolonging the moment, kissing him then pulling away; a bit of fake coquetry around the far side of the table, touching herself for a moment through the silk of her camisole top then poking out her tongue.

Declan had seized hold of her and pulled her across the table, then grabbed her hair and swung her hard against the wall, his hand pushed up between her legs from behind.

'Playing games, huh?' Laughing. 'I know that's what you like. Playing games.'

Sitting there, she remembered, with a quick aftershock, the force of her orgasm when she'd come.

Overwhelmed.

Out of control.

Was that what she needed now? The way it had to be? Lowering the window further, she tossed out her half-smoked cigarette and a moment later lit another. *A kiss and a cuddle and that was enough.* Turning the key in the ignition, she slid the car into gear.

26

'I think she was having an affair,' Helen said. 'I'm sure of it.'

'Sure?'

'Pretty sure.'

They were in a lay-by off the A10, the Ely to Cambridge road, leaning back against Will's Astra, late in the afternoon, the sun's strength just beginning to fade. Helen's VW was immediately behind. Will was eating a bacon roll from the van permanently parked at the lay-by's edge, a polystyrene cup of dubious coffee resting on the car roof. Helen stood nursing some tea and smoking her second cigarette.

'*A kiss and a cuddle*,' Helen said, '*and that was enough*. All those years. I don't believe it.'

'Everyone's not the same,' Will said.

'Meaning?'

'Meaning everyone's not the same.'

Helen took a mouthful of tea, made a face, and tipped the remainder out on to the ground.

'Supposing you're right,' Will said, 'we've no proof.'

'I know.'

Paul and Linda Carey's house had been searched from top to bottom: diaries and items of correspondence had been taken away, along with two laptops and both mobile phones. So far nothing untoward had been found. Friends, colleagues and acquaintances had been interviewed. Nothing. *Nada*. If Linda Carey had been having an affair she had gone to exceptional pains to keep it quiet.

'How come,' Will said, 'we've turned up diddly-squat and yet her husband, presumably, found out?'

'Maybe she told him,' Helen said.

'After going to so much trouble to keep it quiet? Why do that?'

'She was about to leave him, that'd be my guess.'

'And that would be enough?'

'Don't you think?'

Will nodded. There were cases like that, he knew. Jealous husbands, possessive men. It was usually the men. Leave me and I'll kill you. If I can't have you, nobody else will. Try and take my children away and I'll kill them, them and you, too. Stick the kids in the car and drive off the edge of the cliff. It happened. All too often. At least, in this instance, the child was still alive. He took the last bite of roll, screwed up the paper it had been wrapped in and tossed it, together with his now empty coffee cup, into a nearby bin. Conjecture was one thing, proof another. They hadn't yet found it. But if it was there they would.

Helen stubbed out her cigarette. 'Time to go?'

Will reached a hand carefully towards her face, the backs of his fingers just brushing the spot on her cheek where the bruise still lingered.

'Walked into the well-known door, I suppose?'

'Exactly.'

Will shook his head. 'What's going on?'

'Nothing. Nothing's going on.'

He raised his hand towards her face again and she swung her head aside. 'That isn't nothing,' he said.

'For God's sake, Will. I tripped and fell, okay? Heels, I was wearing heels. Always a mistake. It's no big deal.'

She started to walk away and he caught hold of her arm. 'You had an argument? Some kind of a row?'

'Who?'

'You and Declan.'

'I told you.' She stared at him, unblinking, until he let go and stepped away. 'Interrogation over?'

Will unlocked his car and pulled open the door. 'Just take care.'

She stood there, watching, as he drove away.

Two days later, one of the young detective constables who'd been going through the material taken from the Carey home intercepted Helen on her way back to her desk.

'It may be nothing, but . . .'

Linda Carey had been in the habit of logging appointments on her laptop and then transferring that information to the calendar on her mobile phone. The majority of these fell into a pattern: a succession of regular work meetings, visits to the hairdresser or the dentist or to the beauty salon to get her legs waxed, occasional drinks to celebrate a colleague's birthday or promotion, dinner or a visit to the theatre with Paul. The same names over and over.

Before that she seemed to have used a succession of small leather-bound diaries in combination with a computer; print-outs for several odd months had been found – April and November 2002, June, July and August 2003 – along with diaries for 1998, 2001 and 2002.

'Look,' the DC said, 'there's a name here, September 2001, *Terry Markham*, followed by three question marks. That seems to be the first time it appears. There are two *Terrys* after that

– end of September and again in October – then nothing until the following year, April 23rd. After which there's a whole bunch of them – not *Terry* any more, just *T* or, once or twice, *TM* – I'm assuming it refers to the same person – right on through to December. Then they stop.'

'For good?'

The young detective grinned. 'Nothing until this year. Not too long ago, either. Last month. Same initials, *TM*, and a time, *19.30*. Laptop and mobile, the same. On the laptop, as well as the time, it's got *Arts Bar*.'

'The Arts Picture House?'

'Could be. Clocked it first time round, but didn't mean much till I started going through the old diaries. Then I thought, well, worth bringing it to you.'

Helen rewarded him with a smile. 'Three Brownie points and a gold star. Now sod off back to your desk and see what you can turn up on Terry Markham.'

Barbara Connors came round from the side of the house wearing gardening gloves and holding a pair of secateurs. Helen had tried to raise her several times on the phone and failed, but had reasoned that, with a five-year-old to look after, she most likely wouldn't have strayed far.

'I'm sorry to disturb you,' Helen said, 'but the name Terry Markham, I was wondering if it meant anything to you? In relation to your daughter?'

The older woman wiped an arm across her forehead. 'Markham? No, I don't think so.'

'Someone Linda might have known about six years ago? A friend. Possibly someone she met through work.'

'No, I'm sorry. Terry, you say? I'm afraid I can't think of any Terrys.'

'Perhaps you could ask your husband, just in case? And if anything does come to mind, you'll let me know?'

'Of course. I'm sorry you had to come out all this way.'

'Not a problem.'

Helen was hardly back at her car when Barbara Connors came hurrying towards her. 'Wait, wait. There was a Terry. But this was a long time ago, when she was still at school. Terry, yes. Terry Markham. He had quite a thing about her, as I recall.'

27

Beatrice had the next day off from school, an inset day, and Ruth had arranged to be free. 'We'll go out in the car somewhere. Take a picnic, maybe.'

'Mum! Do we have to?'

'You like picnics.'

'Yes, but you know . . .'

'Know what?'

'Cambridge, shopping – you promised?'

'I don't think so. Anyway, what for?'

'A new top, remember?'

'Oh, Beatrice, we can get that any time.'

'Yes, but we don't though, do we? I mean, that's what you say, any time, any time, but we never actually go.'

Ruth sighed. 'All right, next weekend. For definite.'

Beatrice's face registered disbelief.

'I just don't want to waste a whole day trudging round shops, that's all.'

'Okay, okay.' Beatrice sighed and stuck her head back down into her book.

Ruth plugged in the iron, lifted one of Andrew's shirts from the pile, shook it out then smoothed one side along the board with her hand. When they were first married, Andrew had prided himself on the fact that he did his own ironing, and from time to time mentioned it to friends as if it were still the case, whereas, as Ruth had once pointed out, borrowing from a local production of *Hamlet* she'd been hauled off to by Catriona, it was now something honoured far more in the breach than the observance.

'Spoken like a true librarian and a scholar,' Andrew had responded, smiling. 'A quotation for every occasion.'

But he had acknowledged it was true. And, besides, Ruth didn't really mind. In fact, she quite enjoyed ironing: one of those mundane tasks that didn't require too much concentration, allowing her mind to wander.

'This picnic,' Beatrice piped up, having just finished a chapter. 'Where're we going anyway?'

'Oh, I don't know. Take pot luck, shall we? See where the mood takes us.'

'Whatever.'

Dismissed, Ruth returned to her task. The A14 out of Ely and then the A12, if they didn't hit too much traffic they could be in Aldeburgh inside two hours and a half.

They woke to pale skies and drifting cloud, enough of a breeze to bring a little freshness to the air and the hope of some real sunshine later on. Ruth was up early, bustling around, sandwiches to make, a flask for the journey, bottles of water, camera, binoculars, sun screen.

'Pretty optimistic,' Andrew said, seeing the bottle of moisturising sun lotion, factor 20. 'Still, I hope you both have a lovely day. Think of me cracking the whip over my recalcitrant staff when you're skimming stones or whatever.'

Ruth lifted her face to be kissed.

'Beatrice,' Andrew called, 'see you later, sweetheart.'

'Bye, Dad.'

Thirty minutes more and they were on the road, Ruth with the car stereo tuned to Radio 4, more problems of the menopause under lively discussion; Beatrice opted to sit in the back, stretched out, with her iPod shuffle.

The weather seemed to improve the closer to the coast they came and by the time Ruth had parked the car there was barely a cloud in the sky.

'See,' Ruth said, looking up. 'What did I tell you?'

Beatrice treated her to one of those 'I care?' looks she'd been perfecting, but within minutes she'd taken her mother's hand and was chattering away about something hilarious, and, to Ruth, largely incomprehensible, that her friends had been up to at school.

'I think I could just fancy a cup of coffee,' Ruth said, pausing outside one of several cafés on the high street.

'I thought you brought a flask?'

'That was for emergencies.'

They found a seat near the window where they could look out past the striped awning at the passers-by, mostly, it seemed, visitors like themselves. Ruth treated herself to a cappuccino and a freshly baked scone with butter and jam, and Beatrice talked her way into a large hot chocolate with cream and sprinkles *and* a chocolate flake, as well as a piece of strawberry cheesecake.

They walked along the narrow path between the river and the sea, threading their way between brightly coloured fishing boats beached on the shingle, Beatrice ducking down every so often at the sight of a shell to add to her collection.

'Look! Look at this. Isn't it lovely?'

'It's beautiful.'

Ruth pushed the hair back out of her daughter's eyes and smiled.

'What?' Beatrice said, squinting towards the sun.

'Nothing. I'm just happy, that's all.'

'You're crazy,' Beatrice said, and, spinning away, she raced down towards the water's edge, small stones squirting out from beneath her flip-flops as she ran.

They ate their sandwiches in the lee of one of the numerous fishing huts, keeping a wary eye out for the more predatory of the gulls wheeling and gliding above. Once, in Scotland, a herring gull had swooped down and snatched a sandwich from Ruth's hand as she brought it towards her mouth, leaving her startled and shaken and holding an inch of crust.

A light haze was settling over the further reaches of the sea, so that the horizon had all but disappeared and sea and sky were one.

'Come on,' Ruth said, stuffing things back down into the rucksack, 'there's something I want to show you.'

From a distance, the steel constructions rising up from the shingle at the north end of the beach looked like giant fans and then, as they drew closer, like angel wings.

'What are they?' Beatrice asked.

'Wait and then you'll see.'

The nearer they got, the bigger they became, until they stood some twelve feet high at their tallest point and almost as wide.

'They're shells,' Beatrice said.

'That's right, scallop shells.'

'What on earth are they doing here?'

'An artist designed them, Maggi Hambling. A tribute to Benjamin Britten.'

'Who?'

'He's a composer. Was. Used to live near here. A lot of his music was about the sea.'

Beatrice shrugged and pressed her hand against the surface

of the iron shell. 'It's warm.' She leaned her face against it and closed her eyes.

I love you, Ruth thought. So much. I really do.

'Look,' Beatrice said, 'there's writing round the top. What does it say?'

'Read it.'

'*I hear those voices that will not be drowned.*'

'It's from an opera,' Ruth explained. '*Peter Grimes.*'

'By that man?'

'Yes.'

'What does it mean?'

'What d'you think it means?'

Beatrice flapped her hands. 'I don't know.'

'Do you like it, though? The sculpture?'

'It's okay.'

'Some people don't. People who live here. They've poured paint over it and everything. They think it should be taken down or moved.'

'That's stupid.' Beatrice shielded her eyes. 'Can we go now?'

Halfway on their journey back towards the car, Beatrice let go of Ruth's hand and started lagging behind, head down.

'Come on,' Ruth said cheerily. 'Not far now. We're nearly there.'

By the time Ruth had reached the beginnings of the town, Beatrice was a good fifty metres adrift. She swung the rucksack down from her back and sat on a bench to wait.

When Beatrice caught up, she stood, swivelling first on one foot and then the other, looking anywhere but into her mother's eyes.

'What's the matter?' Ruth asked.

No reply.

'You don't want to tell me?'

A shake of the head.

'Come and sit here, then. Let's just rest for a minute before we get back in the car.'

At first it seemed as if Beatrice was going to stay put, but then, grudgingly, she went and sat beside her mother, close but not close enough to be touching, flip-flops trailing on the ground.

'*Voices that will not be drowned*,' she said eventually. 'That's her, isn't it? Heather. That's why we came here, because of her. It is, isn't it?'

'Not really, no.'

'But you've been here before? With her?'

'Yes,' Ruth admitted.

'To look at that – that scallop thing?'

'No, that wasn't here then. But to Aldeburgh, yes. A long time ago.'

Beatrice turned away, back hunched.

'Beatrice, don't . . .'

'I hate her,' Beatrice said. 'I hate her.'

Ruth reached for her and felt her body stiffen, before she turned, sobbing, and pressed herself against Ruth's chest.

'It's all right,' Ruth said softly, her face resting close against the top of Beatrice's head, smelling her little girl smell, the warmth of the sun in her hair.

'It's all right,' she lied.

28

The sign over the door read *Terrence Markham: Bespoke Tailor.*
In the small window to one side a single three-piece suit was
on display, dark blue with the faintest of pink stripes. No price
shown. Helen didn't even want to guess.

The bell above the door gave a reassuringly old-fashioned
tinkle when it opened. A range of suits, carefully graded
from black to the palest grey, hung inside two open closets
to the left of the small interior, rolls of material on shelves
above and below; opposite, there were shirts and socks and,
inside a case, a selection of ties, mostly striped, some bearing
college crests.

The man who glanced up from behind the wooden table
facing the door, where he was measuring a length of cloth,
was five eight or nine, slender, bespectacled; his hair, for a
man not yet quite forty, going prematurely grey.

'Good morning. How can I help?'

'I didn't think,' Helen said, looking round, 'places like this
still existed.'

He smiled; it was a good smile, honest and open, Helen

thought. You'd buy a custom-made suit from this man – if your bank balance could stand it.

'You mean,' he said, 'when anyone can go down to Asda at Burleigh Street or Coldhams Lane and get one off the peg for forty pounds and change.'

'Something like that.'

'A city like this, there'll always be somebody who can tell quality enough to want to pay for it. And be able to. Then, of course, there are the tourists, God bless them, looking for a taste of old English craftsmanship and eager to reclaim their VAT.'

Helen returned his smile. 'You've been here long?'

'Not so very long. Not this time, at least. But the shop, it's been here for years.'

'But not always a tailor's?'

'Oh, yes. Burns Brothers. They had two places in the old days, this one and another on Portugal Street. I worked for them as a cutter after I left school; then again until six or so years ago. Ran this shop for them, in fact.'

'And now it's yours.'

'Maurice, the older one, he died. Leonard decided enough was enough and retired to a place he had in Cyprus. Now, until the bailiffs come calling, it's all mine.' He smiled again. 'And that's a lot more information than you really need.'

'Not at all.'

'What is it, anyway? Something for your husband or boyfriend? A celebration? Birthday? Anniversary?' Another smile. 'Perhaps you're getting married?'

'Not this month.' Helen slipped her warrant card from her bag.

'Ah.' The smile disappeared. 'I wondered. Wondered whether someone would find out, put two and two together and try making five.'

'Five?'

'After that awful . . . after Linda died . . . I kept expecting the police to come round. Every time the doorbell rang, and maybe I'd be in the workshop at the back, I'd walk out here expecting to see two burly men in uniform – Come down to the station – you know, the kind of thing you see on TV. *The Bill.* And then when nothing happened I realised that perhaps nobody knew. So I just kept quiet. I thought it was for the best.'

'For you.'

'Of course for me. There was nothing I could do for Linda now. Nor Paul.'

'And Carl? The little boy?'

Markham raised his hands to his face. 'He's all right, isn't he? I mean, he's being looked after?'

'Yes. His grandparents.'

'He'll get over it in time.'

'You think so?'

'I don't know. I hope so. I can't imagine . . .' He shook his head vigorously, as if to chase out the thought. 'You know,' he said, echoing something that had already passed through Helen's mind. 'I thought at one time he might be mine. Carl. I thought he might be my son.'

'And that's not the case?'

'No.'

'You're sure?'

A different smile this time, wry and slightly sad. 'I'm sure. I even went so far as to ask for proof. The boy's blood type, DNA. He was Paul's son, not mine.' His voice was touched by regret. 'Otherwise . . .'

For one moment, Helen thought he might be about to cry, but instead he took a handkerchief from his pocket – not a tissue, she noticed, but a genuine linen handkerchief – removed his glasses, blew his nose, put the handkerchief away and set his glasses back in place. Control restored.

'There are some questions I'd like to ask,' Helen said. 'Things to get straight. For the record.'

'You want me to come to the police station?'

'At some time, yes, to make a statement. Before the inquest.'

'And now . . . ?'

They walked out on to Magdalen Street and into the grounds of one of the smaller colleges, one of the few where visitors were not charged for satisfying their curiosity about the architecture and generally admiring the view.

Helen thought about lighting a cigarette, but held off for fear some college by-law would be evoked and see them ejected.

Markham seemed to be examining the palms of his hands, the length of his nails. 'We were at school together,' he said finally. 'Linda and I. The sixth form. Different subjects, the same year. I had this stupid crush, followed her around like some demented puppy dog. No wonder she wouldn't give me the time of day.

'I left to study textile design, but, with one thing and another, it didn't work out, and when I came back to Cambridge I talked my way into a job with Burns Brothers. Leonard, for some reason he took a bit of a shine to me, taught me just about everything I know. Linda had gone off to university to do architecture and that was when she met Paul. They got married and went to live somewhere in the north-east, but there were problems – his family, I think – and they came back here.

'By then I'd gone cap in hand off to Italy, trailing after a woman I'd met when she was here at summer school. What a disaster that was.' He smiled ruefully. 'You'd think I'd learn.'

Some people, Helen thought, never did. Herself included.

'Then one day after I returned I was walking by the Backs and I bumped into her. Linda. Literally, almost. I was wandering along, mind somewhere else entirely, and she was reading a book. *Like Life,* it was called. I can remember it now. Short stories, I think. American. After we finished apologising to one another, we started talking, things we'd been doing, filling in the gaps, I suppose. When she said she had to be going I asked if she'd meet me again, a coffee or something, another time. I didn't think for a moment she'd agree, but she did.

'We saw one another once or twice – just talked, that's all it was, nothing happened – you know, nothing physical – but Linda was uncomfortable with it, I could tell, and when she said she couldn't see me again, I wasn't surprised. She asked me not to contact her and I agreed. Then the following April she phoned me, right out of the blue. Said she wanted to see me. I'd been doing my best to forget her and there she was, "Please, Terry, it's important." I didn't know what was going on. It could still have been April Fools' Day for all I knew.

'We met out well clear of the city, close to Wicken Fen. She said she'd been thinking about me. Trying not to. It was a little crazy. Out of hand. We ended up making love there and then in the car. It was as if . . . as if something had been . . . unleashed. That sounds melodramatic, I know, clichéd, but that's what it was like. I'd never known anything like it.

'After that, we saw one another whenever we could. Wherever. Sometimes, when I was looking after the shop and no one else was around, I'd put up the closed sign and lock the door and we'd go into the stockroom and make love there.'

'Paul, her husband, he didn't suspect?'

'I don't know. From what I could tell they were living pretty separate lives by then.'

'But it didn't last?'

Markham shook his head. 'Eight months or so. Not even a year. I met her and it was different again. She was cold, distant. She said she wanted to give her relationship with Paul another chance. I hadn't seen it coming; hadn't seen it coming at all. I got really angry, lost my temper, started shouting. Said she and Paul didn't have a relationship anyway. I accused her of playing games, making excuses, messing me around. Then I threatened to tell Paul what had been going on. She said she'd told him already. Told him she was sorry and promised not to see me again and he'd understood. They were going off on holiday. Egypt. The Red Sea. Make a new start.

'I handled it badly. Sort of fell apart. Leonard, he could see there was something wrong. He had a cousin in South Africa, the same line of business. Cape Town. Go and work for him, he said, a working holiday.' Markham smiled. 'I stayed four years.'

'Why did you come back?'

'My father, he was diagnosed with cancer. We'd never been close – Leonard, he was more of a father to me – but it was serious. He was dying. Things like that – close or not – they make you think, think about your life. I expect that's what made me want to see Linda again, just – I don't know – just see her, that's all. Some sort of unfinished business, I suppose. And they were still living in Cambridge, the same house as before.' He gave Helen a quick sideways glance. 'That's when I found out about Carl.'

'And you thought . . .'

'Like I said, I thought he was mine. My son. He didn't even look like Paul, and besides – the sums, they weren't so very difficult – nine months, it's not hard to figure out. She swore Paul was the father and I wouldn't believe her. Not until she showed me the proof.'

'And then?'

'And then we talked. She told me she was going to leave Paul. There wasn't anything between them any more. She'd tried, but that was it. She was going to go somewhere like Australia, make a new start while she still could. A new life

186

for Carl, somewhere better. This country, she said, it's falling apart. It's no place to bring up a child.'

'And Paul knew?'

A slow shake of the head. 'She was going to tell him when the time was right.'

29

'I always thought architects made a fortune,' Helen said.

She was sitting out on the porch at Will and Lorraine's, Sunday afternoon, the three of them with glasses of wine; in a corner of the garden Jake was banging nails into one side of the den he and Will had been building earlier; Susie was sitting, cross-legged, closer by, nappy hanging down beneath her white dress, using an old tablespoon to shovel earth carefully into a plant pot until it was full, then, having patted it down, just as carefully take it out again.

'Why don't you invite Helen round?' Lorraine had said. 'Sunday lunch or something. I haven't seen her in ages.'

Several weeks later Helen had arrived, carrying a bottle of Californian white wine and a bunch of flowers that had looked much fresher under the supermarket lights than they did out here in the open.

'You see them on television sometimes,' Helen said now. 'Richard what's-his-name, who designed that thing in London . . .'

'The Gherkin?'

'Yes.'

'Richard Rogers?'

'Sounds right.'

'No, I don't think so,' Lorraine chipped in. 'I think that was somebody else.'

'Anyway, whoever it was, jobs like that, or that bridge over the Thames . . .'

'The one that nearly collapsed when too many people started walking over it . . .'

'You can imagine the money that's involved. Millions. They must be raking it in.'

'I don't know,' Will said, 'the bloke who built this place . . .'

'He wasn't an architect,' Lorraine said, 'he was just a builder.'

'Someone would have drawn up the plans, I doubt he'd have done that himself.'

'Maybe so. What's your point?'

'My point is, design something like this, you're on a small percentage of nothing very much. You just think how many architects must spend their time on kitchen extensions and new bathrooms.'

'Why,' Lorraine asked, 'are we talking about this anyway?'

'The woman who was killed,' Helen said, 'by her husband, you remember? That's what she was. She was an architect.'

'This is where the husband killed his wife and then himself?'

'Yes. She was looking to leave him, apparently. Take her kid . . .'

'Their kid,' Will interrupted.

'Okay, their kid. Take their kid, this little boy, and move to Australia. When we checked back on her computer, there were all these hits on the Royal Australian Institute of Architects and other sites where she'd been looking for jobs. The money wasn't great, believe me.'

'But that's why he killed her?' Lorraine said. 'Because she was leaving?'

189

'And taking the boy, yes, that's what it looks like.'

'There wasn't somebody else? She wasn't having an affair?'

'Apparently not. Not then. Not as far as we've found out, anyway. Though she did have this one affair a few years back and she managed to keep that pretty quiet.'

'It's not impossible then?'

'No, it's not impossible.'

'How old was she? Not young.'

'What's young? She was nearly forty. Thirty-nine.'

'Seems a big step to make all on your own, at that age especially.'

'Depends,' Helen said, with a knowing glance towards Will, 'how badly you want to get away.'

'I wasn't going to say anything,' Lorraine said, starting to smile, 'but I have just renewed my passport. Jake's too. Canada, I'm thinking. Or maybe New Zealand.'

'Very funny,' Will said.

There was a shout and a crash from the far end of the garden, as half of Jake's den went tumbling to the ground.

'Especially,' Lorraine said, 'now that Will's other career's come to nothing.'

Will hurried down to rescue Jake, who was sitting amidst pieces of loose timber, crying inconsolably. Susie, lower lip trembling, was looking round, wide-eyed, on the verge of joining in in sympathy.

'A top-up?' Lorraine said, reaching for the bottle.

'I shouldn't,' Helen said. And then, 'Oh, all right. Just a small one.'

'Will?' Lorraine signalled in the direction of his empty glass.

'Why not?' He picked Jake up and gave him a hug. 'We'll build it again next weekend, I promise, and even better.'

'Norman,' Lorraine said a few moments later, 'that's who it was. Norman Foster. Who did the Gherkin.'

'I thought he designed sunglasses,' Will said.

'You mean like Richard Rogers wrote all those songs?'

'What are you two on about?' Helen asked, confused.

'When I first started seeing Lorraine,' Will said, setting Jake down on the porch, 'we used to go out to Saffron Walden to her parents' for lunch on Sundays.'

'Some Sundays.'

'After we'd eaten, her dad would come out with a bottle of sherry and we'd sit round listening to songs from the shows on CDs he'd bought in Debenhams; counting the minutes till we could politely get up and leave. *Rodgers and Hammerstein's Greatest Hits*. I could do you a quick chorus of "Some Enchanted Evening" even now.'

'Don't,' Lorraine said. 'Please, just don't.'

'How about you?' Will said, looking pointedly at Helen. 'Any musical interludes with Declan's parents? Bit difficult, since he's married to someone else.'

'Very funny.'

'Declan,' Lorraine said, 'that's the new boyfriend?'

'Bit of rough,' Will said, before Helen could answer. 'I think that's the term you're looking for.'

'Will . . .'

'How is it going?' Will said. 'Walked into any good doors lately?'

'Fuck off, Will!'

'Language,' he said with a grin, clamping his hands over Jake's ears.

'Just fuck off,' Helen mouthed silently and Will laughed.

'Ignore him,' Lorraine said.

'I wish!'

An hour or so later, the light already slowly beginning to fade, Lorraine and Helen were in the kitchen, belatedly clearing away the lunch things. Will was in the garden, practising headers with Jake, and Susie was asleep on the settee, clutching a white bear missing one ear.

'What was Will on about?' Lorraine asked, rinsing one of the glasses under the tap. 'Walking into doors?'

'Oh, nothing.'

'You're sure?'

Helen scraped away food from one of the plates before slotting it down into the dishwasher.

'You know how Will likes to wind me up . . .'

'He seemed pretty serious.'

Helen sighed and reached for another plate. 'We were just fooling around . . .'

'You and Declan – is that his name?'

'Declan, yes. Declan Morrison. We were just playing games and I banged my head against the wall. It was an accident.' She shrugged. 'I bruise easily, that's all.'

'Games,' Lorraine said. 'What kind of games?'

'Oh, you know . . .'

'No, go on.'

'Go on what?'

'Tell me.'

Helen grinned. 'You're not getting turned on by this, are you?'

'No.'

'Well, it's just . . . just a bit of play-acting, I suppose. I mean, we don't get dressed up or anything.' She laughed. 'The odd bit of fancy lingerie, maybe, but I'm not getting into some French maid's outfit for anyone. It's more, oh, you know, I'll tease him, pretend I'd not interested. Come on all prim and proper. Or carry on as if I'm alone in the flat and I don't know he's there – like when I'm getting ready for bed or getting out of the shower then he'll take me by surprise.'

'Jesus!'

'What?'

'What you're describing. He takes you by surprise. It's a rape fantasy, that's what it is.'

'Is it, bollocks!'

'What else would you call it?'

'A bit of fun?'

Lorraine sighed and shook her head. 'I don't think so.'

'Come on,' Helen said. 'It's a game. I'm pretending. I know it's going to happen. And he doesn't force me, not really. He doesn't hurt me.'

'He doesn't?'

'I told you, that was an accident.'

Lorraine looked at her steadily, then turned aside; there were still a few things on the table that needed to be cleared away.

'Don't you,' Helen said quietly, 'and be honest now – don't you ever have fantasies about being powerless – tied up or something, held down – while someone makes love to you?'

'No,' Lorraine said, perhaps a little too vehemently. 'No, of course I don't. And if I did, I think I'd probably ask for help.'

'A bit difficult,' Helen said laughing, 'when you're hand-cuffed to the bed.'

'Well, now,' said Will coming in from the garden. 'What are you two on about?'

'Oh, nothing,' Lorraine said. 'Just girl talk. Nothing for you to worry your little mind about.'

'And I think,' Helen said, looking at her watch, 'it might be time for me to go. Leave you two lovebirds alone.'

'Alone?' Will said, as Jake came in through the door, dirt on his face and in his hair. 'Aren't you forgetting something?' In the other room, Susie had started to stir.

'See you tomorrow,' Helen said, 'bright and early.' And taking hold of both Lorraine's hands she kissed her on the cheek. 'Thanks for lunch.'

'A pleasure. Come again, okay?'

Helen nodded.

'I'll walk you out to the car,' Will said.

'No need.'

He knew that the moment she was outside she would pause and light a cigarette before driving away.

'You, young man,' Lorraine said, tousling Jake's hair. 'You need a good wash before going to bed. In fact, a bath. That's what you need, a quick bath.'

'Oh, Mum . . .'

'Go on, your dad'll run it for you while I sort out your sister, okay? Okay, Will?'

'Yes, fine. Come on, Jake, I'll race you upstairs.'

Smiling, Lorraine went into the living room and carefully lifted Susie up into her arms.

30

Before the summer months had been overtaken by the outbreak of violent crime that had stretched resources to the uttermost, Will, still bothered – haunted, even – by the thought that he had failed to check adequately into Mitchell Roberts' past, had given one of his DCs the task, laborious and painstaking even in this computer age, of checking for any unsolved cases of abducted or abused girls to which Roberts could have possible links.

He still didn't accept Liam Noble's view that the attack on Martina Jones was an isolated incident. In Will's experience, men with Roberts' predilections didn't get to fifty-plus years of age without accumulating a history of offending. And yet, not only had he never, seemingly, been arrested – nor even questioned – in connection with any similar crime, when his property at Rack Fen had been searched, nothing more pornographic than an old copy of *Penthouse* had been found; no under-the-counter DVDs, no kiddie porn, nothing to fuel the fantasies which had left twelve-year-old Martina naked at the roadside, bleeding and torn.

Will had tried to convince himself that Noble was right and that circumstances – the heat of summer, the isolated presence of the girl – a girl who, despite her age, was not sexually inexperienced – had led Roberts to behave as he had for the one and only time. Behaviour he now deeply regretted. Noble had claimed that Roberts was contrite: he had paid his penalty, his debt to society, and admitted the error of his ways. And according to Roberts' probation officer, since his release he had been punctilious in reporting, had received eloquent testimonials from the garage where he worked, and had in no way suggested a propensity to reoffend.

Maybe, Will allowed himself to think. Maybe.

But then he remembered the lascivious smile that had curled around Roberts' mouth when the older man had confronted him in Cambridge.

'You got children? I'd like to see 'em some time.'

Remembered and became convinced again that Noble was wrong and he was right.

Three cases came up that interested Will particularly – those of Rose Howard, Janine Prentiss and Christine Fell – all occurring within a span of seven years, from 1993 to 2000, and all within a hundred-mile radius of where Martina Jones had been attacked, the sparsely populated hinterland of East Anglia. Janine Prentiss and Christine Fell had been abducted, abused and then abandoned; Rose Howard had, to all intents and purposes, simply disappeared.

Rose Howard had been living on a new housing estate in Peterborough when she had disappeared. Her family had moved there from Corby three years before, when the factory where her father had worked was closed down. She had an older brother, Peter, who hung out with a bunch of dropouts in the town centre and had already been in trouble with the police. Rose tried making friends at her new school, but it was hard, and then, when she went up to the comprehensive – 'Your chance, Rose dear,' the headmistress had said, 'to make a new start' – it had been worse. Though even being bullied was preferable to being ignored. She started to play truant, hanging around the shopping centre and the bus station. One day a man gave her five pounds to put her hand down inside his trousers.

'Where'd you get this from?' her mum said, finding the note, crumpled and green, inside the torn lining of her coat.

When she told her, her mum slapped her and called her a stupid little whore. Her dad laughed and told her to ask for a tenner next time – 'That's closer to the going rate.'

Rose cried: not because of being hit, but because she'd been saving the five pounds for when she ran away. She started stealing from her mother's purse instead; not much, there was never much there, just enough so it would never get noticed. She stole, too, from the other kids at school, money taken from their pockets in the cloakroom or when they were doing PE; once, she took ten pounds from the teacher's handbag when it was left, one lunch-time, on her desk.

Her truancy got worse.

Her mother was told she was in danger of being sent to court if she didn't make sure her daughter attended school.

On a damp and drizzly February afternoon, Rose packed some clothes into a rucksack, along with two Polly Pocket dolls and a CD by Take That she'd stolen from a stall in the market and never played, and started walking along London Road.

She was last seen by the mother of one of the girls in her class, getting into the cab of a small, open-backed lorry carrying sacks of what might have been compost or fertiliser.

That was fifteen years ago: there had been nothing since, so sighting, no postcard. If she were still alive, Rose Howard would be twenty-seven years old.

*

Twelve-year-old Janine had gone missing from her home in Wisbech two years later, 1995. Her parents, who ran a small market garden attached to the property, had left her in the house with her two younger siblings, all three stretched out in the living room, watching TV. Neither parent had gone far, the mother to their shop, filling in for the teenage helper who had failed to arrive; the father to dig in a fresh delivery of bonemeal. They were absent from the house for a little over an hour, in which time Janine went missing.

When the mother came back into the house and asked where Janine was, her younger sister said she'd gone upstairs to wash her hair; her brother, five, engrossed in some animated film or other, didn't seem to have noticed she was no longer there.

Janine was not in the bathroom, nor the bedroom she and her sister shared.

Sometimes, when she was bored, she would go down and help her father but he'd seen neither hide nor hair. Calls to Janine's close friends yielded nothing. Her father drove along the lanes to the east of the town, closest to where they lived: Walsoken, Rosedale, Paradise Farm. Janine had been known to wander off on her own but never far.

'What the hell you do, girl?' her mother would ask.

'Nothin', Mum. Just thinkin' 'bout stuff, that's all.'

Her father tracked back, circled round by Emneth and Oxburgh Hall. Flat landscape, straight roads, tall sky. No sign of Janine.

'I shouldn't worry overmuch,' the police officer said. 'You say she's gone off before? She'll turn up then, I dare say. Come morning, if not sooner.'

Come morning she was still not there.

A search was raised. Neighbours, friends, volunteers. A line of police in special uniforms walked through the fields closest to the house, a fingertip apart. Divers explored two deep ponds less than half a mile distant. Janine's photograph appeared on hastily printed posters attached to bus shelters and telegraph poles. A long-faced girl with long, straight hair, medium brown; grey eyes, tall for her age.

Three days after she disappeared, Janine knocked on the door of a farmhouse near Outwell, some six miles, no more, from her home. Her clothing was torn and her hair unkempt – as if she'd been sleeping in a ditch, thought the woman who answered the door. Janine asked please could she have a drink of water and use the toilet and then would the woman kindly phone her mum and dad and tell them where she was.

The story was slow in coming. Bored with staying indoors, she had gone for a walk along the path through the fields that led on to the road to Paradise Farm and it was there that a van stopped and the driver asked if she were lost. There was a dog in the front with him, a black and white collie, as yet little more than a puppy, and when Janine reached in through the open window the dog had started licking her hand. So when the man said, 'Hop in, why don't you? We'll give you a lift down the turn, me and Ezra here,' Janine had accepted with scarcely a second thought.

'She would an' all,' her mother said later. 'Anything to do with animals, dogs especially, and every scrap of common sense that girl's got flies out the window.'

At the turn in the road, instead of letting her out, the man had swung the van around and driven off in the opposite direction.

All of Janine's screaming had done no good.

When they stopped it was at a pair of cottages in the middle of nowhere, one of which seemed to be tumbling down. The man pushed Janine into a room and threw a bucket in after her before locking the door. 'Do your business in there.'

Later that night he came for her, smelling of drink.

He came back again later still and then again the next day.

There was porridge to eat, lumpy and half-cold, and water

to drink and wash in. A scrap of torn towel to wipe herself dry. Once or twice, she thought she heard a second voice, another man's, though she was never absolutely sure. From time to time the dog whimpered and scratched at the outside of her door.

On the morning of the third day, she was blindfolded and bundled back into the van and driven for no more than forty minutes or so – less than the length of a lesson at school – before being pushed out of the back of the van, still blindfolded, and left.

From there she had walked to the farm.

The man, she told the female police officer who questioned her, was not specially tall – 'fair hair, not dark, fairer than mine' – dressed in old work clothes that smelt, what of she didn't know. 'Not young. Sort of old. But not granddad old. 'Bout like my dad, I s'pose.' He didn't have a proper beard, she said, but needed a shave; his face had been rough against her skin.

'Did he sound like he came from around here?' the police officer asked.

Janine thought he did.

She was unable to identify him from photographs; an attempt to assemble an identikit picture using a police artist floundered and was then abandoned. Two men were arrested and later released without charge; Janine had failed to pick out either one at an identity parade.

The inquiry remained open, the case unsolved.

Thirteen years ago. Janine Prentiss was now Janine Clarke, married with children of her own.

Christine Fell was an only child. Her father was a lecturer at Anglia Ruskin University, specialising in Cell and Molecular Biology and Genetics; her mother a freelance translator from Swedish and Norwegian. When Christine was seven, they bought an old farmhouse close to Chatteris Fen, an area of largely agricultural land, spectacular sunsets and vast, vaulting skies, separated from the city of Cambridge, where David Fell worked, by the Hundred Foot Washes and the River Ouse.

Christine went to a private preparatory school in Ely, where she worked hard and was popular both with teachers and with her fellow pupils. Her mother, Alice, spent a great deal of time driving Christine to music lessons and drama club, as well as to the houses of friends, some of whom lived in Ely, though others were scattered far and wide. Since she worked mainly from home, this was possible and a small price to pay, she felt, for the lovely house they were slowly restoring and the near-idyllic surroundings in which they lived.

Both of them hoped that, when she was thirteen, Christine would transfer up to the King's School, where, in addition to the usual range of subjects, she would have the opportunity of studying Ancient History and Classical Civilisations, Latin, Greek and Chinese. David Fell foresaw a time, not so many years hence, when he and Christine would make the journey into Cambridge together, she as an aspiring young undergraduate, and himself a professor, highly respected in his department.

In June 2000, a light, early summer evening, Alice Fell dropped her daughter off at a friend's house in the village of Little Downham, north of Ely. Her friend's twelfth birthday; Christine was still eleven.

Christine was wearing a new blue dress and yellow cardigan, matching blue shoes. Alice promised to pick her up at half past eight, no later, but a phone call from a publisher for whom she was doing some translating went on longer than expected and it was almost eight-thirty before she finally left home, having phoned ahead and spoken to the parents of the girl whose party it was: Tell Christine not to worry, I'll be there.

Most people having already left, Christine decided to walk

to the end of the lane, just as far as the junction with the main road, and meet her mother there.

She never arrived.

Three days later she was found tied to an old Massey Ferguson square baler inside a disused barn some twenty miles north, close to the village of Wiggenhall St Mary the Virgin. She was still wearing her blue shoes.

31

Janine Clarke was wearing a black suit that could have come back from the dry cleaner's that morning, a small silver brooch in the shape of a flower on her lapel. American tan tights, black shoes with a slight heel. Her hair was worn in a neat bob; two rings, wedding and engagement, make-up tastefully applied.

She held Will Grayson's hand for no more than a moment; slender fingers, long and cold. They had arranged to meet close to the building society where she worked.

'It's good of you to see me,' Will said.

Janine smiled: the same smile, courteous and professional, she gave to customers fifty times a day.

'Do you want to walk, or should we find somewhere to sit?'

'I really don't mind.' She glanced down at her watch. 'I haven't very long, that's all.'

In the marketplace, they found a bench in front of the church. Sheltered from the wind, Will unfastened his jacket; Janine kept hers fully buttoned.

'It's probably the last thing you want,' Will said, 'having to think back to what happened.'

'No, it's fine.'

'If I didn't think it might be important . . .'

'Really, it's fine.' Her words were clipped and sharp and she sat staring out, avoiding his eyes.

'I've read your statements, of course, what you had to say at the time. The man who took you, I just wondered if there's anything you've thought of since . . . ?'

The smile was even more fleeting than before. 'I rarely think about it, I'm afraid. That whole business – it was such a long time ago. It's as if it happened to somebody else.'

Will took the photographs from an envelope and placed them on the bench.

'Do you recognise this man?'

Was it his imagination, or did her body tense?

She lifted one of the pictures with nicely manicured hands and held it in her lap. 'You think this might have been him? The man who . . . who took me?'

'I think it's possible.'

He watched to see if her grip would waver, but her hand remained steady.

'No. I don't recognise him at all. I'm sorry.'

'These were taken some years later. He's older, clearly.'

Shaking her head, she set the photograph back down. 'I'm sorry.'

Will didn't immediately say anything; didn't move.

'The reason you're showing me, this man, he's done something similar?'

'Yes.'

'Another girl?'

'Yes.'

'Young?'

'Twelve years old.'

She turned her face away.

'I think there might have been others,' Will said. 'If he's allowed to remain at liberty, I think there might be still more.'

She looked quickly down at the photographs again, then turned them face down, one by one, on the bench. 'I have to be getting back.' Smoothing down her skirt, she stood.

After another moment's hesitation, Will slid the images back from sight.

'I'll walk with you, if that's all right?'

There were quite a few people about now, shoppers busy in their lunch hour, people carrying take-out food and cups of coffee, grazing as they walked. A pair of young women, steering their buggies against the tide.

'Your little girl,' Will said, 'how old is she now?'

'Don't!' Halting in her tracks, she swung fast towards him. 'Don't do that. Don't you dare!'

'Do what?' Will said, innocently.

'Use my child. Use her to make me feel guilty. Tell you what you want to hear.'

'I'm sorry,' he said, taken aback. 'I apologise.'

They walked on in silence until they were almost level with the building where she worked, a blown-up technicoloured picture of the perfect family in the window, mum, dad and two kids, smiling ecstatically outside their perfect new home.

'Thank you,' Will said, holding out his hand. 'Thank you for your time.'

She didn't take his hand, but turned smartly away and pressed the buzzer to be admitted through the door.

The journey on from Huntingdon to Chatteris Fen was no more than a dozen miles, the road snaking between gravel pits as it wound north, straightening momentarily before rising through a series of narrow bends and running in places above the land, which spread out, dark and anonymous, on either side; not a house in sight, no dwelling, no tree. And then at the last minute, off to the right, Will saw a narrow track, unmarked, and beyond that a pair of double chimney stacks and the beginnings of a pantiled roof.

Alice Fell was waiting for him in the garden at the front of the house, seated inside a wooden structure that looked to Will like an overlarge, open-fronted birdcage, laptop on the table before her, books stacked high on either side.

When she saw Will she saved what she had been working on and rose to greet him. An even-faced woman with short hair sensibly cut, medium height, she was wearing a faded blue quilted jacket and loose, comfortable trousers tucked down into rubber boots. More dressed, Will thought, for gardening than writing.

'Inspector Grayson?'

Unlike Janine Clarke, the edges of her hands were rough, only the fingertips smooth.

'Or should it be Detective Inspector?'

'Either is fine.'

'I was going to have a cup of tea. You'll join me, I hope. I've been putting it off till you arrived. Concentrating on chapter twenty-nine instead.' She inclined her head back towards the table. 'Detective fiction – I don't suppose you read very much of it yourself. Too much of a busman's holiday.'

'Too far from the truth. What little I've read.'

'Yes, well. This fellow I'm translating now – Norwegian – he's not bad on that account. Not bad all told.'

The kitchen had been refashioned with new quarry tiles on the floor, stripped pine cupboards, a large butler sink, solid oak surfaces inches thick; copper-bottomed pans hung from an iron girdle near the Aga. A scrubbed wooden table stood towards the far end, with flowers in a vase.

A tortoiseshell cat had scooted out of the room the moment they'd walked in.

'You found us without any difficulty?'

Will smiled. 'Only just.'

'We did have a sign made. A friend of ours painted it. It was rather beautiful. After two weeks it was pulled down. Vandalised.' She shook her head. 'Even here . . .'

At her suggestion, they took the tea back outside; good strong tea in thick china mugs. Alice Fell pulled out a folding chair for Will from behind where she'd been sitting and set it down close to the edge of the lawn, then moved her own near to it. Behind them a wall of yellow brick could just be seen through a profusion of shrubs and flowers.

'I like to sit here in the afternoons. Catch the last of the sun. Once you reach this time of the year, the nights start drawing in.' A small shudder ran through her, as if, Will thought, watching, someone had just walked over her grave.

He leaned back in his chair and waited, mug held in both hands. The silence around them was almost total. 'Christine,' he said. 'She must be what? Eighteen? Nineteen?'

'She'll be nineteen in a month's time.'

'It's been difficult, I know. You explained.'

Several years in a special school that catered for children with behavioural problems had been followed by an attempt to ease her back into mainstream education that had failed. Christine would sit through lesson after lesson, not speaking, not really following, ignoring those around her until some incident, some stray word, would set her off and then she would unleash such a torrent of anger, every filthy word spat out, arms flailing, that it took at least three adults, frail-seeming as she was, to hold her down. One day she bit one of the teachers, quite badly, in the hand; on another occasion, she stabbed a pupil, a girl, repeatedly, in the arm with a pen.

For a short time after that, she was admitted as an in-patient to the Darwin Centre in Cambridge, since when she'd been attending the Newtown Centre in Huntingdon, where she had regular sessions with a therapist; there was also a community psychiatric nurse who visited her at the house.

'When she wasn't at the centre,' Alice Fell said, 'she used to just sit upstairs. She wouldn't read or do anything. I tried to get her interested in helping me with the garden, but it wasn't really any good. Then this last month or so, since the summer really, she's been working in a charity shop in Ely. As a volunteer. A couple of afternoons, that's all so far. But it's something, a step forward.'

'Is that where she is now?'

Alice Fell hesitated. 'No. She's home. In her room.'

'I'd like to . . .'

Alice Fell was already shaking her head. 'I'm sorry. I thought about what you said, about showing her some photographs. David and I talked it over this morning and we don't think it would be right. Not to stir all that up again.'

'But if she could identify . . .'

'If she could identify the man who abused her, can you imagine what effect that might have? What it would do to her? Forcing her to go through all of that again?'

'I know,' Will said. 'It's a risk, I know. But if this is the man and Christine identifies him, he can be arrested and made to pay for what he's done. Not just to Christine, but to others too.'

Alice Fell set her mug on the ground. 'I can see why it's important. But it's a risk I'm not prepared to take, not on Christine's behalf.'

'What if she were asked? She could always say no.'

'And if she said yes?' She shook her head. 'I'm sorry, Inspector, but I've seen my daughter very gradually edging back towards a point where she might have a real life again. I'm not prepared to jeopardise that, not for anything. If the man in those photographs is the one who hurt my daughter, you're going to have to catch him some other way.'

She walked him to his car and politely shook hands. The cat was in the garden now, curled up between the books on her work table. It was time she collected everything together and brought it all in. She would make Christine some hot chocolate or Ovaltine and take it up to her room. She expected David would ring soon to say he was on his way and she would open a bottle of wine, something full-bodied and cheering, against his return. They might have a fire tonight in the drawing room; it was time.

32

___

It had been put off long enough. Ruth could no longer find a legitimate reason for not taking the train into Cambridge with Beatrice in order to shop. Jigsaw, H&M, Topshop, Miss Selfridge, Monsoon; River Island, Gap, Oasis, French Connection. And not forgetting Tammy Girl. Or the hours – it seemed to Ruth like hours – spent lovingly examining small sparkly items in Accessorize.

'Do you recognise this?' the police liaison officer had asked.

A gold chain with letters spelling out Heather's name.

'She bought it, in Penzance,' Pauline Efford had explained. 'With her pocket money. She thought – she thought it was lovely.'

Ruth kept it wrapped inside a cream all-in-one Heather had worn as a baby, folded now at the back of the drawer in which she kept her own gloves and scarves and a few other of Heather's things: a T-shirt with an embossed Minnie Mouse, a red dress from when she was four, a pair of dungarees.

'Mum,' Beatrice said suddenly. 'Look. Look at these. Aren't

they cool?' She was holding up a pair of earrings: spirals of silver that caught the light.

'Beatrice,' Ruth said, wearily. 'We've been through all this before. You're not having your ears pierced and that's an end to it.'

'That's stupid.'

'No, it's not.'

'Everyone else's got their ears pierced and not me.'

'I'm not sure if that's true. And besides, you know perfectly well you're not allowed to wear earrings to school until year ten, so there's no point.'

'Sleepers? I can wear sleepers, yeah?'

'Beatrice, I don't want to have this argument again. Not here.'

'Don't then.'

Ruth closed her eyes and tried counting to ten. She had been in and out of so many shops, stood patiently outside so many changing rooms; admired, demurred, discouraged, reluctantly approved, finally produced her debit card on so many occasions that her head felt as if it was made from cotton wool. Or worse. And her feet were starting to ache. Calves, too. She wanted nothing more than to catch the bus to the station, get on the train and go back home.

'Here,' she said, taking a ten-pound note from her purse. 'Go ahead. Get them. And don't forget the change. I'll be outside.'

'Ruth,' someone said, as she stepped out through the door, laden down. 'Ruth.'

It was Simon.

'Ruth, hello.'

'My God, Simon! What are you doing here?' She lowered her parcels to the ground. 'I hardly recognised you.'

And it was true. Always thin, he seemed to have become

even more so; his face was gaunt, cheeks sunken in, and his clothes – a mismatching jacket and trousers – hung off him in a way that emphasised his awkward, angular frame. Just the eyes, only the eyes were alive.

'I moved,' he said, breathlessly. 'I thought you knew. Some time ago now. London wasn't . . . wasn't doing it for me any more. All those people, all that noise.' He laughed, a high, nervous trill. 'You were the sensible one, eh? Got out when you could. Up here, the country, you can breathe. And think. Think.' He came closer, an odd little shuffle, head dipping towards hers. 'I've been wanting to talk to you, you know. Hoping I'd bump into you. Now that we're living so close.'

Close, Ruth thought. Close?

Before she could reply there was Beatrice, hair brushed away from her face, holding up the small Accessorize bag, coins close to spilling from her other hand.

'Mum, here's your change.'

'Thanks, darling. I . . .'

'You must be Beatrice,' Simon said, smiling, holding out his hand.

Glancing at her mother anxiously, Beatrice took a step back towards the glass.

'Bea, this is Simon. He . . .'

'Your mother and I were married,' Simon said. 'A long time ago.' He let his hand fall back by his side. 'I've wondered . . . I've often wondered what you'd be like.'

Beatrice looked away.

A couple, arms around each other's shoulders, pushed between them, oblivious.

'She's lovely, Ruth. Lovely.' Smiling.

'We really should be going,' Ruth said, collecting the bags strewn around her feet. 'The train . . .'

'Of course, of course.' He moved closer, the same dip of

the head, quick like a bird's. 'Some time,' he said in a lowered voice, 'we should talk. There are these groups, support groups. People who understand. Understand what you've been going through. What we both have. I think they could help.'

'Simon, thank you. But really, I'm fine. I don't need any help. We're all fine.'

She bustled Beatrice away and when she looked back, some moments later, he was still standing there, neck craned forward, watching them go.

'Mum,' Beatrice said, as they hurried for the bus, tugging at her sleeve. 'That man. You weren't really married to him? Before Dad. That was him? You couldn't have been.'

'It was a long time ago,' Ruth said. 'A long time. He was different then.'

Thinking, no, he's different now.

'And that was it?' Andrew said. 'You didn't find out what he was doing there? Where he's living? Anything?'

They were in the dining room after supper, curtains moving lightly in the breeze. From the squawks and flutters elsewhere, after a certain amount of nagging, Beatrice was practising her flute.

'No. Close, that's what he said. Now that we're living so close.'

'You don't think he's actually here in Ely?'

'I don't know. I didn't ask.' She poured a little more wine into her glass and passed the bottle. 'Quite honestly, the whole thing freaked me out.'

'It was the surprise.'

'Yes, I suppose so.'

'Seeing someone when you least expect it, out of context, it's always strange.'

'Yes, I know. But this . . . And all that stuff about support groups, people who'd understand . . .'

A quick shudder ran through her and Andrew reached across the table and took her hand. 'He probably hasn't got anyone else, poor bloke. Maybe that Internet stuff – I suppose that's what it is – is what he needs.' Smiling, he gave her hand a squeeze. 'It's okay for you. You've got me.'

33

Will had spent most of the morning closeted with the Divisional Commander and other senior officers, discussing the policing of the increasingly diverse communities within the county. After a slight hiccup, the numbers of asylum seekers and economic migrants continued to rise: tensions had already overflowed in certain areas, most recently Huntingdon, where clashes between groups of Poles and West Africans had become worryingly violent and prolific. Elsewhere, significant numbers of Eastern Europeans were becoming involved in the farming and distribution of cannabis. The death of a Lithuanian man, discovered with his throat cut in a field outside Newmarket, was considered by the Major Investigation Team to be the result of a drug deal turned sour.

When, after the best part of four hours and presentations from both the Diversity Steering Group and the Regional Immigration, Asylum and Migrant Worker Group, Will finally stumbled out of the meeting, his tongue was furred by too many cups of instant coffee and his mind numbed by an excess of bullet points, pie charts and well-meaning obfuscation.

He phoned Helen, but, for some reason, her mobile was switched off. Overhead, the sky, which earlier that morning had promised much, was now a meagre veil of grey. There were more papers to attend to at his desk, target assessments, reports, a case that was coming up to trial. Easing the Astra out of the crowded car park, he headed north.

He had seen photographs of Christine Fell taken when she was just eleven: a dark-eyed, willowy girl in school uniform, smiling hopefully at the camera, her life before her. Those taken after the abduction had shown something else: fear, a residue of pain, a knowledge of things she should have neither seen nor known.

What chance that he would recognise her now?

There were more charity shops on the high street than he remembered, each offering a mixture of cast-off clothing, discarded books and CDs, unwanted videos and bric-a-brac, carelessly arranged. Will walked slowly along, peering in windows, half in hope, until there, surely, she was, anonymous in muted colours, standing beside a rail hung with cardigans and fake-leather coats, eyes cast down. She had grown tall, as those early pictures had suggested she might, but the way she stood, stoop-shouldered, disguised her height as best she could.

Will watched as a customer approached her with a question and she seemed almost to flinch, then half-turn her head aside before answering, her voice, Will could tell, kept low. With a shake of her head, the customer moved away, seeking help elsewhere, and Christine was left standing, wringing her hands, willing the floor to swallow her up.

Will pushed open the door and went inside.

Feigning interest, he ran a finger along a shelf of paperbacks: Desmond Bagley, James Patterson, Anita Shreve; several copies of *Bridget Jones's Diary* – Lorraine had read the choice bits out to him in bed.

Jumper loose and at least a size too large, skirt too long, Christine Fell had moved to the cash desk near the back of the shop.

Toys and games were stacked haphazardly close by and Will crouched low, contemplating first a jigsaw for Jake, then, for Susie, a small brown bear missing one ear. The only thing with second-hand jigsaws, he thought, you could never be certain vital pieces weren't missing. After some scrabbling in a plastic box, he found a Matchbox car for Jake instead, a red Jaguar XK with only a single scratch along the bonnet.

'How much are these?' he asked at the counter. Christine Fell glanced up at him for just a moment, then, without looking at him directly, she took first the bear and then the car from his hands and set them down. Her nails, he could see, were bitten to the quick.

'I'm not sure,' she said quietly. 'I think they might be a pound. Let me ask.'

'A pound each?'

'Yes. Is that too much?

'No, no, that's fine.' He took a five-pound note from his wallet. 'I don't have the right money, I'm afraid.'

Her fingers were uncertain on the old-fashioned till; the change, when she held it out towards him, slipped from her hand on to the surface of the desk and rolled from there to the floor.

'Christine,' one of the other staff called from across the shop, 'is everything all right?'

'Yes,' she replied, flustered. 'Yes.'

Will waited while, still fumbling, she retrieved the coins, rewarding her with an encouraging smile.

'I'm really sorry,' she said.

'It's not a problem.'

'I . . . I should have asked if you wanted a bag.'

'Thanks, no. This will be fine.' The car he slipped down into one pocket, the bear into the other. 'And thanks for all your help.'

Hand to her face, she turned, flushing deeply, away.

Back outside, Will hesitated.

If she could identify the man who abused her, can you imagine what effect that might have? What it would do to her? Forcing her to go through all of that again?

He glanced through the window to where Christine Fell still stood.

I'm sorry, Inspector . . . If the man in those photographs is the one who hurt my daughter, you're going to have to catch him some other way.

With a quick shake of his head, Will began to walk away, quickening his pace as he neared the spot where he'd parked the car. A waste of an afternoon. A mile or so along the A10, he spun the car across the central reservation and headed back.

Christine Fell left the shop a little after five-thirty, a long raincoat covering her skirt and jumper, though there was no clear sign of rain.

Will crossed towards her cautiously, not wishing to startle her any more than was necessary.

'Christine?'

Halting, she blinked uncertainly.

'It is Christine Fell, isn't it?'

'Ye . . . Yes. Why? I don't . . .' She gulped in air.

'I was in the shop earlier.'

'Oh, yes, how stupid of me. You bought . . .'

He showed her.

'The bear, of course. And a little car.' She almost smiled. 'Is there something wrong? I charged too much, perhaps, I wasn't sure. Or the change? I gave you the wrong change. I'm really sorry. If we went back, I think there's somebody still there . . .'

But even as she blustered on, words tumbling over one another, she realised it was something more.

'Detective Inspector Grayson, Cambridge Constabulary.' Where there had been a small bear in Will's hand, there was now a warrant card, identification. 'Perhaps there's somewhere we could sit quietly.'

'My mother . . . I'm meeting my mother.'

Will nodded, smiling. 'Just a few minutes, I promise.'

Gently, he took her arm.

The café was on a narrow side street off the main road, the kind that Will didn't think really existed any more; a menu offering Welsh rarebit, poached egg on toast, toasted teacake or scones. Tea came in a pot, coffee – the best Nescafé – with cold milk or warm; none of your highfaluting lattes and cappuccinos here. The walls were painted a bilious shade of yellow, relieved here and there by pictures of flowers that had been fashioned from pieces of coloured fabric and then framed.

The woman in charge broke off from sweeping the floor – they were likely due to close at six – to make a pot of tea for two.

'Sugar's on the table,' she announced, lest it had escaped their notice.

Having unfastened her raincoat, but not taken it off, the edges trailing on the floor, Christine fidgeted with the heart-shaped buttons of her jumper, the folds of her skirt. The tea came in a metal pot with a hinged lid, milk already in the cups. 'I spoke to your mother,' Will said.

'My mother . . .' She looked alarmed.

'A few days ago, she didn't mention it?'

Christine shook her head.

'Didn't want to upset you, I expect.'

'Upset?'

'I said I might want to speak with you . . .'

'What about?'

'All those years ago, the man who abducted you . . . I'd like you to look at some photographs . . .'

Something flashed across her eyes.

'See if it's anyone you recognise.'

'No. No, you can't make me.'

Something clattered behind the counter; Christine loud enough now to be overheard.

'You can't.' There was panic in her voice.

Carefully, Will placed the photographs, three of them, on the table between the teapot and the sugar bowl: Mitchell Roberts in profile and then head on, staring into the camera, all expression sucked from his eyes.

'I won't look,' Christine said, but, of course, she did. How could she not?

'Take your time,' Will said. 'Think. It's important. Do you recognise this man?'

'No,' she said breathlessly. 'No, no.'

'Christine . . .'

She threw herself blindly forward, brushing the photographs from the table with a flailing arm, cup and saucer spinning away and shattering on the floor.

'Go away! Go away! Leave me alone!'

Pulling her coat around her, she was halfway to the door when it opened and her mother stepped in sharply from the street, anger and concern etched in every line of her face.

34

'Christ, Will! What were you thinking of?' Helen said.

They were in Will's office, late morning, door closed. Helen, looking fresh and sparky in a tan skirt and tailored jacket, had brought in two cups of coffee from the nearest Caffè Nero and they sat on the edge of Will's desk, as yet untouched and growing cold.

'Thinking of?' Will said. 'Doing my job?'

'You think? Interviewing a particularly vulnerable witness without her parents' consent . . .'

'She's eighteen. Nineteen, good as. An adult. Come on, Helen, I don't need their consent.'

'Eighteen and in psychiatric care, or did I get that wrong?'

Will shook his head. 'I've just spent the last hour upstairs with the boss getting my balls chewed off – the last thing I need is for you to do the same.'

Helen laughed. 'Wasn't what I had in mind.'

'Very funny.' But he smiled anyway and, reaching for one of the coffees, levered off the lid.

'So how did it go upstairs?' Helen asked. 'You still got a job?'

'Just about. That and a possible harassment suit.'

Helen grinned. 'Shame. I was hoping you'd get a suspension at least. Time for me to step up. Acting DI. Get my feet under your desk.'

'It'll come.'

'I'd just like it to be this side of my pension, that's all.' Picking up the second coffee, she carried it across to the window. Another grey East Anglian day. 'When you showed her the photos – I assume that's what you did, the photos of Roberts – what did she say?'

'She didn't say anything.'

'She didn't recognise him?'

'She shouted, screamed. Didn't want to see. But she knew him, all right.'

'It's never going to be admissible, you realise that. None of it. And if you did ever get her to agree to take the stand, which is unlikely, they'd rip her to shreds.'

'I know.'

Helen moved back away from the window. 'This all should have been sorted years ago.'

'You think you need to tell me that?'

'Why wasn't it, though? I mean, if it was Roberts – one of those girls, one at least. We should have known. Questioned him when we could. Instead of letting him get off as lightly as he did.'

'Yes, well . . .' Will pushed back his chair and stood. 'We fucked up. I fucked up. What more d'you want me to say?'

'Will . . .'

'What?' He was reaching for his coat.

'You're going to go and see him, aren't you? Roberts. Confront him.'

'I might.'

Helen dropped her cup into the litter bin beside the desk. 'Be careful, Will.'

'Careful?'

'Whatever you feel. Guilt, whatever. Don't let him become an obsession.'

'You think that's what this is?'

'It could be.'

Will smiled. 'I'll leave the obsessions to you. More your mark than mine.'

'You think?'

'How is Declan lately?'

He left without waiting for her reply.

Mitchell Roberts checked the pressure in the new tyre and made sure the lug nuts were correctly secured before lowering the chassis back down to the ground. The wrong side of four, and a couple of hours still to go. Wiping his hands down the front of his overalls, he moved away from the work area and, stepping outside, took a packet of papers and a pouch of tobacco from his top pocket.

If Vernon sodding Lansdale didn't like him taking a smoke, then he could just screw himself. Not that Vernon, unless he'd come up worse on the horses that day than usual, was likely to create a fuss. A decent enough bloke, long as you stayed the right side of him, and not above giving work to them as had been inside. Just as long as they pulled their weight. And Roberts did that.

Straightforward stuff, for the most part: bald tyres and blown exhausts. Once in a while, an engine job would come in and Vernon would let him loose. Not much about cars and lorries Mitchell Roberts couldn't fix, folk'd tell you that. Place he'd had out by Rack Fen, before that business with the girl, people'd have him look at their tractors and all sorts, combine bloody harvesters, whatever it was, chances were he'd get it sorted. Not charge the earth, neither, not like some of them.

He lit the roll-up and held the smoke down in his lungs.

That stupid blasted scrap of a girl.

Flirting with him all the time, the way she did. Not above letting him grab a feel, neither, if she thought it'd earn her a free bottle of pop or some of them chocolate buttons.

Prick tease, that's what she was.

Regular prick tease.

Well, he showed her.

Himself, too.

A lesson learned. Prison. He didn't want to go back there.

He was about to head back into the workshop when he saw Will Grayson walking fast towards him.

'Wait up.'

'Can't. Due back at work.'

Will placed himself in his path. 'Take five, you can take ten.'

'Says who?'

'You need to see some ID?'

Smart bastard, Roberts thought.

'Going well?' Will asked.

'The job?'

'What else?'

'Well enough.'

Roberts had let his hair grow out since Will had last seen him, dark at the roots, fair, almost ginger, at the nape of his neck and where it curled around his ears. His teeth were long and yellow and stained with nicotine.

'Money in your pocket,' Will said, 'time on your hands.'

'You say.'

'Five-thirty when you're done? Six?'

'Round there.'

'Plenty of time before dark.'

Roberts made to push past.

'Wiggenhall, what's that from here? Fifteen, twenty minutes, drive?'

Roberts stared back at him. Small, hard eyes.

'Nice round there. Up along the river. Wiggenhall St Peter. Wiggenhall St Mary Magdalen. Wiggenhall St Germans. Wiggenhall St Mary the Virgin. Very holy.'

Roberts blinked.

'That's where you took her, wasn't it? Wiggenhall St Mary. Where you left her, anyway. That barn out past the bridge. Eleven, wasn't she? Eleven years old.'

'Fuck you!'

He made to push past again and Will caught hold of his arm.

'Fuck me? Fuck me? Eleven years old and you left her trussed up with baling wire, blood and shit stuck to her legs and still wearing her best blue party shoes.'

'Fuck off!'

'Liked that, did you? Turned you on? Blue fucking shoes!'

Fear showed for an instant at the back of Roberts' eyes and, before he knew what he was doing, Will had punched him hard in the chest, immediately below the breast bone, sending him stumbling back, then down to his knees.

'Trouble?' called a voice from behind. Vernon Lansdale, car jack in hand, standing by the garage door.

'Not any more,' Will said.

Roberts was breathing heavily, ragged gasps of air.

'Christine Fell,' Will said, leaning close. 'June of 2000. A little over eight years ago. In case you didn't remember her name.' He straightened. 'She remembered you.'

Roberts showed him a broken-toothed grin and it was all Will could do not to put a boot in his face.

'You're lyin'.'

'Am I?'

'Then prove it. Just prove it.'

Will leaned even closer. 'I will. Rose Howard, too. Was she one of yours? You remember Rose?'

No change in Roberts' expression.

'Janine Prentiss, how about her? Young Janine. I met her the other day. Grown up, married, kids of her own. She'll not have forgotten you, either, you can be sure of that. Janine. I'll be talking to her again.'

Now Roberts' grin had all but disappeared.

Will stared at him for a few moments longer, then turned away.

'This place yours?' he asked Lansdale, who was still standing by the garage door, looking on.

'It's mine.'

'Your employment policy – I should get it sorted, if I were you.'

Back in his car, Will flexed the fingers of his right hand, slotted an old *Blondie Greatest Hits* CD Lorraine had bought him into the stereo and turned up the volume.

'Heart of Glass'.

35

Ruth liked Tuesdays. Instead of having to pick up Beatrice from school, she left it to Fiona's mum to collect both girls and take them home for tea, before ferrying them off to their respective flute lessons. Then Ruth – or, occasionally, Andrew – would pick Beatrice up once her lesson was finished. All of which left her with a good two hours to herself, sometimes more.

Quite often she would take a walk along the river, nothing too energetic, just enjoying the sense of space, clearing her head; other times, if the weather were especially nice, she would sit in the garden of the café close by the cathedral and read. Today it was something by Philip Roth she'd pulled off the library shelves and which, truth to tell, she was finding pretty hard going. It certainly didn't chime with her pot of tea and scone with jam and cream. After a few more pages she set it aside.

A man's book, she thought, is that what it was? What was putting her off? For men and about men? She didn't even know if that were strictly true. What was true, though, most of the writers she really liked were women. Not thinking Woolf and Mansfield now, but modern-day. Contemporary. Helen Dunmore. Barbara Kingsolver. Kate Atkinson. Rose Tremain. Whereas Simon, she remembered – and she'd been thinking about Simon a lot lately – had read almost exclusively men: McEwan, Kureishi, Amis. Martin Amis. Simon seemed to like him more than anyone.

Heaven knows why.

He had sat her down once with a copy of *Money* and told her it was the most important book of the last twenty years. What it was, Ruth thought, after struggling through a hundred pages or so, was hostile and unpleasant; very, very unpleasant.

'It's real,' Simon said, when she'd confronted him. 'The real world. In your face. And that's what you don't like about it. You don't want to face up to the truth.'

'That's not so.'

'It's not?' He made a small sound, somewhere between a snigger and a sigh. 'Come on, Ruthie, admit it. Something bad, unpleasant even, you switch off, turn your back.'

Ruth didn't think that was the case. What she didn't want was to have her nose rubbed in it. Remorselessly. As if there were nothing else. Not when she was watching television, not when she was reading. Someone like Helen Dunmore could write about the most awful things – the siege of Leningrad, for instance – without making you feel contempt for the whole human race.

She spread the last of the cream and jam on to the surviving piece of scone and popped it into her mouth, picked up her bag, and headed for home.

Back indoors, she checked the answerphone for messages – none – picked up various bits and pieces of her clothing and deposited them in the dirty washing basket, made sure there was enough pasta for dinner later, and then, after a quick check of her watch, sat down at the computer to go through her emails.

As usual, most of what was waiting in her inbox was unsolicited and unwanted: offers of fortunes to be made, holidays and flights at amazing discount prices; begging letters from Burkina Faso or Mozambique; a once-in-a-lifetime invitation to become a core investor in the Ecuadorian mining industry; wonder drugs for the menopause; marital aids; lottery winnings waiting to be collected if only she would confirm the following details . . .

Ruth consigned all these to the trash and scrolled quickly down through the rest. Catriona asking if she would like to go to London to see a new play at the National; one of the fellow students from her library management course inviting her to join a group of them for a drink; her mother, who had taken belatedly to the Internet, reminding her how long it had been since she had made a visit north. I swear I shan't recognise my granddaughter if I don't see her soon.

Ruth answered briefly – yes, maybe, soon, half-term – wrapping the reply inside a few conciliatory sentences about Beatrice's progress at school.

She was about to close down when a new message announced itself with the sound of a cork being pulled from a bottle – a mail sound which Andrew had set up and which she had found impossible to change.

The sender's name was not one she recognised, but the subject was: *Beatrice.*

Ruth manoeuvred the mouse and clicked the message open.

One after another, images of Beatrice appeared on the screen.

Beatrice – where? – on her way to school, it had to be; Beatrice in Ely with a friend, on a street Ruth didn't immediately recognise; Beatrice, skirt flaring out about her, pedalling furiously on her bike; Beatrice in close-up, head turning towards the camera, as if in response to the camera's click or someone calling her name.

All taken, it seemed, recently; the last few months.

Less.

Below the last picture, a single line of type.

Isn't she lovely?

Ruth felt sick.

Sat there for several moments, face down, head in her hands, not looking at the screen.

When her breathing had steadied, she scrolled quickly back through the pictures, looking for the sender's name. A mixture of letter and numbers without apparent meaning. Hastily, she clicked on Reply, wrote, *Who are you?*, and moved the mouse to Send.

Waited while her stomach churned.

Nothing happened.

Switching off, she reached for the phone, dialled the number for Andrew's mobile, and when he didn't answer left a message for him to call her as soon as he could.

Then she sat in agony till she heard the sound of the car. When she threw open the door, Andrew was walking up the path towards the house, carrying his briefcase, smiling, Beatrice dawdling a few paces behind him, flute case in her hand.

Ruth threw herself at Andrew and clung to his neck, crying.

'Ruth, Ruth. Whatever is it? What's happened?'

'Mum!' Beatrice looked on, alarmed.

'Ruth, whatever's the matter?'

'Nothing. Nothing. It's nothing.' Still crying, smiling through her tears, she stood away. 'I'll tell you later. I'm just being stupid, that's all. Hormonal probably.' Finding a tissue, she dabbed at her face. 'Come on, let's go inside.'

It was a little after ten. Beatrice was in bed, sleeping. Most evenings they would have switched on the TV to watch the news, the headlines at least, but this evening neither of them had moved, the remote untouched on the arm of Andrew's chair. Ruth was sitting, legs folded, on the settee, a glass of wine on the small table beside her, still three-quarters full. When Beatrice had gone to bed – early for her – Andrew had fixed himself a Scotch and water and put a CD on the stereo, piano music, Handel, nothing too heavy. After a while, Ruth had asked him to turn it off.

The email that she'd sent had come bouncing back. A second attempt, the same.

'You sure you don't think we should phone the police?' Ruth said.

'And tell them what? Someone's sent us some pictures of our daughter in an email?'

Ruth sighed and pulled her legs closer.

'You know,' Andrew said, moments later, 'there's probably a perfectly innocent explanation.'

'You said.'

'I mean, they're just pictures, after all. Perfectly ordinary. It's not as if there's anything – you know – funny . . .'

Ruth looked at him. 'Funny?'

'You know what I mean.'

'Don't keep saying that. You keep saying that. You know, you know, as if . . . as if I did. As if we knew anything.'

Andrew stood up to refresh his glass.

'You know . . .'

Ruth shot him an angry glance.

'I'm sorry, but you know what I've just thought. Lyle.'

'What about him?'

'He's just bought one of those new cameras. Digital SLR. Nikon. Fancy lens. Cost him a pretty packet. I bet that's what it is. Lyle, trying it out.'

'Taking pictures of Beatrice?'

'Of course.'

'But why?'

'To surprise us.'

Ruth shook her head in disbelief.

'Showing off, that's what it is. I'm going to call him. I'll do it now.'

But it wasn't Lyle. Yes, he had a new camera. D60. Ten million pixels. Fantastic. But Beatrice? No. No way.

Andrew stood in the middle of the room, glass in hand, listening to the silence in the house. 'I could have sworn,' he said, after a moment. And then, 'Who else? Who on earth?'

Hugging her legs tighter towards her, Ruth is thinking of Simon, but doesn't say.

She's lovely, Ruth. Lovely. A smile in his eyes.

36

All evening Lorraine had been singing the words to 'I Got
You, Babe'. Not the whole thing, just snatches of it, verses,
occasional lines. Stupid, dumb song! She never heard the
original, not at the time. Sonny and Cher, is that who it had
been? Ten years before she was born. UB40 with Chrissie
Hynde, that was her. Back when she was ten. What was it?
Something about having someone to understand? Holding her
hand? As soon as their singles compilation had come out she'd
talked her dad into buying it for her birthday. She still had it
somewhere. 'Stop Your Sobbing', 'Kid', 'Brass in Pocket', 'Back
on the Chain Gang'. Those were the tracks she'd played again
and again. Close on twelve she'd have been by then and old
enough to want Chrissie Hynde as some kind of role model.
Gelling her hair, miming along in front of the bathroom mirror.
  'Hey!' Will said, coming into the kitchen from the stairs.
  'What?'
  'What you doing?'
  'Nothing, why?'
  'Standing there, staring off into space.'

'I was thinking.'

'What about?'

'Doesn't matter.'

Will shrugged. 'Susie'd wet her nappy again.'

'Our fault for letting her have that drink last thing.'

'You want anything?'

'How d'you mean?'

'I don't know. Tea, coffee, something stronger.'

'Stronger?'

'I could open another bottle of wine. Beer in the fridge.'

'I don't think so. You go ahead.'

He fished out a can of Carlsberg, poured some – less than half – into a glass, wiped the top with the heel of his hand and, taking a swig from the can, passed the glass along. 'Split it, okay?'

'Sure.'

What Lorraine really wanted was a spliff, something to relax her before bedtime, help her sleep.

'You want to sit?' Will asked.

'Why not?'

The living room was dark save for what little light shone in from outside, the curtains open out on to the garden and the fields beyond, and neither of them made any attempt to switch on a light. Seated at the opposite end of the settee, Lorraine kicked off her slippers and swung her legs round so that they were resting in his lap.

When he began, slowly, to stroke her feet, not quite a massage, not exactly, she leaned further back and closed her eyes.

Not sure how long she'd been asleep, she jerked awake when he stopped.

'You ready for bed?'

She held out a hand and he pulled her to her feet.

'Helen,' she said, 'is she still seeing that guy?'

'What made you ask that all of a sudden?'

'I don't know. Is she?'

'Declan? Maybe. I don't know.' He shrugged. 'At least she hasn't come into work with any bruises lately.'

'It's not funny.'

'I never said it was.' He pointed at the glass on the floor. 'You going to finish that?'

Lorraine shook her head.

He drank the last of the beer, carried the glass through to the sink and rinsed it under the tap.

'Door locked?' Lorraine asked.

'Safe and sound.'

Following her up the stairs, he pulled her blouse out from where it had been tucked into her jeans, dipped his head and kissed the soft rise of skin between hip and rib.

'What's that for?' Lorraine asked, surprised.

'Later,' Will said and smiled.

Helen had arranged to meet Declan late on in the Horse and Feathers, a sprawling roadhouse out towards the ring road, some fifteen minutes' drive from the house he still shared, despite a host of pillow-talk promises, with his wife and two kids, one his, one hers. There were other children, Helen knew, other mothers, some acknowledged, some not.

She arrived at the pub a little late, fully expecting Declan to be there already, bellied up to the bar. The young woman serving, doubtless augmenting her student loan, set aside the book she was reading long enough to fix her a large G&T.

Angled above her head, one giant TV was showing an omnibus rerun of *Friends*, the other was promising highlights from a Blue Square Premier clash between York City and Mansfield Town. Two fruit machines by the far wall were burping flashing lights across the tawdry furnishings.

A middle-aged couple sat ignoring one another at a side

table, the man in a sports jacket and tie, eking out his pint; the woman, her hair freshly done that morning in the same style as the last twenty years, was sitting with what looked like a snowball in front of her, barely touched.

Another five minutes Helen thought and she was going to risk calling Declan's mobile and find out what the hell was going on. In the event, he rang first.

'Helen?'

'Yes?'

'You in the Feathers?'

'Only for the last half-hour.'

'Look, I'm sorry, I've got this situation . . .'

'Situation?'

'The littlest, Annie, she's not well, some kind of tummy thing. I may have to take her to Accident and Emergency if it doesn't get any better.'

'Can't your wife . . . ?' Helen didn't like to use her name.

'She's out. Some do with her mates from work. Promised to be back before now, the cow.'

'Declan . . .'

'Look, just hang on for a bit, eh? I'll call you if I can get away.'

Helen didn't think so. Letting the phone fall back into her bag, she took one last glance around the vast, almost empty bar.

'Look on the bright side,' one of her girlfriends had said, 'at least you don't have to wash his pants.'

There were worse things.

The last time he had come round to her flat, two nights before, Scotch and vodka and who knows what else, after a lot of fooling around, she'd slapped his face, not once, but twice, and then when he'd laughed and punched her back – not the face, but the body where any bruises wouldn't show – she'd hit him a third time and heard her own voice shouting,

'Go on then, fuck me! Fuck me, you bastard!' – and remembering it now she'd hated herself almost as much as she hated him.

It was way past time to call it a day.

Back home, she poured herself a large glass of red wine and settled down to watch a DVD of *My Best Friend's Wedding* she'd picked up at the supermarket for less than a fiver. Dermot Mulroney not unlike Declan minus the odd ten kilos.

It was close to one when her phone finally rang, Helen well into her second glass of Cabernet and contemplating turning in.

'Declan,' she said, before he could speak.

'Yes?'

'It's over.'

'Is it, fuck!'

She switched off her phone, freshened her glass, watched the predictable end of the movie and got ready for bed. Declan wouldn't like being dumped, she was certain of that. He'd try phoning, intercepting her at work, being angry, being nice, doing whatever he could to change her mind. But, as long as she stood firm, he'd soon grow tired of making a fuss – a fool of himself, that's how he'd see it in others' eyes – and start spreading the word that he was the one who'd dumped her, just a slag after all. Then move on to someone else.

At a little after two and still awake, Helen got up and took two paracetamol, tried to read, finally got to sleep somewhere around a quarter to three. By five o'clock, still with a slight head, she was wide awake again.

'You look like shit,' Will said cheerfully a few hours later, stopping off at Helen's desk on the way to his own.

'Thanks a lot.'

'Good night?'

'Not so's you'd notice. And anyway, what have you got to be so cheerful about?'

'Oh, you know . . .'

Helen thought she might. The phone on her desk rang and she picked it up.

'Are you here?' she asked Will, her hand across the mouthpiece.

'Depends. Who is it?'

'Janine Clarke.'

37

Superficially, Janine Clarke looked much the same as she had the day Will had met her in Huntingdon: the same black suit, or similar, the same silver brooch – a gift, he guessed from her husband, a recent anniversary, perhaps, or birthday. Her hair was neatly cut and in place, make-up understated and precise. The smile she gave him as she came forward to shake his hand was the same assured professional smile as before. Except for the eyes. Nervous, flickering and dark. Afraid of where they were going, what they were going to see.

Her hand was warmer than before, almost clammy, and Will felt the smallest tremor before she slipped her fingers free from his.

'Janine. Thanks for coming in. This is my colleague, Helen Walker. Helen – Janine.'

Janine gave Helen a quick, buttoned smile.

'Why don't we go into my office?' Will said. 'Less chance of being disturbed.'

'Can I get you anything?' Helen asked, when they were inside. 'Tea? Coffee?'

'Just some water, please. If that's all right.'

While Helen was out of the room, Will asked Janine about the drive over, how things were at work, her kids.

'Two, isn't it?'

'Yes. Drew and Damien. Drew's almost five, Damien's three.'

'And Drew's a girl?'

'Yes. After Drew Barrymore, that's where we got the name.'

'Of course. My little one's Susie. After Lorraine's grandmother. Susan. No one glamorous, I'm afraid.'

'Lorraine, that's . . . ?'

'My wife, yes.'

Helen returned, balancing two Styrofoam cups of coffee and a bottle of still water with an empty cup over the neck.

'I don't want you to get the idea I always do this,' Helen said. 'Go get the coffee.'

'True enough,' Will said, playing along. 'Usually she sends me.'

Janine rewarded them with a wan little smile.

'You remember that scene in *Working Girl*,' Helen said, 'where Melanie Griffith's just been promoted and this woman who's going to be her assistant says, "Coffee," and Griffith starts to get up as if she has to fetch it, because that's what she's always been used to. You remember that?'

'Yes,' Janine said uncertainly. 'I think so.'

'And then she tells her – Griffith this is – she tells her assistant she doesn't ever expect her to fetch her coffee unless she's going to get some for herself. I always liked that scene.'

Will prised open his coffee and took a sip before pressing the lid back into place. 'So,' he said, letting it hang in the air . . .

Janine twisted the top of the bottle, breaking the seal. Despite the double glazing, there was a constant rise and fall of traffic from the street, and from beyond the door, only slightly dulled, the sounds of footsteps, telephones, voices, other doors being opened and closed. 'When we . . . when we talked before,' she said, 'and you showed me those photographs . . . what I said about not knowing him, it wasn't true. I knew him. Of course I did. As soon as you showed me. But I didn't want . . .'

Hand shaking, she poured some water into the cup and held it close to her face.

'You said he'd done something, something else, something similar, and you thought he might again . . . I thought about that afterwards, I couldn't get it out of my head. What you'd said about that and my daughter . . .'

Setting down the cup, she took a tissue from her bag.

'The photos . . . he was younger then, of course, and his hair – he had more hair, I think – and his face, it was a nice face. I remember thinking that, that day, the way he looked at me from the van. "You lost?" he said. Local, that's how he sounded. "You lost?" Smiling with his eyes. And he had this dog with him, a collie, on the seat alongside. Only young, a puppy. I reached in to stroke him and he growled a little, I remember, and the man said, "Go on, he's just showing off, he won't bite," and so I stroked him and he licked my hand and the man asked me where I lived and when I told him he said, "Hop in, why don't you? We'll give you a lift down the turn, me and Ezra here."' She closed her eyes. 'He seemed so nice. Friendly and nice. A bit like my dad.'

There were tears now, the beginning of tears, but she choked them back, twisting the tissue tighter and tighter.

'It's okay,' Will said quietly. 'Take your time.'

She sniffed and drank some water and waited until her breathing was more under control.

'I wonder,' she said, 'thinking back over that afternoon the way I have – it must have been a thousand times – I wonder

241

how I could have been so gullible. So stupid. I mean, I knew. I knew about men like that. Oh, not in any detail, but I knew about, you know, not taking sweets from strangers, getting into cars, my mum had drummed it into me enough times. And I heard things on the news. I wasn't some ignorant totally innocent kid. I knew.'

The tissue shredded apart in her hands.

'I knew.'

She lowered her head and Will and Helen exchanged a quick glance.

'Just to be absolutely certain,' Helen said, 'the person Inspector Grayson showed you in photographs previously is the same person who drove off with you in the van? Held you prisoner?'

'Yes.' Not looking at her when she replied. 'Yes.'

Will placed the photographs – one, two, three – on the desk. 'This person here?'

'Yes.'

'Mitchell Roberts?'

'If that's his name, yes.'

'And you'd be prepared to swear to that, in court if necessary?'

'Yes.' This last little more than an exhalation of breath.

Janine lifted the cup of water, took a couple of sips, and then set it back down.

'You sure you wouldn't like a coffee?' Helen asked. 'If you're going to make a formal statement you might be here for quite a while.'

'All right then, if it's no trouble.'

'I'll go this time,' Will said and Helen laughed.

'He's just showing off,' she said.

Janine allowed herself a smile. Try as she might, she could not stop looking back at the photographs, one glance after another.

'Mitchell Roberts, you said? That's who this is?'

'Yes.'

'This other time, the one the Inspector mentioned . . .'

'A young girl. He assaulted and sexually abused a young girl. She was twelve years old.'

'Like me.'

'Yes, like you.'

Janine slid her face down into her hands and, this time, when she started to cry there was no holding back.

Helen waited, then offered fresh tissues.

Will came back into the room with coffee in a borrowed china mug. 'I didn't know if you wanted sugar?'

Janine shook her head.

Will slipped the photographs back into their envelope and out of sight.

'I'm sorry,' Janine said, wiping away the tears.

'No need.'

She took another tissue and dabbed at her eyes, her make-up blurred.

'I'm okay now, it was just . . . you know . . . having to remember.'

'I understand.'

'There was one thing I wanted to ask,' Helen said. 'If that's okay? In the reports of what happened, you mentioned hearing someone else's voice?'

'Yes, that's right.'

'Another man?'

'Yes.'

'But you didn't see anyone? Other than Roberts?'

'No. And whoever this person was, I don't think he was there all the time. Maybe only towards the end.'

'And how did he sound? What kind of voice? Young? Old?'

'Not young. Just ordinary. Middle-aged, I suppose. Maybe a little older.'

'Older than Roberts?'

'Possibly.' She lowered her head. 'I'm sorry, it's all such a long time ago and I've spent so long trying not to remember, shut it out of my mind.'

'Yes, of course.'

'It could have been this Roberts talking to himself. You've got to remember, I was frightened. Terrified. I could even have made him up, this other person.'

'Why? Why might you do that?'

'Because it would mean I wasn't alone there with this man, with Roberts. Because if there'd been somebody else there, he might not have done the things to me that he did.'

Helen looked away.

'The one time I'm sure I did hear someone else was towards the end of the second day, the day before he let me go.'

'What happened?'

'There was an argument. Men shouting. Just two of them, I think. But I suppose it could have been someone going past.'

'You can't remember what they were shouting about?'

'No, I'm sorry.'

'And was this the second day, you said?'

'Yes. I remember being frightened because he – Mitchell – he sounded so angry and I thought . . . I thought when he came in it would be worse. I thought he'd be angry with me.'

'And was he?'

'No. That was the funny thing. He kept asking me was I all right, was I all right? And he was less rough, almost . . . gentle. When he . . . When he . . .' She looked away.

'It was after that you were released?'

'The next morning, yes. He put a blindfold round me and led me out to the van. The dog was there. Ezra. I heard him barking, really close, and then he pushed his nose up against me, but the man shooed him away. And then he picked me up and put me in the back of the van. I wanted Ezra to come with me, but he wouldn't let him.'

She looked at Will directly.

'Will you catch him, do you think? Before he does it again?'

'Yes,' Will said. 'Yes.'

No doubt in his voice at all. This time they had to get it right.

38

They were in Will's car, Helen driving, his request.

'Just as long as you don't get it into your head I'm some kind of chauffeur.'

'Chuff-er,' Will said.

'What?'

'Chuff-er. That's what Jake called it. It was in this little book he was reading. Chuff-er.'

'He's reading already?'

'Ages now.'

'Off to university soon, then.'

'Not exactly.'

'Some kids nowadays, they can't read when they leave primary, never mind start.'

Will grinned. 'Takes after his old man.'

'His mum, you mean.'

She changed down for a slow right-hand bend, one of the few twists on an otherwise straight road. Deep ditches on either side, fringed with reeds. Above them, the sun leaked here and there through a grey wash of cloud.

'I should have brought Roberts in last week,' Will said. 'When I had the chance.'

'Nothing to hold him on, he'd've walked. Mind you, that might have been preferable to thumping him one.'

'I should never have told you.'

'Guilt.'

'You think?'

'Either that or you were showing off.'

It had made him feel better, Will thought, and that was the truth. Even if, the moment after he'd let fly, he'd known it to be a mistake. Losing control, that was for other people – people he looked down on, even despised – not himself. And Roberts knew. Enjoyed it even as he experienced the pain. The grin that had spread, snag-toothed, across his face.

'You ever hit your kids?' Helen asked.

'No,' Will said, too quickly, 'of course not.'

'Not even Jake?'

'No. Least, not really.'

'Not really? You mean as in pretend?'

'I mean maybe, you know, a quick clip round the back of the head sometimes to gee him up. But not hard. Nothing serious.'

He could see her looking at him from the corner of her eye, the kind of look she shot suspects when they thought they'd put one over on her.

'Once,' Will said, 'just once. He was throwing this real tantrum – oh, two, close on two years ago – screaming and yelling and just wouldn't stop. No idea now what had set it off. Thrashing his legs and kicking his feet on the floor. I told him and told him. In the end I whacked him twice across his backside hard.'

'What happened?'

'What happened? He stopped.'

'And you've felt bad about it ever since.'

'Not really.'

'Not much.'

Will found something interesting to look at through the side window; a tractor, dark rusted red, making its slow way across a field, a small flock of gulls in its wake. There were times now, if he lost his temper, when Jake would look at him in real fear.

'It must be hard,' Helen said. 'Bringing up kids. The whole discipline thing, trying to teach them what's right or wrong. Everything.'

'S'okay for you, you're not . . .' He stopped. 'You're not seriously . . . ? You and Declan?' He laughed. 'You might've picked someone who'll likely still be around for the christening.'

'Very funny, Will. And, anyway, that's over.'

'Since when?'

'Since I told him.'

Will looked at her sideways-on. 'You had a row?'

Helen shook her head. 'Just got fed up with being pissed around.'

'Not before time, some would say.'

'Yes, well, we haven't all got your clear mind and great self-control. Now can we just drop it? Change of subject? Okay?'

'Okay. Kids, though . . . seriously.'

'Will . . .'

'No, it'd be good. I can just see it, you and a little one.'

'Will . . .'

'Best not leave it much longer, mind.'

She brought her fist, knuckles extended, down hard against his leg, just behind his knee, and Will cried out.

'Hey! You didn't have to do that.'

'Yes, I did. Now you want more or are you going to shut up once and for all?'

'I'll shut up.'

'Good.'

They drove the rest of the way in silence.

Though she'd never for one moment seen Declan Morrison as the prospective father of any child of hers, it had been Declan who'd brought the subject, most recently, to mind. They'd been at her flat one evening, post-coitally quiet and nicely buzzed; close to one another on the sofa and watching, for God's sake, *Match of the Day*.

Helen never watched *Match of the Day*.

'You ever think about having kids?' he'd said, apropos of nothing, unless it had been the sight of Theo Walcott shimmying his way between a bunch of hapless defenders, then slotting the ball home from the edge of the D.

'Not really,' she'd said, not strictly true. She did think about it from time to time. Of course she did. Seeing some baby go past in a sling; a toddler wobbling his first uncertain steps. And her friends, some of them, had been nudging her lately, how her biological clock was ticking, counting down.

'You should,' Declan had said. 'You'd be a great mum.'

'Like bollocks, I would.'

'No, I mean it.'

'Declan, you're drunk.'

'Doesn't mean I'm wrong.'

On the television, Walcott was brought down inside the area and the penalty was converted, four-one; Declan poured them both a generous shot of Black Bush to celebrate and the remainder of the evening blurred into incoherence, but, come morning, the thought was still there.

So did she want children or not?

Children of her own.

Just one, surely? One would do.

The desire was there, mostly deep down, but so were the doubts. The fear. She thought of five-year-old Carl Carey, orphaned and growing up with ageing grandparents in their neat little semi-detached; growing up to the knowledge of what his father had done. *Paul — he was besotted, he really was.* So besotted he had slashed the mother's throat almost from ear to ear then hanged himself rather than risk losing the son he loved so much.

She thought about what had happened to Martina Jones, Christine Fell and all the rest. The responsibilities were too vast, the possibilities of failure, of loss, too great.

39

Vernon Lansdale's garage came into sight on the near side of the road, a rusting circular sign, advertising speedy tyre and exhaust repairs, swinging slightly in the breeze. There were four pumps, arranged two and two, the last marked diesel only. Currently no customers. A single-storey shop and reception stood square-on to the forecourt, with a double-length workshop beyond. Logs were stacked to one side of the shop door, sacks of potatoes on the other.

From his perch behind the counter, two cushions on a low-backed stool, Lansdale looked up as the car turned in, then went back to his paper. Only when Will and Helen entered did he relinquish his interest in the sports pages, that day's racing from Uttoxeter.

'He's not here.'

'Who?'

'The man you're looking for.'

'Day off?'

Lansdale shook his head. 'Quit.'

'When was that?' A frown on Will's face.

'Couple of days after you beat the shit out of him.'

'He give any reason?' Will asked, ignoring Helen's glance. 'Other than that?'

'Any reason at all.'

'No. Took what was owing, bought some tobacco, packet of Rizlas and left. Not seen him since.'

'You're certain of that?'

'No cause to lie.' Lansdale coughed something into a piece of rag. 'Told him I'd go witness if he wanted to swear out a complaint, assault, but he said he weren't interested.' This looking straight at Will, as if daring him to contradict.

'How about friends?' Helen said. 'When he was here. He ever mention any names?'

'Not a great talker, Mitchell, you got to understand that. Did his job, kept his mouth closed pretty much.'

'But did he ever meet anyone here? Anyone call by to see him?'

'Not as I noticed.'

'You would, surely?' Helen said. 'Place this size.'

'Not here all the time, though, am I? Off site once in a while, have to be. Pick up parts, supplies.'

'And you'd not close down?'

'An' lose trade?'

'So, what? You'd leave Roberts in charge?'

'Why not? He can work the till as well as me. And, yes, before you ask, I checked it after. First few times at least. Not a penny short.'

'But you think,' Will said, 'when you were off away, he might have met someone here, that's what you seemed to imply.'

'I'm not implyin', as you put it, nothing of the sort. What I can't see, I can't swear to. That's all. No more'n that.' Lansdale treated him to a lopsided grin.

'If I find out you're holding something back . . .'

'What? You'll thump me too?'

'Come on, Will,' Helen said, seeing him tense up. 'Let's go.'

'You think he's lying?' she asked, once they were back at the car.

'I think he likes pissing us around. Whether it's any more than that, I don't know.'

Helen reached for her bag and found her cigarettes. 'What's his story anyway?'

'Lansdale? Did some time a while back, selling on vehicles he knew to have been stolen, something of the kind. Clean since, by all reports. Seems to like having the odd ex-con around, working.'

'Reminds him of happier times.'

'Maybe.'

Helen snapped her lighter shut. 'So, Roberts, what now?'

'We can check his lodgings, home address.'

'You think he'll still be there?'

'I know,' Will said. 'Don't hold my breath.'

The landlady was tall and beanpole thin, greying hair pinned back from her face, fifteen years or more since she'd seen Govan, but the accent would still take the shine off a coat of good paint. 'Mitchell, aye, he's moved on right enough. Good few days now. Shame, too. Not a whit of trouble, not like some. Sneaking this and that into their rooms. Manners, an' all. There's some . . .' this with a sharp glance towards Helen, '. . . as don't hold with men opening doors and the like, not any more, but to me it shows respect.'

'He'll have left an address,' Helen said, straight-faced.

'Somewhere.'

In amongst a litter of fliers for take-away pizzas and tandoori specials was a piece of pink card, creased at the centre, advertising floral tributes and bouquets, funerals a speciality. There was an address written on the reverse: 47 Bellamy Street.

Will didn't have a great feeling about it and when they

arrived he was proved right. Bellamy Street was a cul-de-sac, number 47 just two houses before the end. A large skip outside was filled with old boards, bits of broken lath, plaster and brick. In the front garden, a portable toilet stood next to bags of sand and cement. High on the scaffolding, a workman was removing the guttering from below the roof. Sacking hanging down across empty windows, plywood for a front door, the place was little more than a shell.

Of Mitchell Roberts, no one had seen hide nor hair.

They managed to catch Nina George, Roberts' probation officer, just as she was leaving, scarf loose at her neck, bundling files into the rear of her Nissan Micra. 'Yes,' she said, in answer to Will's query. 'His six months was up. Clean sheet. Every appointment kept. I don't think he was ever even late, not by more than a few minutes. Same where he worked, apparently. Punctual, reliable. Employer swears by him.'

'You know he's quit?' Will said. 'Chucked it in.'

'The garage? Lansdale's? No, no, I didn't.' She brushed a length of hair away from her eyes. 'I must say I'm surprised.'

'And now he's left his approved lodgings, you do know where he's gone?'

'Oh, yes. Of course. East of the city somewhere. Out towards the airport. I've got the address on file.'

'Bellamy Street?'

'Yes, that's it.'

'You checked it out?'

'Well, not exactly. Not yet, at least. Why?'

'We've just come from there. Number 47. The entire building's more or less gutted. Enough Polish workmen to start their own soccer team. And Mitchell, no one in the street's ever heard of him. He's scarpered. Off the leash and gone.'

'I'm sure there's some explanation . . .'

'Yes,' Will said. 'Yes. I'm sure there is.'

They left her standing there, confused, thoughtful, buttoning and unbuttoning the front of her new wool blazer, a bargain from TJ Maxx.

40

Beatrice had worn her down, almost to the point of capitulation.

'Mum, why? Just tell me why?' 'Why not?' 'Why though? It's not as if I've never been there for a sleepover before. I have, twice, and she's been here.' 'Go on then, give me one good reason? Just one. You see, you can't.' And finally: 'That's stupid! It's just so unfair.' Followed by the ritual flouncing out, tight-lipped and fierce-eyed; the stomping upstairs and the slamming of doors,.

'I do think,' Andrew had ventured, looking up from his newspaper, 'she might have a point.'

'You think I'm being unreasonable?'

'Well, perhaps a little. After all, she's right in a way, we have let her stay there before. Sasha's, isn't it? Just a few streets away, not exactly the end of the world.'

'Andrew, that's not the point.'

He folded his paper. 'What is?'

'I don't know, it's just . . .'

'It's those photos, isn't it? They've got to you. That bloody email.'

'Yes, I suppose so.'

'There haven't been any more?'

'No, I'd have said.'

'Nothing else out of the way, unusual?'

'No.'

'Nobody hanging round?'

Ruth shook her head.

'When is it she wants to go?' Andrew asked.

'This Friday.'

'That's when I've got this meeting. This damned steering committee. I wish I'd never joined. But I could easily drop her off on my way. Arrange to pick her up again Saturday, not too early. Or they might agree to drop her round.' He smiled. 'We could both do with a bit of a lie-in.'

'I don't know.'

Getting up from the chair, he kissed her gently on the forehead. 'I do understand, you know. I know sometimes you think I don't, but I do. Really. But you can't keep her too close. You've got to let her start to live her own life; grow up in her own way.' Taking a pace back, he squeezed her hands and smiled his reassuring smile. 'It won't happen again.'

Ruth gazed out of the first-floor window at the rain as it fell in long, slanting lines across the yellow curve of the street light and collected in small puddles close to the kerb. Not really hungry, she had made herself a sandwich earlier and eaten it at the table with a glass of wine and that day's paper. It was not yet nine-thirty and she had phoned Sasha's house three times already, checking everything was okay; each call more needless, more irritating than the last.

'Ruth,' Sasha's mother had said finally, 'you are all right?'

'Yes, yes, I'm fine. I'm sorry, I'm being silly. I promise I won't phone again.'

Instead she had watched ten minutes of some moronic

television programme before switching it off and picking up the new Marilynne Robinson novel she had grabbed for herself the minute it had arrived at the library. She had liked *Housekeeping* so much, but this was different, more difficult to get into; the characters, to her eyes, unwieldy and distant.

After half an hour she gave up and went upstairs, thinking she would take advantage of being on her own and have an early night. But in the bathroom, getting ready, it didn't feel right: she should wait for Andrew to come home. It's what he would expect.

She was standing at the bedroom window, peering through the curtains, when she first heard the noise.

A sound like a single footstep from the floor above and then, as she listened, the click and small echo of a door being opened and then closed.

Her skin froze.

The backs of her arms and legs.

She waited, straining to hear a sound. There. But no, that was nothing, someone walking by on the street outside. She could feel her pulse, faintly against her skin. She turned towards the bedroom door, partly opened out on to the landing. A soft fall of light becoming shadow.

The telephone was across the room, beside the bed, but who would she call? And why?

It was nothing. Beatrice had left her window open upstairs; a door closing in the wind.

The street outside was deserted now, save for a fox trotting along, almost daintily, close to the far wall, its coat shiny and darkened by the rain.

She was on the landing before she heard another sound. Something tapping. There, again. It must be the wind, she thought, that's what it was, a night like this, it had to be the wind. If she went up and closed the window it would stop.

Still she hesitated.

There were several items of Beatrice's discarded clothing on the stairs – nothing unusual about that – and she stooped to pick them up: a pair of pants, a T-shirt, a single sock.

The door to Beatrice's room was closed.

My Room, read the handwritten sign. *Private Property! Keep Out!*

Ruth went in and switched on the light.

Everything was as she'd last seen it; a mixture of meticulous order and utter dishevelment. Both sides of her daughter's character. For a moment, she smiled.

The window, as she'd assumed, was open at the bottom, curtains shifting a little in the breeze, the window itself rattling against the frame. That was what she'd heard. That and the door.

As she slid the window shut, something moved for a second in the shadowed glass, quick, behind her head.

'Mum?'

Ruth's breath caught for a moment in her throat.

When she turned, there was Heather standing alongside the bed, one of the small stuffed animals that still littered the area around Beatrice's pillows in her hand.

'This used to be mine,' Heather said.

'I know.'

'And now it's Beatrice's.'

'Yes.'

Heather held it, soft and ragged, to her cheek, a black and white dog with worn fur and one buttoned eye. 'She won't be playing with it for much longer.'

'What do you mean?'

'You know. Growing up.' She smiled. 'Setting aside childish things.'

Ruth reached out and took it from her hand. Lucky, that's what she'd called it. Lucky.

'I thought I heard someone earlier,' Ruth said. 'Walking around. Was that you? Were you here?'

'Mum, I'm always here, you know that. You don't always see me, that's all.'

'Heather . . .'

But when Ruth stepped forward she was gone. There was just the small dog, there in her own hand.

She set it down on the bed and switched out the light, pulling the door firmly closed behind her.

Andrew would be back soon and until then she would listen to music, play patience, try not to look too often at the clock.

When Beatrice arrived home, shortly after eleven the next morning, Ruth threw her arms round her and held her tight.

'Mum! Mum! You're strangling me, okay?'

'I'm sorry, I'm sorry. I'm just pleased to see you, that's all.'

'Okay, but it's not like I've been away for a fortnight. Just chill, yeah?'

'Yes.' Aware of the daft grin that was plastered across her face. 'So did you have a good time, you and Sasha?'

'Yeah, fine.'

'So tell me, tell me all about it.'

'Mum . . .'

'I'm interested, that's all. Is that such a bad thing?'

'Hello? Sleepover. Staying up late, watching videos, midnight snacks, talking. Girl talk. Remember?'

'Not really, no.'

'Tough, Mum. Too late now.' And with that she disappeared up to her room, only to return some minutes later, just this side of aggrieved.

'Mum, you haven't been in my room while I was at Sasha's?'

'No.'

'You sure?'

'Yes, why d'you ask?' Hoping that she wasn't blushing.

'Doesn't matter.'

'Beatrice . . .'

'No, it's okay.'

Three mornings later, already past the time she should have been ready for school, Beatrice called down the stairs.

'Mum! You haven't seen my new top?'

Ruth looked up from buttering her toast. 'Your new what?'

'My jumper.'

'Which one?'

'The one we bought in Cambridge. Stripes, you know? Black and gold?'

'The one that makes you look like a bee.'

'I can't find it anywhere.'

'You've looked in the washing basket?'

'Not there.'

'How about with the ironing?'

'I've looked there too.'

'Beatrice, I don't know. It's probably somewhere in your room.'

'It was. But it's not.'

'Well, if you put your things away more carefully . . .'

'Mum, I've been looking for the last half-hour.'

'Well, I'm sorry, I can't help. Why's it so important, anyway?'

'Because I want to wear it, of course.'

'Well, you'll just have to wear something else, won't you? And do hurry up, or else you'll be late.'

Beatrice said a rude word beneath her breath. 'Yes, Mum, just coming.'

41

Liam Noble was at his desk a good thirty minutes later than usual, no one thing in particular to blame: the traffic certainly, thanks to a lorry shedding its load across two lanes of traffic; his children also, the middle one throwing a wobbly about something that had happened the previous day in the class-room – neither he nor his wife had been able to get out of him what exactly it was – and not wanting to go into school at all, clinging to the banisters so hard his fingers had to be prised away; and then, as if that weren't enough, the clothes dryer had delivered all three of his shirts back to him with a speckling of dark brown adorning each one. So there he was, conscious of starting the day late and wearing an ancient cotton shirt with fraying collar and cuffs that he normally kept for knocking around in the garden, and there waiting for him was Will Grayson, with a face like barely concealed thunder.

It started before Noble had time to take off his topcoat or close the door. Accusation upon accusation: inefficiency laced with wide-eyed optimism and a refusal to look at the facts.

'All right, all right. I said, all right!' Noble as close to shouting as he normally came. 'Mitchell Roberts, I know, I know. It looks like you were right and I was wrong. Now we're agreed on that, can we dispense with all the rhetoric and work out what can be done to see the situation rectified?'

'And that's it?' Will threw up his arms in disbelief. 'A nice quick admission of guilt and a line gets drawn under everything? Well, I don't think so.'

'No? What is then, Will? A bit more grovelling, will that do you? Preferably in public and down on my knees? Or perhaps you want more? The rest of my time on the force spent counting coffee spoons and delivering lectures on road safety and the Highway Code? No? Resignation, then? Is that it? You want to see me fall on my sword? Live up to my name and do the noble thing? You and your lot don't come out of this exactly spotless, you know.'

His sting drawn, Will pulled round a chair and sat, waiting for Noble to do the same.

'I know some of it,' Noble said. 'The bare bones. His probation officer called me at home. That business about the address is a major cock-up if ever there was one. Should have been checked out by one of us first thing.' He let out a short, heartfelt sigh. 'You'd better tell me the rest.'

Will laid it out: the positive identification that pointed at Roberts as responsible for the abduction and sexual assault of a twelve-year-old in 1995; the very real possibility that he had been involved in two similar incidents in 2000 and as far back as 1993.

Will told him about his meeting with Christine Fell, her mental state, her reaction to the photographs.

'And the earlier case? Peterborough.'

'Rose Howard. That's the one I wouldn't swear by. The circumstances of the abduction are similar, but because the girl's never turned up, there's too much we don't know.'

'Peterborough to London, couple of lifts down the A1 and she could still be there now, late twenties, living a life.'

'And never as much as phoned home, never got in touch?'

'It happens.'

Will knew. How many hundred a year simply walked out and never came back. Crossed the line into another life. What he'd been able to glean of Rose Howard's home life from reading the reports, it hadn't exactly been the stuff of happy families. For a while the investigation team had looked at the father, but other than him being a callous and work-shy loud-mouth with an over-fondness for drink, they'd never found anything they could prove.

'These other instances,' Noble said, 'there's a pattern. He keeps his victims for a relatively short time, two or three days, then lets them go.'

'Maybe with Howard something happened. She tried to get away or, whatever he was doing, the abuse, it went too far.'

Noble narrowed his eyes. 'You think somewhere there's a body?'

'I think it's possible.'

'Long time to stay buried.'

We are, Will thought. In truth we are.

Noble walked him back out to his car. What had promised, early that morning, to be a better day – the sun, flame red, rising above the field edge as Will had set out on his run – had withered into the same overlapping grey as so many days before.

'You've thought of this, I'm sure,' Noble said, 'but if Roberts is a serious serial offender, some of those gaps are difficult to explain.'

'Could be he was lucky,' Will said. 'Nobody found out, complained. Either that or he left the area, tried it on elsewhere.'

Noble nodded. There was a third possibility, they both knew, without wishing to spell it out. Just as Rose Howard's body could have been lying hidden in the vast East Anglian landscape all those years, waiting to be found, so could the bodies of others, their names as yet unknown.

Helen was waiting for him when he got back to Parkside, something of a shine in her eyes.

'Good night?' Will said with a grin.

'Good morning.'

'How come?'

'I got to thinking about our meeting with Vernon Lansdale yesterday. More I thought about it, more it seemed he was most interested in winding you up. Pissing you off.'

'So you thought you'd try your feminine wiles instead? The soft approach.'

'Something like that.'

Will went round behind his desk and pulled out his chair. 'Any luck?'

'After a lot of pussyfooting around he came up with a name. Someone ringing the garage a couple of times to speak to Roberts. Hayward. W-A-R-D. At least, that's what it sounded like to him.'

'He have a first name?'

'Lansdale wasn't sure. Something beginning with P. Peter. Paul.' A smile spread across her face. 'I ran it through the computer, just in case. There's a Paul Heywood. E-Y not A-Y. Double-O-D. Heywood. Two offences against the Obscene Publications Act, offering obscene videos for sale or rent, 1997. Fine and six-month suspended sentence. One offence of sending indecent literature through the post, 1999, further fine, probation. 2005 – and here's where it gets really interesting – he was prosecuted for having indecent photographs of children in his possession, with a view to distributing them to others. When it came to trial, the distribution charge was

dropped – not clear why – and he pleaded guilty to possession. Protection of Children Act, 1978. Sentenced to eighteen
months. Released after ten.'

'And this was when?'

''05.'

'Which would have meant he was inside at the same time
as Roberts.' Something akin to a smile moved across Will's
face. 'They met in prison.'

Helen nodded. 'Three months in the same wing, Lincoln.'

'Nice, very nice. I don't suppose the computer spewed out
an address at the same time?'

'Not difficult. Like Roberts, he's on the Sex Offenders'
Register. Address in Norwich. I've asked the local nick to
check.'

'Good work.'

'Thanks.' She took a seat on the corner of Will's desk.
'Perhaps, after all this time, Mitchell Roberts is running out
of luck.'

'Luck?' Will arced his arms up above his head and released
a slow breath. 'If we're right and Roberts is a serious offender
with a string of sexual assaults going back fifteen years and
only one arrest, one conviction – that's got to be down to
more than luck.'

42

They met Roy Cole at the police station on Bethel Street, a large squared-off brick building with flat windows that resembled a warehouse. Cole a detective sergeant with fifteen years' service and one of those young-old faces that never really seemed to change, the same at seventeen as it would be at seventy-two, just the body around it showing signs of age. He greeted both Will and Helen with a firm enough handshake, the smell of tobacco redolent on his clothes.

'So,' Cole said, 'Heywood, he's been a bad boy?'

'Not necessarily,' Will said. 'His name came up as part of an investigation, could be nothing more to it than that.'

'Like I said on the phone,' Helen offered, 'it's just a matter of asking a few questions.'

'Only we've been keeping half an eye, try and make sure he doesn't get up to any of his old tricks. Not that that's so easy, mind. His kind, devious don't come into it. They want to get their kicks jerking off to kiddie porn, not a lot we can do about it.' Glancing at Helen, he added a quick, 'Sorry,' misreading her expression.

'It's okay, Sergeant,' Helen said, 'I'm familiar with the concept of jerking off.'

Flushing, Cole led the way out on to the street. 'Just as easy to walk from here. Place where he works, stacking shelves, unloading deliveries. Parking's a bastard at the best of times.'

Will fell into step, Helen a pace or so behind.

'This inquiry,' Cole said, 'same kind of malarkey as before?'

Will outlined the basic details, no more than was strictly necessary.

When they arrived, Paul Heywood and three others – two spotty youths and an older man with a club foot, all wearing brown overalls – were out in the loading area at the rear, taking a cigarette break.

'Paul,' Roy Cole said, beckoning him over. 'Someone wants a word.'

Hesitant, Heywood moved away from the wall where he'd been leaning, taking one last drag at his cigarette before dropping it to the floor.

He was just above medium height, lean-faced, a tattoo fading on his neck just below the chin, hair long enough to be pulled back into a ponytail, the residue of a cold sore on his upper lip. Pale grey eyes.

'I haven't got long,' he said. 'My break . . .'

'Don't worry 'bout that,' Cole said. 'And you lot, bugger off back to work.'

Heywood blinked in Will's direction; glanced once at Helen then looked quickly away.

'We won't keep you long,' Will said. 'No more than we need.'

Heywood blinked again, said nothing.

'Mitchell Roberts,' Will said, 'I understand you and he are pretty good friends?'

'Who's that?'

'Roberts, Mitchell Roberts.'

'No, I don't think . . .'

'You don't remember?'

'No, I don't think so. Sorry, no.'

'You're sure?'

'Yes, I . . .'

'That's just bollocks,' Helen said, with a sudden step towards him. 'Sheer unadulterated bollocks and you know it.' She moved closer, her face level with his. 'You think we came all the way out here to be fed crap like that? You think this is some kind of joke, so you can stand around, take the piss?'

Shuffling his feet, Heywood looked hastily this way and that, anything rather than look her in the eye.

'You and Roberts were banged up together, Lincoln. Same wing. For all I know you even shared the same cell. You probably did. All those cosy little chats. Magazines someone had smuggled in and you'd paid dear for stuffed under the mattress. That what it was like? I'll show you mine, you show me yours? Yes, Paul? Was that it?'

'No, no . . .' The sweat was starting to pour off him now.

'What?' Helen thrust her face even closer. 'You didn't know him? That what you saying? What you're telling me?'

'No, I did, I did, it's just . . . what you said . . . it wasn't . . .'

'You did know him?'

'Yes.'

'Inside?'

'Yes.'

'And later, after you both got out, you kept in touch?'

A hesitation, then, 'Yes, yes.'

'And what? You exchanged letters? Phone calls? Emails? What?'

'Sometimes I . . . I phoned him. At the garage, where he worked.'

'Often? How often?'

'Not much. Not a lot. Three or four times, that's all.'

'Three or four times?'

'Yes.'

'We can check, you know that.'

'No, that's all it was, I swear.'

'And that was when you arranged to meet?'

Heywood blinked away sweat from his eyes.

'That was when you arranged to meet him?' Helen asked again.

'No, I didn't . . . I haven't seen him. Haven't seen him, not since Lincoln. I wouldn't . . .' His throat was dry, the words sticking to the roof of his mouth. 'I mustn't, you know . . .' A quick glance towards Cole. 'I mustn't have contact with . . .'

'With perverts like Mitchell.'

'Yes.'

'Birds of a feather,' Helen said.

'Huh?'

'You and Mitchell, your kind, flocking together.'

Heywood rubbed the palms of his hands down the sides of his overall.

'Where is he?' Helen said. 'Mitchell? Even if you're not meeting him, you must know where he is.'

'No. He never told me. Cambridge, that's all I know. Hostel somewhere.'

'Not any more.'

'I don't know, I . . .'

'Done a bunk, hasn't he? Gone.'

'I didn't know.' With an effort, he looked into Helen's face for the first time. 'On my life, I don't know where he is. Till you said, I didn't even know he'd gone. And that's the God's honest truth.'

'If I find out you've been lying . . .'

'I'm not, honest.'

'If I do . . .'

Heywood shook his head.

Helen took a card from her bag and pushed it down into

the top pocket of his overalls. 'If he does get in touch with you,' she said quietly, 'you'll let me know?'

Heywood nodded.

'Paul?'

'Yes. Yes, I will.'

'I've got your word?'

He nodded again.

Cole looked over at Will as Helen stepped away. 'Okay,' he said, 'Paul, you better be getting back to work.'

Without another word, Heywood turned and slowly walked towards the door of the loading bay.

Cole waited until they were outside on the street before reaching for his cigarettes, lighting one for Helen first and then himself.

'I don't know about Heywood,' he said, 'but you scared the shit out of me.'

'That mean you believe him?' she asked.

Cole allowed himself a smile. 'Trouble with people like Heywood, they spend so much of their life mired in lies, telling the truth, it's the most difficult thing in the world. But we'll keep a tighter watch where we can. Roberts, we've got his details. Shows his face and there's a good chance we'll know.'

Back at the police station, they shook hands.

'Sure you don't want to stay for a jar?' Cole asked.

'No, thanks,' Will said, 'better be getting back.'

'No peace for the fucking wicked.'

'Say that again.'

'I suppose you'd like me to drive?' Helen asked, when they were back at the car.

'You mind?'

'Long as I can have another cigarette first.'

Will fished out a packet of mints from the glove compartment and they stood either side of the car, Helen thoughtful, smoking.

'How long is it now since Rack Fen?' she asked. 'Martina Jones?'

'Three years, close on four.'

'And those other incidents, the biggest gap between them is what? Five years.'

Will nodded.

Helen let fall her cigarette and ground it beneath her heel. 'Time then, not exactly on our side.'

43

Ruth had been looking forward to this for some time now, a day school at Tate Britain on the paintings of Bonnard and Vuillard. Ruth loved them both: the richness of Vuillard's interiors, the sense of people being caught, unawares, in the middle of some small domestic task; Bonnard's use of colour, the intimate portraits of his wife, Marthe, whom he had met when she was just sixteen and painted obsessively up to the time of her death almost fifty years later. There would be lectures by experts, slides, analysis, an opportunity to look round the galleries, hopefully ample time for discussion.

She kissed the still-drowsy Beatrice goodbye and reminded her about her flute lesson that evening.

'Mum, I know.'

'And Daddy's picking you up afterwards, okay?'

'Mum!'

Ruth planted another kiss on her forehead and hurried away.

'You'll miss your train,' Andrew shouted from below.

'No, I won't.' Bag on her shoulder, pausing for just a moment in case she'd forgotten something, Ruth scurried downstairs.

'Enjoy it,' Andrew said, aiming a kiss at her cheek. 'What time will you be back?'

'Not late. Not as long as the train's on time. Probably not so long after you.'

'Okay. Good. I'll start dinner.'

'You won't forget to pick up Beatrice?'

'No. Now for heaven's sake, go.'

A smile, a quick wave and she was out of the door.

'Bea,' Andrew shouted up the stairs, 'soon be time you were getting up.'

The day came close to living up to Ruth's expectations. Both speakers were good, pitching their talks at round about the right level and avoiding the worst excesses of critical theory. The way in which the relationship between the two artists' work was explored was, Ruth thought, exemplary. And what fascinated her perhaps most were the series of self-portraits Bonnard had made in the years between his wife's death and his own; Bonnard shaven-headed, close to emaciated, dark holes where once had been his eyes: a ghost of himself while he was still alive.

Only the final discussion had disappointed, and then only marginally — too many of her fellow students intent upon showing the extent of their own knowledge rather than contributing to something new.

As a whole, she felt, as she relaxed in her seat on the train, it had been worthwhile. Eminently worthwhile. So much so, that when she went to the buffet car for a cup of coffee, she treated herself to a glass of wine instead.

When she arrived home, still in high spirits, she was surprised to find Andrew's car not there. Perhaps the flute lesson had overrun. Sometimes it happened.

Letting herself in, she dumped her bag and went upstairs to change, wanting to get out of the clothes she'd been wearing all day.

She was just pulling on a fresh jumper when she heard the car pull into the drive, then Andrew's key in the lock.

'Hi!' she called down. 'I'm home.'

And heard the door close.

'I'll be right there.'

Andrew was standing, whey-faced, at the bottom of the stairs. 'Beatrice, is she here?'

'No, of course not. She's supposed to be with you.'

'I went to collect her and they said she'd gone. I thought she might have come back on her own.' His voice was harsh, breathless. 'I've been home once already. I just drove around again.'

'Fiona's,' Ruth said. 'She'll have gone to Fiona's.'

'I've checked already. Phoned. She's not there.'

He looked up at her helplessly: a look Ruth recognised. She caught hold of the banister rail to stop herself from falling. It couldn't . . . it couldn't be happening again.

IV

44

Will still had not been able to speak to the mother. Ruth Lawson was upstairs, asleep, sedated; a friend – Catriona – sitting with her lest she wake. Not a good time to wake alone.

When he had first arrived, Ruth had been frantic, distraught, unable to sit for more than a few moments at a time; angry, tearful, lashing out, her face devoid of colour: several times she had been physically sick. At one point earlier, her husband, Andrew, had had to struggle to keep her from pulling out clumps of hair, punching her own face with her fists. All she had done when Will tried to talk to her was scream in his face; scream and cry.

Now it was close to eleven: four hours since the alarm had been raised, five since Beatrice Lawson had last been seen.

Her flute lesson had finished, as was usual, just before six o'clock, after which she had returned her flute to its case, put on her coat, collected her blue book bag, and gone outside to wait for her father to arrive.

That much was known.

Officers were out in force in the area close to where the music teacher lived, knocking on doors, asking neighbours what they might have seen. Plenty of people returning from work at round about that time, plentiful passing traffic, plenty of cars. Preliminary inquiries had been made of the music teacher, as well as Beatrice's friend, Fiona, and her mother.

There were two possibilities, Will thought: either the girl had got fed up with waiting for her father, who had, by his own admission, been close to fifteen minutes late, and started to make her own way home, or she had accepted a lift from somebody else. The one didn't preclude the other.

Special attention was being given to the route she would most likely have taken had she decided to start walking home alone, a journey that would have taken her, if she didn't dawdle, somewhere between twenty minutes and half an hour. All well-used roads, especially at that time of the evening; no ginnels or cut-throughs, only one small patch of open ground. Alternatively, she could have caught a bus from the far end of the street into the centre, and then another bus from there to within a few hundred metres of her house.

Check, check and check again.

Andrew Lawson sat with his face in his hands, trying not to look at his watch, glance up at the clock. The police family liaison officer, Anita Chandra, made him cups of tea which he set aside without drinking.

One of the first things Will had done, after speaking to the father, had been to join in the careful search being made of the house: room after room, the cupboards, the garage, the garden shed.

No stone . . .

Beatrice's own room was on the second floor and Will

had stood there for some minutes, alone, slowly taking it in: the photographs pinned up haphazardly — Beatrice in a riding helmet, in her costume on the beach, at what looked like a party with her friends — posters on the wall; tights and leggings hanging, entangled, from the back of the bed, bits and pieces of clothing scattered across the floor. Books and comics, magazines. Several pairs of trainers, two pairs of Crocs, yellow and green, pink wellingtons. Bits and pieces of jewellery, bright and cheap, dangling from three lengths of coloured thread. The top of her desk was crowded with notebooks and folders, pens and pencils crammed into a jar; two dictionaries, one English, one French; a pale blue diary with a padded cover and a clasp and catch that clicked open at a touch. The last few days were blank. The rest would be read through carefully, each name, each possibility checked.

There was a small clock radio beside the bed; no computer, no TV.

She could have arranged to meet someone, Will thought, that was the other possibility.

So much yet they didn't know.

Helen had driven out to the music teacher's house earlier that evening, a thirties two-storey semi with a broad bay window on the ground floor and wisteria growing up at either side of the front door and branching off towards the furthest corner of the roof. There was parquet flooring in the hallway, knick-knacks artfully displayed, a three-piece suite in the living room that had served them well, manufactured in the days when things were made to last.

Leslie Huckerby, nervous-eyed, bald, bespectacled, grey cardigan unfastened, shook Helen's hand and gestured towards one of the armchairs. 'Please. Please sit down.'

His wife, Marion, soft and round, asked Helen if she would

like some tea. 'Or coffee, if you'd prefer. We only drink it in the morning ourselves, but if that's what you'd like it's no trouble. Or there's Ovaltine. Leslie and I . . .' She stopped. 'I'm sorry, I . . .'

'Tea,' Helen said briskly. 'A cup of tea would be fine. Just milk. Thanks.'

'It's upset her terribly,' Huckerby said when his wife was out of the room. 'Of course it has both of us. To think that she could walk out of here and . . .' He lowered his gaze. 'You hear of so many awful things happening. Every time you open the newspaper or switch on the television. The news, nowadays, I don't mind telling you, some evenings it's more than Marion and I can bear to watch.' He smiled diffidently. 'I'm sorry, I'm babbling and you're not here for that.'

'It's all right,' Helen said. 'I understand.'

'You must ask me what it is you need to know.'

Notebook open, Helen checked the times the lesson had begun and ended, the normal arrangements by which she arrived and departed.

'Beatrice, did you notice anything different about her today?'

'You mean the way she was dressed or . . .'

'No, no. The way she was, her manner. Did she seem upset at all?'

'I don't think so, no.'

'Distracted?'

'No more than usual. She has some natural talent, Beatrice. A good ear. But her concentration, I'd have to say, is not of the best. And if something doesn't come quickly, well, she can become discouraged quite easily.'

'But she keeps coming.'

'Her parents are keen, the mother especially. I expect Beatrice herself has little choice.' He shifted his position slightly on the settee. 'I doubt if she'll carry on much beyond eleven or twelve.'

'There's wasn't anything especially difficult in today's lesson that might have got to her in some way? Made her angry or annoyed?'

'No, not at all.'

'She didn't go storming off?'

'No. Quite the opposite, if anything. There was a little piece towards the end that she played quite well and I was able to tell her so. It pleased her, I think. She even suffered my usual lecture about practising little but often without rolling her eyes the way she often does. "Goodbye, Mr Huckerby. See you next week." And then she was gone.'

Behind his glasses he was suddenly blinking back tears.

Marion Huckerby came in with a tray. 'We haven't much in the way of biscuits, I'm afraid. Just a few shortbreads.'

Helen had forgotten the smell of Ovaltine – malty, is that what it was? – evenings at home after she had got ready for bed and come back down in her pyjamas, back when she herself was twelve or thirteen.

Another life.

'Beatrice,' Helen said, 'would you say she was young for her age?'

'No,' Leslie Huckerby said, 'I don't think so.'

'Mature, then? Grown up?'

'I don't know, it's difficult to say. Since I stopped teaching full time, going into schools every day . . . they all seem to grow up so fast. Not that I got the impression she was especially into make-up or boys, not like some of them.' He shook his head. 'Just a normal, bright girl with a good head on her shoulders.'

'You don't know,' Marion Huckerby said, 'what might have happened?'

'After she left here, no,' Helen said. 'Not yet.'

'I'm sure she'll turn up.'

'Let's hope so.'

'"Bye, Mrs Huckerby," she said, cheerful as anything.'

'You saw her go?'

'Yes. I was sitting here, in this chair, where I am now. She put her head round the door to say goodbye.'

'And was that normal? I mean, did she usually . . . ?'

'Oh, yes. If the door was open and she could see me sitting here on my own. Sometimes, if her father was here before the lesson ended, they'd hurry off, but otherwise she'd say goodbye and then go and wait for him outside.'

'She never waited in here, or in the hall?'

'Not usually, no. If it was raining, maybe, but no, she'd go out there and wait. It was never more than a few minutes.'

'Before her father arrived?'

'Yes. Sometimes I would hear his voice, or occasionally the car, but not always.'

'There's so much traffic at that time of the evening,' Leslie Huckerby said. 'I've had to have double glazing put in upstairs where I give the lessons, otherwise that's all you could hear, cars, cars, cars.'

'So you wouldn't have heard anything yourself?'

'Not really.'

'Unless you came downstairs.'

'Yes, but I wouldn't, you see. Oh, I might pop to the loo, but otherwise I'd be getting ready for my next lesson. Sorting out music and so on.'

Helen nodded. 'This evening,' she said to Marion Huckerby, persevering, 'after Beatrice had gone outside, do you remember hearing anything? A voice, maybe? Someone calling Beatrice? Saying her name?'

'No, no.' Flustered. 'I . . . I don't think so.'

'Nothing?'

'I'm sorry, no. I wish I did, I wish I could help.'

'And you don't know how long it was she stood there, outside the house, waiting, before she left?'

Tears welling up, a catch in her throat, Marion Huckerby shook her head, 'I'm sorry, I'm sorry.'

Her husband reached across and patted her hand. 'It must have been getting on for a quarter past when her father rang the bell,' he said, 'so she must have left before that. When the doorbell went I thought it was my next pupil, a little early. Marion called up to me, thinking for some reason Beatrice might have gone back upstairs. That was the first time we realised something was wrong.'

Will had taken Andrew Lawson through the circumstances of his daughter's disappearance not once now, but twice, returning to check certain points a third time. Lawson's eyes were glazed over, his body limp, a mixture of tiredness and delayed shock; his answers repetitive, monotone.

He had left his school some five minutes later than he'd intended, delayed dealing with a particularly truculent parent, and then been slowed down again by the build-up of traffic, finally arriving at the Huckerby house at approximately fifteen minutes past six. He couldn't be more exact than that. Instead of being on the front path waiting, as he'd expected, Beatrice was nowhere to be seen. Thinking she'd gone back inside – possibly to ask one of the Huckerbys to call him on his mobile – he had rung the bell and when Mrs Huckerby came to the door, told her he'd come to take his daughter home.

Very quickly then, he'd confirmed that she was nowhere in the house or garden, no sign of her on the street. Phoning home in case, somehow, she was already there, all he'd got was his own voice on the answering machine. His assumption then had been that, fed up with waiting, she'd got into a huff and started to walk. It didn't occur to him then that she might have caught a bus.

Getting back in the car, he drove home along the route she was most likely to have taken. It was only at this point the idea came to him that she might, somehow, have gone back to her friend Fiona's. Fiona Davies. But when he phoned to check, Fiona's mother had said no, she had collected both girls from school as usual and taken them to the Huckerbys'; when she had picked up her daughter at the end of her lesson, Beatrice had still been there waiting for hers to start, she had passed her on the stairs.

No, Andrew confirmed, Beatrice didn't have a mobile of her own. Nor had she ever left without waiting for him before, no matter how late he had been.

'Is it possible she could have arranged to meet somebody?' Will asked.

'Somebody? Who?'

'I don't know, a friend from school maybe? A boyfriend?'

'She doesn't *have* boyfriends.'

'Somebody she'd met through the Web, perhaps? Some chat room or other?'

'No.' Andrew shook his head strongly. 'We were always very careful about how and when she used the computer. And besides' – the incomprehension clear on his face – 'how could she be meeting someone else? She knew she was meeting me.'

Past midnight, Will was standing in Beatrice's room, only a small corner light shining. Earlier he had read through the remainder of her diary, looking for names, assignations, anything that might provide a clue to what had happened, where she might have gone. With her father's permission, he had searched through drawers, read letters, old cards, scribbled notes pushed down into books. Her bank book from the Nationwide showed forty-three pounds in her account, untouched since January of that year. As far as her father knew, none of her clothes were missing, other than the things she had been standing up in. There was nothing, so far, to suggest the girl had planned to leave of her own accord. No suggestion that she had been unhappy either at home or at school.

Looking down into the rear garden, the light from Helen's cigarette was like a firefly against the shadowed grass. Most of the surrounding windows were dark.

Will went down.

'You should go home and get some rest,' Helen said when she saw him. 'A couple of hours while you can.'

'Maybe,' Will said.

By mid-morning they would have posters bearing Beatrice's picture ready for distribution; a second canvass of the neighbours would begin; bus crews would be interviewed. Officers would start interviewing Beatrice's teachers, her fellow pupils; Will himself, most likely, Will or Helen, would follow up the initial questioning of her friend Fiona Davies and her mother. With any luck, by then he would be able to speak to Ruth Lawson as well.

That evening, motorists who regularly passed the Huckerbys' house on their way home would be stopped and questioned. If there were no trace by the end of the day, a composite fingerprint and DNA profile of Beatrice would be produced.

More officers would be drafted in.

Standard operating procedure.

'She vanished,' Will said. 'Ten, fifteen minutes and she vanished.'

Helen stubbed out her cigarette. 'Home,' she said. 'Go home.'

'How about you?'

Neither of them moved.

The liaison officer came quietly out from the house.

'This friend of the mother's, sir, Catriona, have you talked to her at all?'

'No, why?'

'I think you should.'

45

Ruth swam. She swam steadily out from the shore, long slow strokes that pulled her through the water, pushed against the tide. Legs kicking strongly in tandem with the movement of her arms, head turning, roll of her body from side to side, the splash of water into her face and along her back.

Turning, she trod water and looked around.

She had no idea she'd swum out so far.

People like stick men running along the shore.

Waving, some of them. Waving at her?

Raising an arm, she waved back and as she did so the water rose up into her face, stinging her eyes, splashing up into her mouth and nose. Salt in her mouth and sour.

For a moment she choked, unable to breathe.

Then gradually she eased herself around and struck out again, more leisurely this time, a steady breaststroke instead of crawl, her hands parting the waves, small curtains of green.

Glass green.

Green and blue and green again.

The ocean.

She had the ocean to herself.

The horizon a dark line that trembled like a note from a violin.

She swam on, steadily, but her legs were beginning to ache now, a heaviness in her arms.

How much further did she have to go?

Twenty strokes more, ten, and then she'd rest, tread water again, float on her back and let the waves take her, carry her along.

There.

The water slid across her face and she felt herself begin to slip beneath the waves.

This was what she'd wanted all along.

This.

She closed her eyes.

Down.

And down.

Pressure now on her chest and lungs, and suddenly she had to fight to breathe, twisting and thrashing with her arms, struggling to claw herself back up to the surface, but the weight of the water pressed her down.

The more she fought, the more something was holding her back, like hands, hands pressing, holding her beneath the waves.

Hands.

Children's hands.

And their laughter.

The water roared in her ears till she thought that they must burst.

No air . . .

Her lungs . . .

Somewhere above her, sun on their faces, they laughed on and splashed and kicked and played their little games.

Called her name.

One final thrust and then her heart would break.

46

'It's unbelievable,' Helen said.

'I know.'

'That poor woman. No wonder the state she's in.'

Will nodded. No wonder indeed. First one daughter, then another. Helen was right, it beggared belief.

They'd found an all-night garage not far from the house and bought coffee from a machine, sat drinking it in Helen's car, windows wound down for the smoke from her cigarette. The coffee was acrid and stale but they drank it anyway.

'The other daughter,' Helen said, 'Heather, was that her name?'

'Yes.'

'The same father or . . . ?'

'Different. Remarried.'

'And this was thirteen, fourteen years ago?'

''95. Summer of '95.'

'She fell down a mine shaft, that's what this Catriona said?'

'Something like that, yes. She didn't know for certain.'

'But it was an accident?'

'Apparently. We'll get the details tomorrow.'

Helen smiled wanly. 'Today.'

Already the sky was lightening, the first strands of red and orange visible through the false dawn of street lights and forecourt signs. Helen dropped the butt of her cigarette into the dregs of her coffee and it hissed.

'You think about it,' Will said, 'from the moment they're born. The first time, almost, you hold them. Everything so . . . so bloody fragile. And you become terrified. Something happening to them. Something happening to you.'

He looked out of the window, distracted, another car pulling in at the pumps.

'I remember once, this was before we'd moved, I'd taken Jake out in the buggy, one of the first times it must have been. We were just in the park, this little park not so far from where we lived, and I thought, as I was pushing him, I thought what if something happens to me now – I don't know what, a heart attack, anything – and he's just left here all on his own, strapped in, and nobody will know. Not who he is or anything.'

He shook his head.

'It's stupid, absolutely bloody stupid, no rhyme nor reason. Nothing was going to happen to me, nothing was going to happen to him. But once they're born, it all changes. You change. You think differently.'

Helen lit another cigarette.

'Being on your own with them,' Will said, 'that's the worst. Like, one time, Susie had this coughing fit. That's all it was. Lorraine was out somewhere with Jake and I was on my own with Susie – she couldn't have been more than a few months old – and she started coughing and no matter what I did – patting her back, trying to get her to drink water – it just wouldn't stop and I was going frantic. I thought, she's going to die. I couldn't think rationally, not at all. I just stood there holding her, listening to that horrible brittle cough, and feeling

293

her pressed against me, her chest against my hand, each time . . .'

Breaking off, he turned away, eyes closed, not wanting her to see his face, and Helen rested a hand on his shoulder and squeezed.

'Come on,' she said, 'we ought to be getting back.'

The ambulance was outside the house when they returned. Ruth Lawson, parchment pale, was being stretchered along the path from the front door, loosely strapped beneath a dark blue blanket.

As Will hurried from the car, breaking into a run, the liaison officer crossed the square of lawn to intercept him, dew glistening on her shoes.

'What the hell happened?'

'Overdose, sir. Sleeping pills. She'll be all right.'

'How . . . ?'

'She went to the bathroom. After she'd just got out of bed. I should have gone with her. I'm sorry.'

Will nodded. For a moment, he saw Andrew Lawson's face at one of the downstairs windows, a blur. Helen was by the ambulance, talking to one of the paramedics in hushed tones.

'How's the husband?'

'In shock, I think. Their friend Catriona's with him for now. But she's been up more or less all night. She's out on her feet.'

'Get back in there. He'll want to go to the hospital, I imagine. If he's not up to it, see if there's somebody else who can come and sit with him here. Then you get off and catch some sleep yourself.'

'It's all right, sir, I'm fine.'

'Like hell you are. Go home, set the alarm. We'll need Lawson to make some kind of a statement this afternoon. I'll want you back for that.'

'What if the girl calls, sir? Calls here?'

294

'I'll make sure there's someone by the phone. Now off you go. And stop sirring me all the bloody while.'

'Yes, sir.'

'Make me feel old before my time,' Will said, but she was already hurrying away.

Mid-morning, Andrew Lawson sat with Will on a bench in the hospital grounds, head bowed, a cigarette in his shaking fingers, the first time he had smoked in years. His face was grey, heavy bags of skin beneath his eyes; he looked, Will thought, at least ten years older than his actual age. Ten years virtually overnight.

It had taken a deal of persuasion to prise him away from his wife's bedside, Ruth out of danger and deeply sleeping, no movement save for the occasional flicker of the eyelids, the silent opening of her mouth to call what might have been a name.

'I should never have left her,' Lawson said, not for the first time. 'If I hadn't left her this would never have happened.'

'Don't blame yourself,' Will said.

'Earlier,' Lawson said, continuing as if Will had never spoken, 'when Catriona and I were both sitting there, she seemed to be having some kind of nightmare, thrashing around with her arms and kicking out – she kicked the covers right off the bed – but then she settled and she looked almost peaceful and I thought it would be all right. I went into the spare room and lay down. Just ten minutes, just to close my eyes.'

He looked up at Will.

'When they found her – when the police officer found her – I was terrified I'd lose both of them.'

Still burning, the cigarette fell from his hand.

'Beatrice, that was my fault too. Talking to that stupid man on the telephone in my office, on and on about some perceived wrong that had been done to his son. And I was being so bloody professional, doing my best to listen calmly, placate him, when I should have told him to get off the bloody phone so I could collect my daughter. My own child.' He pushed a hand up through his greying hair. 'I was more concerned with him and his son than I was with my own child.'

'You were doing your job,' Will said.

'Is that it?' Lawson said, tears in his eyes. 'My job? My sorry bloody job.'

He lowered his face into his hands and cried.

Knowing how he felt, Will waited, time ticking by. He had spoken earlier to the press officer, the conference called for later that afternoon, in time to get fullest coverage on the evening news. Will still hoped he could persuade Andrew Lawson to be there, sit on the platform at least, perhaps say a few words, the usual heartfelt platitudes. They would be using two photographs of Beatrice, one taken on a recent holiday, showing her happy and smiling, the other the orthodox head-and-shoulder shot school photographers seemed to specialise in, designed to reduce everyone to conformity. After some discussion, they had decided to release a picture of Beatrice and her mother also, the two of them in the garden outside the house where they lived, Ruth with her arm around Beatrice's shoulder, holding her close, mother and daughter, pride and love in her eyes.

Helen had gone to talk to Gill Davies and her daughter, Fiona, Beatrice's friend, about the afternoon of music lessons, the hours before Beatrice had disappeared. Neither of them could venture reason or explanation for what had happened or why. Beatrice had been just the same as usual and nothing that she'd said to Fiona had suggested either that she was nervous or upset, nothing out of the ordinary at all. Nothing about arguments at home, no plans to do anything after her lesson other than meet her father in the usual way. No secret boyfriends, at least none that she had confessed to Fiona; no one that she met through some Internet chat room and kept hidden from her parents.

Things had been fine at school, Fiona said, Beatrice had been getting on with everyone, no big feuds, no rows, no dramatic fallings-out. Both her class teacher and the head teacher confirmed this to be the case: Beatrice was able, occasionally a little bit bolshy, but mostly keen and enthusiastic, popular with the other girls; even the boys grudgingly thought she was okay.

Bus drivers, neighbours – no one had apparently seen anything.

'Finally heard back from Devon and Cornwall Police,' Helen said, catching Will ten minutes before the press conference was due to start. 'The other daughter, Heather. It was an accident, right enough. Got lost on the coast path in heavy mist, fell down the shaft inside this old engine house. Two days before she was found.'

'Poor kid.'

'Poor mum.'

Will nodded agreement, straightened his tie. 'How do I look?'

'You really want me to tell you?'

'Wish me luck.'

47

Cordon walked up from the harbour, the last ragged echoes of sun setting, soft-edged, over his shoulder. Recognising his steps on the cobbled street, the dog barked in lazy anticipation, then was quiet. When Cordon opened the door, she was sprawled along the sofa, barely raising her head towards his hand.

'Good to see you, too,' Cordon said.

In a short while he would take her for a walk, out across the fields and then down on to the coast path towards Mousehole, the pair of them shadows in the near-full dark. Before that he needed to change out of his work clothes, sit a while and clear his head, relax. When Jimmy Lambert had finally thrown in the towel and buggered off to Portugal and an apartment complex where he could play golf and swap lies with the other ex-pats, the organisation and personnel of his CID squad had fallen prey to a strategic review and Cordon had found himself being rationalised sideways into the glories of Neighbourhood Policing; his duties to oversee the activities of the one uniformed sergeant, two young PCs and a brace of eager community support officers who made up his team, their role to address low-level crime and disorder issues and respond to the changing needs of the local rural community.

Cordon's first instinct had been to say balls to that and walk away, but the same stubborn streak that had set him so many times against his senior officers wouldn't now allow them the satisfaction.

He stuck.

Did his job and to hell with what anyone thought, those officers, younger and less experienced, building their careers working high-profile cases and skewering him with smug glances on those rare occasions their paths crossed, sad old geezer put out to grass.

Cordon poured himself a small glass of Scotch and pressed Play on the stereo and, as he sat back, the sound of Eric Dolphy's saxophone, rising and falling through a set of loops and spirals as he reinvented 'Tenderly', rebounded round the room. The evening breeze, Cordon thought, more than caressing the trees; the whisky warm against his throat, harsh and slightly sweet to the taste.

As the track changed and snare drum and cymbal launched Dolphy and Booker Little into the album's title tune, 'Far Cry', and first Little's trumpet then Dolphy's piercing saxophone soloed, Kia shifting uneasily on the sofa, Cordon caught himself remembering Letitia's *What the fuck d'you call that?*, distaste registering on her face.

Letitia.

At four in the morning, on the way home from a night's clubbing and buoyed up by too many pills and too much alcohol, she had let herself into his flat and slipped into his bed, and it had been with great difficulty that, after a brief tussle, he had pushed her back out; Cordon, like most men, especially at this hour, ruled by his dick more than he'd like to admit.

He knew there were others who would have called him a fool, after all she was not a child any more, far from it, but knew also that, by his own lights, he had been right; just as he knew, somewhere at the back of his mind and in his groin, he'd always regret an opportunity not taken, little enough love in his life, little enough abandon.

That morning, when he'd been making coffee, and she'd come in from the bathroom after spending the rest of the night on the floor, towel wrapped round her, hair wet from the shower, he knew that it had changed between them, irrevocably.

'Last night,' he said, 'what was all that about?'

No reply. She drank her coffee, said no to toast, and when she stood up to go, she left his keys beside her cup.

For a short while after that, Kia's replacement walker was a scrawny fifteen-year-old lad who'd been shooting up since he was twelve, sharing needles with his elder brother, mugging middle-aged men cruising the car park toilets on their way home from work.

'Bum boys now, is it?' a DS from Penzance station said to him one day in the police canteen. 'Bit of a change from drugged-up tarts.'

Cordon punched him hard enough to drop him to his knees, then hard enough again to break his nose.

Now, night and morning, time hanging on his hands, he walked the dog himself. And returning this particular evening, he refilled her bowl with water, drank a glassful himself, pulled off his boots and switched on the TV to watch the news.

The disappearance of young Beatrice Lawson in Ely was third item on the news, behind the newly released unemployment figures and the deaths of two British soldiers, killed when their armoured vehicle hit a mine in Afghanistan. Cordon recognised Ruth Lawson instantly, though to him she was Ruth

Pierce. Older now, of course, but happy and smiling along-side her daughter in the photograph on the screen.

Cordon remembered talking to her last on the park bench in St Just, the grey walls of the surrounding buildings echoing the grey of the day. Ruth still struggling to come to terms with what had happened, struggling to understand.

The girl, it seemed, had gone missing in the middle of the town, still daylight, early evening, no otherwise suspicious circumstances, no sightings, no clues. Other than the fact that the girls were the same age, there were no obvious compari-sons with Heather Pierce's disappearance and death save one.

Cordon muted the television sound and reached for the phone. Detective Inspector Grayson was not currently avail-able; if he would care to leave a number, someone would get back to him first thing.

'It's the DI I need to speak to,' Cordon said.

'Of course, sir,' said the duty officer. 'I'll see your message is passed along. Priority.'

And pigs, Cordon thought, might fly. By rights, he shouldn't have had another drink, but who was to tell him no?

48

Frank Nicholson worked nights: security officer at a small industrial estate on the outskirts, seven p.m. until six the following morning. Forty-nine years old, he'd been doing the same job now for twelve years. Signing in, signing out. When he'd started, there had been two of them, his co-worker a paunchy ex-policeman whose breath smelt of onions and cheap Scotch and whose clothes gave off an odour of cigarette smoke and alcohol from the far side of a room. The one time there had been a serious attempt to break into the site, the former copper had been asleep and snoring in front of a small bank of CCTV screens and it had been Nicholson who had contacted the police and then disabled the intruders' van so that, when the sirens sounded, they had to make off, virtually empty-handed, on foot. Two were caught, one escaped; Nicholson was praised and his admittedly meagre salary raised, his colleague sacked.

Now, save for Saturday nights and holidays, when one or other student took his place, the site was his. His domain. He'd had jobs before, more than a dozen, and none had stuck, but this was different; he liked being alone, the chance to read and think and regulate his own life, the routine.

Every morning, when he arrived home, he would change out of his uniform, put on the kettle for some tea, get himself a bowl of cereal and switch on the TV. He was watching the local news when the picture of Beatrice Lawson in her school uniform came up on the screen. Nicholson waited until that segment had finished, set his cereal bowl aside and reached for his phone.

The response to the broadcast the previous evening – Will, at the press conference talking earnestly to camera, Andrew Lawson, distressed and brokenly articulate, at his side – had been immediate and confused. Sightings of someone who looked like Beatrice as far away as Lincoln or Newcastle upon Tyne; a woman who swore she had seen her getting on to a bus in the town centre a little after seven o'clock; two motorists who thought they might have driven past her on their way home, both of these within half a mile of where her music lesson had taken place. Then there were the usual crazies, the mystics and soothsayers, the same sad and dismal crew who hoped to piggyback into the limelight on someone else's misfortune.

All calls, all information, however suspect, was logged, prioritised and checked. The lead about the bus, which had initially seemed the most promising, already looked to be a false trail; the driver remembered a schoolgirl well enough – some query about her travel pass – but the uniform, as he described it, was different, the girl older and with reddish hair. One of the other local sightings, however – someone answering Beatrice's description walking quickly along the next street to the music teacher's house – stood up under questioning. Admittedly, the driver hadn't seen the girl's face, and nor could he describe what she was wearing in any detail, but both place and timing made sense.

Walking. Walking quickly. Walking where?

*

When Frank Nicholson's call came in, it was quickly shuffled to the top of the deck; by nine o'clock it was on Helen Walker's desk and thirty minutes after that a car was collecting Nicholson from his flat in Ely and bringing him to the police station in Cambridge. Helen picked him up from the waiting area downstairs and walked him to one of the empty interview rooms, having sent a young officer scurrying in search of a can of Sprite, at that hour, when asked, her visitor's drink of choice.

The man who sat opposite her was fleshy-faced, but otherwise not noticeably overweight, medium-height, medium-aged, tiredness evident in his eyes and the way he sat, slightly slumped, against the back of the chair.

'So, Frank,' Helen said, 'last night, tell me exactly what you saw.'

Nicholson leaned forward and told his story. If it ever came down to it, he'd be a good witness, Helen thought.

The nub of it was this: his route to work took him along the street where Beatrice had her flute lesson and, as he approached the junction at the end, already indicating left, he had been forced to slow down because of a car parked near the corner, the driver behind the wheel, the road sufficiently narrow that he had to wait for a space before pulling out and around. It was as he did this that he saw a girl, carrying a flute case and a blue book bag and answering Beatrice's general description, standing beside the car.

'The parked car?'

'Yes.'

'But you didn't actually see her getting in?'

'No, not exactly. Not, you know, closing the door and everything, there wasn't time, but, I mean, she must have done, I'm sure.'

He took a quick drink of Sprite and wiped a hand across his mouth.

Helen spun her pen around on the pad of paper before her, waiting till he'd settled. 'Tell me again,' she said.

Nicholson cleared his throat. 'Okay, like I said, the way the car was parked, over by the kerb, a steady stream of traffic coming the other way, I had to wait for a gap until I could go past. That was when I noticed her standing on the pavement beside the car. She had a bag under her arm – blue, it was, a blue bag, I'm pretty certain – and something like an instrument case in her hand.'

'What was she doing?'

'Standing. Just standing.'

'Talking to whoever was in the car?'

'Not then. At least, I don't think so.'

'And you saw her face?'

'Not clearly. Not then. But as I pulled out to go past, she was leaning down towards the car. That was when I saw her.'

'And it was the same face you saw this morning on the news?'

'Yes.'

'This face?'

Helen slid a photograph out from her pad and across the desk.

'Yes.'

Helen could feel her stomach tensing; the adrenalin starting to flow. A tingle at her nerve endings. 'You said she was bending down towards the car?'

'That's right.'

'So as to speak to whoever was in the vehicle?'

'I imagine so, yes. The driver, I think he was leaning across, across the passenger seat, you know?'

'He?'

'Sorry?'

'You said, he.'

'Yes.'

'It was a man, you're certain of that?'

'Yes.'

'But you never saw his face?'

Nicholson shook his head.

'And the way he was talking, he could have been just asking for directions?'

'Yes, I suppose so.'

'What then?'

'There was a gap in the traffic and I pulled round him.'

'And you never saw the girl actually get into the car?'

Nicholson hesitated; reached again for the can of Sprite but didn't drink.

'Frank?'

'No, I'd already gone past. But that's what she must have done.'

'Why must?'

'When I turned left on to the main road, I glanced back and she wasn't there.'

'You didn't see her in the front seat of the car?'

'No, but where else she could have gone? She couldn't have just disappeared into fresh air.'

'He's not some fantasist?' Will said. They were in his office, some twenty minutes later, Nicholson waiting downstairs in case Will wanted to question him himself.

'No,' Helen said. 'I don't think so, no.'

'And the car, what kind of car?'

'Corsa, he thinks.'

'He thinks?'

'Vauxhall Corsa. Dark green. Not new.'

'Registration?'

Helen shook her head.

'How about the driver?'

'Only saw him from behind. Dark coat, maybe. Fairish hair.'

'Young? Old?'

'Not young, he thought. Fortyish? Just an impression. No real way to tell for sure.'

Will looked out through the window on to an abundance of grey; the weather forecast had promised rain before midday. Running that morning, he had been aware of more than usual dampness in the air.

'One witness,' he said, 'sees her walking away from the place where her father was meant to collect her, walking fast. Now another places her at the end of the same street, about to get into a car. Take these as gospel and we're left with this: is she striding out because she's angry with her father for being late and leaving her in the lurch, or is she hurrying off to meet someone she's arranged to see?'

'But who?'

'A boyfriend?'

'Old enough to drive a car?'

'Why not?'

'Will, she's barely ten years old. He'd have to be seventeen at least.'

'Someone she's met through some chat room on the Internet? She could lie about her age and so could he.'

Helen sighed. 'It's happened before, God knows.'

'Anyway, we're getting the home computer checked. There could be contacts she made without her parents' knowledge, some forty-year-old pretending to be less than half his age.'

'Then surely, when she sees him, she's going to know. She's not stupid. She's not going to get into the car.'

'Depends how persuasive he is. How well she's been groomed.'

Helen took a cigarette from her bag and held it between her fingers, unlit. 'What if,' she said, 'she goes storming off in a huff, figures she'll make her own way home, and then this man stops her, says he's lost, asks her the way? Once they're talking, he asks her where she's going, makes out they're both heading in the same direction and offers her a lift?'

'Like Janine Clarke,' Will said. 'That's what he did. Got her talking, offered her a lift.'

'He? You mean Roberts?' Helen's skin ran cold.

'Hop in, that's what he said. Only difference, he had the dog for bait.'

'You don't really think it's him?'

'Janine Clarke. Christine Fell. Possibly Rose Howard, too. Young girls out walking alone. It's what he thrives on, what he does.'

'But we've no proof.'

'Not yet.'

Helen was shaking her head. 'Will, you can't . . .'

'Mitchell goes missing, goes underground, and then this.'

'We still don't know . . .'

'We can find out. I want to know where Mitchell is. If he isn't involved, then fine. Meantime, everything else goes on. Push Nicholson about the car, see if we can't get it identified, track it down. Chase IT about the Lawsons' computer while you're at it. I've got a meeting with Liam Noble in an hour, run through the sex offenders' list. Then I'm going to talk to the girl's father again, hopefully the mother, too.'

'She's out of hospital?'

'Later today, with any luck.'

Will's phone rang and he picked it up. A DI Cordon from the Devon and Cornwall Police, wanting to speak to him personally, the second time he'd called. 'Tell him to leave a number,' Will said. 'Tell him I'll call him back.'

49

As Sex and Dangerous Offender Intelligence Officer, with a responsibility for overseeing the management of high-risk offenders in the division, statistics and figures were a part of Liam Noble's daily life.

A total of just over fifty thousand offenders were released across the country annually, under probation or police supervision. Thirty-one thousand of these were sex offenders, who were obliged to sign the register and notify the police of any change in their circumstances. In the previous year there had been a twenty-seven per cent increase in the number of offenders who had breached those requirements – more than a quarter – and, as far as Noble could see, there was every indication that the current year's figure would be the same or worse. A figure that, as he knew Will Grayson would be quick to remind him, included Mitchell Roberts.

To make matters worse – from the public's perception, at least – of those offenders classified on release as being of the highest risk – around a thousand – close to ten per cent had reoffended the previous year and been charged with serious crimes, up to and including rape and murder.

Mitchell Roberts, as Will would again point out, had not even been considered dangerous enough to warrant high-risk status. Instead, he had been allowed, all too easily, to slip through the net.

With what result?

Noble knew, of course, about the disappearance of the young girl, Beatrice Lawson, in Ely; he had liaised already with officers working on the inquiry, providing them with the necessary information about individuals on the local sex offenders' register. Will Grayson had asked to see him personally, nonetheless.

Noble thought he knew why.

Will surprised him by smiling broadly as they shook hands, asking after Noble's family, cracking a few caustic remarks about the soccer team he had supported since a child. A cheerfulness Noble didn't quite trust.

'The list you sent across,' Will said. 'Possibles in this Beatrice Lawson business. Four or five we're checking into. Worth a look. Anything there, we'll be sure to let you know, keep you in the loop.'

Noble nodded his thanks. 'How's it going anyway?'

'One positive sighting so far. Getting into a car at the end of the street the evening she disappeared.'

'Planned? Someone she knew?'

'Doubtful. Nothing we've turned up suggests she intended to run away. No clothes taken, money, nothing of the kind.'

'Stranger then?'

'Looks like.'

'She'd get into a stranger's car?'

'Her father says not. Says he and her mother drummed it into her practically since she could walk. Everything else we've learned says sensible girl, head on her shoulders.'

'Even so,' Noble said, 'it happens.'

'Christine Fell,' Will said, 'she got into a car. Got fed up with waiting for her mother to collect her from a friend's house after a party and walked down the road to meet her. Not unlike Beatrice Lawson. Next time anyone saw her she was trussed up, near-naked, in a barn out in the middle of nowhere, somebody's sex toy for three nights and days.'

'Eight years ago,' Noble said. 'I've read the file.'

'Then you know.'

Noble held his gaze, returned his stare. 'Nobody was convicted, Will, not even charged. Case is still open. I don't know any more than anyone else. Precious little.'

'I talked to her. Christine. Showed her the photographs. Saw the look in her eyes. It was him, no doubt.'

'Roberts?'

'Roberts.'

'You don't know that.'

'I do.' Tapping his fist against his chest, above the heart. 'In here I do.'

'That's not enough.'

'It is for me.'

'This man in the car – did anyone recognise him? D'you have a description?'

'Not really, no.'

'Not really or not at all?'

'Middle-aged, not young certainly. Probably fair-haired.'

'Could be a million people.'

'Could be Roberts.'

'You've traced the car?'

'We're working on it.'

Noble threw up his arms. 'Damn it, Will, you've got nothing.'

'He's in breach, right, Roberts? Moved and failed to tell the police where he is. Worse, given a false address.'

'That doesn't tie him into this.'

'He's slipped under the radar. Gone AWOL. Ask yourself why. And Beatrice Lawson or not, while he's at large he's a potential danger. So let's get on top of that. Our duty to the public, surely, let it be known he's at large. Our responsibility. Mine. Yours. Yours especially. Nothing breaks in the next couple of days, get the press office to talk to the media. Something like this, they'll lap it up for sure.'

'All that'll do,' Noble said, 'is drive him further underground.'

'Maybe. Then again, maybe not. If he has taken the girl, it just might get him rattled, smoke him out.'

'Dangerous tactics, Will. What if it misfires?'

'Forty-eight hours' time, it might be all we've got.'

Ruth Lawson left the hospital leaning on her husband's shoulder, one hand gripping his, Anita Chandra walking anxiously a step behind. As they slowly neared the car, the liaison officer shooed off an opportunistic photographer, knowing others were even then milling around the Lawson family home, joking, laughing, talking into mobiles, leaving their empty Styrofoam cups to blossom in the shrubbery.

Ruth looked drained of all life, her skin like unprimed canvas; all trace of colour gone, save for an ill-judged attempt to apply lipstick to her mouth. Once inside the car, strapped in, she closed her eyes and pressed her finger ends, nails bitten down, hard into the palms of her hands.

Andrew leaned across and kissed the top of her head and her hair was like wire wound tight.

The shout went up as the car appeared at the corner of the street and the news cameramen and photographers dropped their cigarettes to the ground, clicked shut their mobile phones and hurried out into the road, jockeying for position.

'I'll go first,' Anita Chandra said. 'Try and keep as close to me as you can.'

Questions rained on them as they stumbled forwards, Ruth loosing her footing more than once, only stopping to catch her breath as they reached the front door.

'How does it feel?' she shrieked back at them, flailing away from her husband's grasp and turning round to face the pack. 'How does it feel?'

Taking firm but careful hold of her arm, Anita Chandra ushered her inside.

'I'm all right,' Ruth said, once the door was closed. 'I'm all right. You can let me go.'

They were just quick enough to catch her as she fell.

When Will finally got to talk to Trevor Cordon it was past two o'clock. After listening to him carefully, he thanked him for his call, apologised for not having got back to him sooner, and went in search of Helen.

He found her sitting on a bench on Parker's Piece in the early afternoon sunshine, lunching on a can of Coke and a cigarette. Two cigarettes.

'Your lucky day,' Will said.

'I won the lottery? Not before time. Either that or Leonardo DiCaprio's seen my entry on Facebook and wants to meet.'

'Not exactly.'

'Then do tell.'

'You're off to Cornwall. Bit of a holiday. Tomorrow, first thing.'

'Am I, bollocks!'

'What's the matter? I thought you'd be pleased.'

'Pleased? All that bloody way.'

'It's not exactly the ends of the earth.'

'As good as.'

'Nonsense. Train from London, Paddington to Penzance. Be there in five or six hours.'

'You see what I mean. Ends of the earth.'

'Like I say, think of it as a holiday. Well-deserved break.'

'Great. Send Jim Straley, he needs it more than me.'

'Afraid not. The ACC's cleared it with their top brass. You're the one expected. Red carpet, I'd not be surprised. Open arms.'

Helen stubbed out her cigarette. 'And this is the death of the other girl? Heather, was that her name?'

'Yes.'

'I thought that was all kosher.'

'It still may be. This DI I spoke to, Cordon. He was running the investigation when she disappeared. Several days before she was found.'

'Inside some mine shaft? She'd fallen?'

'Engine house, apparently. Left over from the old tin mines. It's the fallen part Cordon reckons is open to question. Never quite believed it was that simple.'

'But if he was Senior Investigating Officer . . .'

'Powers that be wanted it pushed through without a fuss, at least that's what he reckons. Cordon always figured someone else was involved in the death, without ever being able to prove who it might have been. Coroner returned an open verdict, that was the best he could get.'

'And since then?'

'Pretty much nothing, as far as I can tell. Cordon himself seems to have been shunted sideways, out of the firing line.'

'This was all what? Twelve, thirteen years ago?'

'Thirteen. 1995.'

Ignoring Will's faint look of disapproval, Helen reached for another cigarette. 'I can't see what my travelling all the way down there now's going to achieve.'

'Maybe nothing. But if the same woman loses two children in suspicious circumstances, we need to make good and sure there's no connection. Just in the merest chance there might be.'

'Covering our backs then, that's what this is?'

'How about conducting the fullest possible inquiries? You should be pleased – you're the one accusing me of concentrating too much on Mitchell Roberts, having tunnel vision.'

'Yes,' Helen said, getting to her feet. 'I'll try and think of that when I'm stuck on some train in the middle of nowhere, with no buffet car and the toilets blocked to overflowing.'

One of the IT officers who'd been examining the Lawsons' family computer waylaid Will as he was heading back into the building.

'Something you might find interesting.'

50

There were still a few journalists and photographers kicking their heels outside the Lawson house, local for the most part, stringers hoping to sell something on to one of the nationals. But without any apparent breaks in the investigation, and lacking the parents' desire to expose their grief to the cameras and talk tearily of their missing 'little angel', media interest was already waning.

One or two, recognising Will, perked up when he arrived, homing in on him for news of some dramatic development, but he hurried past with a promise that he'd be making a statement later.

'How are they?' he asked the liaison officer when she opened the door.

'Much as you'd expect, I think.' She just managed to swallow the 'sir'. 'They seem lost. Lost in their own home.'

'The mother . . . ?'

'Fragile. Bit out of it, really. Not saying very much at all.'

Ruth Lawson was sitting in an armchair, a thin blanket round her shoulders and another across her lap, though, to Will, the room seemed warm. Her husband, unshaven, came over from the window and shook Will's hand as he entered, then waited for Will to sit before finding a place for himself.

Anita Chandra stood close to the side wall, careful to keep out of everyone's direct eyeline, not wishing to distract from what Will had to say.

'There's been a development – how relevant, it's difficult to say – but a witness has come forward, claiming to have seen a girl resembling Beatrice getting into a car at the end of the street where her music teacher lives.' He paused, waiting for the information to settle. 'We're following this up as diligently as we can.'

'A car,' Andrew said. 'I don't understand. I mean, how could she? What car?'

'In all probability,' Will said, 'a green Vauxhall Corsa.'

'She wouldn't,' Andrew said. 'She wouldn't get into a car with someone she didn't know. She just would not.'

'And you don't, either of you, know of anyone who owns such a vehicle?'

'No,' Andrew said. 'No.'

Ruth said nothing. Will wasn't even sure if she'd heard or understood.

'Friends? Family? Neighbours, possibly. Someone who knew Beatrice and might just have been passing? Known her well enough to have stopped and offered her a lift?'

'No,' Andrew said again, his voice thickening. 'Of course not. And if it was someone we knew, they'd have told us, surely? When they heard what had happened, they'd have told us right away.'

Unless they had reasons of their own for not doing so, Will thought. Neighbours, family, friends: despite the occasional predatory figure like Mitchell Roberts, he knew that was where most child abusers were found. And the closer to the home, the more dangerous they could be. Access, opportunity. Fantasies that, all too easily sometimes, became realities. Little games that got out of hand.

'And anyway,' Andrew said, 'if that was what happened, she'd be here now. They'd have brought her home.'

'Unless she asked them to take her somewhere else.'

'Somewhere else? What somewhere else?'

Will shook his head. 'I don't know.'

'You make it sound as if she had some secret life. A life we knew nothing about.' He broke off to catch his breath. 'She was just an ordinary girl. She went to school. She played with her friends. She didn't have secrets from her mother and me. She did not.'

But children do, Will thought.

And still Ruth said nothing. Very little seemed to register on her face. Will wondered again how much she'd actually heard of what had been said; how much she'd taken in. He wondered if it was her medication keeping her in that state or something deeper.

'I wanted to let you know this,' he said, 'before the information is released to the media. We'll be asking for anyone who might have noticed a young girl getting into a green Corsa that evening to come forward. Anyone who might have seen her as a passenger. Either myself or Anita here will keep you up to date with any developments.'

'Thank you,' Andrew said, starting to stand, to show Will to the door.

'There was one other thing,' Will said.

Andrew looked back at him apprehensively, flinching as if waiting to be hit.

'Photographs,' Will said. 'There were some photographs of Beatrice on your computer, fairly recent by the look of them. You sent an email asking the sender to identify themselves. As far as we could tell, there was no reply.'

Andrew blinked and sat back down. Ruth moved her hands across her lap, pulling the blanket tighter.

'We've done our best to track down the sender ourselves, but so far without much luck. The account's been closed. We're still checking, of course, but our IT people keep getting stalled. I wondered if you could help?'

Andrew cleared his throat, coughed into the back of his hand. 'Not really, no. We don't have any idea. We did think, rather I did, it was a friend of ours – Lyle, Lyle Henderson – it's his wife who was here, sitting with Ruth, Catriona – but no, it wasn't, not at all.'

'And why,' Will asked, his pulse quickening slightly, 'did you think it was your friend Lyle?'

'He'd bought a new camera, that's all. Fancy digital SLR. I thought it was his way of trying it out, showing us how good it was, what it could do.'

'You asked him?'

'Yes, of course.'

'And?'

'And he said, no. Nothing of the kind.'

'A keen photographer, though, your friend Lyle?'

'More that he likes expensive toys, I'd say. Boys' toys, isn't that what they're called? MP3 players, mobile phones, computers. Stuff for that boat of his.'

'Boat?' Will caught the flicker of interest on Anita Chandra's face as she listened.

'Motor launch, moored down at the marina.'

'Beatrice,' Will said, 'has Lyle ever shown any interest in photographing her before?'

'Not especially, no. I mean, he's taken pictures of her, pictures of us all. Out on the river, that kind of thing. Just snaps, really. Nothing out of the ordinary. You know, friends.'

'He and Beatrice, they got along?'

'Yes. Difficult not to get along with Lyle. Life and soul of the party, you know what I mean. Always wants everything to go with a swing. Now I think of it, I suppose Beatrice did find him a bit much sometimes. He'd tease her, you know, nothing malicious, but she didn't like that, being made the centre of attention.'

'This teasing, was it ever physical?'

'Not really. Oh, he'd tickle her sometimes, threaten to pick her up and throw her into the water, that kind of thing, just, you know, fooling around.'

Lagging behind his words, Andrew's face showed an understanding of what he'd been saying, the implications.

'You don't think Lyle – you can't . . . you can't think he'd have had anything to do with . . . with what might have happened? He's not – no, it's impossible.'

'He's not what, Mr Lawson?'

'Not, you know, interested in young girls.' Andrew shook his head vigorously. 'Not in that way. I mean, you'd know, wouldn't you? I'd know. All the time we spent together, I'd know.'

Will smiled reassuringly. 'I'm sure you're right. But we'll likely have a chat with your friend Lyle anyway. Background as much as anything else. You can let us have an address, of course?' He got to his feet. 'Just one final thing. And this is hypothetical, nothing more. But if Lyle were driving along and stopped to offer Beatrice a lift, would she be likely to accept?'

'Well, yes, in all probability, yes. But the car you described, that's not what Lyle drives. And besides, he would have told us straight away.'

Will held out his hand. 'As I say, Mr Lawson, it's all just hypothetical. Thanks for your time. Doubtless we'll talk again.' He ducked his head towards Ruth. 'Mrs Lawson, goodbye.'

She looked at him as if seeing him for the first time.

On his way out of the room, Will gave Anita Chandra enough of a glance for her to know she was meant to follow him outside.

'Lyle Henderson,' he said, once they were out in the hallway. 'Has he been here at all?'

'He came to collect his wife after Ruth Lawson was taken into hospital.'

'Not before that?'

'No. The wife, Catriona, she was here on her own.'

'She didn't happen to say anything about where her husband was, why he hadn't come with her?'

'No, not a thing. And I didn't ask . . .'

'Relax. No reason you should.'

'You think he might be involved?'

Will made a face. 'I never really trust things that just fall into your lap. But we'll check him out as a matter of course.'

She nodded. 'She's gone, hasn't she?' she said quietly. 'Beatrice. She's been taken. There's no other answer.'

Will glanced back towards the room where both parents were still sitting. 'It's difficult, what you've got to do. Not encouraging them to harbour too many false hopes; not letting them despair. It's hard.'

'It's what I trained for.'

'I know. And you're doing a good job, I can tell.'

'Thank you, sir.' Blushing a little, looking away.

'See if you can find some way of being alone with the mother. Draw her out a little if you can. Get her to talk. About anything at first, it doesn't matter.'

'You think she knows more than she's saying?'

'I don't know. Possibly not. Maybe all she's suppressing is her grief. But maybe not. Maybe there's more.'

The door to the living room opened and Andrew Lawson stood there, drawn by the sound of voices. Will raised a hand in his direction and moved off to run the narrow gauntlet of reporters and cameramen waiting outside.

Brightly, Anita Chandra swivelled round. 'Shall I make us all some tea?'

51

A young gardener, plugged into his iPod, and wearing a Chemical Brothers T-shirt and grey-green combat trousers, was trimming the Hendersons' hedge. Possibly the last cut of the autumn. Leaves were collecting in twos and threes across the lawn, waiting to be raked. Lyle Henderson himself, not content to leave all the work to the hired help, was repotting a plant with a bright orange flower, with a view, Will thought, to moving it under glass against an early frost. What the plant was he had no idea.

The house was flat-fronted and square, ivy and wisteria growing up and across the weathered brick. A good hundred and fifty years old if not more, Will reckoned, built close to the cathedral and the motte and bailey of the old castle, a stream that doubtless trickled into the Ouse running past the bottom of the garden.

When Catriona Henderson came to the front door in response to the bell, she was wearing a black and white striped cook's apron, hair tied back with a wisp of brightly coloured scarf, flour on her hands and sprinkled along her arms.

Nice, Will thought, this glimpse into how some people lived.

After enquiring about Ruth and asking for any news of Beatrice, she showed Will into a long, glass-fronted room overlooking the garden, which had been added before planning regulations and conservation orders began to bite.

'Lyle,' Catriona called, pushing open one of the windows, 'the Detective Inspector is here.'

'You'll excuse me,' she said to Will. 'But if I don't go now there'll be a small disaster in the kitchen.'

Lyle Henderson kicked off his boots at the door and padded in thick socks across to the drinks cabinet by the side wall.

'Not over the yardarm yet, but all that work gives me a thirst.' He held up a bottle of Bombay Sapphire gin. 'There's beer in the fridge, if you'd prefer.'

'Neither, thanks.'

'Catriona offered you coffee, tea?'

'She did and I'm fine.'

Henderson poured a generous helping of gin into a tall glass, added a quick splash of tonic water and a slice of lime and then two cubes of ice from a vacuum container that had recently been refilled.

'So,' he said, lowering himself into one of a pair of matching, cushion-covered, wicker armchairs, 'this is about poor Beatrice, of course. How can I be of help?'

'Just background, really. Filling in a few dots.'

'Fire away.'

'The Lawsons, obviously you know them well.'

'Pretty well. Ruth more than Andrew, truth to tell. She and Catriona palled up when she came here from London. That dreadful business before. She'd recently got divorced, making a new start. Catriona helped to take her out of herself, get over what had happened. Try anyway.'

The ice cubes clinked as he raised his glass. Through the

window, Will could see the gardener pausing to fidget with his iPod, only one short stretch of hedge left to do.

'Andrew, you didn't get on with him so well?'

'Not that. No, good chap, Andrew. We introduced them, after all. No, it's more a matter of however well you think you know them, how much time you spend together, there's always something – I don't want to say deep down, bit of a cliché, but you know what I mean – something, I don't know, that stays hidden.' He sipped his gin and tonic. 'Makes him sound sinister, doesn't it? And that's not what I meant at all. Keeps his feelings pretty much to himself, maybe I don't mean any more than that.' He laughed. 'Not like me. I'm pissed off or elated, everyone bloody knows it within half a mile.'

He grinned across the top of his glass.

'You enjoyed being with them, though, as a family?' Will asked. 'Spent time together, that sort of thing?'

'Oh, yes.'

'Beatrice, too?'

'Of course.'

'And you got on with her okay?'

'Beatrice? Yes, real sweetheart. Mind of her own of course. Drove her mother mad. Anything she really didn't want to do, you could see her digging her heels in and then the sparks'd fly.'

'They'd argue?'

'Cat and dog, sometimes. Never last, mind you. Half hour later, she'd be sweet as can be.'

'How did Andrew deal with it? When his daughter was in one of those moods?'

'Left it to Ruth, mostly. Stood back, you know? Had too much of that at school, I should think, every day. When he did step in it was a bit heavy-handed. You know, laying down the law. Headmaster in him, I suppose. Easier for me, got like that I'd just try and jolly her out of it, pull silly faces, make her laugh. If we were out on the boat, offer to dump her in the water, that kind of thing.'

'Pick her up and swing her around.'

'That kind of thing, yes.'

'Horseplay.'

'If you like. Just a bit of fun.' He stopped, as if wondering if he'd said too much.

'She likes you, then?' Will said. 'Beatrice?'

'Far as it goes, yes. I'd say so.'

'Trusted you?'

'I suppose so. Yes. In a way.'

'She didn't ever say anything that might have suggested she was especially unhappy? Thinking about running away?'

'No. And if she had, by now I'd've said.'

'Nothing about boyfriends, things she might want to have kept from her parents, but might have felt safe telling you?'

Lyle shook his head. 'That's all still to come. Some poor lad's heart to be broke there and no mistake.'

'Where were you, I wonder, around the time she disappeared?'

'Where was I?'

'Yes.'

'Look . . .'

'It's just routine. Like I say, filling in the dots.'

'What are we talking, then? Six, six-thirty. I'd still be out at the golf club. Over towards Shelford Bottom.'

'Need floodlights, I'd've thought, that time of night.'

'There are floodlights in the driving range, of course, but no, by then I was in the club bar. Bit of a card school, I'm afraid. Time I got back here, eight-thirty, nine, Catriona was already at the Lawsons, sitting with Ruth.'

'Was there anybody else here, then, when you returned?'

'No, of course not.' He set down his glass. 'It's no crime you know, enjoying the company of your friends' kids. Larking around. Having a laugh. Not a crime.'

Will looked back at him evenly, waiting.

'Your lot, that's what you'd make of it.'

'My lot?'

'You know what I mean. As much as look at someone the wrong way, never mind actually touch them, bit of play fighting, anything like that, ordinary decent fun, and you'd lock 'em up and throw away the key. Paedophilia, all the rage nowadays. Look twice at a kid under sixteen and you're a bloody paedo.'

'Beatrice Lawson,' Will said, 'is a lot less than sixteen.'

'Okay,' Lyle said, pushing himself hurriedly to his feet. 'That's it. Talk's over. On your way.'

'Please sit down, Mr Henderson. There are still some things I want to ask.'

'Anything else you've got to say, you can do it with my solicitor present . . .'

'There were some photographs Andrew Lawson thought you might have taken . . .'

'Bollocks! There were no bloody photographs. Not of mine. I've told him that and if he told you any different he's got his head up his bloody arse further than I'd thought. Now get out of my house and don't come back and if a word of what you've been suggesting gets out I'll sue you and the whole bloody Cambridgeshire force so fast you won't know if you're on your heads or your bloody tails. Now, go on. F-off, go!'

'Lyle,' Catriona said, opening the door, 'what is all the shouting? I could hear it right in the kitchen.'

'The Detective bloody Inspector is just bloody leaving.'

'Oh, I see. There's some apple and blackberry pie just due out of the oven. I was going to ask if . . .'

Her husband's glare stopped her in her tracks.

'Thanks for your time, Mr Henderson,' Will said. 'Mrs Henderson. I'll be back.'

*

'You really like him for this?' Helen asked.

They were in the back room of a small pub not too far from Parker's Piece, Will having called her on his way back down to Cambridge and arranged to meet.

'I don't know. There's something there, I'm sure of that. Just talking about himself and Beatrice and it was as though I'd pushed a button. Suddenly went apeshit. Total overreaction.'

'Unless . . .'

'Exactly. Something pressed a nerve, no doubt about that.'

'Guilt, probably. From what you've said.'

'You think he could have taken her?'

Helen raised an eyebrow. 'Not necessarily. But there could have been a bit of fooling around. You know, pinching and tickling that went too far. Might have scared the life out of him if it did.'

'Might have got off on it, too.'

'All the more reason to be frightened.'

Will supped from his pint. There was a steady hum of voices from the main bar, intermittently interrupted by sudden laughter or a bellicose shout.

'This boat of his,' Helen said. 'Moored on the marina? Big enough to keep someone hidden?'

'Apparently. I've had a couple of lads down there, nosing around. Everything short of going on board. Pretty certain she's empty. From what people say, Henderson's not been down there in a while.'

'And the car?'

'He drives an old Volvo, built like a small tank. No way that could be mistaken for a Vauxhall Corsa. But the Mrs, Catriona, she's got a Polo.'

'Still not the same.'

'Close enough if you're not big into cars and, anyway, it's only seen out of the corner of an eye.'

'Colour?'

Will held it for a beat. 'Green.'

Helen could feel the muscles of her stomach tighten. 'Surely she'd have used it to go to the Lawsons?'

'I checked with Anita. She came by taxi.'

'So Henderson could have driven home, swapped cars, and got to the end of the street in time to pick up Beatrice?'

'Yes, in theory. But why, unless there'd been a previous arrangement?'

'Or unless he knew her father was going to be late.'

'The phone call. You think Lyle could have made the phone call that kept Lawson talking?'

'Or got somebody else to, why not?'

Will half-laughed and shook his head. 'Too many crime novels, that's your trouble.'

'Nothing wrong with that. Besides, do their research nowadays, some of them.'

'I dare say. But this is real life, not fiction.'

Helen grinned. 'So you say.' She pointed at Will's almost empty glass. 'Want another?'

'Best not. And anyway, shouldn't you be getting home to pack?'

'You sure you still want me to go? Mitchell Roberts, now Henderson. You'll want to talk to the wife, too. Might be useful, having me around for that. Under-represented as we are.'

'We?'

'Women, Will. Not too many of us around the squad room, in case you hadn't noticed.'

'There's Ellie Chapin.'

'She's just a baby.'

'Not exactly.'

'Now, Will, you've been peeking . . .'

'Time she stepped up. Got out from under your shadow.'

328

'Is that where's she's been?'

'I think so. This'll do her some good. Give her something to get her teeth into.'

Helen sniggered.

'You've got a filthy mind,' Will said, not quite able to suppress a grin.

'Guilty.'

'And besides, you're always telling me how difficult I'll find it when you've spread your wings and left the nest. Time maybe for me to put it to the test.'

'Maybe it is at that.' Helen got to her feet. 'Come on,' she said, taking hold of his glass. 'A quick half in here?'

'All right. Why not?'

52

Fourteen minutes past two: Ruth was suddenly awake without knowing why. Asleep beside her, Andrew lay turned in on himself, the faint whistle of his breathing the only sound.

When she slipped out of the bed, the air in the room struck cold and she took down her dressing gown from the hook behind the door and slipped it on.

The door to Beatrice's room was closed.

For a moment, she stood wrapped in the silence of the house, no thought of Andrew, herself alone: the handle of the door smooth and cold against her hand. When she eased it open, was it her imagination or did the small figure standing in front of the mirror flinch?

Ruth allowed her eyes to close and slowly open.

Seeing what she saw, she thought her heart had stopped.

The cord jeans they'd bought from H&M that day in Cambridge, the ones Ruth had tried so hard to talk her out of, the ones with the butterflies and flowers patched on to the legs; the tie-front top she'd ordered for her from the Mini Boden catalogue, expensive but at least she knew it wouldn't fall apart.

Her daughter at the mirror, brushing her hair.

'Beatrice.'

The word seemed to break upon the air.

'Mummy!' As she turned, Heather smiled and put her arms out for a hug. 'I thought I'd try on some of Beatrice's clothes. They're a little small for me, of course, but never mind. And look, I've been practising doing my hair just like hers, you see?'

Ruth could see nothing, blinded by tears.

'Don't cry.' Heather slid a hand into hers, the fingers warm, warmer than her own. 'You know I hate it when you cry.'

Ruth dabbed a tissue at her eyes.

'That's better. See.' Again, she held out her arms. 'You can give me a hug, you know. I won't break.'

Feeling the bones beneath the flesh, Ruth held her daughter fast, afraid still to tighten her arms too much or press too hard. Heather's breath was warm on her neck, her lips warm and slightly damp on her cheek, one quick kiss as she pulled away.

'Beatrice,' Ruth said. 'Have you seen her? You have, haven't you? Can't you tell me where she is?'

Heather's smile was momentary and sad.

'Don't ask,' she said. 'You must never ask. You know that, don't you?'

'But Heather . . .'

There was no one there. The clothes, newly folded, at the foot of the bed, the brush on the small dressing table, the echo of her daughter's breath still alive on Ruth's skin.

Don't cry. You know I hate it when you cry.

53

They went in just before dawn. Will Grayson, Ellie Chapin
and a complement of a dozen officers at the Henderson home;
DS Jim Straley and six more at the marina. Lyle Henderson,
irate in blue and gold striped pyjamas, shouting and shaking
his fist; his wife, Catriona, running first down then upstairs
with her voluminous nightgown billowing around her, exposing
stringy calves and plumpening thighs.

'You've got no right,' Henderson blustered. 'No right at all.'

Will waved the warrant in his direction and pressed on. In
every room of the house, doors were being thrown open,
cupboards explored, drawers emptied out on to beds, on to
the floor.

'Room upstairs, sir,' said one of the officers. 'Rear of the
house. It's locked.'

Henderson was in the kitchen with his wife; Catriona now
wrapped in a towelling dressing gown, the pair of them
stranded mid-tile, neither willing to look the other quite in
the eye.

'Key,' Will said, holding out his hand.

'What? What key?'

'Upstairs back. We need access.'

'No need. Hardly ever gets used. That's why it's kept locked.'

'Key,' Will said again.

'I've told you, there's nothing there. A few bits and pieces, that's all. Old business stuff. Files.'

Will was still holding out his hand.

Henderson sighed and stepped back. 'The key's in the front room, the bureau.'

'Please go with the officer, show him exactly where.'

Over by the kitchen window, hands in her dressing-gown pockets, Catriona stared out at the first signs of daylight, yellow and silver-grey, beginning to show low in the sky.

'I'm sorry,' Will said.

She gave a quick, dismissive nod of the head and nothing more.

The room upstairs held two bookshelves, a desk and office chair, a double-height filing cabinet, several suitcases in varying sizes resting one on top of another, and a narrow cupboard that proved empty save for one fishing rod, a tennis racquet, and several old pairs of golf shoes; leaning haphazardly against the far wall was a stack of magazines, mostly *Maritime Journal* and *Power and Motoryacht* by the look of it, along with a few copies of *Country Life*.

On the desk was an iMac 7.1 OS X computer and a laser jet printer; there was a portable hard drive in one of the desk drawers.

'Is this the only computer in the house?' Will asked.

Henderson shook his head. 'Catriona has a laptop.'

'Make sure the officers take it with them when they leave.'

'You can't . . .' Henderson began, then stopped.

The bookshelves held a set of *Wisden* going back to 1958, a history of Rolls-Royce Aerospace, assorted books on fishing and golf, several racing mysteries by Dick Francis and, on an upper shelf, two large-format books, *Lolita's Sisters* and *The Dreams of Young Girls* – airbrushed, soft-focus photographs of barely pubescent girls, alone amidst picturesque woodlands or curled lazily in pairs across wide, ornately furnished beds, their near-naked bodies lyrically draped with wisps of filmy cloth.

'That's art,' Henderson said, when Will held the books out towards him.

'Yes,' Will said, slapping one of the books shut. 'I can tell.'

He was back outside when Straley called from the marina. 'Boat's clear, sir. Not a sign.'

'Make sure it's checked out, inch by bloody inch.' Will snapped his phone shut. 'Ellie,' he said, addressing Chapin, 'why don't you suggest the Hendersons get properly dressed and then see they're ferried down the station. Separate cars.'

Having established that he was not under arrest, merely assisting the police with their inquiries and that he could leave at any time, Lyle Henderson insisted on having his solicitor present before agreeing to answer any questions.

In the circumstances, Will was not unhappy about this: it would allow time for a first cursory examination of whatever files were held on their computers, whatever might be nestling on the portable hard drive.

It was the best part of an hour before the solicitor arrived, sporting a well-cut grey suit with a mustard yellow check waist-coat and bright blue tie, silver hair expensively cut and neatly brushed, black shoes polished to within an inch of their life.

He greeted Henderson, if not like an old friend, then someone with whom he'd shared a drink at the nineteenth hole or possibly sat across from, enjoying a hand of bridge.

Will's hand he shook briskly, his tone businesslike, just this side of affable; a request for ten minutes alone with his client to which Will acceded.

The interview began with Will going through what had previously been established about Henderson's friendship with the Lawsons, continuing with his whereabouts on the evening their daughter had disappeared. All very low key, matter of fact.

Bored, the solicitor examined his nails.

'You like her, the daughter, Beatrice?'

'Yes. Yes, of course.'

'Have fun together, on the boat, messing around?'

'Sometimes, yes. Look, we've been through all this before.'

'And she was okay with that? Enjoyed it? Played along?'

'Yes. Like I told you before, she could get into moods sometimes – I suppose all kids do – and if Andrew or Ruth said anything, she'd only get worse. Sullen didn't come into it. Face like thunder. With me, most times she'd snap out of it, come around. Made her laugh, I suppose.'

'Like you said, bit of horseplay.'

'*You* said.'

'Even so, that's what it was. Something physical.'

'Not always.'

'Slap and tickle.'

Before Henderson could respond, the solicitor laid a warning hand on his knee. 'I think we could move on from this particular line of questioning, Detective Inspector, don't you?'

'You and Catriona,' Will said, 'you've never had children of your own?'

Henderson shook his head.

'Any special reason?'

'Inspector . . .' the solicitor said, beginning to voice an objection.

'Never got round to it, I suppose,' Henderson said. 'Busy lives and then – you look up and it's too late.'

'You like children, though? Young people.'

'Yes, we both do.'

'Enjoy their company.'

'Yes.'

'The pair of you?'

'Yes, I said.'

'In the same way?'

Henderson's mouth opened as if to speak.

'My client can't be expected to answer for his wife,' the solicitor said.

'I'll be happy if he answers for himself.'

'Yes,' Henderson said a moment later, without much conviction. 'In the same way, of course.'

'She shares your taste, then, for eroticism?'

No reply.

'Mr Henderson?'

'Not necessarily, no.'

'She found it offensive, perhaps?'

'Inspector, you can't . . .' the solicitor tried, but again his client cut him off.

'Not really, no.'

'But you,' Will said, 'you'd no such qualms?'

'You make it sound as if this was something that happened all the time.'

'Looking at pictures of young girls.'

'Young women.'

'*The Dreams of Young Girls*, that was one of the books on your shelf.'

'Exactly. One book.'

'Girls not so very much older than Beatrice Lawson.'

'Damn you!' Henderson banged both fists down on the table and scraped back his chair. 'I'll not sit here and listen to your filthy innuendoes. Not another minute more.'

'I think,' the solicitor said, rising easily to his feet, 'this interview seems to be at an end.'

Will let them get almost to the door.

'A shame,' he said. 'I was hoping we'd have time to discuss some of the items we recovered from your hard drive.'

Henderson stopped mid-stride.

'Your solicitor can probably tell you about the work of CEOPs, the Child Exploitation and Online Protection Centre. Several items we found might come into their jurisdiction. Interest them at least. Short sections of video you seem to have downloaded.'

'All right,' Henderson turned back into the room and approached the table.

'*Sexy Girls Doing Homework.*'

'I said, all right.'

'*Putitas de Secondaria*. My Spanish is pretty negligible, but I think I can work that one out. More schoolgirl stuff.'

Henderson sat back down, avoiding Will's gaze, head in his hands. Alongside him, his solicitor drew a slow breath, leaned back, and, with a deft tug at his trouser leg, crossed one long leg slowly over the other. It was going to be a longer morning than he'd imagined.

Despite her husband's angry advice, Catriona Henderson had agreed to talk to the police without the presence of a solicitor. Perhaps knowing she was going to be interviewed by a female officer made her feel more at ease; then again, she might have felt she had nothing to hide.

Ellie Chapin had been on the force for three years, a detective for less than eighteen months: still, to some extent, feeling her way. Dark hair worn quite short and parted to one side, with a fringe she was forever brushing away from her eyes, she was in her late twenties and looked younger. To her embarrassment she was occasionally asked for ID when buying drinks at the bar.

An inch or so above medium height, not a scrap of extra fat on her body, she was wiry and deceptively strong. A runner's build. On the track, at five thousand metres, she was regularly pushing to get under sixteen minutes. Cross-country, sloshing through winter rain and mud, she usually finished ahead of the pack. At university, she'd captained the women's athletics team and come close to being selected for the World Student Games.

If Catriona – a big, confident woman with a big voice – thought she was going to get an easy ride, she was mistaken. Other issues aside, Ellie felt she had a point to prove. One of the more experienced male officers sat alongside her, but with instructions not to interrupt unless absolutely necessary. This was strictly her show.

'How would you characterise your husband's relationship with Beatrice Lawson?' Ellie asked.

'I don't know if I would,' Catriona replied.

'Try.'

'I don't know if they had a relationship.'

'They spent time together.'

Catriona shook her head. 'Not really. We all spent time together, the four of us, Ruth and Andrew, Lyle and myself. Two couples. That was the relationship. Sometimes, when it was appropriate, Beatrice was there too. Sometimes not.'

'She'd be with her babysitter, childminder?'

'I imagine so, I really don't know.'

'But you all went out together on the river, days out, excursions?'

'Sometimes, yes.'

'And on occasions like that, what would you say about your husband and Beatrice? I mean, did they get on?'

'Yes, I suppose so. As much as a fifty-something-year-old man can get on with a ten-year-old.'

'She felt okay with him, then? I mean, not intimidated or anything, the way some girls are?'

'No, I don't think so.'

'Friendly? Relaxed?'

'Yes, if you like. You could call it that.'

'And were you ever aware of your husband behaving towards her in a way you might consider inappropriate?'

'Inappropriate?'

'Yes.'

'Of course not.'

'You're sure?'

'Of course I'm sure.'

'You do know of your husband's interest in young girls?'

'His what?'

'His interest in young girls, photographs and so on . . .'

'Photographs, that doesn't mean—' Abruptly, she stopped.

'Doesn't mean what, Mrs Henderson?'

'It doesn't mean that he . . . This has nothing to do with Beatrice, nothing at all. They're just pictures, that's all they are. If he takes pleasure in looking at them, so what? It isn't any crime.'

'There are laws.'

'And these are books you can buy in any bookshop.'

'Laws about indecent images of children.'

'Now you're talking nonsense.'

'Am I?'

'Of course you are.'

'I have to ask you, Mrs Henderson, have you seen the images your husband has downloaded from the Internet?'

'No, of course not.'

'Young girls, not much older than Beatrice. Dancing round in little netball skirts. Showing themselves to the camera. Getting naked in the shower. Touching themselves. Touching each other.'

'Stop it.'

'There's one little film, not much more than a few minutes long. This girl with two grown men . . .'

'Stop.'

'At one point, the camera zooms in on her face and you—'

'Stop!' Catriona threw up her arms and flailed at the empty air. 'Stop it, please.'

Ellie glanced at the officer beside her. 'Mrs Henderson,' she said, 'if you'd like to take a break . . .'

'Perhaps if . . .' Catriona began. 'Perhaps if I could speak to you on your own?'

She looked away. Ellie nodded and, without comment, the officer got to his feet and left the room.

'There now,' Ellie said. 'Just take your own time.'

There were damp patches darkening beneath the arms of Catriona's blouse and Ellie was just beginning to sense the sweat from the other woman's body.

'Would you like some water?' she asked, but Catriona began talking as if she hadn't heard, her voice, unlike before, low and subdued.

'When I first found out . . . when I first found out what . . . what made him excited, turned him on, we'd been together, married for years, and when he told me, at first I thought it was a joke. And I suppose he tried to make a joke out of it. Asking me if I still had my old school uniform, stuff like that. I remember telling him not to be so stupid, but at the same time seeing that it had made him – just talking about it had made him excited. And then, one day he came home with this adult size girl's gym kit, you know, green PE skirt, white Aertex blouse and little white socks, God knows where he got it from, some fancy-dress shop, I suppose. He asked me to put it on, that night, and got really angry when I said I wouldn't. Really, really angry, so then I did, and after that he kept asking me and asking me and bringing home other things to wear with it, like crotchless panties, and then he started wanting to take photographs, and I saw myself, one evening, there in the mirror, this fat, overweight, middle-aged woman

340

posing on top of the bed in all this stupid gear, bits of flesh sticking out everywhere, and that's when I told him, no, no more. I'm not doing this any more. And the next day I took the uniform and everything and lit a fire and burned it and said, there, that's the end of it.

'I told him it didn't matter what he did, his photographs and magazines and whatever, as long as he kept it to himself. That's why I insisted that room be kept locked. Then I didn't have to think about it. I didn't have to know.

'But I asked him once – we were talking quite honestly, one of those times, quite rare, when you felt you really could – and I asked him if he ever felt tempted – you know, you read about these men going off to Thailand and places, sex tourists, is that what they're called? – I asked him if he ever felt he wanted to go somewhere like that, and he looked at me as if it were the most horrific thing he'd ever heard. Fantasy, he said, that's all it is. Fantasy. I'd cut off my hand before I'd touch a child. That way.'

She waited, holding Ellie's attention. 'If you think Lyle had anything to do with whatever's happened to Beatrice, you're wrong.'

By mid-morning, Henderson's solicitor had had enough. 'My client's given you all the time you could reasonably expect and more. Answered every question fully and fairly. It's quite clear to me you've got nothing to charge him with. As far as the disappearance of that poor girl is concerned, he clearly has no involvement whatsoever.'

'There is the matter of the material on his computer,' Will said.

'Pretty tame as things go these days, don't you think? Boundaries change, Detective Inspector, what's acceptable and what's not. I wonder sometimes, all those free-minded liberals back in the sixties, demonstrating for free speech, *Lady*

Chatterley and all that, what they think about the permissive society now, what it's all come to? Every second or third word out of people's mouths a swear word, children too. And what you hear on the radio, read in the newspaper. All there, nothing barred. The culture we live in, it makes me shudder. But we're its servants, you and I, in different ways. Nothing we could do, even if we chose, to stem the tide. I doubt very much if the CPS would think it in the public interest to prosecute my client for possessing material anyone with a few pounds and an evening to spend can see at his local Odeon, but that decision is not mine.'

He held out his hand.

'The girl, Inspector, I hope you find her. And alive.'

54

Helen was surprised at how quickly the first part of the journey passed. She read a little, fetched an indifferent coffee from the buffet and later a somewhat less indifferent tea, gazed out of the window, read a little more. The train was pulling into Bristol Temple Meads almost before she'd realised. The next section, on towards Exeter and Plymouth, took them through increasingly attractive countryside, steeply undulating hills with pockets of woodland in between, the leaves turning all shades of orange and brown.

At Plymouth there was a stop to change crew which allowed passengers time to stretch their legs on the platform, time, in Helen's case, for a cigarette. She was just climbing back on to the train when she glimpsed, several carriages down, someone who looked enough like Declan Morrison to raise goose bumps on her arms. Declan following her down to Cornwall in what? Some ill-considered cockamamie attempt to get her to change her mind? In the weeks since she had told him it was over between them, he had tried waylaying her at work, sent emails, phoned; once, very late, and very much the worse for drink, he had turned up at her flat at two in the morning, brandishing protestations of love and the last bouquet of tired flowers from the petrol station down the road, and she had been tempted, sorely tempted, but had finally stood firm.

'All right, all right,' he had said, dumping the flowers outside her door and wandering off, grudgingly, home to his wife and kids.

But men like Declan Morrison, Helen knew, never really meant 'all right'; never conceded defeat, the chapter closed, until they had another woman secure in their sights.

She sat with those thoughts long enough for the train to have traversed the bridge high across the Tamar and swung left, following the curve of coast towards St Germans; at which point she got up from her seat and walked back through carriages, prepared to face it out.

Of course, it was not Declan Morrison, nor anyone, at close sight, who looked very like him; enough of a resemblance, perhaps, to explain why at first glance she had made the mistake – the build, the set of the shoulders, the shape of the head, even the slow spread of a smile when he realised he was the subject of her gaze.

With scarcely a pause, Helen moved on towards the buffet car and something to sustain her for the remainder of the journey, her relief undercut by the realisation that to have jumped to the conclusion meant she had not yet swept Morrison from her mind.

A little unfinished business yet.

Back in her seat, she picked up her book again and tried to read – a novel one of her friends had recommended – but her concentration had gone. Instead, as the train, slower now, shuttled between one small West Country station and another, she found herself thinking back to the summer, Paul and Linda Carey and Terrence Markham and the slow, dawning impossibility of fulfilment, happiness; two people dead and a child orphaned, young Carl growing up in his grandparents' house without ever, perhaps, really understanding why.

'Oh, Christ!' she said out loud, slamming her book shut and startling the passengers opposite.

It's hopeless, isn't it, she thought, finding any kind of happiness with someone else, anything that lasts. Most of her fellow officers were separated or divorced, already on to their second marriages some of them and eyeing up the third; even her girlfriends, the ones she met each month for a drink and a good old natter and a Greek or Turkish meal, most of them were single through choice or circumstance, still licking their wounds, some of them, from their last encounter.

Amongst most of the people she knew, only Will and Lorraine seemed to be hanging in there, holding it all together, waving the flag for marriage, kids, a home, a life. While other men of Will's age and rank were going over the side like rats from a sinking ship, taking any comfort they could find, Will, damn him, didn't show the least inclination to play away from home.

He'd look – she'd seen him casting the odd appraising glance in young Ellie Chapin's direction when she'd first joined CID – but having looked, he'd happily set the thought aside. And when Helen herself flirted with him, as she did, sometimes outrageously, he would play along, safe in the knowledge that a game is what it was and words and looks, for him, were never deeds.

Sometimes, Helen thought, she almost hated him for his – what was it? – steadfastness, she thought that might be the word.

Looking up, she saw that they were pulling into Truro; time to go and rinse her face, refresh her make-up, return her thoughts to the job in hand.

She felt an unexpected tug of pleasure as the train passed the causeway out to St Michael's Mount, the sun glancing off the tops of the waves dipping in towards the shore, and then they were slowing into the station at Penzance and she was collecting up her things and descending on to the platform amongst the returning locals and the late holidaymakers and there, beyond the barrier, tall, angular and unsmiling, was the man she was to meet.

Cordon held out a hand for her to shake, reaching for her bag with the other. His hand was warm and rough. 'Welcome to Cornwall.' A hint of a smile now, just in the eyes. 'Brought some decent weather with you, I see.' There was enough of a burr in his voice to suggest Cornish born and bred.

'You want to go to your hotel first, get that settled?'

'I'd like a drink.'

They walked along past the harbour car park and up some steps on to a partly cobbled road, Helen pausing once to light a cigarette. Cordon finally stopped outside a small, flat-fronted pub and, transferring Helen's bag to his other hand, pushed open the door. Once inside, he indicated a low-ceilinged side room, empty save for some unwashed glasses and a marmalade cat that jumped soundlessly down from one of the chairs and slunk reproachfully away.

'What'll you have?' he asked, bending his head in the arched doorway, more or less his first words since the station.

'Let me.'

'No, it's okay.'

'Gin and tonic, then.'

'Large?'

'Please.'

While he was off at the bar she sat looking at the framed photographs on the wall, black-and-white images of fishing boats returning to harbour, the lifeboat being launched into a maelstrom of rain and spray.

Cordon returned with their drinks, a pint of bitter for himself which he sampled before sitting.

'Your hotel's not far from here. Nothing special, but it's quiet and clean. You can move on if it doesn't suit.'

'I'm sure it'll be fine.' This where you live?' she asked.

'The pub?'

'The town.'

'No, Newlyn. Just round the bay. Penzance is too full-on for me.'

She thought he was joking, but wasn't sure.

'The girl,' Cordon said, 'the one as has gone missing . . . ?'

'Still no sign.'

'Not run off, that's not what you're thinking?'

'Doesn't seem likely.'

'Taken then.'

'Most probably.'

'How long is it now?'

Automatically, Helen glanced at her watch. 'Seventy-two hours, come six o'clock.'

'Three days, then.'

'Yes.'

'Leads?'

'Nothing definite, nothing to hang on to. Someone in for questioning this morning, friend of the family – spoke to my DI from the train, they're checking his alibi. May turn out to be something, but . . .' She shrugged.

Cordon lifted his pint.

The cat slipped back into the room, jumped on to one of the empty chairs, turned around twice and settled, head down, a paw across its eyes.

'You're wondering if there might be a connection with what happened here?'

'Not at first. Not till you got in touch. First we heard from your force, accidental death. Then, whatever you said to Will . . .'

'That's your DI?'

'Will Grayson, yes. Whatever you said to him, made him think it was worth checking over.'

'Two girls, similar age, same mother – one hell of a coincidence.'

'And, clearly, you don't believe the accident story.'

'Didn't then, don't now. But what I don't have is an alternative version of events. Just this feeling. Sits here . . .' he tapped his fist against his chest, '. . . like bloody indigestion. Won't go away.'

'Not after all this time?'

Cordon shook his head.

'You've been over it again? You or someone else? Cold-case stuff?'

Cordon smiled. 'Put it forward, didn't I? Open verdict, after all. This pair come down from Exeter, spent half a day at best going through the evidence, transcripts of interviews, what-have-you, talked to Jimmy Lambert – he was my DS at the time – over a couple of pints in his local – this was before he sodded off to Portugal – talked to me, that was about as far as it went. Not worth expending further resources on reinvestigation. Stuck in my craw, that did, I don't mind telling you. Got a pal of mine to run a story in the *Cornishman*.' He laughed. 'Might as well've had my name on it. Took a bollocking for that an' no mistake.'

'Made a difference, though? The publicity?'

'Did it, buggery! Silent as the bloody grave. Did a little reinvestigating of my own after that. Contacted the family of the girl who'd been with Heather Pierce the afternoon she got lost – Kelly, that's her name, Kelly Efford – the pair of them caught in a sea fret out on the coast path. Parents living apart by then, going through a divorce.'

'They ever suspects?'

'We looked at the father, of course we did. Didn't seem to be anything there. Talked to him this time and he was in a bit of a state, family breaking up and everything. Preoccupied. Had no more thoughts about what had happened that day than he did at the time.

'The one we did like, real oddball, recluse, living in this shack out on the cliff, went to see him and, if anything, he was more eccentric than before. Chunnering away to himself half the time, humming these old songs. Music hall, stuff like that. Ask him a question and you'd be as like to get the bus times from Zennor to Godrevy or a chorus of "Oh, Mr Porter" as a straight answer.

'He admits finding the other girl, Kelly, and taking her in. Peeled her wet clothes off her, kept her overnight in his bed. No sign he laid a hand on her save for that.'

'And Heather?'

'Never saw her, so he says, and try as I might, I could never prove different.'

'Nothing in the forensics?'

'Not significant. Nothing you could build a case on.'

'This was how long ago?

''95.'

'Been a lot of developments since then. Low Copy Number DNA. Could be worth getting the evidence re-examined, clothing and such. My DI's got a contact in FSS. Least he did. Might be able to get something pushed through sharpish.'

Cordon was shaking his head. 'If we could get the go-ahead, maybe. But last time I tried, after that cold-case team come in, response was the same as before, not worth expending further resources. Nobody else was pushing and I let it lie – not so long after I was put out to pasture. The beauties of rural neighbourhood policing.'

Helen grinned. 'What's that? Spot of sheep rustling?'

'Nothing as exciting. Now you're here, of course, bit of added muscle. With this second disappearance, we might swing something.'

He finished his pint; Helen's glass was already empty. 'How d'you want to play this? Check through the evidence? Interviews? Either that or I can take you out where it happened. Start from there.'

'Let me get the facts straight first. Go over what you got at the time.'

'Fair enough.' Cordon rose to his feet. 'Let's get you checked into your hotel, police station's not much more'n a stone's throw away. Find you a desk to work from.'

Helen lowered her hand to give the cat a stroke as she went past and it hissed her away.

'Like that down here,' Cordon said, 'the natives. Some of them. Don't take to incomers so easily.'

All of the faces in the main bar turned to watch them as they left.

55

Ruth's parents had wanted to hurry down to be with her the moment they'd heard: the combination of their granddaughter's disappearance, quickly followed by their daughter being taken into hospital, had them searching through train and bus time-tables, then checking road routes in the unlikely eventuality they should decide to drive. Cumbria to Cambridgeshire, a lengthy journey across country in potentially heavy traffic, was a daunting prospect for a couple well into their sixties, whose normal car use didn't extend much beyond a weekly trip to their nearest Booths supermarket.

A phone call from Andrew had alerted them to the situation and then later calls had kept them in the picture, assuring them the best thing they could do was to stay put and let Ruth get over the worst of the shock before coming to see her.

He couldn't ward them off for long.

One bus, a change of trains and a taxi from the station and there they were: Ruth's father – tall, slightly bent and balding, with an abstracted air that made him look like a retired professor of philosophy – her mother, grey-haired, dumpy, nervously smiling at anything and anyone. When they saw Ruth they both began crying, her father embarrassed, looking away, her mother reaching out both arms to take her in an awkward hug.

Andrew hovered anxiously, ready to offer tea or perhaps even sherry; concerned that her parents' arrival would upset Ruth more than she was already.

After an hour or so, practically all that could be said had been said. The four of them sat in uneasy silence in the living room, the day outside waning away.

Abruptly, Ruth's mother got up and began collecting the cups and saucers, prior to taking them out into the kitchen. Andrew asked her father if he'd like to take a look at the rear garden, still quite a bit in flower, extraordinary for the time of year. Anita Chandra came back into the house with the final editions of the papers; one of the tabloids had linked Beatrice's disappearance with the death of Heather Pierce, thirteen years before. *Mother's Double Tragedy* was the headline above a recently snatched shot of Ruth returning from the hospital, enlarged here into a blurred close-up, mouth open, eyes dark with tears. The same shot appeared on the front page of several other papers as they scrambled to keep up with a rival's scoop.

It was a miracle, Anita thought, the story had taken so long to break. Now the house, more than ever, would be under siege, the phone ringing off the hook, the numbers of journalists and cameramen outside increased, requests for interviews more insistent than before, the press office struggling to cope.

'No,' Andrew said angrily, 'I've said it before and I'll say it again. I am not prepared for my wife to appear in front of the camera and be gawked at by millions as if this were some kind of ghastly reality TV show.'

Ruth said nothing, nodded agreement, took another pill. Exhausted from the journey, her parents called it a night early, a bed made up in the spare room.

At one-thirty, Ruth was up again, her face in the bathroom mirror pinched and pale. Dressing gown belted round her, she went, barefoot, to the kitchen. Since Beatrice had disappeared, she had scarcely eaten, certainly not a proper meal, a biscuit here, an apple there, a corner of cheese. Now she took down a bowl and filled it with corn flakes, shook on a shallow spoonful of sugar, poured milk, and, finally, sliced a small banana across the top.

She was just sitting at the counter when Anita Chandra entered quietly.

'I thought I heard someone.'

'I couldn't sleep. I thought I had, but then, when I looked at the clock, I realised it had only been a couple of hours. And then I thought I was hungry.' She nodded in the direction of the cereal bowl. 'Join me.'

'No, thank you.'

'This used to be my daughter's favourite snack, before going to bed.'

'Beatrice?'

'Heather. Sometimes after she'd been packed off to bed, she'd sneak back down and you'd hear these noises in the kitchen. Like having mice, Simon would say, gnawing away at the cereal supply. I think he quite liked it, the idea of her tiptoeing down.' She smiled sadly. 'I was always more concerned with her going back to bed with sugar all round her teeth.'

'Simon – that's Heather's father?'

'Yes. I thought, when he heard what had happened, he might have been in touch. Simon. I mean, he must know, mustn't he? He must see the papers, watch the news.' She picked out a piece of banana with her spoon. 'He didn't look too well the last time I saw him, maybe that's the reason. Or perhaps he just doesn't want to intrude.'

The kitchen clock ticked.

'How long ago was it that you saw him?'

'Just this summer. We bumped into him, Beatrice and I. In Cambridge.'

'Is that where he lives?'

'I don't really know. He didn't say. Just that he'd moved – left London – and wherever he was living now, it was close. Close to us.'

'Here in Ely, then? That close?'

'I don't know. I don't think so.' From her expression Anita could tell she was thinking of something else. 'The photographs,' Ruth said. 'The photographs of Beatrice that were on our computer. You know about those?'

'I think so, yes.'

'I thought at the time – I never said this to Andrew, he was so certain they'd come from Lyle – but I thought – I don't know why – but it might have been Simon.'

56

Mist hovered pale grey over the fields, grey hardening to a purplish-blue at the furthest edges. Will, wearing a bright reflective top and with fluorescent strips fixed to the backs of his running shoes, ran easily within himself, letting his thoughts jog down, arranging and rearranging. Beatrice, cross at her father's lateness, stomping off in a show of temper; the outstretched hand, the waiting car; Lyle Henderson locked in his room with his images of young girls; the lewd grin on Mitchell Roberts' face — *You got children? I'd like to see 'em some time.*

At first, he'd thought the breaking news, linking Ruth's first daughter's death with Beatrice's disappearance, would be enough to consign the appeal for information about Roberts' whereabouts to small print on centre pages, but now he reasoned some enterprising news editor would happily link two and two and weld them into something closely resembling four. What price the police-released photograph of Mitchell Roberts and one of Beatrice Lawson ending up on the same front page of the *Express* or the *Sun*?

Back home, he dropped his running gear in the washing basket and stepped into the shower. Lorraine, he could hear, was already bustling the kids through their early morning routines, getting ready herself between times, nothing fancy, a touch of mascara here, a brush through her hair.

By the time he got downstairs, dressed in a dark blue shirt and grey trousers, a blue and white tie loosely knotted at his neck, coffee was beginning to bubble on the stove and Lorraine was just slotting bread into the toaster.

'You're a wonder, you,' he said, kissing her on top of the head.

'So they say.'

Will kissed her again, close to the mouth and, from behind his Rice Krispies, Jake made a loud snort of disgust.

'How was your run?' Lorraine asked.

'Okay. Slow.'

'You're getting old.'

'Just trying to avoid ending up in a ditch.'

He poured them both coffee and sat down.

'No progress, I suppose? The girl?' She glanced slightly anxiously towards the children, uneasy about discussing Will's cases in too much detail in front of them.

'Nothing really.'

'That man you had in for questioning?'

Will shook his head. When they had checked Lyle Henderson's alibi for the time Beatrice Lawson had gone missing – that he had been playing cards at the golf club until seven-thirty, a quarter to eight – none of the statements from his erstwhile friends had borne him out; no one had seen him in the clubhouse later than half past five.

Will's hopes had flared.

Henderson had been dragged back in, his solicitor summoned. Faced with the testimony, he had sheepishly admitted the truth: after leaving the golf club he had driven to a discreet brothel on the outskirts of suburban Cambridge and paid for sex. The madam, who ran the place with all the efficiency and cleanliness of a cottage hospital, recognised her client immediately.

'Oh, yes. Humbert-fucking-Humbert. Twice a month regular.'

When Beatrice Lawson had been, in all probability, stepping into a green Vauxhall Corsa, Lyle Henderson was being serviced by a twenty-seven-year-old part-time hair stylist wearing a gym slip and bottle green knickers.

'There's no need, is there,' Henderson asked, 'to tell my wife? I mean, you know, the details.'

'I'm sure,' Will said, 'she can work them out for herself.'

He was upstairs in the bathroom, brushing his teeth after finishing breakfast, when the phone rang and Lorraine answered.

'For you,' she called up the stairs. 'Anita Chandra?'

As Will left the house some ten minutes later, a blade of blackbirds scythed up into the morning sky.

By the time he reached the Lawson house, Ely a relatively short drive away, the media were out in all their glory. Stopping at the newsagent's on the way, he'd been pleased at how well his expectations had been met. Turn from the photo of the missing Beatrice Lawson on page one – the picture of her in her school uniform the press seemed to love – and there on page three was Mitchell Roberts, with the headline *Missing! Wanted by Police!* and details of the offence for which he'd been convicted. Let the readers make whatever connections they would.

Will had elbowed his way inside the house and was met by Anita Chandra in the hall. 'I didn't know, sir. I wasn't sure if it was important or not . . . I mean, it might be nothing . . .'

'No, you did right.'

'She's up, Ruth. Been up for an hour or so. I told her you were coming.'

'How's she seem?'

'A little better, I think. Calm, even.'

Tranquillisers, probably, Will thought. 'The living room?'

'Yes. Oh, and Mr Lawson, Andrew, he wants to go into his school, just for a couple of hours. Says it's important. I think he could do with the break.'

'Okay, arrange a car. Do what you can to get him past that mob outside. And last night, getting her to talk, well done.'

'I didn't do anything really, she—'

Will stopped her. 'Praise in this job, little enough and far between. Don't knock it back.'

Ruth had taken her parents a cup of tea and encouraged them to stay in bed longer, though since then she thought she had heard her father pottering around in the bathroom. Andrew had been at the computer, mainly responding to emails from his deputy, and was preparing to leave. Ruth had made herself a mug of Ovaltine and was sitting, legs pulled up, on the settee, with John O'Conor's recording of the 'Nocturnes of John Field' curling out across the room. In normal times, if she'd worked herself up into any kind of a state, the sound of the piano, delicate yet somehow assured, would have been enough to calm her, but these were not normal times.

Earlier, she'd been leafing through a book about Bonnard and his house in the south of France that she'd bought at Tate Britain the day Beatrice had disappeared, but instead of the richly coloured reproductions showing the Mediterranean gardens and the shimmering light above the sea, it was the desolate self-portraits he had made towards the end of his life that she returned to again and again, his jaundiced face like skin stretched across a skull, dark pits for his eyes. Looking at them, she could not shake Simon from her mind, the sunken cheeks, the air of hopelessness, almost of despair.

When Will came in, she started to get up, but he signalled for her to stay where she was.

'How are you feeling this morning?'

'I don't know. More myself, I think.' She brought her feet round on to the floor. 'Anita said there isn't any news. That's not why you're here.'

'I'm afraid not.'

'I'm almost relieved. It's what I'm frightened of most. Each day that goes by. You or someone else like you, walking in to tell me Beatrice has been found.'

He knew what she meant; knew she didn't mean found alive. He glanced down at the book he presumed she'd been reading earlier and the artist's face that looked back at him was both familiar and shocking: the face of a man who had seen so much loss, so much of the horrors of the world, he couldn't stand to see more.

He pulled round a chair and sat down.

'According to Anita, you think it might have been your ex-husband who took those photographs of Beatrice and emailed them to your computer?'

'Yes. It's possible.'

'I wonder why you didn't say anything about that before.'

'I suppose – I don't know – I didn't want to get Simon dragged into all this. There didn't seem to be any point. I mean, he's got troubles of his own – and I didn't want to think in any way he was involved.' Looking down, she brushed something non-existent from her skirt. 'They were only photographs, after all.'

'And a message,' Will said. 'Wasn't there some kind of message?'

Ruth looked at him before speaking. '"Isn't she lovely?" That's all it said. "Isn't she lovely?"' She waited for Will to respond. 'That doesn't mean . . . It doesn't mean anything.'

But Will was thinking of the expression on Mitchell Roberts' face the time he had watched him in the park, returning a hat to a little girl in a purple anorak: the appreciation, the anticipation of pleasure that had animated his face. *Isn't she lovely?* Will could imagine the words forming, unspoken, inside Roberts' head, caressing the roof of his mouth and falling soft against his tongue.

'The images,' he said, 'you'll have to remind me – they weren't all taken at the same time? Nor at the same place?'

'No. A couple were outside her school and the others, yes, in different places. Different times, too.'

'And they were all taken without Beatrice's knowledge?'

'As far as I know, yes.'

'Or your own?'

'Of course not. Until we bumped into him that day in Cambridge I had no idea Simon was anywhere around. As far as I knew he was still living in London.'

'You hadn't been in touch?'

'No. Not for years.'

'Then meeting him as you did . . .'

'It was a surprise, I told you. A total surprise.'

'Accidental, d'you think? Coincidence? Yourself and Beatrice running into him like that?'

'Yes.'

'How long was it after that meeting the photographs arrived?'

'Not long. A matter of days.'

'In which case, they would have been taken, most of them anyway, before you met.'

Ruth hesitated. 'I suppose so, yes.'

'Then he had to have been following her for quite some time.'

'I don't know.'

'Stalking her.'

'No. That sounds so . . .' She shook her head vigorously. 'Not like that, no.'

Will reached out and closed the book, set it carefully on the floor and moved to sit facing Ruth on the settee. 'As far as you're aware, did Simon have any contact with Beatrice at all? Before that meeting?'

'Good heavens, no.'

'You're sure?'

'Of course.'

'If she'd known he was photographing her, following her – that anyone was – she'd have told you? You or Andrew?'

'Yes, yes, of course she would. But what you're suggesting, about Simon. That he might have been stalking her, it just doesn't make any sense. He's not . . . well, he's not like that, not like that at all.'

'Nevertheless, there has to be an explanation for the photographs. If he didn't take them somebody else did, someone he knows. Has contact with.'

Ruth clasped herself and, for a moment, closed her eyes once more, as if doing so could shut off the thoughts beginning to race around her mind.

'We need to talk to him,' Will said. 'It could be there's a perfectly innocent explanation.'

'I'm sure there is. There has to be.' She was beginning to be aware of the perspiration on her skin.

'You don't have an address? Anything recent?'

'No. Nothing. His old address in London, of course, I could give you that. But otherwise . . . "Living close," that's what he said. "Now that we're living close." I don't know anything beyond that.'

'And Pierce, that's his surname? Simon Pierce?'

'Yes.'

'And is he likely to be working somewhere up this way then, do you think?'

'I imagine so. He was working in local government before, but now . . . He'd always talked about going back to being an accountant. Freelance, you know? Part time. I never thought he'd do it. I thought it was one of those things people say. A kind of safety valve, I suppose.'

Will nodded to show he understood. 'When you were talking about him before, you said something about troubles. Troubles of his own.'

Ruth was slow to answer, composing her thoughts. 'It was after the accident. To Heather. We . . . I suppose we dealt with it in different ways. Simon was very closed off at first, holding it all inside. Trying to talk to him about it, about what had happened, it was almost impossible. As though he wanted somehow to push it all away as if it hadn't happened. He didn't even want to talk about Heather. And I . . . I was in a state, the least little thing would set me off crying, and then he'd get angry. Tell me not to make a fuss, make a scene, why didn't I get a hold of myself?

'I went to stay with my parents for a while, I thought that would be easier. But they – my father especially – every time I broached the subject they'd smile and pat my hand and start talking about something else.'

She swallowed as if her mouth were going dry.

'It got so that I'd start talking to people on buses, complete strangers. I thought . . . I really thought I was going mad. And then Simon told me he'd found this group through the Internet, for families who'd lost their children. Accidents or illnesses, mostly. He'd found it easier, not having to speak directly, just emails. Back and forth, all the time. He wanted me to get involved and I did and it helped, for a while anyway. Helped to know there were lots of others going through the same thing. It was somebody there who suggested therapy, put me in touch with someone they'd been seeing, and that's what I did. And it was really useful. It helped no end. I was starting to feel like, well, like a normal person. I mean, the grief over what had happened was still there, I was still grieving, of course I was, every day, but that seemed almost normal now. As if I could go back to getting on with my life. I tried to get Simon to do the same as I'd done, see the same person, but by this time there were a couple more groups he was involved with – he'd be at the computer all the time, every minute he wasn't working – and he said he didn't need to see any kind of therapist, he was getting all the help he needed as it was. But it had become a kind of obsession. I never-saw him. We never had meals together any more. Not even conversations. Half the night he'd sit up and not come to bed until three or even four and then he started sleeping in the spare room next to his wretched computer. And it was affecting him, you could see it was, not getting enough proper sleep and hardly eating. It was having an effect on his work, too. I think he'd had at least one official warning. When finally I left him, I don't think he really noticed. This whole business had taken him over. And then, when I saw him again, this last time, he looked truly awful, truly ill . . .'

The door opened suddenly and Ruth's father took two steps into the room, mumbled an abrupt apology, and withdrew.

'We'll talk to him,' Will said. 'Simon. If he's in the area, he shouldn't be too difficult to find.'

'You don't think . . . ?'

He smiled gently. 'I don't know.'

'Our friend Lyle,' Ruth said, 'Anita told me you were speaking to him. Was he able to help at all?'

'No, not really.'

'I'm sure he would have if he could.'

'Please don't get up,' Will said. 'I'll find my own way out.'

When he'd gone, she stayed exactly where she was, unable to move. The music had long since finished and slowly now the ordinary sounds of the house were starting to build around her: the quiet opening and closing of doors imprisoning her inside her own thoughts. *Isn't she lovely?* No matter how distressed, how sick he had become, Simon could have had no part in Beatrice's disappearance, surely?

Sitting there, alone, Ruth began to gouge her fingers into the soft skin around her eyes, as if to blind herself from what she feared but feared to see.

57

Helen woke without knowing immediately where she was. A quick glimpse of the floral-patterned curtains, the kettle on top of the chest of drawers with its attendant tea bags and sachets of instant coffee, and, from outside, the raucous call of seagulls, provided the answer.

How had Cordon described it? Clean and quiet. Well, it was certainly that. The landlady had greeted her with a cup of tea and two Garibaldi biscuits and a warning about not smoking in her room. As if.

Helen had spent the remainder of the previous day reading through the notes summarising the investigation into Heather Pierce's death, Cordon trying none too success-fully not to editorialise over her shoulder. Eventually she had asked him if there weren't something else he could more usefully be doing, whereupon he'd informed her he would pick her up at her hotel at nine the following morning and left her alone.

As far as Helen could tell, the investigation seemed to have been carried out pretty much by the book, the only serious blip being the failure to discover the girl's body during the initial search.

Apparent failure.

It was this, the possibility that the body had not been present when the search originally took place, which had given rise to Cordon's doubts. For Heather to have fallen down the shaft of the engine house on the evening she disappeared would have meant her body being overlooked; for the body to have been introduced later raised the questions of how and by whom? And where she had been in the meantime.

As far as Cordon and, to a lesser extent, the coroner were concerned these were questions to which there were, as yet, no satisfactory answers. For the senior officers at the time the answer had been simple: the first search had been inefficiently carried out and the body had simply been missed.

Carelessness. Inexperience. No crime.

Helen read the statements made by Francis Gibbens, the man who had found – and saved – the second girl, Kelly, and by Kelly's father, Alan. Alan Efford. Both, she thought, were witnesses she wouldn't mind talking to further herself. But by then she could feel her eyes starting, involuntarily, to close and knew she was on the path of diminishing returns.

No mini-bar in her room, she had bought a half-bottle of common-or-garden Scotch on the way back to her hotel and, after a quick nightcap, surprised herself by falling asleep within minutes.

For the journey down she had worn a denim skirt over thick black tights, a short leather jacket over a pale blue top, soft comfortable shoes. This morning she wore blue jeans, not her best, and a pair of sturdy boots, a grey marl sweater beneath an oversize green anorak which had been left behind by a previous short-lived boyfriend.

'Well,' as she liked to say to her friends, 'when a man turns up wearing walking boots for a first date you know he's not going to hang around for long.'

Cordon was waiting outside, the engine of the four-by-four quietly running.

'Dressed for it, I see,' he said.

'What did you expect? High heels? Four-inch stilettos?'

'It's been known.'

The interior smelt of dog and something damp she couldn't identify. In a matter of minutes they were shed of the town and heading out across the peninsula on a road that lifted them up on to flat fields and moorland, past places with names like Bosvenning and Deveral Common and Jericho Farm.

'So what did you reckon?' Cordon asked.

'I can see why you were concerned.'

'Concerned? A stubborn bastard with his head located somewhere up his arse was how my boss put it. Words to that effect.'

'Some might take that as a compliment.'

Cordon grinned.

Just short of the small town of St Just, he swung left on to a narrower road that wound abruptly through a series of tight bends before petering out into a muddied track. A few hundred metres along, Cordon brought the vehicle to a halt just shy of a five-barred gate.

'We'll walk from here.'

Two fields across and they were standing on a ledge of flat rock high above the coast path, heather spreading out below, a blaze of purple and rusted orange broken here and there by jagged outcrops of granite. Above, the sky was so bright and clear a blue it hurt Helen's eyes to look: ahead, as far as the eye could see, was the ocean.

'It's beautiful,' she said. 'I never realised it was so beautiful.'

Cordon grunted with something like satisfaction and clambered down, striding out without bothering to look back or offer a hand. Helen scrambled and slid, then jumped and set off in his wake. At least she wasn't being patronised.

The engine house stood out in silhouette, its tall chimney suggesting the ruins of a church perched high near the cliff edge.

Almost there, Helen thought, but, deceptive, the path rose and fell several more times, dropping down sharply towards a stream bed where the land briefly levelled out, each ascent steeper than the last and causing her to stop and catch her breath, the muscles at the backs of her calves beginning to tighten and ache.

'How you faring?' Cordon asked, as she reached a crest and bent low, arms on hips, breathing heavily. 'Maybe time for a cigarette?'

Straightening, Helen gave him a scathing look and pushed past, Cordon laughing as he followed behind.

By the time they had reached the engine house, swathes of white cloud had begun to wind themselves across the sky. Despite the autumn sun, the stonework was cold and rough to the touch. Helen moved to the open doorway and peered cautiously inside. Gradually, as her eyes became accustomed to the change in light, she was able to make out the edges of a platform, twenty feet or so down, and beyond that only the interior of the shaft and the falling dark.

'This is where she was found?'

'Down there, aye. Pure bloody chance. One of the search party lost his footing – round about where you are now.' Helen inched a step or two back. 'Lucky for him, that ledge down there broke his fall. The girl, Heather, she was right there in front of his eyes. To all appearances, she'd fallen, same as him. Cracked her head against some old machinery, part of the original winding wheel.'

'Was that what killed her?'

'A serious blow or blows to the head, that's what the coroner said. Most likely sustained when she fell.'

'Most likely?'

Cordon nodded. 'The official version, you'll have read it yourself.'

'The two girls became lost when this sudden fog came in off the sea, disorientated, frightened. Maybe they get separated by accident, possibly they split up on purpose, searching for the path. Kelly takes a tumble down the cliff and ends up near this man Gibbens' shack, Heather gets as far as this and what? Takes shelter? Inside it'd be pitch black. She'd fall easily.'

'Agreed.'

'And the estimated time of death suggests she died on that first evening, that first day, two days before the body was found.'

'Yes.'

'So, according to your theory, where was the body all that time?'

'I don't know.'

'Someone killed her, though, that's what you're saying? Killed her and hid the body, then came back for it later and disposed of it inside here.'

'More or less, yes.'

'It's easy to hide a body, out here in the open? Keep it hidden even though the whole area, this whole stretch of coastline's being searched?'

'I could take you to ten tunnels within five hundred metres, opening, some of them, right out on to the cliff. Some are hidden by bracken, a few, the larger ones, fenced off. You likely saw a warning sign or two on the way along.'

Helen moved towards the open doorway. 'I do need a cigarette.'

'Be careful where you toss it away.'

A container ship was making its way north-east along the horizon, a couple of small fishing boats close in.

'If the body was that well hidden,' Helen said after some

minutes, 'why come back and move it? Why take that risk? Do you think, whoever it was, they wanted it to be found?'

'Maybe. Either that or lost for ever. If it hadn't been for that piece of ledge, I doubt there's much to break your fall till the bottom of the shaft.'

Helen held the smoke down in her lungs before releasing it slowly.

'Suppose you're right for a moment, just suppose. Do you think the murderer was someone already known, someone you've already interviewed, had in for questioning? Or do you think it was someone as yet unknown?'

'It could be the latter,' Cordon said. 'In which case, at this remove, unless we were to come up with some new evidence, it's unlikely we'll ever know who they are.'

'And if it's not? Who's your money on then?'

Cordon stepped away. 'Gambling's for fools. Let's go and talk to Francis Gibbens.'

Gibbens was on the slip of beach below his makeshift shack, trousers rolled up above his knees, paddling in the tide. When Cordon called out, he turned and raised a hand to shield his eyes, recognising him straight off and slowly making his way back on to the sand.

'Who's she?' he said, indicating Helen with a nod of the head.

'A colleague.'

Helen introduced herself and held out a hand.

Gibbens sat on a rock and began to dry his feet with a scrap of towel that had been wrapped around his neck like a scarf.

'Salt water,' Gibbens said, 'good for my rheumatism. Bunions, too. Bastard things.' He looked up. 'I doubt you're here to pass the time of day.'

'The occasion you rescued the girl,' Cordon said. 'My colleague'd like to hear how it was.'

Gibbens looked at him sharply, snapping the towel tight. 'No. That's not what you want. It's the other girl, isn't it? The other girl you're interested in, Heather, what happened to her.'

'Why do you say that?' Helen asked.

''Cause it's never been rightly settled, has it? Stumbling into that old engine house in the dark, layin' there for days. More to it'n that.'

'Is that what you believe?'

'He does. Ask him.'

'And you? How about you?'

'What I believe don't matter. Just an old fool, livin' on his own.' He slid his feet into what looked like two left shoes and tucked the towel back round his neck. His trousers were still halfway up his legs.

'Eliot,' he said. 'Walking crab-like along the beach with the bottoms of his trousers rolled. Before he become a poet he was on the music halls, you know. Wearing a black face, like them minstrel shows. "Little Dolly Daydream". That was one of his numbers. "I Want My Girlie", that was another. That and "J. Alfred Prufrock", of course. Come on up and I'll set the kettle on, make tea.'

The interior was dark and dingy and seemed more disordered than when Cordon had last visited: bits of flotsam and jetsam on most surfaces and patched here and there across the floor; ancient hardback books with their pages stained and wrinkled as if they'd been submerged in salt water. Over to one side, a vintage wind-up gramophone rested on top of a metal trunk, several small piles of scratched and chipped seventy-eights ranged alongside.

'Sit,' Gibbens said expansively, gesturing towards a ramshackle selection of chairs. 'Sit.'

But when Helen went to do so, a black cat with a torn ear hissed and showed its claws.

'Manners,' Gibbens said and, lifting the animal clear, he shooed it outside. 'Getting old, that's her trouble. Not used to the company, neither.'

'Still got your goats?' Cordon asked.

'Just two. Out along the cliff somewhere.'

'Thought the council'd have hounded you out of here by now.'

Gibbens laughed and settled the kettle on a small Calor gas stove. 'So did they. Till this lawyer took an interest. Out to make a name for himself, I reckon, threatening to take 'em to the Human Rights Commission an' all sorts.' He laughed again, a rough cackling sound that set Helen's teeth on edge like chalk being scraped along an old-fashioned blackboard.

The tea, when it came, was black and strong.

'There's sugar if you'd like,' Gibbens said. 'No milk.' He chuckled. 'Milkman forgot to call again, I'm afraid.'

They sat for a while listening to the sea's rise and fall and the melismatic cry of gulls wheeling overhead. If I lived here, Helen thought, all on my own save for a few animals, I'd go crazy too. If that's what he was.

'You're right,' Cordon said, 'it's what happened to Kelly's friend that we're interested in, the pair of them lost they way they were. Fret coming in the way it did.'

Gibbens said nothing, hummed bits and pieces of melody, some old, mostly forgotten tune.

'You were out there when it started to come down.'

'I was?'

'You tell me.'

Gibbens shook his head. 'Right in here. Sittin' where you are now, matter of fact. *Crime and Punishment*, you remember? Part three, chapter six. Raskolnikov's workin' himself up into a muck sweat on account he thinks the police suspect him of murder.'

'And do they?'

'Don't they always?'

'Correctly or not?' Helen asked.

'Don't rightly want to say. Shame to spoil it for you, give away the plot.'

He's crazy, all right, Helen thought. Crazy like the proverbial fox.

'I did go out,' Gibbens said suddenly. 'Wasn't too thick then, not down here at least. Like blasted night up around the path. Walked up a short ways, got so I couldn't see my hand afore my face. Come back down. Shut it out.'

'What made you go out in the first place?' Cordon asked.

'Curious, I suppose.'

'That was all?'

'That and the noise.'

'Noise?'

'Someone calling.'

'Calling what? Calling a name? Calling for help?'

'Name. Least I think it was.'

'Which name?'

'I don't rightly know, not for sure.'

'Kelly?'

'I don't know.'

'Heather?'

'Could've been. Can't rightly say if it was or not.'

'But if you heard it?' Helen said.

'What I heard, something like a name. The way it was said. Like someone calling a name.'

'Just the one person calling out? One voice?'

'Maybe two.'

'Two?'

'First one and then another. Not at the same time, like. One louder than the other.'

'Which?'

'The first.'

373

'Could one of them have been a girl's voice?' Helen asked.

'Not to my hearin', no.'

'When you heard this shouting,' Cordon said, 'what did you do? Did you call back?'

Gibbens shook his head.

'Do anything?'

'No.'

'So why have you never mentioned this before?'

Gibbens looked at the floor, at his feet crammed into two left shoes. 'Didn't think it were important. Folk lose their way in fog, call out. Nothin' more'n that.'

'One of those folk,' Cordon said, his voice hardening, 'ended up unconscious in your bed. The other one turned up dead. I'd say that was important, wouldn't you?'

Gibbens looked at him then. 'Wouldn't have changed nothin', would it?'

'Wouldn't it?'

'She'd still be dead.'

'I'll ask you again, why didn't you tell us this before?'

Gibbens looked away again. 'Didn't want to get involved any more'n I was.'

'That all?'

'What else?'

'Feeling guilty, maybe?'

'What of?'

'I don't know. Keeping quiet. Not going to help sooner than you did. Thinking if you had, Heather Pierce might still be alive.'

All expression fell from Gibbens' face. 'Got one death on my conscience already. Don't need another.'

Helen looked across at Cordon, who shook his head.

'Kelly's father went out looking for her,' Cordon said, 'before calling us in. Her brother, too. You think it might have been them you heard, father and son?'

'Could well be.'

Cordon set down his cup, the tea barely touched. 'Francis, we'll be getting on. Thanks for your time. Thanks for the tea.'

Gibbens barely inclined his head, made no move to see them to the door. Outside, the sky was still as clear and blue as it had been before.

'His son,' Cordon said, 'he took his own life. Hanged himself.'

'Poor bastard.'

'Yes.'

'You think that's why he's shut himself away?'

'Reason enough, don't you think? Something like that happens – more you dwell on it, my guess, the more responsible you'd feel – shutting yourself off from the whole damned human race must seem a pretty good idea.'

He started to walk, striding out, and Helen fastened the zip of her anorak to stop it flapping around her and set off in his wake.

58

It was the fifth day after Beatrice Lawson's disappearance, the fifth morning, and less misty than the one before. No time for Will's morning run. From where he sat, in the first of two cars pulled over beside a strip of narrow road near the middle of Padnal Fen, he could see the light beginning to break over the lee of the eastern horizon, the contours of the land taking on slow definition. The former smallholding Simon Pierce had bought nine months before had stood vacant the best part of a year, its previous owner bowed down by growing debt and isolation, the grudging nature of the land. The squat, square house stood unsheltered from the wind, save for a break of stubborn trees to its northern side: the house and its few, huddled outbuildings the only habitation within sight. One of those, Will imagined, was sheltering the vehicle registered to him: a grey N reg. Toyota Corolla. For it to have been a green Corsa would have been too much to hope for. Officers were still checking through the list of Vauxhall Corsa owners in the county: green, a popular colour where that particular model was concerned.

As Will watched, a light came on at one of the upstairs windows, pale against the gathering sky. Ellie Chapin sat, tense, beside him; Jim Straley and two other officers in the car behind.

'Do you think she's there?' Ellie said, breaking the silence.

'I don't know,' Will said.

If Helen were here, he thought, she'd have the window wound down, smoking a last cigarette.

While the upstairs light still burned, another came on below.

'Let's find out,' he said.

The man who came to the door was wearing a T-shirt and jeans and rubbing the sleep from his eyes. His feet were bare. His hair, which he'd allowed to grow quite long, was tousled and uncombed. There was little flesh on his arms and what there was hung pale and loose. His face was sallow, his eyes dark and flickering, as if blinking himself properly awake.

Will identified himself and the two officers standing immediately to either side.

'Beatrice,' Pierce said flatly. 'That's why you're here.'

'Where is she?'

Pierce took a step back into the quarry-tiled hall. 'You'd best come in.'

Will's heart made a jump, as if Pierce were about to show them where she was.

They followed him into the big kitchen, Will and Ellie Chapin. Straley remained outside with the other officers who were already heading towards the outbuildings. On a blackened range at the furthest end of the room, a kettle was whistling softly, releasing steam.

'Where is she?' Will said again. 'Is she here?'

'Here?'

Will moved towards him and as he did so, Pierce began to laugh.

'Funny?' Will said angrily. 'You think this is funny?'

'It's you,' Pierce said. 'Imagining . . .' He wiped a hand across his mouth. 'You know, don't you, what happened to my daughter? My own little girl. You know what happened to her?'

Will nodded.

'You know how she died then. On her own. Terrified. In the dark.' He tugged at the sleeve of his T-shirt, scratched at the inside of his arm. 'She was frightened of the dark, did you know that? Did she tell you that? Ruth, her mother. Did she tell you our little girl was afraid of the dark?'

'Mr Pierce . . .'

'Yes?'

'Do you have any idea where Beatrice is?'

'Of course I don't!' It was a scream, the words torn from somewhere inside. 'Of-course-I-don't.' Each word separate, proclaimed.

He swayed a little, suddenly unsteady on his feet, and reached out to the table for support.

'D'you think that I – after what happened to Heather – the loss we suffered, still suffer – you think that I could take it into my head to harm . . .'

He turned aside, head down.

'Not necessarily,' Will said, 'to harm.'

'No, of course. Not harm. Help. Be kind. Kind to Ruth. Kind.' When he turned back, there were tears in his eyes. 'She never got over it, you know. Losing Heather. She says she did, but it's not true. I know. You don't get over something like that, do you? You can't.'

He looked at Ellie Chapin. 'Have you got children?'

She shook her head.

'Have you?'

'Yes,' Will said. 'Two.'

'Then you'll know.'

'*You got children?* Roberts' voice a hollow echo Will could not ignore.

'I've tried to help her,' Pierce said. 'I really have.'

'Her?'

'Ruth. Because I know – I'm the only one who does – I know how she's feeling.'

'And you've helped, tried to help?'

'Yes.'

'Exactly how?'

'Spread the word, of course. About Beatrice. These groups, on the Internet, here and abroad. Europe. Everywhere. Dedicated to helping parents, families, find missing children. Ever since that little girl in Portugal there've been scores of them, hundreds. You see . . .' His eyes, big eyes, were fixed on Will, almost imploringly. 'Whoever's taken her, Beatrice, by now she could be anywhere. You must have had sightings, I'm sure. Amsterdam. Greece. Turkey. People who've seen her, somebody like her.'

'And you do all this from here, communicating with these various groups? From here on your computer?'

'Yes, of course.'

'You what? Register her as missing?'

'Yes, well, not officially. I'm not supposed to do that, officially. That would have to be Ruth and I don't think . . . When I've mentioned it before, tried to get her interested . . . But now, well, perhaps she'll think differently. Or you, one of you, you could suggest . . .'

The words trailed off to silence.

Ellie Chapin lifted the kettle from the stove before it boiled dry.

'A photograph,' Will said, 'before you could post Beatrice as missing, even unofficially, you'd need a photograph.'

'Yes, I suppose . . .'

'But that's no problem for you, you've plenty of photographs. Dozens of them, filed away. On a memory stick somewhere, is that where they are? Good, too, not just snaps. I've seen them, a selection anyway. The ones you sent to her mother. It was you, wasn't it? "Isn't she lovely?" That's what you said. Your message. Anonymous. Secret. Why didn't you want her to know? Her mother? Why go to all the trouble to keep your identity secret? Was it because of how it would look? What people would think? Something strange, something not right? Abnormal? A grown man sneaking round taking pictures of his ex-wife's ten-year-old daughter?'

Pierce had backed away as far as the wall and now stood cowering, his arms wound round his head, eyes clenched shut.

'Where is she?' Will demanded. 'Tell me where she is. You know, don't you? You know.'

'No, no. I don't, I don't.'

Backing away, he fell sideways, catching his head on the edge of an open cupboard door, and lay there in an untidy, angular ball.

'Shall I help him up?' Ellie Chapin said.

'Let him be.'

Moments later, Jim Straley pushed open the kitchen door, holding a plastic evidence bag high in one hand: inside, crusted with dirt and torn at the sleeve and the neck, was a child's black and gold striped top.

59

When Ruth saw the top, she burst into tears. And then, as she listened to Anita Chandra explaining where it had been found, she slumped backwards into a chair, still crying, riven by incomprehension and despair.

Andrew went to put an arm around her but she pushed him away.

'It means she's dead, doesn't it?' Ruth said, sobbing, the words a blur. 'That's what it means.'

'No, no,' the liaison officer said. 'It doesn't have to mean that at all.'

'Don't lie. Don't lie to me.'

'It means we have every chance of finding her. Now more than before.'

'But Simon . . . ? That's where . . . ? I don't understand.'

'We don't know yet exactly what the circumstances were, the jumper being in his possession. On his property. We're talking to him now. As soon as there's anything definite, of course we'll let you know.'

'Perhaps,' Andrew said, 'you'd like to go and lie down. Just for a while. I'll bring you up some tea.'

Ruth nodded and, like a child, suddenly exhausted, allowed herself to be led away.

From the moment he had entered the police station, Simon Pierce had been different: calmer, controlled, at times almost obsequiously helpful – as if he were an active part of an ongoing investigation, instead of, for now, its focus.

Seated alongside Jim Straley in the back of the car, he had been quiet, only passing comment once or twice as they crossed the fen, once remarking on the level of water in the drainage ditch that ran into the Lark, once pointing out a brace of pheasants startled up from near the edge of a field as they passed. Otherwise, he sat silent, close to smiling.

'No,' had been his response, when asked if he would like time to contact a solicitor. 'I don't think that will be necessary, do you?'

Will didn't like, didn't trust, what was happening. Had all the histrionics before, the pathetic collapse, been an act, or was this now? It was almost as if this was what he had been waiting for, preparing, trying out his own lines. Another side of the same coin.

At Will's insistence, the duty solicitor was summoned: a greying, former newspaperman named Matthew Oliver, who had come late to the law, and existed in part, Will assumed, from selling titbits of information to his erstwhile colleagues. Oliver was cherry-faced, balding, what remained of his hair left to curl over the dandruff-scattered collars of his ageing suits. Appearances to the contrary, he was nobody's fool.

Before the interview, Will had spoken with Ellie Chapin. The top, they'd established, had been bought by Ruth and Beatrice at H&M in Cambridge on the same day they had met

Simon. Coincidence or something more? Beatrice had first noticed it missing almost two weeks later.

'I got the impression,' Ellie said, 'there's something about it the mother's not saying.'

'About the way it went missing or what?'

'I don't know.' She shook her head. 'I'm sorry, it's most likely nothing.'

'No. If you feel there's something there then probably there is.'

Ellie looked back at him gratefully.

'We'll talk to her again,' Will said.

Simon Pierce had pulled on a fraying cotton sweater over his T-shirt before leaving the house, a tweed jacket with patched sleeves and a pair of worn-down leather shoes; he was still wearing his jeans. He sat upright, expectant, waiting for it all to begin. His chair pulled slightly back, Matthew Oliver tapped the end of his biro against a spiral-bound reporter's notebook and counted the cracks in the ceiling, a new paint job that had settled badly.

With Jim Straley sitting alongside him, Will introduced those present for the sake of the tape and gave time and date.

The black and gold jumper lay, covered, on the desk between them.

'This garment, which has been confirmed as belonging to Beatrice Lawson, how did it come to be in your possession?'

'Was it in my possession?'

Will drew breath. Was that the way it was going to go?

'It was found on your property. Amongst rags and sacking and a few old clothes in an outbuilding that looked as if, until recently, it had been used as a henhouse.'

'They stopped laying,' Pierce said.

'What?'

'When I took the place on, the owner, the previous owner,

he said they'd give you several dozen eggs a week, no problem. But a fox took a couple, the best layers, and that was that. Can't fly, you see. Got wings, but can't fly. Helpless.'

If he's playing clever buggars, Will thought, I'll have him.

'What was the building used for more recently?' he asked calmly.

'Recently?' Pierce pushed out his bottom lip. 'Nothing special. Storing bits and pieces.'

'That's all?'

'That's all.'

'And can you explain how Beatrice Lawson's top came to be found there?'

Pierce shrugged.

'In words, please,' Will said. 'For the tape.'

'Of course,' Pierce said, abruptly smiling. 'For the tape, I just shrugged, indicating that I don't know.'

Will wanted to slap the smile off his face. Beside him, he could sense Jim Straley's hands being made into fists.

'Think again, Mr Pierce. How did this garment come to be found where it was?'

'I'm afraid I don't know.'

Will leaned forward. 'Right now, there's a Scene of Crime team going over not just that barn, but every inch of your property. What do you think they're going to find?'

Pierce shook his head. 'No comment.'

'I'm sorry?'

'No comment.'

'Your ex-wife's young daughter goes missing, she's been missing now for five days. Some of her clothing is found on your property and you've no comment?'

'I'm afraid not.' This time the smile was less certain, the voice less cocksure.

'It's within my client's rights . . .' Matthew Oliver began, finally stirring.

'I think your client's all too aware of his rights,' Will said. Then, abruptly. 'We'll take a break.'

'You can't,' Pierce said. 'We've only just started.'

But Will was already out of his seat and turning towards the door. A pace further and he swung back fast, leaning down towards Pierce in his chair. 'If you know where Beatrice Lawson is, for Christ's sake, tell me now.'

Pierce reared back, alarmed. 'I don't. I swear.'

Straightening, Will pointed a finger. 'If her life's in danger because you know something you're not saying – some stupid little game you're playing – you'll regret it every minute you live.'

The two officers stood outside in the corridor, anger still bright in Will's face.

'I thought you were going to smack him one,' Straley said. 'More to the point so did he.'

'We'll give them five minutes,' Will said, 'then go back in. There was no sign of a car out there, that's right, isn't it? This Toyota registered to him?'

Straley shook his head. 'Couple of old tyres in the tall barn. Oil on the floor.'

'Okay. We'll see what he has to say.'

'I'll get four teas, shall I? Take 'em back in?'

'Why not? Just make mine a coffee, okay?'

Pierce's Toyota Corolla, Pierce told them when the interview resumed, had been towed into the garage six days before, the day before Beatrice went missing: problems with the transmission. Vernon Lansdale's garage just the other side of Ely. Immediately, a nerve began vibrating at the side of Will's head. The same garage where, until recently, Mitchell Roberts had been working. Too much of a coincidence, surely, to be purely accidental?

'Why there?'

'Huh?'

'Why that garage? Why there?'

'I'd stopped there a couple of times before. Just for petrol, least that's what I'd thought, but the man, Vernon, he noticed one of my tyres was practically flat. Had it fixed for me straight away.'

'He didn't fix it himself?'

Pierce shook his head. 'Someone in the workshop.'

'Someone? Who?'

'I really don't know.'

'You talk to him at all? This man in the workshop?

'No, not really. Just, you know, what's wrong? How long will it take?'

'That was all?'

'Yes, of course that was all. What more was there to say?'

Will excuse himself and returned minutes later with a photograph of Mitchell Roberts.

'Is this the man?'

Pierce looked at it carefully. 'It might be.'

'Only might?'

'Yes. I said, all we did was exchange a few words. He got on and changed the tyre, I stood around outside, that's all it was. Why? Why's it so important?' He looked back down at the photo. 'Who is he, anyway?'

'You've not seen his picture? Recently?'

'No, where?'

'In the paper, on the news.'

Pierce smiled a wan little smile. 'I don't keep up, I'm afraid.'

Will slid the photograph from sight. 'Last Tuesday evening, between five-thirty and seven, where were you?'

'Tuesday?'

'Tuesday.'

'Home, had to be.'

'Had to?'

'The car went off to the garage around ten that morning.

Vernon came out with the truck and fetched it himself.' He gestured with his hands. 'No transport out there, you're snookered. Not that I mind. Always plenty to occupy my mind.'

I'll bet, Will thought. Half an hour later, he called another break. If Helen were there, he would have happily handed the questioning over to her like a captain switching his bowlers when a batsman becomes entrenched: change of angle, change of pace.

As it was, Jim Straley would have to step up.

'Take Ellie in with you,' Will said. 'Concentrate on the photographs. When he took them. Why. Why send them to the mother. I'm going to go and talk to her after I've checked out the garage. Meantime, let's hope Scene of Crime turn up something fast.'

60

Will stopped off at Lansdale's garage on the way into Ely. The youth who came out to greet him was seventeen or eighteen, straw-haired, wearing blue overalls a size too large, iPod headphones dangling from the top of the bib. Vernon, he said, never worked Sundays if he could avoid it. Well, nor did Will, but this was different.

At the sight of Will's warrant card, the youth gave over Vernon's mobile number, but there was no answer and Will left a message, asking Vernon to call him back as soon as possible.

'How long've you been working here?' Will asked.

'Sundays, must be best part of a year.'

'You know a man called Roberts used to work here till recently?'

'Mitch, is that?'

Will nodded.

'Seen him once or twice, not for a while. He quit, Vernon said. Said as how he might train me up, take his place, like.' The youth smiled hopefully.

'Still got a Toyota here, being worked on?'

'Corolla, N reg.' He nodded in the direction of the closed workshop. 'Still waiting on parts.'

Will took one of his cards from his wallet. 'Vernon comes back, calls in, whatever, just in case he hasn't got my message, get him to call me. Okay? It's important.'

'Right, right.' As Will turned back towards his car, he slipped his earpieces back into place, nothing more to do than watch him go.

Ruth had been thinking about Simon off and on all of that day, thinking about him seriously for perhaps the first time since their divorce. When it had become clear, in the wake of Heather's death, that their relationship was not going to survive – that what had happened had only served to accentuate the differences that had been growing between them for some time – her assumption had been that it would be Simon who would move on most easily; Simon who would find a new partner, remarry, perhaps even have another child.

When she had met him in London and told him of her relationship with Andrew, the fact that she was the one going to marry again, he had taken it almost with aplomb. Congratulations. A smile. Slightly sardonic, perhaps, but a smile nevertheless. And then, more or less nothing. He had slipped out of her life and she had let him. Moving to Ely as she had done, she had chosen to sever almost all ties with her old life. She supposed that was what happened, especially after something as traumatic as the death of a child. The more you were together, the more you remembered.

Even the Effords' marriage had not survived. There had been a letter from Alan that had somehow found her, forwarded from address to address; he was living in a two-room flat in north London, near the Archway, and seeing the children at weekends. The tone of his letter was regretful, almost desperate. Why don't we meet up? It would be good to see you again. She hadn't replied.

When the doorbell went now she paid it little attention; either Andrew or Anita would answer it, assuming Anita was still around.

A few moments later, Andrew opened the door to the living room and ushered Will inside. 'The Detective Inspector wants to ask us some more questions.'

Ruth smoothed down her skirt and waited while Andrew sat beside her, a hand on her shoulder.

Will sat opposite.

'Is it about Simon?' she asked.

'Not directly, no. I just wanted to ask you again about the top that we found. You said it went missing, I think, seven days after the photographs appeared on your computer?'

'Yes, as far as I can remember.'

'And your assumption was what? That it had been lost somewhere?'

'Yes, I suppose so. I mean, we searched, Beatrice and I. You have to realise, this wasn't the first time something like this had happened. Clothes put away in the wrong place, stuffed down for some reason beneath the mattress, not put away at all. When it still didn't turn up, I imagined it had been left at school.'

'She wore it to school?'

'Sometimes. There is a uniform, but it's fairly basic, and on Fridays, within reason, they can wear what they choose. I told Beatrice to check in lost property, make sure no one had taken it by mistake. She'd been for a sleepover at her friend Sasha's just a few nights before and I rang Sasha's mother to check she hadn't left it there. There was nothing. It seemed to have just disappeared.'

'You never thought it had been stolen?'

'No, not really, only . . .' She shook her head.

'Yes?'

'It doesn't matter, it's nothing.'

'Please. Whatever you were going to say, it might be important.'

Ruth looked away. There were goose bumps on her arms. 'Andrew, I'm sorry, but perhaps I could talk to the Detective Inspector alone?'

'I don't see why. I mean, surely there's no need . . .'

'Andrew, please.'

'All right, if that's what you want.' He looked back at her from the door, a long look of disappointment and gathering mistrust, then closed it quietly at his back.

Alone with Will, Ruth hesitated, uncertain how to begin.

'It was the evening I spoke about,' she said eventually. 'When Beatrice was at Sasha's. Andrew was out, too, some meeting, so I was all alone in the house. That wouldn't usually bother me, in fact sometimes I quite welcome it, the chance to be on my own – but this particular evening, I don't know why, I was feeling edgy, nervous almost. Worried about Beatrice, probably, not that there was any need. I mean, she was fine. I'd phoned to check. Happy to be where she was. But then I heard this noise. Upstairs, at least that's where I thought it was coming from. Upstairs in Beatrice's room.'

'What kind of a noise?'

'A footstep, that's what it sounded like. Someone walking. And then a door, a door closing. I went up and there was nothing, just a window that had been left open, banging, but somehow I couldn't shake the feeling that somebody else had been there, in the house.'

'You mean, broken in?'

'Yes, I suppose so.'

'And it couldn't have been Andrew? Come home early without saying?'

'No, not at all. He didn't come back for quite a while afterwards.'

'He didn't know about it then?'

Ruth shook her head.

'Why didn't you want him in the room when you told me?'

'It's not that simple.' She pressed the palms of her hands together. 'Not easy to explain.'

'That's okay. Take your time.'

'It's Heather.'

'Your other daughter? The one who died?'

'Yes.'

'What about her?'

'Sometimes she . . . she comes to see me. She . . . I don't know how to say it . . . she just appears. And we talk.'

'And that's what happened that evening?'

'Yes.'

'And you think that might have been what you heard? Heather?'

'Yes.'

'Upstairs in Beatrice's room?'

'Yes.'

'But you're not sure that's what it was? The sound you heard?'

'No, you see, whenever I've seen her before, she just, well, like I said, she appears. There isn't any sound. It's just suddenly she's there.'

'And then what happens?'

'We talk. Usually we talk. Sometimes we hold hands. And then, after a little while, she goes.' Ruth pressed her hands against her face. 'You think I'm crazy, don't you? Making all this up. Another middle-aged neurotic woman.'

'No, I don't think that at all.'

'But you don't believe me.'

'That doesn't matter. What I believe.'

'Andrew would tut-tut and tell me I've been under a strain and I should go back to the therapist. Get some more help. Get it all washed out of my system.' She pushed her fingers up through her hair. 'I don't want her out of my system. I've lost her once and I don't want to lose her again. Especially not now.'

Looking back at Ruth, Will realised he had no idea how to respond or what to say.

61

By the time Will returned to the police station where Simon Pierce was being held, the first thorough search of the house and outbuildings at Padnal Fen was still continuing, without any further sign of the missing girl so far being found. Samples of what might be human blood, taken from the former henhouse, had been sent to the lab, but more in hope than expectation.

No longer a game, if that's what it had been, Simon Pierce had gradually confessed to having followed Beatrice over a period of several months, sometimes taking photographs, sometimes merely watching from a distance. At no time, he said, had he attempted to speak to her; at no point had he made any direct contact whatsoever. The facade of confidence he had sat behind when the first interview began was starting to crack, but, to Will's regret, there was still nothing that made his connection with Mitchell Roberts any more than tauntingly coincidental.

An examination of the two memory sticks found with his computer revealed several hundred images of Beatrice, all apparently taken without her knowledge. There were more on the hard drive, some repeated, some different. It was a small selection of these that he had sent to Ruth.

'Why try and disguise where they'd come from?' Straley had asked. 'Why not make it clear they were from you?'

'I didn't think she'd like that.'

'The photos or the fact that you'd sent them?'

'That I'd sent them.'

'Why was that?'

'I don't know. The time I met them, her and Beatrice, in Cambridge, she didn't seem very happy to see me, that's all.'

'Why do you think that was?'

'I don't know.'

'And Beatrice? Was she happy to see you?'

'She didn't know me.'

'She didn't recognise you?'

'How could she? She didn't know who I was.'

'Until then.'

'That's right.'

'Surely she must have seen you following her around?'

'I wasn't following her around, not in the way you make it sound.'

'What way's that?'

'You make it sound nasty, unpleasant.'

'It wasn't?'

'No.'

'Spending all that time trailing after a young girl, barely ten years old?' Straley could scarcely keep the disgust from spilling out of his voice.

'Stop it,' Pierce said. 'Stop it. That's not what it was like at all.'

'No?'

'That's your mind, not mine.'

'Tell me what it was like then. Make me understand.'

Pierce took one long, shallow breath and then another. 'I just wanted . . . I just wanted to get to know her. What she was like. There's no harm in that. No harm at all.'

'Where is she now?' Straley asked.

'I don't know. Don't you think I'd tell you if I did?'

Not surprisingly, the media had got hold of the fact that the police were holding somebody and they were clamouring for details; Will had agreed to a press conference being scheduled for later in the day, but without any intention of giving up Pierce's identity. Once that became public, and his former relationship with the missing girl's mother became known, speculation would be rife and the pressure on Pierce himself intense. So much sound and fury serving only to disguise the truth.

Right now, Pierce having his regulatory meal break, sitting opposite his solicitor, toying with sausage and chips. Jim Straley and Ellie Chapin were in Will's office, drinking coffee; that is, Jim and Will were drinking coffee, Ellie was drinking from a flask of ginger tea she brought in each day from home.

'Ellie,' Will said, 'see what you can find out about these Internet groups Pierce is involved in. Fathers without children, that kind of thing. Talk to Liam Noble, he might know something. Either that or point you in the direction of someone who does. Okay? Jim, you come back in with me.'

On the way to the interview room, Will took Matthew Oliver off to one side. 'If your client's name gets out before we release it officially, I'll know who to come looking for. Understood?'

'Me?' Oliver said, widening his eyes. 'As if.'

Simon Pierce sat apprehensively now that Will was back conducting the interview himself; there was a splodge of something that might be have been ketchup on the front of his cotton sweater.

'Can you imagine what it'd be like,' Will said, starting speaking almost before he had sat down, 'if we allowed your name and what we're holding you for to get beyond this room? An article of clothing belonging to the missing girl was found hidden on your property, right out in the back of beyond. You know what crowds are like, you've seen them on TV, all that righteous anger. You'd be lucky to get out of here in one piece.'

Pierce's eyes were shut tight.

'Threats, Detective Inspector?' Oliver said. 'Intimidation?'

'Simply wanting your client to appreciate the facts.'

'My task, I believe.'

'Then do it. While there's time.'

Oliver sighed. 'Perhaps my client and I might be allowed five minutes to talk?'

'You've just had forty, for God's sake.'

'Then what's five more?'

'Use them wisely.' Will pushed back his chair.

Outside, they walked to the end of the corridor, down on to the lower landing and looked out at the traffic making its slow way along Parkside and turning off towards the Newmarket Road. On the piece of open ground opposite, the trees had now lost most of their leaves.

'Think he'll come clean?' Straley asked.

'I think it's time he did.'

Back in the room, Pierce kept his eyes firmly fixed on the floor and it was Matthew Oliver who spoke first.

'My client regrets that due to the emotional state he has been in following the disappearance of his former partner's daughter, he has not been able to provide you with all the facts you require. He hopes that once these are made known and the situation resolved, he will be able to put this whole unfortunate episode behind him and you and your colleagues will be able to devote all of your attentions to where they are most needed, recovering this poor missing girl.'

Oliver leaned back and Will didn't know whether he was supposed to applaud. 'Nice speech, Matthew. And mostly without notes. Now can we get down to it?'

Pierce started talking without looking up. 'It was a Saturday. Saturday morning. Beatrice had gone into Ely with her friend, Sasha, and her mother. I think that's what her name was. Sasha. They did some shopping, bits and pieces in the market, then they went to the bookshop and after that they went on to the café near the cathedral and sat outside. It was a nice day.'

He was looking at Will now, rather at a space between where Will and Jim Straley were sitting, his voice low, low key, as if telling something that had happened to somebody else.

'They stayed there for quite a while. The girls had hot chocolate with lots of whipped cream. And there was a dog, someone at the next table had a dog. Silly little dog, barking and yapping, tied up, and they loved it. Both girls loved it. Patting and stroking and laughing when it got wound up in its own lead. Finally the mum had had enough. "Come on," she said. "We're going." And she hurried them off.

'That was when Beatrice forgot her jumper, top, whatever you call it. She'd taken it off and put it on the back of her chair. I waited to see if they were going to come back for it and when they didn't I just went over and picked it up. I'm not even sure what for. I suppose I thought I might send it back in the post with a little note or even take it round. Give it to her the next time I saw her out with her friend. But I didn't. Didn't do any of those things. I kept it.'

He focused on Will now, on Will directly, and his eyes were luminous and large.

'It's pathetic, isn't it? That's what you think. Pathetic and perhaps a little sad. But that's all it is. You read about it, there are instances, lots of them, it's common. People in my situation.

Who've lost children. Transference, that's what it's called. They transfer their feelings on to someone else. And with me, I suppose it was Beatrice.'

'Tell me about the jumper,' Will said.

'Can I have a drink of something? Some water?'

'Once you've told me.'

The solicitor moved as if to intervene and a quick look from Will settled him back down.

'All right,' Pierce said, blinking. 'When I . . . when it became obvious I wasn't going to send it back – it had been too long – I thought, I'll burn it, but then I couldn't do that, so I just bundled it up with a lot of other old things, stuffed it into the corner of the henhouse and forgot about it.'

'You forgot?'

'Yes. More or less, yes.'

'But when you read about Beatrice going missing, saw it on the television, whatever, surely you realised the police would come out here, wanting to talk to you and that it might get found?'

'No, why should I? It's not as if I'm involved.'

'You sent those pictures. You involved yourself.'

'I got someone to send them for me.'

'At your instigation.'

'Yes.'

'Who is this person?'

'A friend.'

'A friend you met through the Internet?'

'Yes.'

'And his name?'

'I don't know. His real name, I mean. He calls himself Don, but that's not his real name, almost certainly not. Privacy, you see, the beauty of sites like that, you can say what you really feel without anyone knowing who you are.'

'So where does he live? This Don?'

'I don't know. It could be anywhere. Another country. Just down the road.'

Will pushed a pad of paper and a pen towards him. 'The details, write them down.'

'They're on my computer, all of them.'

'Write them down.'

Pierce looked round at his solicitor, who nodded, and began to write.

Will and Matthew Oliver were standing outside, on the edge of the car park at the rear of the building, Oliver smoking a cigarette. A faint rain had started to fall and was misting over the roofs of the cars.

'You'll release my client. Now that he's been fully cooperative.'

'On the contrary, I shall be seeking authorisation to hold him for a further twelve hours.'

'On what grounds?'

'That I have reason to believe he has either had some involvement in Beatrice Lawson's disappearance or has some knowledge of who was.'

'It doesn't hold up. Doesn't wash.'

'Doesn't it? By his own admission, he stalked her for weeks. Months. Surreptitiously took pictures. Stole an article of her clothing. And you expect us to believe it was just some innocent bit of – what did he call it? – transference? Something he's got over and put behind him? Come on, Matthew, you know better than that. And now let's get in out of this rain.'

Due to a multiple pile-up on the nearby A46 between Cambridge and Newmarket – two families, including small children, having to be cut free from their cars, and one virtual decapitation – the press conference was less well attended than of late. If there were no positive new developments soon, this was how it would be: the story relegated to the bottom of page five, a brief item on the television news, squeezed between the comic human interest and the sport.

Will made his announcement as concisely as possible and waited for questions.

Since the police had seen fit to request an extra period of time for questioning, did that mean charges were imminent?

No, it did not.

Surely it was in the public interest to release the name of the man they were holding?

No, it was not.

Did the fact that they had a suspect in relation to young Beatrice's disappearance mean that they were no longer looking for Mitchell Roberts with the same urgency?

Absolutely not. While he remained at large, Roberts still posed a serious threat to the community.

But there's no indication that he is involved in the disappearance of Beatrice Lawson?

Not as yet.

Will was briskly to his feet, the press officer alongside him raising her hands to make clear that the conference was over.

62

Helen watched Will's press conference on the small set in her hotel room, the indoor aerial reducing him to a barely recognisable blur. She had spoken to him twice during the course of the day: once to get the name of his contact at Forensic Science Services in Birmingham, the second time for a more detailed update of the investigation into Beatrice Lawson's disappearance than she would get from the television news. The initial euphoria the team must have felt when the article of Beatrice's clothing was found seemed to have quickly dissipated; had she been wearing the garment at the time she went missing, were there any evidence to suggest she had it with her that evening, the discovery would be more important than it had at first seemed. On balance, however, Simon Pierce's version of how the top came to be in his possession was the most likely. A somewhat sad, she supposed, confused man's souvenir.

Try as he might, and tantalising as it was, Will had failed to make any more of the chance meeting between Pierce and Mitchell Roberts, and although they were continuing to question him and check his contacts, Helen knew that, unless some new piece of evidence were found, at the end of the thirty-six hours Pierce would be released.

She poured herself a small measure of Scotch and diluted it well with water. She'd agreed to meet Cordon for a drink later – a drink and maybe something to eat – and she didn't want to get started too early. The bulk of the day they'd spent, the pair of them, first assembling a case for sending Heather Pierce's clothing off to Birmingham, then arguing it with Cordon's superiors. Only when that had been grudgingly agreed did Helen pursue the name Will had given her of the woman he knew at FSS.

Initially, it had been like chipping away at granite: surely she understood . . . like to help but . . . adherence to policy . . . dangerous precedent. In the end, Helen had begged Will to find the time and call her himself. What their relationship had been, she didn't know, except that it went back some time; and if he had made it work for him once before, maybe he could do so again.

'Okay,' Will said, when he rang Helen back to report. 'She says she'll do what she can.'

'That's it?'

'If she can find a way of slipping it up the list, she will.'

'Which means what, in terms of time?'

'Way things are now, weeks instead of months. Two, three weeks at the very best. She can't promise any more than that.'

'Christ, Will, what did you do? Lead her on and then not follow through?'

Recalling the conversation, Helen laughed again and headed for the shower.

They went to a pub down by the harbour, locals for the most part, mixed with a sprinkling of visitors, Cordon stopping to speak to several people at the bar before carrying their drinks across. Tribute ale in tall glasses. Pints.

'Is there anywhere people don't know who you are?'

'This town? Likely not.'

'Is that why you live somewhere else?'

'Newlyn? Stretch a leg, you kick someone else's backside. No place to hide there.'

'Doesn't that get to you?'

'Used to it, I suppose.'

'Must make your job more difficult.'

'Sometimes it does. Sometimes the opposite. People get to know who they can trust.'

'And they trust you?'

'Some do.'

Helen took a long drink from her glass. 'I'd hate it, all this small-town stuff, everyone knowing your business, knowing who you are. Cambridge is just big enough, most times you can stay under the radar.'

'Misbehave in private.'

'If you like.'

A man in a dark blue roll-neck sweater and blue trousers – fisherman's wear, to Helen's mind – came over and, with a nod in her direction, leaned towards Cordon and began a hushed conversation from which she heard no more than the odd word.

Cordon sat giving the man his full attention, his face in profile from where Helen was sitting, angular cheekbones in a lean face, brown eyes flecked with – what was it? – green; a nose that had been broken, at least once she thought, when he was younger.

What was he now? Early fifties? Thirty years in, he could have retired. And done what?

The man who'd been talking squeezed Cordon's shoulder and walked off, back to the bar.

'What was all that about?' Helen asked.

A smile came slow to Cordon's face. 'The price of fish.'

She didn't know whether to believe him or not. Probably not.

Somewhat to Helen's consternation, Cordon suggested an Indian restaurant a short walk away from where they were, along a narrow side street leading off the promenade. But the interior was happily devoid of flock wallpaper, the service attentive without being smarmy, and the food – well, the food was far better than she had anticipated, the tandoori king prawns in particular. The wine list even offered up a more than decent Côtes du Rhône that didn't cost the earth.

'So,' Cordon said, tearing off a piece of naan bread and using it to mop up some of the pepper and coriander sauce from his plate. 'Do you think you'll bother to go and see Alan Efford or not?'

They had discussed this earlier, the possibility of Helen changing her ticket and breaking her journey in London, taking the opportunity to talk to Efford about the events, as he remembered them, of thirteen years before.

'I think I might.'

'He's not going to tell you anything much you don't know now you've read through the transcripts.'

'Probably not.'

She poured a little more wine into both their glasses; no point in leaving it to be thrown away.

'I never got the impression,' Helen said, 'that you fancied him for it.'

'Efford? No, not really. We considered him, of course – bound to have done. But aside from anything else, when it came to opportunity there wasn't a great deal.'

'According to what Gibbens had to say, there was at least one person in the area where the girls went missing. He heard them shouting.'

'I know. Efford admits to being there, going out along the

405

path when it was first clear what had happened. That the lad had come back without them.'

'How did he feel about that?'

'Lee? Like a dog wandering round with his head down and his tail between his legs. Guilty as buggery, and no mistake. Leaving them out there on their own the way he did.'

Cordon said yes to banana fritters and ice cream and Helen abstained.

'You want a brandy or anything?' he asked.

'God, no!'

Back outside, the air struck cold but clean and an almost perfect half-moon sat high above the bay. There were couples sitting huddled together on the benches spaced out the length of the promenade; further along, a man in silhouette, the glow of his cigarette small and bright, stood careful guard over a pair of fishing lines cast out to sea.

'Come on,' Cordon said. 'It's a fine night. Let's walk.'

'Where to?'

A few hundred metres on, the path dropped down to run close along the shoreline, virtually the only sound now the soft rattle of pebbles as they rolled rhythmically back, released by the incoming tide. The lights of Newlyn curved ahead, rising up, one above the other, to the point where land and sky invisibly met.

Helen paused to light a cigarette.

When she offered one to Cordon, he shook his head. 'Not far now,' he said.

The pub was long and low and close to the sea wall, plenty of cars parked outside, an orange glow from the windows, music tipping out.

'You do like a bit of jazz?' Cordon said.

'Not especially.'

'You'll like this.'

She followed him through the door. At the far end of the

narrow room, two musicians were just visible through a crowd of people, guitar and saxophone, the number they were playing winding to an end. As it finished, a couple sitting near the side wall got up to leave and Cordon commandeered their seats.

'What would you like?' he asked, nodding towards the bar.

'I'll get these. What'll you have?'

'Another pint'd be fine.'

Helen ordered that and, after a moment's thought, a large whisky for herself. In for a penny . . .

The duo were playing a ballad now, one of those old songs that had been around forever, the tone of the saxophone sinuous and warm.

'Your local?' Helen asked, looking round.

'More or less.'

There'd been the usual nods in his direction as they moved through the room, the occasional hand raised in greeting.

'The landlord,' Cordon said, 'that's him playing the guitar. Feller with him, the sax, comes down from London. Regular. Good, don't you think?'

Helen didn't have a clue. She didn't even know what kind of saxophone it was. Tenor? Alto? Still, she supposed it was pleasant enough.

'Last time he played here,' Cordon said, 'I was with my son. Over from Australia.'

'That's where he lives?'

'Lives now. Been all over. His mother and I split up before he went to university and he's been pretty much on the move ever since. South America, southern Africa, now Down Under. All a bloody long way away.'

When she asked him more, he replied haltingly, switching the subject as soon as he could, asking her about Will and what he was like to work with.

That tune finished and another started.

Cordon's turn to go to the bar.

After the last number, the landlord came over and lightly punched Cordon's shoulder, shook Helen's hand.

'Something wrong here,' the landlord said with a wink. 'Too good-looking for him by half.'

While Cordon stopped for a brief word with the sax player, Helen stepped outside for a cigarette. When she looked up, the sky was brimmed with stars.

'There's usually a taxi just over the bridge,' Cordon said, emerging. 'Get you back to the hotel.' The light from the pub doorway favoured the contours of his face.

'How about some coffee first,' Helen said. 'You think you could manage that?'

The dog met them at the door, tail wagging energetically as it raised its head towards Cordon's hand.

'Let me just put the coffee on,' he said, 'then I'll walk her round the block.'

'Show me where it is,' Helen said. 'I'm sure I can manage.'

She looked around the interior while he was gone: CDs alongside the stereo, alphabetically arranged; a small stack of paperback books on the floor beside one of the chairs; a pile of clothes, folded at the end of the neatly made bed; a few framed photographs on the wall. A single plate and bowl left on the drainer to dry. What the hell am I doing? Helen asked herself. The coffee was just starting to bubble as Cordon and the dog returned.

'You're pretty tidy for a man living alone.'

'Place this small, hard not to be.' He ran fresh water into the dog's bowl.

'How d'you like it? Being on your own?'

'You get used to it. You want milk in this?'

'Uh-uh.'

'Sugar?'

'One.'

'How about you? You living with someone?'

'Not so that I've noticed.'

'How come?'

'Last time I tried it was a fiasco. Six months with me and he buggered off to Canada. Joined the Mounted Police.' She laughed. 'We make a pair, you and me, anyone who gets too close ends up fleeing to the ends of the earth.'

With some little difficulty, Cordon hoicked the dog off the settee so they could both sit down.

'You're seeing someone, though,' he said.

'Am I?'

'I imagine.'

Helen grinned. 'Another bloody disaster! Men, the ones available, the ones you might fancy, they're either gay or they're married and looking for a bit on the side.'

'Like your DI?'

'Will?'

'The way you were talking about him before, I thought . . .'

'Will's so married it runs through him like a stick of rock. Shame, sometimes, but there it is. Besides, screwing around on the job . . . Disaster, like I said.'

Cordon smiled. 'There was this woman officer, she's moved on now. Dyer. Ann Dyer. Young but ambitious. Confident. It was obvious she'd be going places. Anyway, she said . . . a number of times, she said, after work, when we were clocking off like, come for a drink, why don't you? And I'd find some excuse. Not sure why, but I did. But she kept on asking, so finally I said yes and it seemed fine, we got on pretty well, and as we were leaving I asked her, did she, you know, want to come back, back here, and she laughed. Laughed in my face. "A drink, sunshine," she said, "just means a bloody drink."'

'And that's supposed to make me feel sorry for you, I suppose?'

'Not at all.'

Leaning across, she kissed him on the mouth.

'What's that for?' he asked, surprised.

'Don't worry, I don't do sympathy. I wanted to do that outside the pub, but I didn't want to embarrass you in front of your friends.'

He grinned. 'I wish you had, I could've lived off it for months.'

'Tell them about this.' She kissed him harder this time, kissing till he kissed her back. Her arms going round him, his around her until they slid awkwardly sideways and he had to stretch a hand down to the floor to stop one or other of them tumbling off the settee altogether.

A few moments later, he eased himself away.

'What's the matter?'

'I don't know. I . . .'

'Look, I just want a nice, uncomplicated fuck, okay?

The hesitation was only slight. 'Okay.'

The dog padded away to the far end of the room and lay down facing the other way.

63

They were at the station early, the train already at the platform, Helen was standing just outside the entrance and having
what would be her last cigarette before arriving in London
and sipping from a cup of coffee from the station buffet. Cordon
had been awake before her, up and out with the dog and back
again before she'd made it to the shower; coffee then and toast
and some music on the stereo she'd asked him to turn down
or off and he'd opted for the latter.

'Force of habit. Either that or the bloody news and most
days that's too depressing to want to listen to.'

She was looking at one of the photographs: a young man
with sun-bleached hair, stripped to the waist, holding a surfboard high above his head and grinning at the camera.

'Your son?'

'Yes.'

'Not bad-looking. His mother's genes, obviously.'

'Fuck off.'

'You ever been out to see him?'

Cordon shook his head.

'Perhaps you should.'

The dog had come with them in the car and now mooched around the platform end, occasionally breaking away to chase seagulls from the station entrance.

'I'd better go,' Helen said, dropping the end of her cigarette down into the cup and closing it with the lid.

Cordon took it from her and dumped it in the nearby bin. 'If you get anything out of Efford . . .'

'I'll let you know.'

'Otherwise . . .'

'As soon as the results come in from FSS, you'll be in touch?'

'First thing.'

Taking hold of his arm, she kissed him quickly on the cheek. 'Close cooperation between forces, something to be encouraged.'

'So they say.'

Midway down the platform, she turned to wave but Cordon and the dog had already gone.

Archway was a part of north London Helen didn't know. Small shops and workmen's cafés and youths in hoodies hanging round on corners, stirring themselves occasionally to spit on the pavement or readjust a low-slung crotch. Wan-faced men with ratty dogs sat close to ATM machines, begging. Four lanes of choked traffic going nowhere fast. Just a short way up the hill beyond the tube station entrance, Dick Whittington had heard Bow Bells summoning him back to become Lord Mayor of London: if he'd seen this lot, Helen thought, he'd have kept on going.

Alan Efford's flat was on the top floor above a kebab shop, the smell of slow-cooked slabs of meat and chilli sauce following Helen up the stairs.

The contrast to how Cordon lived couldn't have been greater. Cardboard food boxes from KFC and McDonald's in the corner beside the sink, empty cans of Carling Black Label and Magners cider, a plate with the remnants of the previous night's ready-cooked meal still on the table. Clothes, unironed and possibly unwashed, hung from the backs of chairs; others were still stuffed down into the bag from the launderette. Perched on top of the microwave, a small television was tuned to the horse racing, the commentary a low litany of runners and riders.

Helen did well not to wince away from the smell of stale air and hopelessness as Efford stepped back from the doorway to allow her in.

He was unshaven, hair akimbo, most probably, she thought, not long out of bed. What had once been a good denim shirt was now stained and coming adrift at one of the seams.

'Thanks for agreeing to see me,' Helen said.

Efford shrugged. 'When you rang me, out of the blue like that, I thought maybe you'd found out something new. You or what's that other copper called? Cordon? Something about what happened to Kelly's pal. But it's not that, is it?'

'Not exactly, no.'

'Yeah? What is it then?'

'You said we might have discovered something new – you don't think it was an accident, then?'

'Yeah, I do. I mean, you know, what else? But that Cordon, he wasn't havin' it, was he? An' you keep seeing it, don't you? Nowadays. On the telly. That programme – what is it? – *New Tricks*? *Old Tricks*? – one of those. Where these old geezers start rootin' around these old cases. Cold cases, that what they're called?'

Helen nodded.

'That what this is, then?'

'Sort of, yes.'

He looked at her for a moment, as if making up his mind. 'Look, you want to talk that's fine, but not here. Don't mind taking your life in your hands, there's this caff over on that sort of island by the pub. Quiet and they don't care how long you sit. Tea don't taste like piss, neither. I'll meet you there. Ten minutes. Okay?'

'Why can't we go together?'

Efford grinned and raised an arm, sniffing the air. 'I stink, right? Stink an' I look like shit.'

'That doesn't matter.'

'Does to me. Woman like you. Fit. Don't want be seen having breakfast with a dog like me.'

'It's already afternoon.'

'Still breakfast time. An' don't worry. I ain't gonna do a runner. Ten minutes, right?'

It was twenty and Helen was beginning to look at her watch anxiously when Efford finally walked in. The café itself was not quite what she'd expected, more like one of those little faded hippy places you found in the back streets of Cambridge, piss-poor paintings on the walls and students pecking at their laptops and sipping long-cold cups of cappuccino.

Lunch over, most of the mosaic tables were empty and Helen had chosen to sit near the window with the latte she'd ordered. A quick call to Will on her mobile was diverted, so she left a message, arranging, hopefully, to meet him later, if not first thing next morning.

When Alan Efford did arrive, grinning as he pushed open the door, there'd been something of a transformation. Newly shaved, hair gelled into place, he was wearing black cords and a white shirt, creased but clean, and Helen could see in his day he'd been a handsome man. Still was.

God, she thought, don't tell me I'm getting a thing for older men.

'Want another?' Efford asked, nodding towards her mug.

'Thanks, I'm fine. But you get what you want, I'll pay.'

He took her at her word. Scrambled eggs, bacon, tomatoes, mushrooms, toast. And tea.

Helen let him eat.

When the plate was half empty, she said, 'You heard about Ruth?'

'Heather's mum? No, what about her?'

'It was in all the papers, all over the TV. Her daughter from her second marriage, she disappeared. Almost a week ago. I'm amazed you didn't know.'

Astonishment was clear and unfeigned on Efford's face. 'I saw something, about a kid going missing. I never . . .' He pushed his plate aside. 'Poor Ruth! That woman . . . You can't imagine . . .' He shook his head. 'I liked her. She was all right. A bit stuck up, of course. Didn't ever really approve of her Heather pallin' round with our Kelly. Never said, like, but you could tell. When it happened, it all come out. Not from her, but her old man. Simon? What a prick! Ain't got a degree an' a public school fuckin' education, in his book you ain't worth the time of day.' Efford drank some tea. 'He was right, of course, in his way. Not about all of that education malarkey, but right about it bein' my fault what happened.'

'You think so? Really?'

'Never should've let 'em go. Never should've trusted that son of mine to look after 'em. Which he should have done a sight better'n he did. Even so, my responsibility, not his. Should've been me gone out there with 'em or not at all.'

'You went out after, though. As soon as you realised what had happened.'

'Fat lot of good that did. Couldn't see a bleedin' thing.'

'The man who found Kelly later on, he heard you shouting.'

'Good on him. 'Cause they didn't, the girls. Like hollerin' into some blanket. Voice got swallowed up till you couldn't hear a bloody thing.'

'He said he heard two voices. Least he thought he did.'

'That'd be Lee then. He went out after me. Stayed till the police come, more or less.'

'He didn't see anything?'

'Fog was still thick as pig shit, wasn't it? Didn't start to clear for ages.'

Helen took a sip from what remained of her coffee, now lukewarm at best. 'There's nothing about the whole business you've thought of since? Something you might not have mentioned at the time?'

'Such as?'

A quick smile crossed Helen's face. 'I don't know.'

''Fraid not.'

'Eat up,' she said. 'Shame to let it go to waste.'

'Don't seem right,' Efford said, when he'd finished. 'Not being able to light up after a meal. Makes you feel like a bleedin' criminal.'

They went and stood outside, Efford bumming one of her cigarettes. The traffic, red buses prominent, was still making its gradual way around the patch of some dozen or so buildings on which they were marooned.

'Lee,' Helen said, 'you see much of him?'

'Now and then. Works not far from here. Paint shop down Holloway Road. Just serving, you know? Mixin' the colours when it's called for. Stuff like that.' He shrugged. 'It's a job.'

'And Kelly?'

'Married, i'n't she? Couple of kids already. Two different fathers, but that's the way it goes. Got a flat over by Camden. Any luck, this one might stick around. The dad. Not short a bob or two, either. Where he gets it, mind . . .'

'You think she'd talk to me?'

'She might. Yeah, she might. I could give her a bell.'

'Okay, thanks. And Lee?'

'I don't know. With him I'd be less certain. I said something

416

about it once, I remember, an' he shut me right off. Didn't want to know.'

'Still feeling guilty.'

'I s'pose so. Not that he should.'

'You'll phone Kelly?'

'I'll do it now.'

'I need to get back this evening, but I could talk to her tomorrow. Any time after around ten, ten-thirty.'

Efford already had his mobile in his hand.

Back in Cambridgeshire, Lorraine had collected Jake early from school, taking time off herself so as to take him to the dentist, early afternoon the only appointment she'd been able to get. Together then, they'd picked up Susie from nursery and walked her home, Jake kicking pebbles along the road, shouting every time he scored a make-believe goal.

Indoors, Lorraine settled him down in front of CBeebies and changed Susie before getting the pair of them something to drink and making up a snack plate they could share: grapes, pieces of cucumber, slices of carrot, some segments of a tangerine.

It was while she was doing this that she first saw the man in the field. Just standing there, hands in pockets, looking up towards the house, towards the window. When she looked again, he had gone.

64

That same morning that Helen was travelling up from Cornwall, Ellie Chapin, after consulting the Child Exploitation and Online Protection Centre the day before, made her preliminary report about the Internet sites Simon Pierce had been accessing. The majority, it seemed, were legitimate, either spreading the word about missing children across the World Wide Web, or offering help and support to parents whose children had either died or gone missing. But there were others, around the fringes, whose activities were more suspect. Instances, as yet anecdotal rather than proven, of sex offenders infiltrating groups, either to obtain images or gain information they might conceivably use for their own ends.

The site on which Pierce had met the go-between who'd sent the pictures of Beatrice to her mother, was called *Little Angels*, presumably after the term many parents used to describe their lost or missing children.

As far as Ellie had been able to discover, the site made available a host of images of young children, mostly, but not exclusively, girls, in addition to stories, some quite salacious and all purporting to be true, about what had befallen children who had either run away from home or been taken.

Attempts, through the server, to track down the owners of the site, had been met with a mixture of obfuscation and outright refusal, and emails sent to the address from which the photos of Beatrice had been sent had either bounced back or remained unanswered. Nothing in Pierce's involvement, however, suggested anything that transgressed legality; none of the images stored on his computer were sexually explicit or in any way improper.

His story as to how he came by the article of Beatrice's clothing stood up, as did his alibi, such as it was, for the evening she had disappeared; his car had been in a garage some miles away and there were no records – this had been scrupulously checked – of any of the local taxi firms picking up a fare at or near his address.

By eight o'clock that evening, thirty-six hours after he was arrested, Simon Pierce was released without charge.

Nowhere to go. No credible sightings, no new information. The continuing trawl of Vauxhall Corsa owners had yielded nothing other than a few false leads. When Will met Helen later, two dodgy coffees and a shared margherita pizza in a small café near the police station, Beatrice Lawson had been missing for almost exactly six days.

'Sorry,' Helen said, curling up a slice of pizza before bringing it to her mouth, 'but I'm starving.'

'You didn't eat?'

'I forgot.'

'How was it anyway?'

'Cornwall?'

'What else?'

'Windy. Beautiful in its way.'

'Not what I meant.'

'I know.' She severed another slice of pizza, ready for eating. 'The girl's death, in a way I think Cordon's right. More questions than answers. And I can understand the coroner delivering an open verdict. But that doesn't mean it has to be murder. I met the guy who was their prime suspect – a real fruitcake, but did he kill the girl? No, I doubt it. Not many other possible suspects, and those there are don't stack up. So, barring the chance there was some pervert out lost in the fog at the same time, accidental death is probably what it was. Slipped and fell. It happens.'

She caught at a string of cheese that had detached itself and wound it round her little finger. Will, more decorous or perhaps less greedy, used his knife and fork to cut off a bite-sized piece.

'Nothing you could see to tie it in with what happened here?'

'Aside from that poor mother? No.'

'Waste of a journey, then, really?'

Helen raised an eyebrow. 'I wouldn't say that.'

'Meaning?'

'Oh, you know . . .' A smile playing round the corners of her mouth. 'It's always interesting, meeting people from other forces, seeing how they work. Just in case, this promotion, I have to look outside. And what happened – what might have happened – it's interesting enough. If it's okay by you, I was going to go back down to London tomorrow, talk to the friend of the girl who died. Family she was staying with. Maybe the brother.'

'You think it's worth the time?'

'I don't know. Possibly not. But if you don't need me here . . . And I sort of said to Cordon that I would.'

'Beholden to him, are you?'

Helen stuck out her tongue. 'It'll cross a few Ts. After that, it's just a case of waiting for the DNA results to come through.' She tasted her coffee and spooned in more sugar. 'But you.

What you told me about Pierce having his car serviced at the same garage where Mitchell Roberts worked – when you first heard that, you must have nearly wet yourself.'

A wry smile came to Will's face. 'You're right there. Though it did seem almost too good to be true. And of course, it was. No way Roberts was still around when Pierce's car was taken in for repair.' He shook his head. 'One of those coincidences that get the juices flowing but turn out to be nothing.'

By the time Will arrived home, Jake had taken himself off to bed in a sulk because Lorraine had refused him seconds of ice cream for pudding.

'I didn't think you liked it at the dentist?' she'd said.

'I didn't. I hated it. He was horrid. He hurt me.'

'Jake, he did not. He was very careful. But if you don't want to see him again soon, you're going to have to do what he said and cut out all the sweets and chocolate and eat less sugary things altogether. Which includes ice cream.'

If looks could kill, Lorraine would have been dead where she stood.

Added to which, Susie, as if absorbing the prevailing mood, had taken to grizzling and refusing whatever blandishments her mother could contrive.

All it needed was for Will to come home with a face like stone, which, of course, he duly did.

'Perfect!' Lorraine exclaimed when she saw him.

'What? What did I do?'

'Nothing,' she said, summoning a smile. 'Sit down and I'll get you a drink. Dinner won't be more than twenty minutes or so.'

The evening passed unremarkably enough: food, settling the children off to sleep, a second glass of wine, the same old mindless TV. In the bathroom, Lorraine kissed Will on the back of the shoulder in passing and, in bed, after she'd finished reading, she rested what might have been an exploratory arm on his side, but Will was tired and not in the mood and feigned not to notice.

Half an hour later, turning heavily, Lorraine spoke to him out of the darkness. 'Will, are you sleeping?'

'I was.'

'This afternoon, when I got back with the kids, there was someone out there in the field.'

'What kind of someone?'

'A man.'

'What doing?'

'Nothing. Just standing.' She touched his elbow. 'I think it could have been Mitchell Roberts.'

Will was instantly awake.

'Roberts? You're certain? You're sure?'

'No, of course I'm not sure. I'd have told you before if I was.'

'Why the hell didn't you phone me at the time?'

'I just said. Because I wasn't certain. And anyway, it wasn't as if he actually did anything. He just . . . looked. I turned my head away and then he was gone.'

'Out in the middle of a field, he can't have just disappeared.'

'But he did.'

'And you didn't see fit to say anything about it until now.'

'There's no sense getting angry.'

'Isn't there?' He hurried downstairs and came back with the copy of the newspaper that had Mitchell's photograph on the front page.

'Is this him? The man you saw?'

Lorraine looked at it hard and sighed. 'I don't know.'

'Think.'

'Jesus, Will! I am. But it was getting dark, I couldn't see properly. It . . . it might have been him, yes, but I'm sorry, I just can't be sure.'

Will set the paper aside, switched out the light and reached for her hand; for a while, neither of them spoke.

'If it was him,' Lorraine said, staring up into the dark, 'what does it mean?'

'It means he knows where we live. Most likely where Jake goes to school. When you're home and when you're not.'

Lorraine shivered and squeezed his hand. 'What does he want?'

'I don't know. To frighten us, probably. Frighten you. Get back at me.'

'He wouldn't hurt us, would he? Hurt the children?'

'He might.'

Will moved so that his arm was close around her, her face pressed fast against his chest.

65

No way Lorraine wasn't going in to work. 'Will, no, listen. I've already taken three days off this month, one yesterday to take Jake to the dentist . . .'

'That was half a day.'

'. . . and two when Susie was sick. I can't afford to take any more. And this is a busy time.'

'According to you, it's always a busy time.'

'Well, it is. There are still overseas students whose grants haven't been settled, applications starting to come in for next year. If I don't keep on top of it, they'll let me go.'

'So fine, let them.'

'No. Not because of this. Someone standing in a field.'

'Someone?'

'Yes. I don't know who it was or what they were doing there.'

'You did last night. Mitchell, that's what you said.'

'I said it might have been.'

'And now?'

'I'm just not sure.'

'Jesus Christ!' Will slammed his fist down on to the break-fast table and one of the bowls jumped on to the floor and smashed.

Immediately, Jake started to cry, and seconds later Susie followed suit.

'I don't see why you're so angry,' Lorraine said, stooping to pick up the pieces.

'Then you're stupider than I thought.'

'Thank you. Thank you very much.' With a clatter, she dumped the broken china in the bin.

'That man, Roberts, d'you know what he's done? What he's capable of doing?'

'Yes. Yes, I think I do.'

'And you're prepared to take the risk?'

Lorraine counted up to ten. 'I'll talk to the school, and the nursery. Make sure both the children are kept inside and prop-erly supervised. If they're not prepared to do that they can come to work with me. We'll manage somehow. All right?'

'Fine!' Will pushed past her and wrenched open the kitchen door. 'But on your head be it!'

'You're so worried,' Lorraine snapped, 'do your job, why don't you? If it's Mitchell out there, and he's so bloody dangerous, why don't you catch him?'

From the look on Will's face, she thought he was going to hit her and she flinched. Susie's tears became breathless sobs. Jake hid his face in his hands. The door slammed so hard a sliver of frame cracked away and Lorraine was left shaking, the sounds of frightened children filling her ears, hands across her chest clasped tight.

Dressed and out of the house with just a quick kiss on the children's heads, a nod towards Lorraine, Will called in a few favours from the officer in charge of Ely police station on Nutholt Lane. A patrol car would pass through the village at regular intervals, with a constable being stationed outside the primary school at the middle of the day and immediately after school.

As soon as Lorraine had mentioned any possibility of children being endangered at the nursery, they had insisted she keep Susie away, and so, loaded up with picture books, crayons and toys, Lorraine had bundled her into the car and taken her down to the college where she worked. She rang Will on her mobile as soon as she arrived, wanting to make the peace, but failed to get through.

Will was in the car, driving towards Norwich with all possible speed, the Last Shadow Puppets CD on the stereo, loud as it would go.

Roy Cole met him at Bethel Street with something like anticipation bright in his eyes.

'Same place as before?' Will asked.

'The same.'

This time they took the car, Will filling in the details as they drove.

On arrival, Cole tossed the cigarette he'd been smoking into the kerb, left the car parked outside the store with its blue light flashing and within minutes he had Paul Heywood relieved of his duties and out in the delivery yard, hunch-shouldered, hands clasped in front of his crotch as if expecting to be kicked.

'Remember the Detective Inspector here?' Cole asked, his face no more than an arm's length from Heywood's own.

'Ye-yes.'

'He asked about your pal, Mitchell Roberts, you remember that?'

'Yes.'

Cole reached around and caught hold of the man's ponytail, jerking hard. Pain narrowed Heywood's eyes. 'This time you better tell him the truth.'

'I did – I did.'

'This time you better tell him fuckin' everything.' One quick tug and he let him go. 'I'm just going out here for a smoke, leave you two alone.'

Nervous, Heywood wiped at his watering eyes: when Will moved towards him, he tensed and closed them tight.

'Mitchell Roberts,' Will said, 'when you talked to him on the phone. From the garage. He ever mention a man named Pierce, Simon Pierce?'

Heywood shook his head.

'Simon Pierce, you're sure?'

'Yes, he never . . . I never heard that name before, I swear.'

'Okay.' Will rested a hand, not heavily, on his shoulder and Heywood juddered as if he'd been struck.

'You don't like to get hurt,' Will said, smooth and quiet, a friend enquiring of a friend.

'No, no.'

'Happened sometimes when you were inside, I suppose?'

'Yes.'

'Happened quite a lot.'

'Yes.' Heywood was sweating now, a shiver running through him with every word.

'Roberts, he helped you out sometimes, I dare say?'

'Yeah. Yes, he did, he was a mate.'

'And sometimes not.'

Heywood's eyes leapt nervously around.

'Sometimes not,' Will repeated.

'No.' Eyes cast down. 'No, sometimes he couldn't. Sometimes he . . .'

'Sometimes he stood and watched.'

'Yes.' Heywood crying now, shaking against Will's hand that still rested on his shoulder as if in consolation.

'You wouldn't like to go back . . .'

'No. No.'

'I'm sure we could arrange it, DS Cole and I. Arrange for you to go back inside, see all your old friends, those that are still there, spend a little time together, enjoy each other's company.'

'No, please, please.' He took hold of Will's arm and squeezed. 'Please don't.'

'Tell me then what you can about where Mitchell goes, where he stays. Whatever you can remember, places, names . . .'

Heywood let go of Will's arm and swayed an awkward step backwards, before finally steadying himself, steadying his breathing. 'He talked once about Cleethorpes and then this other place where he stayed, west of here, Wisbech, some name like that? Liked it round there, I remember him saying. Congenial, that was the word he used. Never heard it before or since. That's how it stuck in here.' Tapping the side of his head. 'Congenial.'

'Stayed,' Will said. 'Stayed on his own?'

'No. That'd be with them diddicoys, wouldn't it? Got on with them, some of 'em at least. Gyppos, you know?'

Will knew. He nodded once at Heywood and pushed his way through out of the yard and on to the street, where Roy Cole was just finishing his cigarette.

Duncan Strand, the Gypsy and Traveller Liaison Officer for the Cambridgeshire force, was in his office at the Huntingdon headquarters when Will phoned, but due to leave for a meeting in Leicester within the hour. Will checked his watch; no way of reaching there in the time. Instead, he pulled into a lay-by and gave Strand such details as there were. A group of travellers, sticking to the east of the country. Cleethorpes to Wisbech. From north-east Lincolnshire, on the estuary of the Humber, down to Wisbech, an inland port amidst the Cambridgeshire Fens. Wisbech, where, thirteen years before, twelve-year-old Janine Prentiss was abducted and held prisoner for three days. Three days and nights.

'I'm not sure how long he might have stayed with them, Roberts,' Will said, 'could have been just a matter of a few days, could've been longer.'

Up to then, prison aside, he had always reckoned Roberts for a loner, but now . . . *Congenial*, the word resonated with Will too.

'Llewelyn Jones,' he said. 'Ring a bell?'

'Loud and clear. Other side of Peterborough, last I heard. Could've moved on.'

'You'll check?'

'Do what I can.'

Mitchell Roberts' profile would be readily accessible on the force computer; no need for Will to spell out the urgency of the situation. He broke the connection and pulled back out on to the road. He was no more than fifteen miles further along when his phone rang and he snatched it up, thinking it was probably Strand calling him back.

It was Lorraine.

Someone answering Mitchell Roberts' description had been seen close to the perimeter of Jake's school.

To hell with safety, Will speed-dialled as he drove. By the time he arrived in the village, some forty-five minutes later, several police vehicles were ahead of him, parked up on the verge, and the school was virtually sealed off. Inside, lessons were going on, but not as usual. Jim Straley hurried across to meet him, the local DI matching him stride for stride.

'Your boy's safe,' Straley said. 'Nothing happened. This man – could have been Mitchell, but it's still not certain – he was spotted hanging round the back of the school first, out where the playground butts up against the first field. Then later, just coming up to the end of lunch break, he walked right up to the front gate. Teacher on duty asked him what he thought he was doing and he just backed off. Wandered away, calm as you like.'

'I thought there was meant to be an officer out here all through lunch-time?' Will said.

'So there was. Answering a call of nature inside.'

'My wife?' Will asked.

Straley nodded in the direction of the school. 'Inside. I offered to escort her and the kids home, but she said she'd wait for you.'

Will found Lorraine in the head teacher's office, Susie playing with the polished stones of her necklace, Jake sitting subdued, cross-legged on the floor, his head in a book. The head teacher was elsewhere, playing a maths game with year five.

'Oh, Will!'

Bending low, he hugged her close; her and his daughter both.

'I should have listened, I'm sorry.'

'No. We were neither of us thinking straight. Besides . . .' straightening, '. . . it's okay.' Suddenly, there were tears pricking his eyes and he turned towards Jake. 'Come here, you. Put that book down and give your dad a hug.'

'Dad,' Jake said, brushing against his father's face, 'are you crying?'

'What have I got to cry for?' he said, but for now he couldn't stop.

When Jim Straley knocked on the door and beckoned Will outside, they were all standing, wrapped around each other, in a cluster.

'One of the local PCs found a witness, doing a spot of fishing out beyond the village. Reckons he saw a man answering Roberts' description run across the field ahead of him, cross the stream by a bridge lower down and head off north towards some farm. Whiteside Farm, something of the sort?

'Whiteside, I know it, that's right.'

'Apparently, there's a track runs up from there to the main road?'

Will nodded. The A1101.

'This fisherman, he thinks he may have heard an engine, starting up. Quite heavy, he reckoned, the way it turned over, like maybe an old van.'

'Not much likelihood of CCTV.'

'Depends which way he went and how far. If he's gone south towards Mildenhall, down past the airfield, good chance I'd say. But if it's the other direction . . .' Straley shook his head.

The other direction, Will thought. Up through Littleport and across the northern reaches of the Hundred Foot Washes towards Wisbech.

Was it coming together at last?

Some of it, at least.

'Come on,' he said, putting his head around the head teacher's door. 'We're going home.'

66

The youth Helen stopped to ask for directions – knock-off sports gear, Nike trainers, Adidas cap – tried to sell her a wrap of china white before realising his mistake. The moment he did, he was off, as Helen's dad might have put it, like a blue-arsed fly.

Her dad had lived on estates like this growing up, block after block designed by someone with a set of Lego and sod-all imagination, each, save for the name, indistinguishable from the next.

The board showing the layout was so covered with graffiti, it was all but impossible to decipher. Dogs growled and snapped from walkways crowded with prams and pushchairs and uncollected waste. Children cried and women shrieked.

The woman Helen finally found to ask was dressed head to toe in a black hijab, only her face and hands showing. Her voice was so soft, Helen had to lean towards her to hear, but the instructions were accurate and clear. Kelly's flat was on the seventh floor, reached, when it was working, by a lift redolent of stale urine with sweet hints of marijuana. Bottle it, Helen thought. Eau de Despair.

In contrast, Kelly was bright, chirpy, well turned out, make-up carefully applied, hair razor cut close to her head, dark with a pinkish tinge.

'Got lost, did you? Took me bleedin' forever. Still go the wrong way sometimes, end up back where I started. Come on, come on in.'

The tiny hallway was home to a double buggy, myriad boots and shoes, assorted boxes and an overflow of toys. More toys in the living room, but those not in use were neatly stacked; flowers on the table, slightly wilted, but flowers nonetheless. Attached to the wall, a large-screen television angled down. Regardless of whatever was going on around him, a boy of between two and three sat on the carpet studiously building a tower of coloured bricks and screaming with delight each time it collapsed.

'I'll make us a cup of tea in a minute. Everett's gonna take the kids for a walk, i'n't you, Everett? Give us a bit of peace.'

The man who'd appeared in the doorway was big and black and cradling a baby of some nine or ten months against his chest.

Seeing Helen, he smiled. 'You police, right?'

'Right.'

'But not from here, like?'

'Not from here.'

His smile broadened. 'That's all right, then, i'n it?'

Shifting the child from one arm to the other as if she were a doll, he bent down towards Kelly and kissed her on the neck, running a hand across the stubble of her hair. 'Later, babe.'

Kelly squeezed the muscles of his arm, kissed the baby's head, picked up her son and kissed him too, then, making sure Helen was comfortable, went off into the kitchen to make the tea.

A lot of kissing, Helen thought, trying not to look at reflections of herself in the blank screen of the TV.

Kelly soon returned with mugs of tea and slices of cake – 'Reduced at Iceland. Past its sell-by date, who cares? Live dangerously, eh?'

After a quick swig of her tea, Kelly reached for her cigarettes, offering one to Helen before lighting up herself.

'Can't get away with this when Everett's here. Goes ballistic.' She almost giggled. 'Not a pretty sight.'

'You been together long?'

'Since before Tracey was born.' She drew hard and held the smoke down in her lungs. 'Never thought he would. Never thought he'd stay. Goes to show, don't it? Men, you never can tell.'

True there, Helen thought. 'You happy to talk about Heather?' she asked.

'Happy? I wouldn't say that. I will though, not that I think it'll help. That night . . .' She shivered, remembering. 'She was my best friend, you know. And that last year, before, you know, we went away, we was round one another's houses all the time. Well . . .' She laughed. 'More hers than mine. I think her mum preferred it that way. Less chance of catching nits or some awful disease. First thing you got round there, "Take off your shoes, girls, and leave them in the hall, then go upstairs and wash your hands." She laughed again. 'After that we'd get a biscuit, right? One biscuit on a plate, two if we were lucky, and some juice in a glass with a straw. "Make sure you don't make any unnecessary crumbs." She was nice, though, Heather's mum. Stuck up, of course, but that weren't her fault. Way she was brought up. Like me, common as muck.'

She was pretty, Helen thought, Kelly, when she smiled. She would have been pretty back then, herself and Heather, both teetering on the edge of adolescence.

'Were there many boys down there on holiday?' she asked. 'Where you were staying?'

'At the camp? A few, yeah. This little gang.'

'Your age or older?'

'Older. Fourteen, fifteen.'

'Fanciable?'

'You're kidding, right? I mean, you know what boys are like, that age. All football, cars and computers. Video games. They'll crack dirty jokes, all right. Make remarks.' Kelly had another drag at her cigarette and picked up her tea, holding the mug in front of her in both hands. 'Nearest they get to girls, most of 'em, is jerking off to some tart, wiggling her arse on MTV. Watching late-night porn.'

'Your brother, Lee, the same?'

'When he wasn't tryin' to peek through the bathroom door, yeah.'

'So there was nothing going on between any of you?'

Kelly shook her head. 'We'd tease one another, yeah? Me and Heather. This one fancies you, that one. But I doubt they ever did. Why would they? Not a decent pair of tits between us. Anyway, why d'you ask?'

'Oh, just trying to get a picture.'

'You think something happened, don't you? Somethin' more'n Heather fallin' down that bloody mine or whatever. Well, it didn't. Take my word. We went out when we shouldn't. Stupid, right? Fog or fret or whatever they call it, come down so fast we was lost, turned around, not a fuckin' clue where we was. Stayed there waitin' for it to clear an' all that happened, it got thicker and thicker. In the end it was Heather who said she was going to go back down the path, see if she could find some spot where it weren't so thick. "You stay here," she said. "Stay right here. Then I'll know where you are." I never saw her again, not till the funeral.'

'You didn't hear anyone shouting?'

'Once or twice, yeah. And I called back, didn't I, but I might as well've saved my breath.'

'You didn't see your dad? Your brother?'

435

'I didn't see fuckin' anythin' till I woke in that old geezer's bed. Saved my fuckin' life, that's what he did. Could've been two funerals, not just the one.' She looked at her watch. 'I've got this mate comin' round. Half an hour or so. I could put her off, if you like?'

'No, it's all right,' Helen said. 'Half an hour'll be fine.'

Over another cigarette, they went over the events of the holiday once more; talked about Heather's relationship with her own family and with Kelly's, too.

'I thought I might try and have a word with your brother,' Helen said. 'Before I go back.'

Kelly gave her a look that said, suit yourself.

'You don't get on?'

'Not so much that. Don't see him too often, that's all. Him and Everett . . .' She shook her head. 'Doesn't matter. Way it is. He's got his life, I got mine.'

She showed Helen to the door. 'Don't get lost now. Sure you know the way?' She told her just in case. 'Walk through on to Camden Road and then a bus towards Holloway. Get off at the Nag's Head an' turn left. Up past the Odeon. Can't miss it. Piece of cake.'

She gave a little laugh and Helen smiled and thanked her again. This time Helen took the stairs. Not just Will and Lorraine then, she thought, happy with each other, happy with their kids. Some people, she supposed, just took the cards life dealt them and got on with it as best they could. Somehow it made her feel good.

She found her way past the cinema easily enough and there was the paint shop, stretching the best part of a small block. She thought she knew which one of the assistants, all wearing brown overalls, was Lee Efford but asked just to be sure. Five eight or nine, not as tall as his dad, short hair, stubble, a tattoo on the side of his neck, brown eyes.

'Yeah?' he said, when Helen came up to him, not quite looking her in the eye. 'Help?'

'Lee? I've just come from your sister's.'

'So?'

'I thought maybe we could have a little talk?'

He looked at her then. 'Police, i'n it? What the fuck now?'

'If you've got a break coming up? I don't want to make a fuss.'

Grudgingly, he looked at his watch. 'Half an hour, three-quarters. I'll see you in the park, just round the corner. Back of here.'

Helen bought a newspaper, a packet of mints and a fresh pack of cigarettes and found a bench in front of an all-weather football pitch on which a parcel of kids who should certainly have been in school were practising penalties. There was a paragraph about Beatrice Lawson's disappearance towards the foot of page seven. A man who had been helping police with their inquiries had been released. Police would neither confirm nor deny that he had any family relationship with the missing girl. The search for the owner of a green Vauxhall Corsa spotted in the area where Beatrice had last been seen was continuing. That was all.

Forty minutes later, she'd convinced herself Lee had done a runner, which would have been interesting in itself, and there he was, walking reluctantly towards her, coat collar up.

When she offered him a cigarette at first he shook his head, then, when he saw her light up, changed his mind.

'What's this about then?'

'What do you think?'

'It's not that business with the car?'

'What business's that?'

One of Lee's mates had stolen a car and the pair of them had gone joyriding, fine until the driver lost control doing handbrake turns round the back of the Emirates stadium, two in the morning. Police were called in time to pick up Lee and his pal legging it in the general direction of Highbury Corner.

Both of them arrested and bailed, probation and an official warning respectively.

Helen listened, letting Lee talk. 'It's not about that,' she said.

Lee flicked the butt of his cigarette out towards the centre of the path and watched it smoulder.

'Kelly,' he said, 'she reckons I don't think about it, what happened. Just 'cause I don't go on about it like she does, she an' my dad. It's like, when they're together, right? One or other of 'em has to start talkin' about it. Heather. Poor Heather. As if I didn't care. An' now there's that other girl, gone missing. Saw it on the telly. Her mum, it's the same, yeah?'

'Ruth, yes.'

'Poor cow. And the girl, no one's found her, right?'

'Not yet.'

'You know what?' Lee braced his back against the bench. 'Those blokes, blokes who do stuff like that, I'd castrate 'em, right? Either that or stone 'em, like they do out in – where is it? – Afghanistan, places like that. Stand 'em up and have people throw stones at 'em till they're fuckin' dead. Sweet.'

Helen watched as two young women – girls – walked past, pushing buggies, chatting, not a care in the world.

'You went looking for her that day, that afternoon?'

'Heather? Yeah.'

'You and your dad.'

'I dunno. He might've, I dunno. Never saw him, did I? Couldn't see a bloody thing.'

'You tried.'

He swivelled sideways. 'Lot of fuckin' good that did. Lot of fuckin' good it did her.'

Five minutes later, Helen was walking on through the park and out towards Tufnell Park Road, the tube to King's Cross and then the train. Did she know anything she hadn't known before, anything she hadn't learned from reading the reports

Cordon had made sure were clung on to, listening to the tapes? She wasn't sure.

Back in Cambridge, she checked the messages on her computer and cleared her desk as well as she could. Will, she learned from Ellie Chapin, was in the north of the county, some panic at his son's school, she wasn't sure what, but she didn't think anyone was injured or hurt. Helen called his mobile and got no reply; she didn't know if there was anything of much use she could tell Cordon, but rang him anyway and they had a brief conversation.

She tried Will's home number, but no one was picking up. Time to go home herself.

When she arrived, there was Declan Morrison, leaning up against the wall, a bottle of Scotch, to which he seemed to have been liberally helping himself, in his hand.

'Peace offering,' he said, waving the bottle in her face.

If there was one thing Helen didn't want, it was this. 'Go home, Declan.'

'Been waiting for you,' he said, beaming his lopsided grin. 'Hours and hours.'

'Go home.'

Stepping around him, she slid her key into the lock.

''S'up?'

'Nothing. I'm tired. Now go home to your wife and kids.'

'Jus' lemme in for a lil' while. Jus' for a lil' drink.'

'You've drunk enough.'

She'd learned to read the moment when his expression changed, when the face tightened and fists were formed and half-drunken good humour hardened into anger that was as unpredictable as it was brutal. With a quick movement, Helen knocked the bottle from his hand and as it shattered, she wrenched open the door and jumped inside. Slamming the door shut, she turned the key, slipped the bolt and reached for her phone. As Morrison beat his fists against the woodwork, she gave her name and address to the emergency switchboard, along with enough detail that the urgency was clear.

Stripping off her clothes as she went, she switched on the shower and stepped in, the first sounds of police sirens lost beneath the wash of water as she raised her face towards the spray.

67

———

'Why's he doing this?' Lorraine said.

'To show that he can.'

'But why?'

They were still sitting at the table in the kitchen, plates cleared away, glasses of wine recharged, the children upstairs and asleep long since; Jake, especially, exhausted by events he didn't really begin to understand.

'He's convinced I'm out to get him. Some sort of personal vendetta.'

'And he thinks this will make you stop?'

'Maybe. Who knows?'

'But it's not just you, he must see that. It's the police, everyone. Whatever he does to you, to us . . .' Lorraine rested her face in her hands. 'It doesn't make any sense.'

'People like Roberts don't make sense. Except to themselves. Some psychiatrist, maybe.'

He drank a little more wine. He should have responded to Helen's call, he knew, but it could wait. Would wait. Morning would do. He should hear something definite back from Duncan Strand by then. Noon at the latest.

'I don't want any more of this,' Lorraine said, tapping the rim of her glass.

'Here then.' Will held up his own glass and she tipped it in.

Beside him at the sink, she rested her head against his shoulder, arm around his waist. 'If anything had happened . . .'

'Sshh.'

'But if . . .'

'You best stay home with them tomorrow, both of them. Till this is over. Once you explain to the college, they'll understand.'

Lorraine nodded. 'Okay.'

'And don't worry. There'll be someone on duty near the house all day.' He nodded towards the blackened window. 'You won't be on your own.'

'I know.'

He pulled her closer to him. 'You'll be safe here.'

Unseen, something moved in the dark space outside and, with a rasping screech, a barn owl flew up into the night sky, its white face turned towards the moon.

Ruth was unable to sleep. Fractured images of her children pressed down. Beatrice's smile became Heather's pain; Heather's laughter became Beatrice's tears. One moment she was holding Heather's hand, walking along the beach at Aldeburgh, sun shimmering down. But when the child spun away and ran, laughing, only to turn and poke out a tongue, it was Beatrice's face, Beatrice's voice, jubilant, taunting. 'Neh-neh-ne-neh-neh! Hate you! Hate you! Can't catch me!'

Beside her, Andrew lay with one arm stretched towards her, as if to keep her at bay. His breathing was even, heavy, broken only by an occasional whistle of air. Gradually, over the last days, he had become more distant, withdrawn; making time still to be with Ruth, and ensure, as far as he could, that she was coping with what had happened, but making time, Ruth thought, is what it was. More and more, he was reimbursing himself in the surety, the safety of his work.

It was as if, Ruth thought, part of him, the part that was missing his daughter, was becoming numb: inviolable to pain, inured from hurt. As if he already knew he would not see her again, alive, and was protecting himself as best he could. Living already with his grief.

Ruth touched his shoulder and was surprised by the warmth of his skin. Perhaps what she'd been thinking wasn't true; perhaps it was unfair. Leaning down, she kissed his arm and slid from the bed. Her dressing gown was behind the door. In the bathroom, she splashed cold water on her face and pulled a comb through her hair. Cleaned her teeth. Half past two. In the soft glow of lights from the town, from the landing window she could see the slow movement of clouds across the sky.

The moon was three-quarters full.

In the kitchen, she made peppermint tea and, on an impulse, buttered toast.

Heather?

When she turned towards the door there was no one there.

Taking tea and toast into the living room, she switched the radio on low, somebody playing Bach, the cello suites, she didn't know who. Carefully, she took down the book she had bought in Paris, *Voyage à Giverny*, paintings made in Monet's garden, water lilies, wisteria, clumps of hollyhocks and climbing roses. So beautiful. Unreal. Tears ran down her face. That holiday, sitting with Simon outside the café at night, almost as happy as she had ever been, waiting, unknowing, for the phone call that would tear her life apart.

Andrew found her there, sleeping, at five, and half-carried, half-led her back to bed. When he left, almost three hours later, she was still sleeping, exhausted.

There was only one cameraman outside the house, tired, bored; he didn't even bother to raise his camera when Andrew drove past.

Ruth didn't know where she was when she woke; voices disturbing her, voices in her head. One voice. Simon's. On and on, calling her name. She pulled the duvet up over her head to shut it out.

Pebbles, then; pebbles against the window.

Pulling aside the curtain, she looked down.

Simon was standing on the narrow path between the front door and the gate. Looking up now, waving, calling her name.

Simon, wearing an old duffel coat and khaki trousers, the coat, which might have fitted him once, now several sizes too big, so that he resembled nothing as much as a barely animated scarecrow, flapping one arm.

Go away, Ruth thought. Just go and leave me alone.

But he wasn't going to go away.

Quickly, she dressed, pulling on a shirt and sweater, an old pair of jeans. She opened the front door, put it on the latch, and stood outside on the step, letting the door close to behind her.

The air struck cold.

Dressed, her hair unbrushed and uncombed, she felt exposed.

'What do you want?' Even her voice sounded strange.

'Ruth . . .' He took a step forward. 'I would have come sooner, but . . .' He looked at the ground. 'I just wanted to say . . . say how sorry . . . how very sorry I am about what's happened. Really very, very sorry.'

'Thank you.'

'I know . . . of course, I know . . .' His fingers were plucking restlessly at the wooden toggles at the front of his coat. Fiddling. Fiddling. The light she'd seen in his eyes before had been replaced by something else.

'Aren't you going . . . ?' He looked beyond her. 'Aren't you going to let me in?'

'No, I don't think so.'

A car went slowly past without stopping; on the lawn, a blackbird searched for worms: the lone photographer had long since packed up his gear and gone.

'But I . . . we . . . I can help you, help you understand. You know I can. I know what it's like, after all. What it's like when this happens. Something like this. Your little girl.'

Ruth shuddered inside.

'And there's nobody,' he continued. 'Nobody else. Not Andrew. Not that really understands. How can they? How? But you and I, we know. We know.'

'Simon. Go home. Please. Leave me alone.'

'Ruth, please . . .'

She reached behind her for the door. 'I'm going back inside now.'

'Ruth, you can't.' He started towards her, his eyes pleading. 'You need me. You really do. I can help you find her. You'll see.'

She slammed the door hard and moved quickly away, his last words unheard.

'Ruth, I know, that's the thing. Beatrice. I know where she is.'

68

A clear night, untrammelled by cloud, had brought the temperature down. Six degrees, maybe less. Will had had second
thoughts about going in to work and leaving Lorraine and the
children alone, but she had told him the last thing she wanted
was him, under her feet all day, pining to be somewhere else.
'Mitchell, from what you've said, you're close to tracking
down where he is. Sooner you find him, sooner we can all
get back to normal. And besides, we'll be fine, you said so
yourself.'

When Will crossed to meet Helen at the lay-by, he could
see the ghost of his breath on the air. Helen with the almost
ritual tea and cigarette, leaning against her car in the same
way. How many days had started this way?

'We're going to have to stop meeting like this,' Helen said,
with a smile.

'I thought we had.'

'Miss me, did you?'

'Not really.'

'Someone around to pick up the pieces, hold your hand?'

'Wind me up, you mean.'

'Besides, you've had Ellie. Younger than me, and prettier.'

Will shook his head.

'What's the matter?' Helen laughed. 'Doesn't she do it for you the way I do?'

'Thankfully, no.'

Helen nodded in the direction of the van, where a small knot of lorry drivers stood, hands in pockets, waiting for bacon rolls, the smell vying with the scent of diesel on the morning air. 'You getting anything?'

'I don't think so.'

Helen lit another cigarette. 'I heard what happened yesterday. Out at the school. Lorraine and the kids, they're okay?'

'Pretty much.'

'There's no doubt it was Roberts?'

'Doesn't seem to be.'

'It's personal, isn't it? With him. Getting back at you any way he can.' She moved a piece of gravel around under her foot. 'Maybe if you hadn't pushed him so hard, going after him the minute he got out . . .'

'What was I supposed to do? Do nothing?'

'You needled him. Got under his skin.'

'Of course I got under his fucking skin! You want another Christine Fell out there? Another Martina Jones?'

'No, but this way . . .'

'This way, what?'

'Maybe that's what we've got.'

Will threw the contents of his cup, virtually untouched, towards the verge and started back towards his car.

'Will, for God's sake . . .'

Handle on the car door, he stopped: his breathing was heavy in his chest and he could feel the accelerated beat of his heart.

Helen held her tongue: pushing Will any further would only make him more defensive still. She took a last drag at her cigarette and stubbed it out. 'Our meeting with Duncan's at ten?'

'Quarter to.'

'We'd better go.'

The office of the Gypsy and Traveller Liaison Officer was a Portakabin round at the back of the main police headquarters building. Somebody's idea of a little joke.

'It's only temporary,' Duncan Strand said, when he stepped outside to welcome them. Wispy hair hung too long over his collar and, wearing faded brown cords and a grey cardigan over a plaid shirt, he could easily have passed for a traveller himself. Which was almost certainly the point.

'How long have you been out here?' Helen asked.

'Best part of three years.'

There were small advantages. On days like this, Strand and his part-time civilian assistant could keep the doors and windows closed and, with the aid of a couple of small oil-fired radiators, build up a pleasant fug inside; tea and coffee they could make whenever they wanted; if they chose, they could unplug their phones and let the rest of the world go by and not too many people would be the wiser.

Detailed maps of the county and its borders were pinned to the walls, sites used by groups of travellers, along with patterns of travel, were clearly marked: those which were licensed by the local authority and those which, although unofficial, were returned to again and again.

'Since you rang,' Strand said, 'I've done some asking round. About Roberts, like you said. It's difficult to pin anything down. A few people grudgingly admit to knowing him, no more than that.'

Will was looking at the map. Amongst the unofficial sites was the one near Littleport, where Martina Jones' grandfather, Samuel, and the rest of the extended family had made camp, just a few fields away from where Mitchell Roberts had his garage at Rack Fen.

'Jones,' Will said, 'nothing linking him and Roberts? That you know?'

'Samuel Llewelyn? It was Roberts who assaulted his grand-daughter, wasn't it?'

'Yes. Went down for it as well.'

'And you think Jones'd befriend him after that? With the girl maybe still around?'

'Who knows?'

'Very much the old-fashioned patriarch is Samuel. Likes to rule the roost. Not the kind to forgive easily, I'd have thought.'

Will looked back at the map. Jones and his clan sometimes travelled quite large distances, out of the county both north and south; but, closer to hand, they seemed to trace a familiar circuit across the Soke of Peterborough and the Bedford Levels. In his mind, Will superimposed the locations of crimes in which he thought Roberts might have been involved: Ely, Wisbech, Peterborough itself.

'You know where Jones is now?'

Strand went and sat by one of the computers. 'Last we heard, he was back Peterborough way, just north of Flag Fen.' He crossed to the map. 'Off this B road here, the 1040.'

'And this was when?'

'Few weeks back now.'

'So he could still be there?'

'Or gone.'

'You won't object if we drive up?' Will said. 'Take a look?'

Strand held out both hands, palm upwards. 'Be my guest.'

The encampment was bigger than before: seven caravans in various stages of disrepair, two ageing camper vans and a flatbed truck. The usual assemblage of barefoot kids, mangy dogs and half-wild cats; adults who melted from sight the moment Will and Helen arrived. One of the children, eight or nine years old with a lean face and large eyes, was squatting by a smouldering fire, attempting to cook a small fish he'd hooked out of the stream that trickled near the field end and impaled on a stick.

'Fuck off, coppers,' he said quietly as they walked past.

'They learn early,' Will remarked.

'It's that air of authority,' Helen said. 'Recognise it anywhere.'

'Well,' a voice boomed from behind them. 'Detective Inspector Grayson, as I live and breathe.'

'See what I mean,' Helen said.

Jones was wearing a patched coat and thick moleskin trousers and leaning on his stick, a scarf tied at his throat. His long, silvery hair was tied back. 'I would say, a pleasure, but I'd be lying. Police, never anything but trouble as a rule. Screw us any way they can. Jealous, see, that's what it is. Freedom. Lack o' rules. My rules aside.' Grinning, he shook his stick. 'You've likely not come to serve a summons though? A notice to quit? Far too important for that. Some other business altogether. Unless you're here to accompany the young lady, of course. Her protector.'

He essayed a mock bow in Helen's direction.

'The day I need protection from the likes of you,' she said, 'I'll quit.'

When he laughed Jones showed a mouthful of uneven teeth, some capped with tarnished gold. 'Well said. Even though we both know it's not strictly true.'

A dog barked and showed its nose at the caravan door behind him and he shouted for it to be quiet. 'Blasted animal! Should've had him put down years ago.'

'Your granddaughter,' Will said, 'is she still travelling with you?'

'Martina? Thanks be to God she's not. Followed her poor

450

benighted mother up to Aberdeen, trailing after some lunatic Scot working the rigs. Not sorry to wash my hands of her. More trouble than she's worth.'

'Your own kith and kin?'

Jones laughed louder than before. 'If I was to take all my kith and kin, as you call 'em, under my wing, I'd need three times this many caravans an' more besides.'

'How did she recover?' Will asked. 'After what happened?'

'Wounds heal.'

'Some,' Helen said. 'Some never do.'

'Believe what you want,' Jones growled.

'Mitchell Roberts,' Will said.

'What of him?'

'I didn't realise you and he knew one another. It never came up at the trial.'

'Knew him how?'

'Well enough to take him in, give him a bed, a roof over his head.'

'You think I'd do that? After what he done to her?' Hawking up phlegm, he spat at the ground. 'Shows his face round here, I'd give him a beating he won't forget.'

'Wasn't always that way, was it?'

'What?'

'You knew him before.'

The expression on Jones' face changed, registering, just for an instant, the merest shadow of doubt.

'Knew his interests, his little peccadilloes.'

'What if I did?'

'Depends how much they were shared.'

'Not by me.'

'No?'

'No.'

'Martina, she wasn't a virgin when Roberts got to her—'

Jones swung his stick round hard and slammed it against

the side of the caravan, causing the dog inside to resume barking. 'You get off my land, the pair of you . . .'

'Your land?'

'I got nothin' more to say to you, now an' forever. You understand me? You understand?'

Turning, he wrenched open the caravan door and, as he did so, the dog, an elderly black and white collie, jumped, slightly arthritically, to the ground and continued to bark.

'Ezra!' Jones shouted from the doorway. 'Get your sorry hide back in here now!'

Instantly, Will heard Janine's voice, shaky despite the intervening years, describing what had happened the day she was released, the moments before she was roughly bundled into the back of a van. *The dog was there. Ezra . . . he pushed his nose up against me, but the man shooed him away.* The dog, a puppy then, thirteen years before, now old and slow. It was possible. '95. Where had Samuel Jones been in the summer of '95?

The patriarch stood, defiant, on the steps outside his caravan, while behind where Will and Helen were standing, a dozen men, emboldened, were starting slowly to advance, some with makeshift weapons in their hands.

'We'll be back,' Will said. 'This isn't over.'

Together, he and Helen walked back through the cordon, which grudgingly opened wide enough to let them go.

'The dog,' Helen said, once they were in the car. 'That's what you're going on?'

'That and the look in his eyes.'

They were back two hours later, three cars and a Transit, crammed, shoulder to shoulder, with uniformed officers. Not a moment too soon. Samuel Jones and his followers had just finished breaking camp and were getting ready to move.

'Going somewhere, Samuel?' Will asked, unable to stem the smile breaking out on his face. 'Freedom of the open road.'

'Go fuck yourself!'

'Maybe later. Now get in the car.'

For some moments it looked as if some of the travellers might be about to intervene, but the police presence was such that they stood their ground and merely scowled, letting off the odd curse. Duncan Strand would stay put, along with the bulk of the officers, and handle the questioning, doing his best to deflate the animosity as he did so.

Unfettered, the collie limped after the car taking Samuel Jones away, barking loudly.

69

Though Duncan Strand's records didn't go back as far as 1995, there was evidence of Jones and his followers staying in the Wisbech area in both 2001 and 2004, on an unofficial site north-west of the Middle Level Main Drain which bisected the land between Wisbech and Downham Market. The site in question was on a piece of low-level ground partly shielded by trees and no more than a mile from the farmhouse in Outwell where Janine Prentiss had reappeared after her abduction.

According to what Janine had said at the time, the van she had been carried in had driven for a long time – almost as long as a school lesson – before she had been let out, still blindfolded, at the end of a lane.

Thirty minutes? Forty? An hour?

Had the van driven straight there or gone round and around? She wasn't sure.

The journey could have begun as much as fifty miles from where she was dropped off or as little as five. A search for buildings similar to the ones Janine claimed to have seen yielded four. Farm labourers' cottages, no longer occupied and left to rack and ruin, were scarcely a rarity.

Of those, two had attracted the most police attention, one close – little more than a mile north of the site the Jones clan had used – the other, further east, across the Drain and within easy distance of the village of Wiggenhall St Mary the Virgin, where Christine Fell had been found tied to a baler.

Look for a pattern, wasn't that what the profilers said?

But both of these cottages had shown signs of having been temporarily used: fires lighted, rubbish strewn around; condoms, cigarette packets, scraps of clothing, animal bones. Neither yielded anything which said without contradiction, this is where Janine had been held.

Samuel Jones sat across from Will and Helen, defiant, head back, clear-eyed, a heavily veined nose that had been broken and reset several times. Lacking his usual stick to hold, he clasped the edges of the table with horned hands.

'Get on with it then! Stop wasting my blasted time.'

'You've got somewhere to go?' Will asked mildly, his voice a contrast to Jones' roar.

'Out of here. Out of this . . . this blasted box. Shut in. Shut in like this, this poxy room.'

'Answer the questions,' Helen said, 'and then you can go. Simple as that.'

'What bloody questions? Roberts? More about him? I told you time enough already, I in't seen him in years, not since I saw him in court the day he was sent down.'

'We believe you,' Will said. 'About that, at least. For now.'

'Then what in blazes am I doin', still cooped up here?'

'Waiting to tell us about before.'

'What before?'

'Let's start with '95.'

'Ninety-five what?'

'1995.'

'What about it?'

'You were staying on a site just north of Outwell, not far from Holly End.'

'Was I? You know more'n I do, then.'

'The same site you used in '01 and '04.'

'What of it? Even if it's so.'

'Roberts stayed with you.'

'Did he?'

'Tell me.'

'Can't tell you what I don't know.'

''95. The summer of '95.'

'Can't recall.'

Helen leaned forward a little, getting his attention. 'You know we're talking to people you travel with? Family, hangers-on. You think their memories'll all be as bad as yours? And then there's your daughter, Gloria. Martina's mother. Shouldn't be too difficult to trace her up in Aberdeen. She'll remember Roberts, I dare say. Just a kid, wasn't she, when she had Martina? Fifteen, sixteen? Reasons, maybe, to remember Mitchell Roberts well.'

Jones' hands were no longer gripping the table, but his thighs, fingers pressing down deep against the bone. The colour was fading from his weathered cheeks.

'No call,' he said. 'No call for any of that.' He cleared his throat. 'Roberts, I met him afore that. When you said. Some few years before.'

'How many?'

'You want me to tell this or not?'

'How many years before?' Will asked again.

Jones released a long, slow breath. 'Winter of '92, it'd be. One of the vans broke down. Peterborough way. Roberts, he was working in this roadside place, petrol and that, just doing odd jobs out back. Bloke in charge said they didn't have no mechanic, nothing like that. Wanted us out of there, not blockin' off his forecourt. Roberts, he said he could get it fixed. "Not on my time," the bloke said, so Roberts said, "Fuck you then, pay me what's due." Helped push the van down to the next lay-by and fixed it there and then. Enough to get us on our way. "What do you want," I asked him, "for that?" "Wouldn't mind a bed," he said. "Just a few days. Place to stay."' Jones ran his thumb over the broken ridge of his nose. 'Stayed a good while longer than that.'

'You became friends.'

'Never that.'

'What then?'

'He was a good mechanic, natural. Good with his hands. Caravans an' that, they'd taken a beating over the years, never been replaced. Roberts, he worked on 'em. Bought this little van for himself and drove all over, scrounging parts. Time he moved on, that'd be the spring, he had most every damned vehicle we had running like new.'

'Spring of '93?'

Jones nodded. 'Didn't see him for a good while after that. Year, eighteen months maybe. Bit of a state then, looked as if he'd been sleeping rough. Didn't stay long that time. Week, little more. Wandered off. Thought that'd be the last of him, but not so long later, another year maybe. Less. Got some money from somewhere. Workin' in a factory. Wisbech. Frozen food. Never stayed with us exactly, not then. Place of his own, don't know where. Still got the same old van.'

'And this was when exactly?'

''95, '96.'

'Which?'

''95.'

'Sometimes,' Will said, 'when he went off in his van, the dog went with him?'

'Dog?'

'You know which one I mean. Your dog. Ezra.'

Jones shook his head, the silver mane of hair shifting on his shoulders. 'Only a puppy then. Took to him for some reason, Lord knows why. Why Roberts wanted him, either? Always been more trouble'n he was blasted worth.'

'Roberts,' Will said, 'wanted the dog for bait.'

The site Samuel Jones took them to was neither of the ones they'd homed in on before, a different direction entirely. South past Three Holes and Lot's Bridge, a quarter-mile beyond the course of the old Roman Road on the edge of Upwell Fen. Two labourers' cottages that had been built not long after the beginning of the previous century and slowly crumbled into decay; the one now little more than a jumble of bricks and mortar, only one retaining wall still standing, the other a largely burnt-out shell, with sections of the roof remaining, the rest open to the sky.

'This was it?' Will said, cautious lest Jones were leading them astray.

'Believe it or believe it not.'

There were farm buildings on the horizon to both east and west, neither within earshot. The land flat and vast. Out here someone could scream loud and long and not be heard. Out here terrible things could happen unseen, unremarked.

'Someone's been here recently,' Helen called from the interior. 'Cigarette ends. Empty cans.'

'This is where he brought her?' Will said, swinging back towards Jones. 'Janine Prentiss?'

'I never knew her name.'

'But you were here?'

He took his time about answering, weighing up, no doubt, the pros and cons. Things he didn't want the police to come back to, probe into too deeply.

'Twice,' he said, eventually. 'When he was here with the girl. Twice.'

'Share her with you, did he?'

Jones let out a howl and, flushed with anger, took a step towards Will, fist raised.

Unblinking, Will stood his ground. 'Tell us what you were doing here,' he said.

Jones waited for his breathing to steady. 'The first time I come for the dog, simple as that. This place was in a fitter state then. Roberts had been living here, off and on, I knew that for a fact. I didn't know about the girl. Tried to keep her hid, didn't he, but I realised what was going on. Said she'd run away from home on account her father had been beating her and he was just giving her shelter. Temporary. Taking her to an aunt, over Newmarket way, that evening.'

'You believed him?'

Jones didn't answer. The wind was raw, cold on the face and hands, particles of dust and dirt in the air.

'I came back out again,' Jones said, 'the next day. Brought the dog with me. The girl was still here. I got a look at her this time, a proper look. Told him if he didn't get shot of her I'd call the police.'

'Get shot of her?'

'To the aunt, like he said.'

'There was no aunt.'

'How was I to know that?'

'You didn't care.'

'I did what I could.'

'You could have taken her there and then. Taken her yourself.'

Jones shook his head. 'I'd got myself too involved already.'

'I'll bet,' Will said sourly.

'What the hell d'you mean by that?'

'Whatever you want.'

The two men glared at one another in pent-up anger. Twenty years younger, no, ten, Jones would have come for him, Will

459

knew, and the warrant card in his pocket would have been no defence.

'Will,' Helen said. 'A word.'

Reluctantly, Will turned away.

Helen walked till she was out of earshot and waited for him to follow. 'You think Roberts could have brought her here? Beatrice?'

'It's possible.' He looked around as, with a loud raucous caw, a crow rose up on the wind. 'If he did, where is she now?'

'The ground in the corner there, near the rubble. It looks as though it's been disturbed.'

'Animals? Foxes?'

'Maybe. But if they were digging down, what were they digging for?'

'Okay. Let's get a search team out here. Dogs. See what they can find.'

There were two crows now, then three, circling above them on the air.

70

The dogs homed in on two locations: the one Helen had noticed, amongst the debris of the building that had mostly fallen in; the other at the rear, amidst what had, presumably, once been a garden and was largely overgrown now with weeds. Will and the crime scene manager walked the ground, discussing priorities: the interior site would be examined first, bricks and rubble carefully removed before Scene of Crime officers in coveralls and surgical gloves started, cautiously, to dig.

It might be possible, in time, to divert some of the team to the second site, so as to begin work there. The entire area had been cordoned off and a white tent erected around the immediate location of the search.

A small generator had been brought in to ensure power was available; lights already rigged.

It was going to be a long day, a long night.

Will called Lorraine twice in the afternoon to establish that she and the children were all right. Helen had accompanied Samuel Jones back to the central police station and was interviewing him again under caution.

'When do you think you'll be back?' Lorraine asked, the second time he rang.

It was impossible to say.

'Later, if I can. I'll do my best.' Even as he said the words, he knew it was less than likely. If a discovery were made, he wanted to be there when it happened.

He spoke briefly to Jake, listened to Susie breathing, and broke the connection. Twenty minutes later, after checking with the senior officer in Ely, he called Parkside and talked to Jim Straley.

'Jim, a favour. The local nick hadn't reckoned on sending anyone out to babysit Lorraine and the kids beyond midway through the evening. Presumed I'd be back by then. Can you organise someone from your end?'

'No need. I'll get up there myself.'

'You're sure?'

'Sure. You want me there for when?'

'Close to nine as you can.'

'Okay, not a problem.'

'Thanks, Jim. I owe you one.' Pulling his coat collar up against the burgeoning wind, Will moved back towards the centre of the site.

'Police investigating the disappearance of the schoolgirl, Beatrice Lawson, are understood to have begun searching the grounds of two long-abandoned farm workers' cottages in the vicinity of . . .'

Ruth pressed the preset button on the radio and the news-reader's voice gave way to a swirl of strings, a melody she instantly recognised as coming from the final movement of Tchaikovsky's 6th Symphony, the *Pathétique*.

Instantly, she switched it off.

Better the silence than that.

Anita Chandra had rung them earlier to prime them on this new development. 'I just wanted you to be aware,' she said.

'In case the media bump it up to be something more than it is. At the moment there's nothing definite to link what's going on to Beatrice, whatever the press might say, nothing at all. But if anything does emerge you'll be the first to know.'

The first to know – she had meant to be reassuring, Ruth understood. The first to know whatever was discovered out in that barren place.

Meanwhile, she moved aimlessly from room to room, avoiding Andrew and the look of helplessness on his face; at least, now her parents had returned to Cumbria she didn't have to cope with their near-silent presence, the assumption – clear in their eyes, but never spoken – that Beatrice was already dead. So she made yet another cup of tea she would forget to drink, picked up this book, then that, and set them both down, unread, while, beyond her sight, the search went on.

Men and women – she supposed there were women – their bodies as covered as if they were contaminated themselves, were down on their hands and knees, no more than an arm's length apart, gently lifting up soil, depositing the least thing suspicious into some sterile plastic bag. She had seen it many times, in so-called entertainment programmes and on the television news. That business out in Jersey, the former children's home, and then the body of that poor girl that had been discovered in the back garden of her killer's house down by the south coast. All so familiar . . .

It was a little over a week since Beatrice had disappeared. By six o'clock that evening it would be exactly eight days.

What if her parents were right and she would never see her daughter alive again?

She knew how that felt.

She went to the living-room window and looked out. All that was visible was her own reflection, pressed back upon the glass. Slowly, silently, she began to cry.

*

Lorraine scraped what Jake had left of his pasta supper into the bin and ran the bowl beneath hot water, rinsing it clean. There had been a time when she would decant all of the children's leftovers, cover them with cling film and put them in the fridge for another day. Of course, what happened was that five days later she found them pushed to the rear and lightly mouldering, and got angry with herself for not making use of them when she could. Now such providential days were over. Whatever was left on their plates, dumped and gone. Move on.

She looked at the clock: Will wouldn't be home now, she was sure. Walking away from a potential crime scene where a body might be found – Lorraine smiled – she knew him better than that.

Both children had gone down remarkably easily; the fact that Will had spoken to them on the phone making his absence at bedtime easier to bear. Before Lorraine had finished reading to them, Susie's eyes had closed and even Jake's had blinked shut once or twice.

All had been silent since.

In the kitchen, she turned the pages of a magazine. Recipes she would never make, clothes she would never wear. When the doorbell rang, she jumped.

Through the security spyhole Will had insisted on being fitted when they first moved in – 'Just in case the natives aren't friendly' – she could see the uniform of the officer outside.

'Only me, Mrs Grayson,' he said, smiling as she opened the door. 'By rights, I ought to be getting off now. Gone nine. Replacement's comin' up from Cambridge. Held up, maybe. I could hang on for a bit if you'd like.'

'No, it's okay. We'll be fine.'

'Long as you're sure.'

Lorraine made sure the door was locked and bolted after he'd gone. Out of habit as much as anything, she checked the windows: all secure. The sliding glass door that opened out into the garden was firmly closed but not locked and she pressed down the metal lever to lock it fast.

There was one of those programmes about moving house on the television, a repeat most likely: a couple wanting to swap their studio flat in some fashionable part of north London for a farmhouse in the Yorkshire Dales, with outbuildings so that she could have a studio for her felt-making, while he ran his computer software start-up company from the barn.

After watching just five minutes – the man, rimless glasses and a Paul Smith scarf, was particularly annoying – she decided she needed a drink. A glass of wine, why not? There was a bottle, already opened, in the fridge.

She was just taking it out when she heard a sound.

'Hello.' He spoke just as she turned.

Her heart seemed to drop down inside her body.

Roberts leaned against the door jamb effortlessly. Scuffed leather jacket and combat trousers, dark trainers on his feet, grey mittens on his hands. Smiling.

'You know who I am?'

'Yes.'

'Seen my picture a time or two, I dare say?'

Lorraine didn't reply, her mind racing too fast, accelerating alongside her pulse. How . . . ?

He read her mind.

'Thought when you slipped the lock on that door there, you was shutting me out.' He laughed, high-pitched and short. ''Stead of which, you was lockin' me in.'

'What do you want?' Lorraine said, not recognising the sound of her own voice.

'Your little ones, both upstairs are they? Safe asleep?'

She made a dash, heedless, past him towards the doorway and the stairs, but he grabbed hold of her arm and swung her back into the room.

'Sleepin' like babies, last time I looked. Regular babes in the wood.' He laughed again, louder, showing long, discoloured teeth. 'We know what happened to them, don't we? Strangers took 'em off to be killed.'

'You bastard!'

Lorraine rushed at him, one hand going for his face, but he knocked her arm aside and pushed her away, shoving hard enough that she lost her balance and collided with the edge of the table, rolling away and half-falling to the floor.

'What I like to see in a woman,' Roberts said. 'A bit of spunk.'

When he threw back his head to laugh, Lorraine's hand closed round the neck of the wine bottle and she launched herself towards him, swinging the bottle hard and fast and smashing it high against the side of his face above the eye.

With a yell, he went stumbling back, half-blinded, clutching at his face, and she yanked open the drawer beside the sink and seized the first implement that came to hand, a long-bladed knife with a serrated edge.

Roberts swore and spat as blood leaked from his face and Lorraine, evading his flailing arm, closed with him again and drove the blade as deep into the pap of his belly as she could, then ran.

Taking the double set of stairs two, three at a time, she burst, breathless, through the bedroom door, her children sleeping sound and undisturbed, Jake with his thumb in one corner of his mouth, Susie clinging to a small brown bear.

Tears flooded her eyes and she had to catch hold of the door to stop herself from falling, her legs giving way beneath her, her breath beating harsh inside her body.

A roar of pain and anger alerted her and she ran back to the head of the stairs in time to see Roberts, face half-masked with blood, blundering towards her; time to lift herself, one hand on the head of the banister, one on the window ledge, and kick out, her right foot catching him in the throat and sending him tumbling, the back of his head striking the wall and then a stair and then the wall again before he was still. Splayed awkwardly, unnaturally, one leg twisted beneath him and still.

He was in that position when Jim Straley arrived minutes later, apologies frozen on his lips as he saw what was before him, this woman he had met once and then briefly, throwing herself into his arms and weeping, her whole body shaking, unable to find the words to explain.

As soon as he felt he could, Straley eased her away and sat her down, handcuffed Roberts to the nearest radiator, phoned requesting back-up and an ambulance, and then phoned Will.

'Will, it's me, Jim. No, listen, everything's okay . . .'

71

'Lorraine,' Helen asked, the first question on her lips next morning, 'she's okay?' The whole police station at Parkside was agog with what had happened; people standing in line, almost, to shake Will's hand and tell him to pass on good wishes and congratulations.

'She's fine,' Will said. 'Still pretty shaken – more, probably, than she'd like to admit, but yes, okay.'

'And the kids?'

'The kids are fine, too. Susie's childminder's agreed to look after both of them for the day. Longer, maybe, if necessary. We'll see how it goes.'

'What is going to happen?'

'About Lorraine? She'll be interviewed under caution this morning. The DS is handling it himself. No way they're going to let me near. Once that's over, I assume she'll be bailed while a file goes to the CPS and they come to a decision.'

'They're never going to charge her – a lone woman protecting her children.'

'I'd be surprised.'

'What she did . . . She was amazing. I mean, Lorraine . . .'

'I know.'

'Proud of her, then?'

'What do you think?' Will found it difficult not to grin. The fear that had knotted his stomach when he'd first heard, fear for his children, for his wife, the guilt at not being there to protect them himself, had quickly been replaced by a sense of almost overwhelming relief. And, yes, pride. Pride in how Lorraine had handled herself, what she had done. 'And Roberts?' Helen asked.

'In hospital under guard. Operation on his stomach last night to stop the bleeding. There's plenty to hold him on for now. As long as Janine Clarke'll agree to give evidence, and I think she will, there's enough to get him put away for a very long time.'

'Any news from the search site?'

He looked at his watch. 'They'll have been back out there early this morning. I'm still waiting to hear.'

Lorraine had met Richard Fincham, Will's new detective super-intendent, just the once before. One of those semi-formal evenings that she more often than not found excuses to avoid. Not that Fincham himself hadn't been pleasant enough. Willowy, prematurely grey, he'd transferred up from Kent, where he'd amassed a reputation for being firm but fair, keen to see correct procedures followed, the right boxes ticked. In his forties still and on his way to somewhere else.

He greeted Lorraine with a warm handshake, his free hand clasping hers as he made earnest enquiries as to how she was feeling in the wake of the previous night's events.

'This is Detective Sergeant Pearson,' he said. 'Judy Pearson. She used to work with me down in Maidstone. I thought it would be useful if she sat in on the interview. In the cause of impartiality.'

Judy Pearson held out her hand. She was in her early thirties, Lorraine thought, stocky, pleasant-faced, little apparent make-up, hair cut short and gelled.

'Not only a matter of being fair and above board,' Fincham said, 'but of seeming so. Just in case things go further than I think they will. Or should.'

He extended a hand, gesturing for Lorraine to take a seat.

'What exactly d'you mean,' she said, 'if things go further than you think?'

'In the event the CPS might decide a prosecution was in order.'

'But I was defending my children.'

'I know, I know. And, as I say, the chances of their coming to that decision are slim indeed. Unless, of course . . .'

'Unless?'

'If Mitchell Roberts were to die . . .'

'Is that likely? The last I heard . . .'

'No, according to the latest information I have, Roberts' condition is stable. I see no particular cause for alarm.'

'But I am under arrest.'

'Technically, yes.'

'So this . . . this is just a formality?'

Fincham smiled. 'A little more than that.'

He sat back. 'Why don't you begin by telling us in your own words exactly what happened?'

Lorraine hesitated. One way or another, she'd been rehearsing this almost since it happened; since she'd woken early that morning, at least. When Will had explained what would most likely happen, that she would be formally arrested and interviewed under caution, she had reacted badly. 'What? You mean I'm going to be treated like some fucking criminal? Well, here, here . . .' holding out her wrists, '. . . handcuff me now and have done with it.' It had been some time before Will had been able to calm her down.

Now, after an uncertain start, she recounted what had happened as clearly, as dispassionately as she could.

'Thank you,' Fincham said when she had finished.

She drank from the water provided and Fincham refilled the glass.

'Judy,' Fincham said, sideways over his shoulder.

Judy Pearson leaned forward. 'Mrs Grayson, when you stabbed Mitchell Roberts with the knife, the knife you'd taken from the kitchen drawer, was he still attacking you at that time?'

'Yes.'

'You – let me see if I've got this right – you hit him with the bottle, in the face, above the eye, and then stabbed him with the knife?'

'Yes.'

'One after another, bottle, knife.'

'Yes, but not right after.'

'There was a gap, an interval?'

'I had to get the knife from the drawer.'

'You had to get the knife from the drawer.'

'Look, I don't understand.' Lorraine directed her remark towards Fincham. 'What's going on here?'

It was Judy Pearson who answered. 'All I'm doing,' she said, 'is trying to establish the sequence of events.'

'You know the fucking sequence of events.'

'There's no need to swear.'

Lorraine swallowed her answer; stared at her hard and was silent.

'Between you striking Roberts to the head,' Pearson said evenly, 'and stabbing him in the stomach, how much time would you say elapsed?'

Lorraine considered. 'I don't know. Moments, seconds. I can't say.'

'And after the first blow, to the head, what did Roberts do? How did he respond?'

'How did he respond? He responded by falling backwards and grabbing at his face.'

'He fell over? To the floor?'

'No, not to the floor. Back against the wall, the kitchen cabinets on the wall.'

'And you?'

'I got hold of the knife.'

'You took the knife from the drawer?'

'Yes.'

'While Roberts was still back against the wall, holding his face?'

'I suppose so, yes.'

'He wasn't attacking you at that time?'

'No.'

'But you took the knife?'

'Yes.'

'Why?'

'Why do you think? To protect myself, of course.'

'But you've said, at that moment, he was standing back against the wall with his hands up to his injured face?'

'Yes, and the next he was coming for me again.'

'He attacked you?'

'Yes.'

'In what manner?'

'What manner? He rushed at me, swinging his arms, striking out.'

'Striking out or trying to grab the knife?'

'I don't know. No. I think he was aiming at my face.'

'And that was when you stabbed him?'

'Yes.'

'In self-defence?'

'Yes.'

'I think,' Fincham said, half-turning towards the detective sergeant, 'Mrs Grayson might appreciate a short break.'

'There's more?' Lorraine said. 'More questioning?'

Fincham nodded. 'Not too much now, I don't think.'

'Then let's get it over.'

'Very well.' He leaned back again in his chair.

'When you were upstairs, Mrs Grayson,' Pearson said, 'with the children, even though you knew Roberts to be injured and, temporarily at least, incapacitated, would it be true to say you still felt yourself to be in danger?'

'Yes.'

'And the children?'

'Yes, of course, my children.'

'Roberts had made threats against them?'

'Yes. And I knew . . . I knew what he'd done. In the past.'

'So when you heard him on the stairs, it's accurate to say you were in fear for their lives as well as your own?'

'Yes. Yes, it is.'

'In what you did, you were protecting them?'

'Yes.'

'And that was why you acted as you did?'

'Yes.'

'Thank you. Thank you very much.' Pearson glanced across at her superior. 'I don't think I have any more questions.'

Lorraine collapsed backwards in tears.

'Mrs Grayson, Mrs Grayson,' Fincham said, resting a consoling hand on her shoulder. 'It's all right. We can stop there. Here.' He took a clean tissue from his pocket. 'You've done well. Brilliantly.'

Lorraine wiped her face and drank from the glass of water he held out towards her. She felt exhausted, drained.

'The law,' Fincham said, sitting back down, 'dictates an individual has the right to use only such force as is reasonably necessary to protect him or herself and their children. I'm satisfied that in this instance, that was the case. And I shall be very surprised if the CPS fail to agree. But that, we shall have to wait and see. Now please, take your time, when you're fit and ready, I'll have someone drive you home.'

Pearson stopped alongside her chair. 'I'm sorry to have to put you through all that. But I thought, anyone who did what you did, could stand up to the likes of me. You're a very brave woman.'

She held out her hand and, after a long moment, Lorraine took it in her own.

72

Will drove out to the cottages on Padnal Fen in a state of no little excitement. According to the text on his mobile, the search had proved positive, discoveries had been made. Beatrice Lawson, was that where she had been hastily buried, killed and buried? At the same time as he wanted, almost more than anything, that not to be the case, but for her to be found somewhere still alive, he knew that with every day the chances of her having been murdered increased.

The crime scene manager stood smoking a cigarette at the edge of the site.

'You've found something,' Will said. 'A body?'

'Not so fast.'

'What do you mean, not so fast? Is it a body or not?'

'Bones, Will. Bones.'

'Go on.'

The manager looked back towards the centre of the site. 'The first location. Inside, if you can call it that. There were signs of an animal – more than one – digging round the edges of that pile of bricks and masonry where a section of wall had recently collapsed. Obviously trying to get at what was buried beneath. We sifted through everything as carefully as we could. Cat bones were all we came up with. Could have been a young fox, there's probably some way of determining for sure if it's of consequence, which I assume it's not. So, it's not your girl, not there, we're certain of that.'

'And the other site?'

'More bones. A skeleton, to be precise. Human this time. Buried a good six foot deep.'

'A girl?'

'Could be. I'd say almost certainly yes, though you'll need the pathologist to be sure. Young anyway, small frame. Barely pubescent would be my guess. Somewhere between nine or ten and twelve, thirteen.'

'How long had she been down there?'

'Again, I'm guessing, but I'd say a goodly length of time. Fifteen, possibly twenty years.'

The same nerve was beginning to pulse at the side of Will's head. ''93?'

'Could be. Could well be.'

Rose Howard, last seen climbing up into the cab of a small, open-backed lorry on the outskirts of Peterborough, with two Polly Pocket dolls and a Take That CD in her rucksack. 1993.

Just for a moment, Will closed his eyes.

With Helen's return, Ellie Chapin had gone back to more mundane things: the tedious but necessary business of check and countercheck, of days spent working computers and telephones. In the days since Beatrice Lawson had disappeared, close to a thousand motorists had been stopped and questioned, more than one hundred and thirty Vauxhall Corsa owners tracked down, seventy-five reported sightings followed up and twenty of those checked out in detail.

Needle, Ellie thought. Haystack.

If she sat at her desk with only her computer as company for very much longer, she thought she might take off her shoe and put the heel right through the screen.

A click of the cursor and the name Walters blinked back at her. Walters, Bernard. An address in Ely, the outskirts actually, north beyond the hospital. Corsa GLS, green, 1196 cc. Two previous attempts to contact the owner made, no response, not at home, flagged for a follow-up call.

What more excuse did she need?

For once the road north was reasonably clear; the sky above a faint blue, barely distinguishable from grey; the temperature a not unreasonable nine degrees. Ellie plugged her iPod into the car's stereo and thumbed the wheel round to Artists and then to Laura Marling – something about her songs, the single 'New Romantic' especially, that caught just the right blend of naivety and determination. Just because I'm young and still maybe just a little bit foolish, doesn't mean you can piss me around. She liked that.

The house, when she came to it, was a surprise. Situated at the end of a street of perfectly normal thirties houses, bungalows some of them, it was an elongated cube of glass and steel with a shallow rectangular pond at the front surrounded by pale grey stones.

The door was at the side, the sign alongside it, so discreet as to be almost unnoticed, read *Bernard Walters, Architect*.

More in hope than expectation, Ellie rang the bell.

The voice, asking the nature of her business, came from a speaker she couldn't see.

'Detective Constable Chapin, Cambridgeshire police.'

'I'll be right down.'

The door swung open on a man wearing a white shirt and pale drawstring chinos, leather moccasins on his feet. Forty? Forty-five? Blue-grey eyes.

'Bernard Walters?'

'Yes.'

'Are you the owner of a green Vauxhall Corsa?'

'Yes, why? Is there a problem?'

'Not necessarily.'

'Then come in, please.' He nodded in the direction of the adjacent house. 'Give the curtain twitchers something to mull over other than stair lifts and Complan. Attractive young woman calling in the middle of the day.' He grinned. 'Lots of scope for addled minds.'

Ellie followed him along a narrow corridor, up a flight of spiral stairs and into a room that took up the whole floor and was part living space, part studio: architectural models on two long tables, blueprints on the walls, computers, green plants, neat piles of magazines, leather and chrome chairs. Choral music was coming from a pair of speakers attached to the wall.

'Coffee?'

'No, thanks, it's fine.'

'Easy to make two as one.'

'All right, then. Thanks.'

While she was waiting, Ellie looked at one of the models, a seemingly large building on several levels, with smaller buildings close by, all surrounded by green space and avenues of tiny trees, matchstick people wandering pleasantly between.

'What's this?'

'A new school.'

'Where for?'

'The Netherlands. I've just come back from yet another series of consultations. Inspecting sites. Money, of course, that's the problem, though not as much as if I were building it here.'

He brought over the coffee in tiny espresso cups, white china with a gold rim.

'And this?' Ellie asked as she sat. 'The music?'

'Pergolesi. You like it?'

Ellie smiled. 'Not very much.'

'"Stabat Mater". Tend to listen to it first thing every morning. Loud. Blows away the cobwebs.'

'And now?'

'Just background. Helps me think.' He reached on to the table for a small remote. 'I'll turn it off.'

'There's no need.'

'It's okay.' The voices died on the air. 'Now, what's this about my ageing car? Crawled through its last MOT, just. Taxed, insured. Not been involved in any accidents as far as I know, not recently, although I can't be sure.'

'How come?'

'Um?'

'How come you can't be sure?'

'Oh, I lent it to a friend. Just for a few days, while I was away. My accountant, actually. He was having trouble with his own car and, living out in the middle of nowhere as he does, he'd be really stuck without one. I gave him a spare set of keys. Asked him to come in and water the plants as payment.'

'This friend . . .'

'Simon.'

'Simon Pierce?'

'You know him?'

'How long . . .' Ellie could feel her mouth beginning to go dry. 'You've known him how long?'

'Ooh, not long at all. The accountant I had before jacked it in. Went off to be a Buddhist. Nepal, somewhere. Simon was local, more or less. Seems decent enough, good at what he does. Very. Little weird, maybe. Borderline strange. Sometimes I feel like suggesting three square meals a day and a good psychotherapist, but then, you know . . . other people's lives. As long as he gets the job done, that's all that matters to me.'

Ellie was sitting forward, her espresso barely touched. 'The dates he would have borrowed the car, could you be exact?'

'Yes. Up to a point. They'd have corresponded with the dates I was away. Monday of last week to when I got back, the day before yesterday. Just over a week. During which he could have taken it at any time. All I know is it was here when I returned.'

'And he had used it? You're sure of that?'

'Yes, I think so. It was parked differently and someone had clearly been in the house.' He smiled. 'None of the plants had died.'

'You didn't check the milometer or anything?'

'Good God, no! But listen, why is this all so important? Was it involved in an accident or something?'

'Not exactly. Not an accident.'

'And you're not going to tell me what.'

Ellie shook her head. 'Not right now.'

'Later, maybe? Some other time?'

'Maybe.'

'Over dinner?'

Ellie laughed. 'I have to make a call.'

'Go ahead.' He was quickly to his feet. 'I'll go downstairs, leave you to it.'

When Ellie followed him down, several minutes later, he was mixing some kind of doughy mixture in a yellow bowl.

'These keys,' she said, 'the ones you gave Pierce, could they have given him access to anywhere else?'

'No, just the car and the house.'

'There are no other keys hanging around?'

'Yes. Yes, of course.'

She followed him back upstairs. On the wall, behind where Ellie had been sitting, was a board from which several sets of labelled keys hung from plastic-covered hooks.

'All there,' Walters said. 'All there except . . . except this one here has been put back in the wrong place.'

'You're sure?'

480

He gave a little self-deprecating laugh. 'Anyone as anally retentive as I am . . . Yes, I'm sure.'

He could have taken them and put them back, Ellie thought, taken them and had them copied. 'What are they the keys to?'

'A house for a client. At Pymoor, just outside Little Downham. Half-finished and he ran out of money.' He shrugged. 'These days, it happens more than you might think.'

'Can you show me on a map?' Ellie said, trying, not altogether successfully, to keep the excitement out of her voice.

73

The house Bernard Walters had designed was on a plot a little way from the centre of the village, past the Methodist Chapel and along a narrow lane shielded by a stand of tall poplars. The basic shell had been erected, the ground floor virtually completed, a mixture of breeze-block and brick, windows now boarded over; sheets of thick polythene flapped loose around the planks and scaffolding on the upper levels.

Will and Helen sat with Ellie Chapin in the first car. Jim Straley and two others in the car behind. An ambulance, just in case, stood round near the Cricket and Social Club on Pymoor Lane.

Save for the wind through the trees, nothing moved.

'You think she's in there?' Helen asked.

Will turned in his seat. 'Ellie, you've got the keys?'

'Here.'

Will took them in his hand and, after a moment's consideration, handed them back. 'No sense us all barging in at once. If she is inside, scare the life out of her.'

'You're sure?'

'We'll be right behind you. Now get along, before I change my mind.'

With a broad smile, Ellie got out of the car and started to walk, slowly, towards the house.

'Sentimentalist,' Helen said scornfully, starting to follow.

'Good management, some might say.'

'Some might say you were trying to earn your way into her knickers. Gratitude fuck, I think that's what it's called.'

'Not that you'd know.'

'Not where you're concerned.'

By now Ellie had reached the door. A brief hesitation, a glance round to where Will and Helen were waiting, and she fitted the key into the lock, turned it, and the next moment was lost to sight inside.

Inside it was black, almost completely dark, just a few narrow shafts of light where the window boards failed to completely fit.

'Beatrice?' She whispered the name, once, twice, once more.

Over by the far wall something stirred.

'Beatrice?'

By now her eyes had become more accustomed to the levels of light.

'Beatrice, is that you?'

Whatever was under the blankets moved, fell back, moved again.

Cautiously, so as not to scare her more than was necessary, Ellie went across and knelt down. A frightened face turned towards her and then away, back beneath the blanket that had been covering her head.

'Beatrice, it's all right. My name's Ellie. I'm with the police. You're safe now. You can come home.'

Slowly, gradually, the blanket came down, and, as it did so, Will appeared, shadowed, in the doorway, and the girl grabbed at Ellie's arm, fingers pressing into the skin.

'It's okay. It's another officer, that's all.'

'You okay?' Will asked.

'I'm fine. We're fine.'

'Okay, then.' The shadow disappeared.

Ellie took hold of the girl's hand. 'Come on, let's go. Let's get you out of here. You want some help to stand? There. There. That's it. Good. I've got you. That's it. Lean on me.'

Seeing them step out into the light, into the middle of that quiet lane, that quiet village, Will had to turn away, lest the tears flood his eyes.

Ruth would say afterwards that the moment she heard Anita Chandra say her name at the other end of the phone, she knew what would follow. Something about the tone.

'Mrs Lawson, Ruth, there's good news.'

And when, not so very much later – though, of course, it seemed an age, an eternity – she saw Beatrice for the first time in almost nine days, her daughter looking pale, nervous and surprisingly small as she walked between Helen and Ellie, holding fast to Ellie's hand, she thought something inside her would break.

Beatrice clung to Ellie's hand almost to the point where Ruth and Andrew stood waiting, both of them with tears threatening to blind their eyes, and only, with a few paces to go, did she dare to let go and launch herself into her parents' arms. The three of them clinging to one another, sobbing, all of them sobbing, Ruth bending low, Andrew on his knees, and Beatrice lost between them, squashed, hugged, loved.

Those were the pictures that would appear in the papers, front page, syndicated round the world, the photographer who'd received the tip-off paying for his information gladly, a nice little earner and why not, spreading joy from Reykjavik to Port Stanley. Good news, not too much of it around.

*

When Will caught up to Jim Straley at Padnal Fen there was no one there: doors locked, windows latched, outbuildings empty. His first thought, somehow Pierce got wind of what had happened and made off while he could. Done a runner, flown the coop. Then Straley pointed back towards the road, a grey Toyota Corolla slowly making its way towards the house, careful driver, thirty miles an hour or less.

They waited, out of sight, while the car came to a standstill and Pierce had got out, reaching into the rear before straightening and starting towards the house, a plastic shopping bag in each hand.

'Terrible, that,' Straley said, 'for the environment.'

Startled, Pierce dropped one of the bags and, for a moment, looked as if he were about to make a dash back to the car. Biscuits, bottled water, Geobars and tinned sweetcorn rolled out on to the dusty ground.

Stooping, Will scooped up a packet of digestives. 'Stocking up?'

'Yes, I just . . . just a few things . . . running low.'

'Likes these, does she?'

'What . . . ? What d'you mean? I don't understand.'

'Beatrice. A fan of these? Plain digestives? Not the chocolate kind?'

'Please, please, I . . .'

'Yes?'

Pierce's eyes were like birds, desperate for flight. His body shook inside his ill-fitting clothes. As Will came close, he turned his head suddenly aside, lurched forward, and was violently sick, vomit trailing from his mouth and nose.

'Jim, take him inside. Get him cleaned up. I don't want him stinking out the car like that.'

74

The doctor who examined Beatrice pronounced her fit and well, physically at least, no sign that she'd been assaulted or abused, a diet largely made up of cereal, tinned peaches, cheese, bread and water and cold baked beans enough to sustain her in captivity. As for the other side of things, he told Ruth, they would have to take them as they came, day by day. Social Services agreed. Watch over her, but not too closely, give her room, time to adjust; let her talk about what happened if she wants to, but never force it, never push. There were people who could help, if necessary, professionals; therapists used to dealing with children, young people, trauma.

What none of them said, not then, not in public: it could have been worse, much worse. Everyone knew, gave thanks as best they could, prayed if they'd a mind.

'Simon,' Ruth had ventured once, 'he didn't touch you or anything?'

'No, Mum.' A quick dismissive shake of the head. 'It's okay.'

She hadn't asked again.

For now it was enough for Ruth to watch her daughter as

she walked across the room, pulled at a strand of hair, kicked her heels, smiled at nothing, frowned. So far Beatrice had said very little about the days spent in captivity, other than how boring it had been.

'Mum, I'm gonna watch some telly, yeah?'

'All right, yes, if you want.'

What Ruth wanted was to take her in her arms and hold her till it hurt. Instead, she went and sat by the window and picked up a magazine. Little by little, step by step: give her time.

Simon Pierce was abject, silent, filled with remorse. Unshaven, unkempt, he sat across from Will and Jim Straley, hands clasped in his lap, unable to look either officer in the face. Questioned, there was none of the self-assuredness he had occasionally shown before.

His solicitor, fresh-faced, eager, being offered such a high-profile case a decided feather in her cap, was anxious to intervene, draw attention to points of procedure, points of law, give her client all the protection he required. She was wearing her best suit, severe yet not too masculine, hair held in place with two silver clasps, a little discreet make-up around the eyes, red lips.

No one in the room paid her more than scant heed.

'I didn't hurt her,' Pierce said. 'I never hurt her, you know that, don't you? I wouldn't. Never. That's other people, other people, not me. I'm not like that. Well, you know, you can see. All that work I've done to try and help. Not so much since I came up here, but before. These groups. *Little Angels.* Others. They always want people who are willing to talk, share. Share their experiences, you see. Those who know, who've experienced that loss. Lost children and lived through it. No matter how bad, how bad it was, come out the other side.'

'Is that what you did?' Will asked quietly. 'Came out the other side?'

'Yes. Yes. After what happened to Heather. I did. I was strong. It was Ruth who couldn't face what happened, wouldn't, wouldn't talk about it, just wouldn't, and so it was all left to me, all down to me. To deal with things, you understand? You see? Not just the funeral, the church, the arrangements, no, after, afterwards, in the house, that bloody house, alone, the two of us and she wouldn't . . .' A sob broke from his throat and he steadied himself against the table edge. 'She wouldn't . . . It was as if she didn't know me any more. She just . . . she turned in on herself, away from me, as if Heather had never been my daughter, as if she'd never had anything do with me. Her loss, Ruth's loss and not mine, and that's when I started to look for help. Started to look for help elsewhere. And work, of course. I tried to lose myself in my work, my job, but it all – I don't know – somehow it all unravelled . . .'

He looked at Will helplessly.

'I thought . . . I really thought, Simon, you're in danger of falling apart, you've got to do something. Do something. And I tried to talk to Ruth then, but it was too late, she said it was too late, she was leaving me, leaving, she wanted a divorce. Well, all right, I said. Okay. I could go along with that. Understand. But then, after she moved away, she started seeing this other man, this Andrew, and the next thing I knew they were getting married. Married, as if we'd been nothing, nothing together, nothing. And she was happy. Happy. As if Heather . . .'

Pulling a shredded tissue from his pocket, he wiped the corners of his mouth, his eyes.

'Then I learned she was going to have this child. A girl. A little girl. As if all she had to do to finally rid Heather from her mind was give birth, put someone in her place. It was all so . . . unfair.'

'Unfair?'

'Yes. She'd forgotten what it was like to suffer, to mourn. To feel that lack every time you looked across the street, every time you opened your eyes. There, in the queue at the supermarket, turning her head. Or on the bus, going into town, laughing with her friends. So, I decided she'd have to learn. Again. What it was like.'

'You wanted to hurt her.'

'I wanted her to remember, remember the pain.'

'And what about Beatrice? What about her pain? Her fear? That child, she must have been terrified.'

'Oh, no. I don't think so, no. At first, perhaps a little, but once she got to know me, know who I was . . . I even think she got to like me a little, just before the end . . .'

He covered his face with his hands.

The solicitor coughed discreetly and looked away.

Don't think, you sad bastard, Will said to himself, I'm going to start feeling sorry for you because I'm not.

There was the usual celebration in the local hostelry, the detective super showing his face for long enough to be noticed and carded as a good sport before making his excuses. Will, on this occasion, wasn't far behind him, arriving home in time to chase Jake up to bed and read another chapter of *Comet in Moominland* before the boy fell asleep.

Downstairs, he joined Lorraine on the settee, where she was sitting with her legs drawn up, watching TV.

'I wasn't expecting you home so early.'

'Yes, well . . .'

'You tired?'

'Pretty much.'

'You look tired.'

Will nodded. 'How about you?'

'Oh, I'm okay, considering.'

'How did it go today? I've scarcely had a chance to ask.'

'It could have been worse, I suppose.' Turning, she stretched one of her legs across his lap. 'Fincham was pretty decent. Unlike that dyke he brought up from Kent.'

Will laughed. 'That what?'

'You heard me.'

'If I'd called her that, you'd have had a right go. Just because she's got short hair doesn't mean . . .'

'Okay, it doesn't. But her – in her case I'll make an exception.'

'I don't know. You should have seen her cosying up to Jim Straley in the pub. Had her hand in his trouser pocket, more or less.'

'That's 'cause she wants to find out if the rumours are true.'

'What rumours?'

Lorraine grinned and held out both hands, palms a good foot apart.

'Yeah?'

'So they say.' She shifted position again. 'Anyway, Fincham made it clear, as far as he's concerned that should be the end of it.'

'Let's hope.' On the screen, someone who might have been Kenneth Branagh was driving around otherwise deserted country roads in a large Volvo, looking concerned. 'You watching this?'

'No.'

Will flicked the remote and went back to massaging her foot.

'What will happen to the man who took that girl?'

'Pierce? He'll be charged with child abduction. No previous, he might even get bail. By the time the psychiatrists have done with him, I shouldn't be surprised if he didn't get off pretty lightly, couple of years at the very most. The right judge, he might not do time at all.'

'He didn't harm her, did he?'

'Kept her a prisoner all that time, locked in a room with precious little light, not knowing what might be going to happen – sounds like harm to me.'

'What was he going to do with her?'

'Let her go. So he says. Tell the mother where she was.'

'And what?'

Will shrugged. 'I don't know. Hope that she'd be grateful, probably.'

Lorraine sighed. 'That poor kid.'

'Yes.'

She bent forward and kissed him, stroked his arm. 'When I think . . .'

'Yes.'

Leaning back, she smiled. 'You know what you were doing a minute ago . . .'

'This?'

'You couldn't do it a bit higher up, could you?'

Will thought that he could.

75

Suddenly, it was winter, or so it seemed. Instead of fluctuating, the temperatures went down and stayed there, five, four, three degrees. The sun, when it appeared, was never more than low in the sky. Standing water was covered with a skim of ice. Night seemed to begin midway through the afternoon. The remains that had been unearthed out at the old labourers' cottages on the edge of Upwell Fen were confirmed as those of Rose Howard: Mitchell Roberts, already back in prison, was charged with her murder.

Will spent more time with Lorraine and the kids than he had before, stayed close whenever he could. Helen was increasingly unsettled, stricken with an itch she didn't know how to scratch.

It was a Wednesday morning when Trevor Cordon called on her mobile and some moments before she recognised his voice. 'The results, DNA, just come through from Birmingham. Thought you might like to know.' Several microscopic samples of blood had been found on Heather Pierce's outer clothing, sufficient to obtain a low-copy profile.

'Might want to meet me, I reckoned,' Cordon said. 'See it through.'

'When?'

'I'm on the train now.'

North London was busy and grey: people hurrying this way and that, heads down, anxious to be out of the cold. Only a bare-chested man, blubber hanging over the top of his jeans and little more than his tattoos to keep him warm, seemed oblivious to the freezing temperature, waving a can of lager high above his head as he wove, unsteadily, between the lines of traffic on the Holloway Road.

'This sample,' Helen asked Cordon when they met, 'enough for a conviction?'

'Not on its own.'

At first, she thought Lee Efford was not at work that day, failing to spot him on the floor of the shop, but, when she asked, she discovered he was out at the back, helping inventory some new supplies.

They went and sat on the selfsame bench, defying the cold. Cordon fetched tea in polystyrene cups from the café on the main road. Their breath hung on the air when they spoke.

No sense in beating around the bush.

'We found blood,' Cordon said, 'on Heather's clothes. No doubt but that it's yours.'

Lee's cup came close to slipping through his hands.

'What you should do,' Helen said, 'tell us what happened. Take your time. We're here to listen, that's all.'

Not quite the truth. Not all.

Lee hung his head, asked for a cigarette and then had trouble getting it to light.

'There's nothin',' he said finally. 'Nothin' much to say. After they got lost, Heather and Kelly, I went out after 'em. My old man, he'd had such a go at me, right? An' I felt, well, guilty, I suppose, though it was their own stupid fault for

493

pissin' me around and that, but still . . . I must've stayed out there for ages an' then I more or less bumped into her, Heather. One minute there was nobody there and then there she was, right in front of me. Cryin' like, in a real state. Reckoned as how she'd told Kelly to stay where she was, not to move, like, but when she got back she'd gone. I told her not to worry. Said I'd wait with her till the fog got better or someone else come out and found us. I didn't know where we was by then, neither, didn't have a fuckin' clue.

'Anyway, we sat down, by this bit of rock – more or less fell over that, too, in the first place. An' we're sittin' there an' I can see she's still really frightened, cryin' a bit, you know, shakin', and then, after a bit, she asks me to hold her hand. An' I do, and I puts my arm round her, just, you know, givin' her a bit of a cuddle, make her feel better, an' then all of a sudden I'm kissin' her, not even meaning to, not thinking about it, kissin' her and she kisses me back. Properly, you know, like she's done it before, and I suppose, after a while . . .'

He stopped and looked at Helen, as if gauging the expression on her face.

'After a while, I started, you know, feeling her up . . . just outside her clothes, but she knocked my hand away and jumped up and started to run, so I grabbed her and that's when she caught me one. Swung right round, yeah, an' hit me in the mouth so's I could taste the blood, an' I spat it out an' called her a stupid bitch and she ran off and I went after her and that was when she fell. Smack against this other rock. I could hear it, right? Even there, in all that fuckin' fog. Smack. Her head on that rock. I felt sick, didn't know what to do. Went chargin' off, fell arse over tip, hurt my ankle, my leg, finally went crawling back. Found her. She weren't breathing. I panicked, right? Thought, you know, no one's going to believe . . . not going to believe it happened like it did. So I more or less felt my way around, not far. Found this sort of

494

opening, covered up, most of it, leaves and shit – I pulled her in there, covered her up best I could. I know it was wrong, I know now . . .'

With trembling fingers, he lit another cigarette.

'I went back out there the next night, snuck out of the tent, didn't think I'd find her, but I did. She was cold. Like some statue. Didn't seem, you know, real. I picked her up and carried her, she didn't weigh a thing. Carried her to that tower, that engine place, whatever. Threw a stone down, so deep you never heard it drop. I thought, if I push her down there no one's ever gonna know, right? No one's ever goin' to say, what happened, it was anything to do with me. Leavin' 'em out there aside. And she was dead now. It couldn't hurt her, right? Right?'

For the first time, Helen glanced away.

'You didn't realise,' Cordon said, 'the body had landed on a ledge?'

'I thought it hit somethin', right? Thought it just, you know, bounced off an' carried on down.' He wiped a hand across his mouth. 'I wasn't gonna hang around an' find out, was I?'

Someone seemed to have done something about the smell on the stairs, Helen didn't know what. When Alan Efford opened the door, just a crack at first, he looked a sight better than he had before; unshaven still, and still in rumpled clothes, but brighter, Helen thought, more alert, as if he might be about to re-engage with the world.

Just as well.

'Hello,' Efford said cheerfully. 'Hadn't expected to see you again so soon.'

He invited her in, offered tea which she refused, listened with growing concern while she spoke.

'And he's where now?' he asked once she'd finished. 'Holloway nick?'

'Yes. Hornsey Road. Making a statement.'

'I should get down there.'

'Yes. He'd appreciate it.'

'I doubt that. But I'm going anyway.' He scooped a coat up from the floor, bent to tie his shoes. 'You?'

'No, I'm done here. I'll be getting back. Just wanted you to know.'

'Yes, right. Thanks.' He shook his head, just the once. 'The stupid young sod!'

'He panicked. He was just a boy.'

'No excuse, though, is it?'

'It might be.'

'How d'you mean?'

'If the rest of the evidence fits his story – and to my memory, it just about does – well, there's no malice aforethought, nothing that could be called unlawful killing, I doubt he's going to be charged with murder. Manslaughter's a possibility – was the girl killed because she was running away, in fear of her life?'

Efford was watching her like a hawk, hanging on her every word.

'No, I'd say the only offence they're going to stand a chance with in court is deliberately hiding the body, moving it first.'

'He'd get jail time for that?'

'Concealing a death from the coroner? Eighteen months if he's lucky, two years if he's not. Either way, best part he'll likely do on remand.'

'Poor bastard.'

'Yes, well,' Helen said, 'at least he's alive.'

She followed Efford down the stairs and out on to the street and, as he hurried away, she crossed and went down into the tube. Any luck she'd catch the next train back to Cambridge with time to spare.

*

496

They were in the same lay-by, the refreshment van long closed for the evening, the almost constant headlights illuminating across their faces.

'We've got to—' Helen began.

'I know, stop meeting like this.'

'People will think we're slipping around.'

'As if.'

Helen's lighter flared in the momentary dark.

'You think the lad'll be charged?'

'Bound to. He's not going to just walk away.'

'You reckon he was telling the truth? Think it happened like he said?'

'Yes, I think so. But then, it's not my call. CPS might see it differently. If he hadn't been chasing after her, she might never have fallen, hit her head.'

'Hard to prove.'

'I know.'

'I ought to be getting back,' Will said.

'There is one other thing.' Her face was suddenly lit up in a glow of amber and yellow, someone going past with their lights on full beam. 'That transfer request I've been on about since God knows when – I've finally put it in.'

'Cornwall?'

Helen laughed. 'The Met.'

'Which section?'

'SO7. Serious and Organised Crime.'

'Promotion?'

'Not right away.'

Will angled his head towards the road, the fast stream of traffic almost uninterrupted. 'Bigger area, more scope. You'll do well.'

'That's all you've got to say?'

'What do you want me to do? Break down in tears? Beg for you to stay?'

'Something like that.'

'Bollocks!'

'That's my expression, not yours.'

'There'll be none of this, you know, hobnobbing at the side of the A10.'

'Why d'you think I'm going?'

To the surprise of both of them, Will kissed her on the forehead; once, quickly, then stepped away. 'Seriously, you'll do well.'

'Thanks.'

'Now . . .' He was glancing round towards his car.

'I know, the family awaits.'

As had become their habit, a habit she would have to break, Helen lit another cigarette and watched him drive away.

76

Ruth had bought the new tabletop easel and a set of canvases on her last trip into Cambridge, taken out her watercolours from where they'd been packed away. Sitting over by the bay window, taking advantage of the light, she was copying Matisse's *Anemones and Chinese Vase* as well as she could. She had a vase of her own on the table, a not dissimilar design and round, like the original. A striped cushion also, though the colours were different. And, anyway, the Matisse had been done in oils. Beautiful, she thought, and beyond anything she could ever hope to achieve. But then, few people could.

She set down her brush for a moment to listen to what was playing on the stereo, one of the *Goldberg Variations*, the 25th, the adagio, the pianist's touch so light, the tempo so slow it seemed as if it might falter and stop, slip over some unseen, unfathomable edge, but of course it never did.

In the small silence between that piece and the next, and before she could resume painting, Ruth thought she heard a noise. A sound, like a door opening or closing, on the floor above.

It had been so long.

Quietly, not hurrying, she crossed towards the stairs.

The door to the smaller bedroom was ajar.

The sound of the piano rose up, faintly, from below.

Ruth eased the door wider and stepped inside. The girl was standing before the mirror, stooping a little, her back towards Ruth, looking at her face in the glass.

Ruth's breath caught in her throat.

'Beatrice?' she finally said.

Slowly, as if time were stopping, the girl turned towards her mother.

'Who else did you think it was?' Beatrice said, and smiled.

VF